THE
LURKIN

Printed in Australia
First Printing: November 2022
Shawline Publishing Group Pty Ltd
www.shawlinepublishing.com.au

Paperback ISBN 978-1-9227-5159-1
eBook ISBN 978-1-9227-5166-9

 A catalogue record for this
work is available from the
National Library of Australia

THE
LURKIN

LOUISE COREE WHITFIELD

Dedication

This book is dedicated to a young boy named Jason who lived for only a brief few years. A child whose light shone so bright that, without knowing, he taught many people some wonderful things about life. His time on the planet was fleeting yet purposeful. May we learn from his existence and evolve into peaceful spirits, dissolving anger and hostility into knowledge, acceptance, and wisdom.

Acknowledgements

I would like to acknowledge those who wish to make peace with themselves as well as those whom they come into contact with. We are all fragile beings on the planet all trying to live the happiest life we can. Those who come from suffering often continue to walk in this valley only causing more misery to themselves and continuing its path of destruction. It is when we tap into our higher selves we can act with love and light instead of anger and hate. Spend time every day meditating and quietening our mind it is here that we will find the sweet solace of nirvana that can influence our every action. Spread love seeds and watch them grow and blossom one human at a time, then one family, then one community, then one state, then one country then one world.

GLOSSARY

Ashanti - Female Fallon who lives in Tremlite

Badon – Town where drunks live from wine made from a fruit called Gogo

Barnio - Garnio who went missing

Berelda - Garnio from Tremlite who becomes Barnio's love

Billop - Small thatched house made of mud and straw

Bulbong - Kangaroo type animal with a large floppy nose

Bulbrook - Possum like animal

Cashan - Scaysborough Judge for baking

Danio - Trehwell Child of Jardjon and Wilmsea who own a tavern in Badon

Dorian and Josat - Brothers who are Fallons with no wings- strong and live in Tremlite though travel far for Jimjam and other fruits their father is named Trinto

Dream Cloud Brew - What the Lola Berries were made into for sale at the Tavern

Elwin - Tremlite leader

Etruscan - Wizard like being

Fallon - Winged creatures who can metamorphose and grow wings only for short flights

Gallan - Etruscan

Gangio - Small, strong and dangerous creature that is like a wolverine

Garnio - A green gangly creature that can move at the speed of light- though only for short periods of time

Garrow - Vindervay that is fond of Nadoo

Gida – Nipoo friend of Nadoo

Gogo - A fruit that a wine is made from in Badon- difficult to conceive children

Haggio - Garnio in Tremlite

Haiton Beterd – A garnio welcome

Heffla - Trehwell whom roams the forests

Isotar - Tremlite leader

Jardjon - Father of Danio

Jenta Jonty - A fallon greeting

Jimjam - Delicious fruit from a tree

Jim Jam - Fruit that tastes like honey

Jyno - Trehwell Male carer of Danio in Badon his partner is Shona

Lolo berry – Hallucinogenic berry discovered by Danio

Marjum - Fruit

Mattock - Sleeping bag

Nadoo - Queen of Nipoo's loves cooking and eating

Nipoo - Gnome like creature

Nomad - Trehwell King - Strong Graceful

Noonan - Cheetah like animal

Perina - Winged Fallon who lost a wing due to a fall on her journey

Rainbow Jewel - Found by Nadoo on her trip to Tremlite

Scaysborough – Council of the Wise

Shona- Trehwell Carer for Danio in Badon, wife of Jyno

Trea and Binea - Planets of Middle Earth like moons

Trehwells - Troll like creatures who lived in Tremlite and Scaysborough

Trulio - Fallon tasting judge from Tremlite

Truon – bird with a large beak that has been trained to talk by the Council in Tremlite

Truscott - Fallon not winged- lives in the moment and always shines

Vik - Vindervay

Vindervay - Small Pixie like creature that blends in with the environment

Vingoo – Lawless band of Trehwells – Gonza, Hely, Trival, Jansto, Pento, Chinto

Wilmsea - mother of Danio

Zaphod - Winged Fallon, lost one wing in a fall- asked Perina to marry him

PART 1

Chapter 1

Perina's Transformation

*The beginning of any journey is made by a conscious
thought and a purposeful action.*

The longest time had passed, and in an enchanting moment,
a ball of silver light travelled through the small funnel-shaped
opening at the top of the sinewy cocoon's entrance. The light
flooded the cocoon's interior, warming the occupant who
began to stir. Tiny particles of energy seeped into Perina's being,
causing her to draw breath once more. She thought the sea was
humming to her, and her last image of her existence that she
could remember entered her mind. She remembered clasping
her hands around the tree's bark, which Zaphod had encouraged
her to do. And, despite the compelling fear plaguing her, she
surrendered herself to the process that Zaphod rightly knew
was her destiny. A supreme sense of serenity encompassed her
being, and with a gentle inward breath, Perina's eyes flickered.

She gasped with sudden horror as her eyes took in her
surroundings. Right in front of her was a brown wall that
resembled dried seaweed; it was translucent enough to only
let in the dullest of light. She tried to move but her movement
was greatly restrained by the vine-like creeper that made it
difficult for her arms to shift from their upright position. She
felt a strange and dull weight on her back. Panic-stricken she

placed all her energy on trying to kick out with her entombed legs, which responded with a few tiny forward movements of her feet. She bowed her head, quickly taking stock of the situation. She appeared to be encased in a tomb-like structure exuding a dank, though not too unpleasant, smell like musty syrup.

An oozing caramel-coloured substance was dripping off the veined walls that seemed identical – dark brown structures with a seaweed-like texture. On the verge of shrieking aloud in terror, she heard a reassuring voice pervade her mind – *when you wake up, remember to use the ring on your toe to release the base of the structure. This will free your hands and allow the walls to collapse. Repeat this to yourself until the dreaming takes over, and you will know what to do when you are transformed.*

Immediately comforted by the warmth of Zaphod's voice, just as she remembered it, she looked down to see the glistening silver ring clamped around her big toe. It had a piece moulded to the middle, jutting out like a large lion's claw. The discussions she had with Zaphod came flooding back to her, making her recall the way she clambered around him, posing question after question. She remembered how Zaphod would respond to each one in his usual manner, with patience and wisdom. Perina never detected any annoyance on his part with the constant barrage of her questions. She remembered positioning her body as per his directions, once she fully understood them, then slowly succumbed to the trance-like state that heralded her to this transformative process.

Once regaining these memories Perina became empowered with renewed vigour. She slowly lowered her right foot under the loop-like vine at the base of her cocoon, successfully placing the silver claw of the ring inside the loop. With all the stamina she could muster, she swiftly raised her leg upright, as previously instructed by Zaphod. In a fleeting moment, her hands were released, and the structure encasing her, began to peel away slowly from the top. In a flurry of seconds, the walls of the cocoon unravelled softly like a lotus bud opening its petals, with Perina standing at the centre like a ballerina in a music box.

The light engulfed her, and it took a few moments before her eyes could adjust to decipher her whereabouts. The ocean glistened before her, as beautiful and appealing as she remembered it. She raised her foot to step off the flower bed-like structure, promptly falling backwards with a thump.

'I told you it would take time to get used to those.' Perina turned her head upwards to find Zaphod clambering through the bushes behind her. Gently taking Perina by her arm, he steadied her to her feet. 'You need to get used to the weight of the wings, Perina, now that you are a fully-grown Fallon.' Perina stared into the welcoming face of her friend, Zaphod. They embraced for what seemed like eternity, gaining comfort from each other's embrace. Perina looked over her shoulder, gasping at the sight of her newly formed wings. 'It's as it's meant to be,' Zaphod said with a laugh. 'These wings of freedom will carry you onward to the next part of the journey. It's as it's meant to be, Perina.'

Chapter 2

The Mystical Land of Scaysborough

Every journey begins with one tiny step.

Fallons are not fairies, which they are often mistaken for. They are human-like creatures that are able to metamorphose and grow wings. Fairies are mythical creatures, whereas Fallons live in the land of Scaysborough. Scaysborough existed in a cocoon of mist beyond the Celleric seas – a town so obscure that time seemed to have chosen it as its resting place. No humans have been there, as the entry to the realm of Scaysborough is hidden inside a cave surrounded by brume in a forgotten corner of a tiny island in a faraway ocean.

Scaysborough residents however have, from time to time, popped through the cave into the Earth's world. They have even carried their wizard boats and visited many countries of the Earth. This is why many humans have recorded seeing fairies, wizards, goblins, and aliens – none of which are the real names of Scaysborough inhabitants though. Once, an Etruscan (humans call them wizards) had brought a human back with him to Scaysborough, after he had visited Earth. Gallon, the wisest Etruscan in the land, interpreted the human for all the residents. How they all laughed when they heard about how nasty trolls are and how shy fairies are, according to humans. The human's account of Etruscans, or wizards as they called them, was probably the most accurate.

Etruscans were human-like creatures, though they had wizened looks and often walked around muttering some puzzle or philosophy, contesting all through wherever they journeyed, both with themselves and anyone they happened to meet.

The Garnios had shrieked with such delight as Gallon told them about the human's version of them. Garnios were green and gangly creatures with large eyes and frog-like hands. They could move faster than light, appearing as though they have, vanished, sometimes leaving a flash of light behind them as they moved. The Garnios had been amused to know that the humans referred to this light as a spaceship and wished they had such a vessel to travel through space. Garnios actually had no need for one though, as they could move from one end of Scaysborough to another in the blink of an eye.

The human had also spoken of gnomes, which in Scaysborough, were called Nipoos. Nadoo was one such creature, and she had laughed so hard on hearing the human's account of gnomes that she fell off the log she had been sitting on and had to be bandaged as she had struck her head on a rock on her way down. Nipoos were actually very brave and hardy folk who would only hid if they sensed extreme danger. They were small and stocky like the humans and had a very good sense of humour. Although, they could also be pretty stubborn and irritable, especially when they were hungry!

The Trehwells, whom the humans called trolls, however had become extremely upset when Gallon read the human's version of them. Some sobbed and some left the gathering in sorrow, retreating to the comfort of their thatched homes at the base of the village's mountain. Trehwells were in fact gentle folk who loved their families, their homes, and their gardens. They only erupted in ferocious fits of anger to protect their loved ones or their belongings. This happened rarely, as the only dangerous creatures in Scaysborough were the Tremlites and the Lurkin.

The Tremlites were a band of mixed residents who lived in the land called Tremlite, including Nipoos, Fallons, Trehwells, and Garnios (which was the same mix of residents in Scaysborough). It was thought by the residents of Scaysborough that the Tremlites were imbued with hatred, jealousy, and bitterness. This was reasoned, because some of them were born into misfortune, some found misfortune along the way of and others were just plain nasty. It was reported that the Tremlites blamed the Scaysborough people for their misfortune, and therefore stole from them, deceived them, and even hurt or killed them at times. No living resident of Scaysborough had actually been robbed or harmed, though stories of such mischief had survived from the accounts of old saints, which had been recounted from one generation to the other.

The other dangerous being was the Lurkin! The Lurkin was the most feared creature in the land of Scaysborough and Tremlite, creating turmoil and angst wherever it went. The Lurkin could (according to the legends) appear anywhere at any time. It would manifest amidst a haze, pretending to be a friend in times of trouble or a foe in times of happiness. It could cast seeds of doubt in those convinced and thwart righteous efforts whenever possible.

The Scaysborough residents believed that the Lurkin spent most of its time with the Tremlites, where it would fuel the Tremlites' anger and hatred, encouraging them to deliver their deeds of evil. Scaysborough folks thought that if it wasn't for the Lurkin, Scaysborough would be a happy land. Scaysborough's council of the wise was of the belief that even the Tremlites would see the error of their ways with the Lurkin gone, and one day, Scaysborough would be able to live in harmonious existence with the Tremlites.

No one in Scaysborough had reported seeing the Lurkin for a

while, and this greatly troubled the council of the wise. At the last council meeting, Nomad, the king of the Trehwells, had stated, 'I fear the Lurkin is planning great trouble like the one it brewed seven summers ago. Only now are our freshwater lakes beginning to show the same abundance of fish and crayfish from before the Lurkin had struck.'

'I fear that another attack might kill the lake altogether,' lamented Nadoo, the Nipoo queen. She was always preoccupied with food, and the real reason she was so concerned about this was that boiled crayfish was her most loved dish, aside from cakes, biscuits, and breads. Nadoo had to wait for five summers before the crayfish and fish restocked themselves – only then could she add these tasty treats to her diet – one that also included edible tufts gathered from the woodland as well as berries, herbs, lettuce, grains, and fruits.

Once on a very early morning, just before the sun climbed the sky seven summers ago, Nadoo and the other Nipoos had gone to the local Scaysborough lake, Lake Argyle, to begin fishing, a ritual they engaged in at predawn. Only this time, instead of seeing the peaceful shores of the lake in stillness and calm, they encountered a deadly scene. All the fish that would ordinarily be swimming happily in the lake were either breathlessly flapping near the shores or washed up dead. Nadoo had scooped up the water and tasted it to see why this had occurred, only to find that the lake's water, which should taste fresh and pure, tasted salty. One Nipoo reported seeing a small figure running towards the Tremlite town, drawing the conclusion that the Lurkin had surely ordered the Tremlites to pour salt into the lake in order to upset, possibly incapacitate, the Scaysborough community. The gathering of Nipoos, not knowing what to do next, sat down in a group and wailed along the shores.

Lake Argyle could have died completely, if it wasn't for Genoa, an Etruscan, who had taken an early morning walk that day to watch the moonflowers nestled along the lake's edge in the light of dawn. This was a spectacle to behold, as when the flowers bloomed, they moved in unison with the sun, shining a bright yellow and giving off a lovely shine just like the celeste moon. Genoa felt rewarded as he absorbed the brimming beauty of the blossoming moonflowers – bending down to admire the beautiful flowers, taking in their glorious scent. As he did so, he heard the flapping noises coming from the lake. Upon turning towards the same, he saw all the fishes flapping in distress and the crayfish scurrying up the banks onto the sand, spitting water out of their tiny mouths. Genoa saw the group of Nipoos sobbing by the shore and heard from one his account of what had happened. They explained to him that the Lurkin had arranged for a Tremlite to pour salt into the lake. At the time, Genoa was unaware that no one had actually seen this happen and that they only imagined so. Genoa advised that he would call for assistance, leaving the Nipoos still immobilised on the shores, wailing ceaselessly.

Genoa ran screaming into Scaysborough. The entire town remembered that early morning, as they were awoken by Genoa urging all residents to come forth. He quickly recounted what had occurred at the lake, and the residents sprang into action. Gallon, the Wisest, took charge, and soon, Nipoos, Etruscans, Fallons, and Garnios alike were knee-deep in water with nets and buckets, catching the aquatic beings that had not yet succumbed to the deadly salt. They were whisked away to buckets and tanks that had been filled with water from the dams in the settlement.

The lake however recovered quite quickly from its salt infusion, and after a few rains, it was ready for the little beings to be reunited with their former home.

The Lurkin was also accused of creating other disasters, such as the forest fires some three winters ago, the mud slides at the Trehwells' billops (billop is what the Trehwells called their round, earth-built homes), and plenty of other mishaps around the village.

At a meeting of the council after the salting of the lake, the Etruscan elders motioned that a group of the bravest residents of Scaysborough venture into the Tremlite camp in an attempt to gather knowledge about what other atrocities the Lurkin might have been concocting with the Tremlites. 'Knowledge is by far the best defence,' asserted Gallon, the Etruscan king. Seven inhabitants attending this meeting felt inspired to volunteer for this daring mission. The seven who were selected for this daunting task included Perina, Truscott, and Zaphod (all of whom were Fallons), Gallon – the wisest Etruscan, Nomad – a Trehwell, Nadoo – Elder of the Nipoos, and lastly Barnio, a Garnio, who was also the smallest and fastest of the lot.

Perina, after volunteering for the mission, had agreed to metamorphose in order to grow her wings, so that she could fly if needed on the journey to Tremlite. Zaphod had metamorphosed some time ago and was well accustomed to his wings. Truscott however did not feel the need for wings; he enjoyed his body as it was and loved walking, climbing, and discovering new things. All of them agreed to embark on the journey in one season's time – during spring in Scaysborough. This would allow Perina some time to get used to her wings as well as learn how to fly and glide under Zaphod's guidance.

Fallons' wings are nothing like the wings of fairies depicted in the books of the humans. They protrude from the middle of their backs, rather like bat wings, and are quite heavy, which take some time to get accustomed to. This is why Truscott, like many other Fallons, do not have wings at all; choosing to stay earth-bound allowed them to run as swiftly as a Noonan (a type of cat like a cheetah).

So, the following months were spent plotting, planning, and training, until the group was ready to set out on their journey.

CHAPTER 3

THE PARTING

*True freedom is the ability to engage in the journeys
our soul yearns.*

The news of the groups parting trumpeted throughout Scaysborough. The courage and bravery of the seven, stirred strong emotions of admiration and awe throughout the lands. The Townsfolk rapidly arranged festivities aimed at heralding the team on its mission and to applaud their valiance. Thousands of residents travelled to the large field at the centre of Scaysborough. The field was as large as ten football fields that the earthlings have. Surrounding the fields were beautiful Colo trees that had large pendulous apple-green leaves and beautiful pink flowers with orange stamens that wafted strawberry scents. Many of the trees, fruits, and vegetables of Scaysborough were similar to the ones on Earth, except they were more colourful, with stronger scents, and nearly all of them bore edible fruits.

The Colo trees themselves yield a delightful berry, which tastes like a cross between an apple, strawberry, and date. They are so delicious! There are also many Earth-like trees on Scaysborough such as mango, banana, plum, and pear. The Etruscans who ventured to Earth would bring back seeds and plants that bore edible fruits and grow them in Scaysborough. However, the Etruscans only brought back a few animals, as they were careful not to upset the Scaysborough animal life. They learnt from the mistakes of humans, as they saw the problems rabbits, cane toads, camels, and other animals placed in an unnatural environment faced in the places that they visited.

As the parting was a grand function, many Scaysborough folk, primarily the Nipoos who loved cooking, baked and baked for days prior to the celebration. The villages turned out scrumptious cakes, breads, cookies, scones, and slices in their large, wood-fired ovens. Both male and female Nipoos liked to cook! As you may have guessed, they were quite rotund, as they loved eating too! Nipoos were smallish creatures – not even a metre tall. They had chubby hands and faces and were usually chirpy, chatty, and smiling. The only time they got grumpy was when the food was not plentiful; then they could start scolding and growling. Luckily, Scaysborough was a land of abundant resources so they were not cross often!

They would often sing as they baked.

Knead, knead, knead
prod, prod, prod
Here's the way to make the brod (Scaysborough folk called bread 'brod')
Spread on the butter
Spread on the jam
Chomp it down happily, as fast you can

They had a lot of songs for everything they made, and Gallon would say this was why the food they made tasted so good, as it was baked with love and happiness. The Nipoos had placed trestles lining the field's boundaries, brimming with food. They shrieked with delight when other Scaysborough residents enjoyed their food, clapping and singing even more. Nipoos often ate as they manned the stalls, just to make sure the food was good to eat, they would say – a quality control measure!

Though, it was more likely that they just couldn't stop eating!

The Garnios entertained the crowd by their amazing speeding light game. As you may remember, Garnios can travel so fast, they disappear in a flash of light. The Scaysborough residents enjoyed guessing where they would reappear. The Garnios however were very tricky and would spring from almost anywhere, at any time, which caused much laughter and frivolity. It was not uncommon for them to appear so fast that you would accidentally bump into them or trip over them, which they did quite frequently as a part of their game. Elwin, who was a particularly large Trehwell, was not amused when one Garnio popped out in front of him, making him trip. Elwin was eating a rather large doughnut at the time, and it's cream splotched all over him and his best tunic. Elwin however couldn't help but join in the laughter when a Fallon, who was flying by, showed him how funny he looked in mirror she was carrying. The cream had landed on his nose, ears, and beard, resembling craggy pieces of icicles. He was a funny sight indeed!

The Garnios were not cruel and went straight to work, cleaning his face, hair, and tunic. They even got him another cream bun! The Garnios did not like being ill-thought of and always made sure the residents who fell victim to their tricks were happy and content before they did another one. Elwin walked away laughing and laughing, thanking the Garnios for their assistance in remedying his attire.

At the centre of the field, there was dancing and merriment with a Trehwell band singing one of their favourite songs. Many Fallons, Trehwells, Etruscans, and Nipoos were dancing, with some Fallons joining hands and flying to the air, breaking into a rhythmical flapping dance. This is how the song went.

Scaysborough Rock, it's here to stay
Scaysborough Rock, its ok

Scaysborough Rock, get down and swing
Scaysborough Rock, it's the feel thing

So swing your partner
Swing your cow
Doe-see-doe if you know how
Scaysborough Rock, it's here to stay
Scaysborough Rock, its ok

You live in a billop, that may be true
But you have the Scaysborough in you
So take off your shoes, let down your hair
You will surely find the Scaysborough in there,

Scaysborough Rock, it's here to stay
Scaysborough Rock, its ok
Scaysborough Rock, get down and swing
Scaysborough Rock, it's the feel thing

So swing your partner
Swing your cow
Doe-see-doe if you know how
Scaysborough Rock, it's here to stay
Scaysborough Rock, its ok

Oh, by the way, a cow in Scaysborough is the same as the human kind. Cows were one of the animals brought to Scaysborough from Earth. Nipoos had found that cows' milk was delicious and could be used to make butter, ice-cream, and many such delights. They pleaded with the Etruscans to let them bring cows to Scaysborough. The Etruscans discussed this at the council of the wise, arriving at a consensus that cows would be permitted to their world, as long as they were fenced and not allowed to journey into the wider terrain for fear of disturbing the natural balance. The Nipoos have kept their word and cared for the cows with love and tenderness, never allowing any to escape. All of Scaysborough enjoys the goods they get from cows – butter, milk, and ice-cream!

The party went on! Scaysborough residents were singing and dancing; the field was brimming with joy and happiness. It was nearing five o'clock when the crowd was suddenly brought to a hush. All eyes turned towards a Gallon walking through the crowd, ringing a large musical bell-shaped instrument creating a beautiful tinkling tune – a well-known signal for all to listen.

The parting speeches had to begin before nightfall to be fair to the Garnios, who would automatically fall asleep after dusk. They could not be awoken until morning, so they usually went back to their cottages well before 7 pm, when the sun would usually set.

The crowd hushed, as Gallon walked around, soon inducing a whispered silence that framed the scene. The crowd seated themselves in lines around the stage at the far end of the field. But, a minor disruption occurred when Perina called out for assistance, as one of the claws of her wings got entangled in a tree on her way down from the aerial dance to country rock music. Zaphod quickly flew to her rescue, untangling her from the branch with ease. Perina was extremely grateful and impressed by Zaphod's strength and agility. This type of accident was rare as Fallons are expert flyers; Perina however was still getting used to her wings.

Once everyone settled down in their seats, Gallon called upon the six chosen travellers to the stage. Gallon, who was revered as the wisest creature in Scaysborough, had not only been chosen for the mission to Tremlite along with these six travellers, but he had also been elected as the spokesperson of the council of the wise.

Complete silence fell upon the crowd as he began to speak. 'As you all know,' began Gallon, 'six of our finest residents and

I have agreed to embark upon a perilous journey to the land of the Tremlites, to try and find out if the Lurkin is planning any mischief. We are gathered here today to set this brave party on its way, with this loving exuberant gathering that we have organised. This energy will bring them good fortune and safety in their voyage.' Directing his speech to chosen six – Perina with her newly formed wings, Truscott, Zaphod, Nadoo, Barnio, and Nomad, Gallon continued, 'May peace and love carry you forward, and may righteous thoughts pave your way.' The crowd chanted these words in agreeance, until Gallon motioned them to stop with the raise of his hand. The six travellers, who had gathered on the stage at Gallon's directions, bowed their heads in gracious acceptance of their well-wishers' words. Gallon then discussed the purpose of the mission, urging all Scaysborough folk to think encouraging thoughts until their return. After Gallon concluded his speech, the music and dancing continued, with the loving solidarity whirling about the wind, tying them all together as one.

Just before the sun began to set, the bell was tolled again, as a warning for the Garnios to get home and for the crowds to disperse back to their billops. Some however remained to assist the team to pack for their departure due the following morning. The seven chosen had decided to camp in the field, where the celebration had just take place, for the night. This also allowed them to test the camping equipment that they had packed for their travels. Each member of the party was weary from the celebrations and set about getting their tents ready for the evening. They carried their supplies in cassocks, which is like a backpack in Scaysborough. Their cassocks were packed with a dome tent, breads, cakes, and fruits as well as a mattock, which is like a sleeping bag.

Nadoo was in charge of packing the food, and they all had more than they needed. The trip to Tremlite would only take about three days. They planned to gather fruits, berries, and other food items along their path for their return journey. Barnio, who knew night was nearing, wished his fellow travellers a good night. 'Good night, Good night, Sleep well, Sleep well,' repeated Barnio flitting this way and that making sure his wishes were bestowed to all. Such was the way with Garnio's, they often repeated words, After ensuring all had collected all ears in the listening, he then settled under his mattock and succumb to sleep.

The other six quickly followed, and the volunteers made their way back to town after wishing them all the best for their mission. It was as though the air of joyous exuberance in the field from the celebrations offered extra calm and peace to the party, which settled them into a deep and peaceful slumber. The travellers needed to sleep well, as they would need their rest to prepare for the following day's perilous journey!

CHAPTER 4

THE PASSING

No one sees from the same eyes, hears from the same ears, feels from the same hands, or interprets from the same brain. Thus, every moment is unique for all beings. It is only silence that brings all of us together, but for that, we must quieten the mind.

All seven of them slept soundly through the night, except for Truscott who awoke in the middle of the night with a startle! He heard a rustling sound that appeared to be coming from some bushes nearby. Truscott sprang up immediately from the warmth of his mattock, venturing outside his dome-like tent to check for any danger. Truscott was perhaps the bravest one of the group; he was strong and true in spirit. He stood almost as tall as a Tamar tree (approximately six-foot high) with an exceedingly muscular physique. Truscott took pride in his body and strength. He was not vain, neither did he show off. Instead, he honoured his body and utilised his strength for helping those around him. He was well known in all of Scaysborough for his kind deeds and virtuous actions and was perhaps the most popular resident.

Truscott became easily embarrassed by the attention of others, and even though he was very friendly, he chose to spend the vast majority of his time alone, working on his body, mind, and spirit to create a perfect harmony. He exercised daily doing a dance like routine, which he averred connected the whole of his body and brought about an innate awareness to all of his actions. He ate good food, sticking mostly to a diet of fruits, vegetables, nuts, and grains, with the occasional meal of fish or meat. He rarely ate sweets and partook in drinking ale only on special occasions; Truscott was also very wise.

Truscott scanned the campsite but couldn't find anything unusual. The planets of Trea and Binea were well alight, and despite the dark sky, these planets emitted enough light for Truscott to be able to see quite well. Scaysborough has night and day as the Earth, though it did not have a moon. Scaysborough relied on the planets for light at night, as one depends on the moon on the Earth. Truscott, who did not take anything lightly, stayed still for the moment to ensure that whatever he heard had passed and there was no danger. Once reassured, Truscott returned to his tent, climbing back inside his mattock very quietly, practising his art of stealth. Although he was a little troubled by the disturbance, he managed to drift back into a peaceful slumber.

The tents of the party were all joined together like a honeycomb. This way they could all be alerted in case any threats or cause for alarm were perceived. Their tents could be assembled in any shape they wished – circular, honeycomb, or a single line, depending on the terrain of the campsite. They were now arranged in a circle with all the entrances to the tents facing a round field in the middle, where all of them would meet for breakfast for the journey ahead.

Barnio, the Garnio who was almost as fast as the speed of light, woke up first, which was his habitual practice. Due to the Garnios' need to sleep as soon as the sun set, they used to make up for the time by rising as soon as the sun peaked through the edge of the horizon. Barnio rose from his sleep, bouncing into action immediately, singing as he went around the tents waking up all the occupants. 'The morning is here; the day is nigh. Let's get going, before the sun gets high.' Barnio danced and chanted this message from one tent to the other. Most of his fellows responded warmly to Barnio's chant, though Nadoo was not quite chuffed.

In her usual manner, Nadoo scolded Barnio for being so bright and cheerful early in the morning. Nadoo was not her happiest in the morning. She was at the best of her tempers by mid-morning, when she felt fully awake and had indulged in a long and hearty breakfast. However after being awakened by Barnio's chant, the rest of the group got dressed promptly and huddled together at the centre of the camp. Nomad set himself to the task of lighting the camp fire, whilst Perina, Truscott, and Zaphod prepared breakfast, which included nuts, grains, fruits, and toast. Gallon was preparing some twine tea at another fire pit, while Barnio was running hither and tither, setting tables and placing cups out for the impending feast. The day was warming up, as the sun crept higher in the sky.

Just as the toast neared readiness and the smell wafted around the camp, Nadoo appeared from her tent. She didn't greet the others, only giving out a grumpy grunt when they offered morning salutations to her. She however ate her food heartily, accepting the offer of tea from Gallon afterwards. Once she had eaten her breakfast and sipped down her tea, she presented the entire group with the biggest smile and engaged in cheerful conversation.

Truscott told the group about his night adventures during breakfast, recounting the noise that had disturbed his sleep.

'Possibly a Bolbrok,' (a possum-like creature) exclaimed Zaphod.

'Or a Truon,' (a large owl-like bird with a huge beak) conjectured Nadoo.

'Could have even been a Bulbong,' (a kangaroo-type creature with a long bulbous nose) Barnio asserted and continued, 'I saw one around this area last week!'

'No, they don't come out at night,' responded Nomad.

'Could it be the Lurkin, the Lurkin,' repeated Barnio quivering a little as he spoke.

Whilst the group continued their discussion, Gallon alarmed somewhat by the mention of the Lurkin, slipped away to explore the bushes where Truscott had heard the noise. In doing so, he happened to find a few yellow threads of callum (a cotton-like fabric). Gallon was deeply troubled by this. The thread could have belonged to a Tremlite spy, as the shade of yellow was not a dye that he had seen in Scaysborough. Scaysborough clothing was spun in the village, which were dyed in different colours from the vegetation that grew in the area. The bright orangish-yellow thread was not from Scaysborough, as no dye of that colour was available there.

Gallon, though worried, abstained from sharing this information with the group, as he felt that it was important for them to start out in high spirits. Gallon placed the threads carefully inside his pocket and rejoined the group. Perina noticed a troubled look on Gallon's face. She however quickly forgot about this, as Gallon looked worried quite often. It was not unusual to see this look on Gallon's face, as he was usually deep in thought, never taking a break from thinking and analysing things. The group, now content after a hearty breakfast, carefully packed their supplies into their cassocks. Cheerful in spirit, they set upon their journey ahead. Gallon however was more solemn and was extra alert to any signs of danger. He stayed at the back of the group, watching out closely for any signs of other travellers or spies.

Chapter 5

The Journey Begins

Trials are journeys for learning, so when obstacles arise,
strive not to despair; instead, look at them with joy,
as an opportunity to learn and advance the soul.

The climb out of Scaysborough was by no means an easy walk. The only traversable path out of Scaysborough was through a spiralling tract that wound around Mistoka Mountain. Since the Lurkin's attack on Lake Argyle, only very few beings journeyed to this remote part. Hence, the track was covered in vines, fallen rocks, and broken branches. This meant the party needed to stop and clear the overgrown track from time to time, delaying their arrival at first destination point of their journey.

Nadoo was the first to complain. 'These vines are so tiresome and cumbersome,' she moaned. Nadoo, despite her short and stout physical built, was decidedly fit and was becoming thoroughly frustrated at the slow pace she had to surrender to. She would normally be climbing at full speed, almost running to her destination.

'Don't worry,' announced Truscott. 'Once we reach the summit, the vines will disappear, and the track will be easier to walk on.' Truscott was the most experienced one, as he was one of the few who had ventured this far as, being a lover of physical fitness and exercise. Truscott would normally step over the vines and climb over the fallen rocks on the path. However, the others, who were laden with the cassocks on their backs and weren't as tall or nimble, were unable to do so.

Even though he did not utter a single complain, the most frustrated member of the group was Barnio, who was used to travelling almost as fast as light. He would ordinarily be at the front of the group, shouting for them to hurry up. Instead, at the moment, he chose to sit back despondently, waiting for a substantial amount of clearing to be done, after which he would rush to the top and wait again. No one seemed to mind this, as they knew he was not very skilled with axes and had very little strength to move rocks. Zaphod was perhaps the strongest one of the group and was the first to plough effortlessly into the rock slides that were blocking their path, splitting large rocks that would usually take the effort of two or three beings. It took several hours for the slow-moving bunch to trudge their way ahead, making it apparent that they would not reach their scheduled destination before nightfall. They conceded that they would need to find a camping spot somewhere along the way.

They were also well aware of the fact that they would need to do this prior to sunset, as Barnio would automatically go to sleep after dusk, due to the sun's direct influence on the Garnios. Truscott, owing to his previous travels to this region, knew of a clearing for them to pitch their tents. The stopped to rest and revitalise themselves with some refreshments; they were valiant in attitude and began to eat and drink in merriment. Nadoo even composed a song, and very soon, everyone started singing it with great delight.

It went like this…

The path may be covered,
The path may be long,
Though the path is travelled

By the fit and the strong.
We have what it takes,
To conquer the quest.
We rely on each other,
To give it our best.

After being refreshed and charged up with courage and comradeship from singing Nadoo's song, the group repacked their belongings and set back on their path, cutting vines, moving rocks, and prodding slowly up the hill. They walked stoically, still in good spirits, despite the slow pace at which were moving. They walked in silence; the only sounds you could hear were the slashing of twigs, the calling of birds, and a few crabby outbursts from Nadoo who was beginning to feel hungry again. Finally, when they were within metres of the clearing that Truscott was leading them to, much excitement gripped the group as could catch a glimpse of the grassy clearing at times through the canopy of trees.

Their joy however turned to shock when all of a sudden, while turning a corner, they were confronted by a huge towering rock positioned smack in the middle of their path. The vines and trees were exceptionally thick in this area; and to the right of the boulder was a steep cliff face with a narrow ledge dropping straight to the very bottom of the mountain. The left side of the rock was equally unpassable; it was smeared in slippery moss and matted creepers that offered no discernible way through its maze of branches. Gallon wore a look of extreme concern over his face as did Barnio, who was now keeping very close watch of the time. It was 6.30 pm, which meant that in half an hour, he would be fast asleep.

Perina and Zaphod tried to fathom an aerial path out of there, but due to the canopy above, the narrow cliff edge would not allow their wings to expand enough for them to take flight. Even if they could do so, flying at that altitude had its own dangers, as the air currents were strong and too treacherous at the peaks. Truscott however was sure footed and spoke to Gallon about the possibility of climbing the boulder, extending ropes to pull the rest of the group up and over. After much consideration and speculation by the two, as well as detailed drawings in the dirt to illustrate the method in question, their ideas were put forth to the rest of the group.

Truscott explained that he would climb the rock and tie ropes to a nearby tree at the top. Zaphod would then climb up, so he and Truscott could pull the rest up the rock. 'You must never let go of the rope,' instructed Gallon. 'You must assist Truscott and Zaphod also.'

'Place your legs on the rock and pull yourself upwards, as much as you can,' Truscott added. All of them agreed, as no one could think of a better plan. So, with good wishes from his friends, Truscott began the ascent.

Truscott was strong and brave, gripping on to the tiny crevices in the rock, whilst finding small bumps or cracks in the rock with his feet to crawl his way up. The group assisted as best they could from the ground, shouting directions to possible footholds. It was a slow, painstaking journey, and Truscott was inching his way to the top, bit by bit.

'A little to the left,'to the left, the left' shouted Barnio, seeing a fitting crevice. Suddenly, the whole group gasped as Truscott's foot slipped from the destined crevice, leaving him dangling from a handhold; his body was swinging over the sheer drop of the cliff face.

'To the left; to the left,' they shouted in unison.

'Believe that you can make it, and you will,' Gallon screamed out.

The entire group started chanting, 'You can do it; you can do it. Find a hold; find a hold.' The positive energy of the group appeared to settle Truscott; he was able to swing his leg over the side of the rock, till his foot found the tiny crevice, and he could control his flailing body once again.

At this point, Truscott stretched his left hand, gripping a long vine hanging atop the rock and hauling himself up. The party cheered in delight.

'That is greaaaaaaaaaaaaaaat,' exclaimed Barnio, collapsing to sleep the very next moment. The group gasped aloud. Due to their concern for Truscott, no one, including Barnio, was paying attention to the time.

'What will we do now?' bewailed Perina, voicing the concern bothering the entire group. 'We can't sleep here! There is no room, and we can't possibly leave Barnio behind!'

'We have to think fast…' shouted Truscott, perched at top of the rock, 'as the light is dimming quick, and we have to set up camp.' Much discussion followed, in raised and furious voices at times, as the light faded into the dark.

As usual, Gallon took charge of the quarrelling group, beginning with the facts. 'It would be too dangerous to sling Barnio over the rock at this time. Garnios never move in their sleep, so there's no danger for Barnio to sleep under the crevice of that large rock.'

'Let me try to carry him on my back.' Interjected Zaphod. Whilst Zaphod knew the wisdom that Gallon was offering, Zaphod also didn't wish to his friend to be left unattended.

'It's worth a try,' chanted the others almost in unison, Gallon however shook his head and said, 'I don't like the chances.'

Before logical thought had a chance to take hold Zaphod's impulsive nature took flight. Only seconds after Truscott had managed to tie the rope firmly to the tree at the top, Zaphod jumped to his feet and said with determination 'I will give it all I can.' The whole group held their breath when Zaphod hauled the now lifeless Barnio over his shoulder. As Barnio was fast asleep his body was weighty and heavy. It flipped and flopped around until Zaphod could manage to hold him under is left wing. He took the rope in his right hand and strained every muscle and sinew to haul his beloved companion up the treacherous incline. He had only managed to get a few feet up the craggy rock face when his foot missed a crevice and his whole body jolted downwards, the strain of the weight of the lifeless Barnio became an overwhelming burden. Zaphod managed to turn to the group with pleading eyes. Gallon swept into action, he grabbed Barnio's legs gently untangling him from Zaphod's hold and steadied the sleeping Garnio to the ground. The flailing Zaphod was able to steady himself and managed to place himself back on the ground.

Gallon who looked squarely at Zaphod though addressed the whole group, 'We will not attempt this again' As you can see there is graver danger in attempting to bring Barnio with us tonight. We will fetch him before first light, before he even misses us. Now let's get him safely set up under the rock ledge.'

Following Gallon's instructions, Perina, Nadoo, and Nomad set to the task, placing Barnio on his mattock, making sure he was comfortable and warm, placing vines over the entrance to keep him safe and undetected from the Lurkin or any of his followers. No dangerous animals wandered in that area, so Barnio was deemed safe until morning.

Truscott led the party up the rock one by one. He made sure that everyone knew the importance of placing their feet firmly before on any ledge they find prior to hauling themselves upwards. He threw down the rope to Zaphod who quickly managed to utilise them in a pulley type fashion to reach the top. Zaphod and Truscott then instructed the group to tie the ropes around themselves, and between Zaphod and Truscott, they heaved all the members atop the rock. Nadoo was the noisiest of all climbing up the rock, she huffed and puffed, thought was possibly the most sure footed of all in the climb. Truscott set to clearing path down the other side of the rock banked by the cliff face, which created a track, almost like a staircase, down the other side.

The group was now safely on the other side of the rock, near a clearing. In the dwindling light, they started setting camp, though all of them felt heavy-hearted about leaving Barnio behind. Gallon tried to comfort them by stating the facts. 'There wasn't enough room on the path for anyone to sleep, and even if they stayed, they would risk rolling over in their sleep and fall straight down the treacherous edge of the cliff to their death.'

The group knew he was right, though somehow, it still felt like they were deserting Barnio. Truscott pleaded with Gallon to be allowed to check on Barnio through the night. But, this was disallowed, as the danger of him slipping or losing his footing, due to the low visibility, was too great a risk. It was decided however that Zaphod and Truscott, both being early risers who awoke before dawn, would venture down to rock to greet Barnio after he woke up, bringing him back with them for a delicious breakfast. Just the mention of food was enough to cheer up Nadoo, who promised to make some cakes in the fire in the morning, with some flour and other foodstuff that she had brought along.

They pitched their tents, placed their mattocks down, and ate beside a campfire, before they retired for bed. At the campfire, Perina said a prayer for Barnio saying, 'May Barnio be safe throughout the night, with us being there to greet him at the beginning of light.' After chanting this prayer in unison, they went off to sleep to refresh themselves for the next day. Gallon stayed awake the longest, checking for any suspicious noise or disturbance, before he too succumbed to tiredness and fell into a deep slumber.

Chapter 6

The Confrontation

Learn to respond, not react.
Discuss and debate though, do not attack.

The group was awakened by the perilous cries of Truscott and Zaphod. 'Barnio is missing; he is not there!' they screamed in distressed voices, as loud as they could. Soon enough, everyone, including Nadoo, emerged from their tents, gathering in a circle to discuss the situation.

'Are you sure he didn't just roll into a crevice nearby?' asked Nadoo with a harrumph; she was a little bit gruff, as she never, ever, ever liked being woken up.

Truscott and Zaphod arrived back in the camp, screeching to a halt as they saw the group. 'We awoke at dawn, just as promised, to meet Barnio,' blurted Zaphod.

'Not only is Barnio missing, so is the large boulder that was blocking the path,' reported Truscott. 'We scoured the entire surrounding area there is no trace of him either.

'It has to be the work of the Lukin,' spat Zaphod through gritted teeth 'How else could that boulder have moved, and why hadn't we heard it.' Despair and fear crept though the group, who stood together now with silent thoughts and whitening skins. It was decided with some trepidation that Gallon, Zaphod, Perina and Truscott would return and conduct another search.

'I will make breakfast whilst you are gone,' motioned Nadoo. Whilst Nadoo was very concerned about Barnio, her appetite never left her. Her motto was that being hungry never helped anyone. She began unpacking the supplies to cook breakfast. She laughed to herself thinking Barnio had woken up and sped off in the wrong direction and would find his way back in time for the pancakes. A whisper of a thought, which appeared to blow into her head like the wind, tormented her slightly. *This would not have happened if Gallon hadn't convinced everyone that it was too dangerous to move him at night.* Nadoo shrugged her shoulders and harrumphed out loud. A tiny seed of doubt in her leader began to grow in her mind.

What seemed like hours had passed before Gallon, Zaphod, Perina, and Truscott returned to the campsite. Breakfast was all laid out, ready to be eaten.

'No Trace. No trace at all,' stated Gallon. Everyone seemed to slump in height at this declaration. Nomad held his head in his hands in despair. Over breakfast, they began to discuss what their following course of action would be. Though each of them knew the importance of eating breakfast, no one was particularly hungry. Even Nadoo was picking at her food, though she was still able to devour about seven pancakes.

'We are not prepared for delays like this. The rations will not last if we stay an extra day here,' reasoned Gallon. No one wanted to leave without Barnio.

'If we hadn't trusted Gallon's wisdom so blindly, Barnio might have been here now,' Nadoo declared openly, at one point in the discussion.

'We all made that decision, Nadoo, and it will not help if we start blaming each other,' Perina responded rapidly.

The other five agreed with Perina, and Nadoo reacted with a grimace and a harrumph.

The group was sitting despondently, when suddenly, they

heard a ruffling sound in the bushes, just beyond the campsite. The group became alert and full of hopeful expectations that it was Barnio speeding towards the campsite to join them for breakfast. But instead of him, a short and stout Trehwell emerged from the path.

'Greetings friends and travellers,' exclaimed the Trehwell in a cheerful tone.

'Heffla, my friend!' shouted Nomad, rising to greet the traveller, welcoming him with a warm embrace and heartfelt pats on his head. Heffla was a traveller who enjoyed his own company and loved the peace of the wilderness, living his days in commune with nature. He had long wild hair and a long and wiry beard. Heffla was introduced to everyone in the party and told the tale of Barnio's disappearance. Heffla stroked his long beard, showing great concern on learning about Barnio's predicament.

'I encountered some Tremlites scouting the woods yesterday. They were many miles from their settlement,' informed Heffla. 'I only hope that they did not discover the sleeping Barnio; who knows how they would treat him.' Although Heffla had lived most of his life by himself, he also had a great distrust for Tremlites, because of the tales he had heard. Thus, he hid whenever he saw any Tremlite and never sought to engage in any conversation with them.

'Oh alas, alas!' wept Nadoo, thinking about Barnio's possible capture. The entire party fervently started discussing what action to take. Heffla had spent many a night in the surrounding woods and was familiar with all the camping areas that the Tremlites could utilise. According to Heffla, the Tremlite settlement was a five-day march from Scaysborough, not three days, as the group had thought previously, and the Lurkin himself roamed about in this settlement. A cold shiver ran through the group just at the name of the Lurkin, making them shudder in unison. Heffla recounted how on one occasion he had ventured into a Tremlite camp on their invitation. He had been walking unusually late in the night, due to a mishap of taking a wrong trail, and was scouring for a place to set up camp in the rapidly fading light. He could hear some voices in the distance and literally bumped into two Tremlites who were gathering sticks.

They had introduced themselves as Dorian and Josat, and upon hearing Heffla's plight to find a camp at this late hour, they invited him to join them. Feeling very tired, Heffla kept his suspicions aside and followed Dorian and Josat to their camp.

Dorian and Josat were Fallons who used to traverse the paths of the forest to gather wild Jimjam (a little white fruit that tasted like honey). They would then sell those fruits in the Tremlite village. Other Tremlites had also been there at the camp, and upon hearing about Heffla's affiliation to Scaysborough, they began to urge him to join them and change his residence to live in Tremlite. They informed him about the treachery of the Scaysborough folk, recounting tales of the many wrongs done by them. They even spoke of an incident concerning a poisoned lake, which Heffla knew had occurred in Scaysborough because of the Tremlites' mischief, not the Scaysborough folk, as they were alleging. Heffla had felt that it must have been the Lurkin speaking through them, as he did not believe their tales and made excuses to retire early to his tent. He took off the first thing in the morning and, upon meeting Dorian and Josat at the fire preparing breakfast, thanked them for their stay, telling them that he was leaving early to make the most of his journey.

The group had many questions for Heffla about the meeting, which he answered to the best of his best knowledge –what did they look like, what did they wear, and so on. As Heffla was describing them, he was aware that they looked like and acted very much like the Scaysborough folk. On being questioned about the Lurkin, Heffla replied, 'The Lurkin is something that cannot be seen or directly heard; it is like a whisper in the wind that enters your soul.' This sent a shiver through the group, and once again, Nadoo thought about what she had considered regarding the mismanagement of protecting Barnio, though she did not utter it aloud this time. She merely swallowed the thought though added it to the discontent that was bubbling and brewing in her belly.

CHAPTER 7

THE DISCOVERY

The only truth you will find is within yourself.
Others' truths are theirs alone.

Dorian and Josat, the Fallons previously spoken about by Heffla, were themselves out, scouring the forest for wild Jimjam as they usually would. This time, they were heading for the trees that grew high up in Mistoka Mountain. They did not travel this far usually, though they had heard that the trees here were full of this delicious, ripe, honey-like fruit. Dorian and Josat were brothers who were often mistaken for twins, as they were similar in size and strength. They were born in the Tremlite settlement, and in spite of being Fallons, neither of them had chosen to grow wings, as they enjoyed their robustness. They maintained their physiques in best shape by lifting heavy stones, running, and climbing. They therefore were said to be the strongest Fallons in Tremlite town, often bedazzling the residents with their feats.

They would often laugh about the time when they had lifted an entire billop (a small cottage), disturbing a Garnio's midday meal. The Garnio, whose table and foodstuffs were unexplainably moving and wobbling about quickly, looked out of the window to see what was happening. It's said that his eyes became so large, it engulfed his whole face, on seeing that his house was being carried around by Dorian and Josat on their shoulders. The brothers were much younger at the time and full of mischief. They were told off so much by the upset Garnio, Jonya, as his home now had cracks and splits after being manhandled by the pair. After the news of the incident reached their father, Tiago, he made them spend the rest of the day repairing the billop, as well as any other odd job that Jonya directed them to do for the following one month. By the end of the month, after completing many tasks, including chopping a nearby mountain of wood for him, they had vowed never to do anything so foolish again. Being made of clay and bound with vine ropes and wax, billops were heavy as an elephant! It's little wonder that, from that day onward, Dorian and Josat were known as the strongest Fallons in the village and were often called upon for heavy work. The brothers, still being young at the time, however did not keep their vow completely.

Apart from being brothers, Dorian and Josat were best of friends, taking pride in their strength, for which they were renowned. They continued to amaze the villagers, lifting heavy logs and boulders. One day, for more merriment, Josat and Dorian lifted two of their father's cow's right over their heads, rested them on their shoulders, and placed them promptly on the cowshed's roof. As you can imagine, they got into a lot trouble from their father, when he ventured out of his Billop to see what all the mooing was about. You can imagine his surprise when he found the perplexed cows on the roof. The brothers were immediately summoned and ordered to retrieve the cows, making sure they place the cows down as gently as they could. Once this was achieved, they had to spend time cleaning out the cowshed. As angry as their father, Tiago, was at the time of the misadventure, he could now be heard laughing out loud while recounting the incident to others. Josat and Dorian were adult Fallons now and had mostly left their mischievous ways behind. But, they still enjoyed showing off their feats of strength, though they were very careful not to upset anyone when doing so.

After becoming adults, Josat and Dorian moved to the centre of Tremlite and bought apartments next to each other in a large and ornate tower that reached up to the sky. Most creatures in Tremlite chose this kind of a dwelling, so there were very few Billops in Tremlite town.

Anyway, as discussed, Josat and Dorian had headed off to collect Jimjam. They would generally leave Tremlite early in the morning, as Mistoka Mountain was a long way from their home. Most beings would take about five days to reach the mountain, but Dorian and Josat could run as swift as a Noonan (a cheetah-like animal) and reach the mountain in about eight hrs. They would usually collect the Jimjam in the afternoon and camp at the base of the mountain overnight, making their way home the next morning. Customarily, a large crowd of residents would be gathered to meet them on their return, eager to barter or buy the delicious Jimjam fruit.

On this day however, Dorian and Josat had left particularly early, as they had planned to run past Scaysborough, being very curious about the settlement. After meeting Heffla, whom they both liked, they were unsure about why Scaysborough folks had such a bad reputation with the Tremlite folk. The brothers did not think that the Lurkin existed, as they had heard many tales but never encountered it themselves despite travelling the land far and wide. Of course, their father, Tiago, forbid them to ever go near Scaysborough, warning them about the dangers. But, of course they wanted to find out for themselves. In Tremlite, Scaysborough folk were said to be proud, haughty, nasty, and untrustworthy. Tiago had told them the tale of his great, great, grandfather, Trinto, who had lived in Scaysborough till he was banished from the town. The story recounted through the generations was that Trinto had been visiting a neighbour and had forgotten to shut the gate of the cowshed. Due to this error, seven of his neighbour's cows had escaped. When the farmer found out about the diminished stock of his cows, he accused Trinto of stealing them.

A trial was held; being found guilty, Trinto was banished from Scaysborough. On his way out of the town, Trinto found the cows. But, instead of returning them, extremely angered about being accused of thievery, he took them with him, vowing to set up a new settlement that he named Tremlite. He sent word to Scaysborough about his plans via a friend who had visited him secretly and the other disgruntled Scaysborough folk came to live in this settlement as well. This is why it's a common practice in Scaysborough to believe that Tremlite is full of criminals, when really it housed the creatures who had been unjustly accused of crimes that they had not committed. If only both the towns knew how similar they were, they would not be such arch-enemies at all!

As you know already, Dorian and Josat were curious about Scaysborough and had set out early, around two am, stocking their cassocks with supplies, running bare chested through the forest, straight towards Scaysborough. They ran like the wind, arriving at Scaysborough before dawn. On reaching a clearing of the forest, they could barely make out Scaysborough's silhouette in the blurry distance, still obscured by the darkness of the ending night.

They decided to creep closer to the town and, in doing so, encountered a curious sight in a field just before the main township. It appeared to be a campsite with a lot of tents joined together in a honeycomb shape. They edged closer to these tents, trying to peer inside in an attempt to see the inhabitants. They could hear loud snoring from one tent, and just as they were about to peer into a window, they heard someone stirring. They ran back to the edge of the forest as fast as they could. On their way, Dorian accidentally tore a part of his bright yellow cassock, and unbeknownst to him, a few strands got left behind on a bush near the tents.

The brothers were disappointed for not having had the opportunity to see more, but they vowed to come back on another occasion, hoping to investigate further. Both of them thought to themselves, *Scaysborough does not seem very different at all from Tremlite, except the buildings perhaps.* It appeared to them that Scaysborough was dotted with small Billops and did not possess the grand tall buildings that Tremlite town offered. Not wanting to be detected, since they were still unsure about how the Scaysborough folk would great them, Dorian and Josat wasted no time in leaving Scaysborough before dawn broke and ran swiftly towards Mistoka Mountain, so that they could fill their cassocks with Jimjam. On reaching the summit, when it was nearing sun down, they had a good view of the valley below and were surprised to see that the track on the other side of the mountain seemed to have been cleared. They were hoping it was Heffla who had cleared these paths, as he seemed to be an affable Trehwell and depicted no malicious tendencies as such.

They reached the Jimjam tree that was glistened mildly in the last gasp of the sun's setting rays and was laden with fruits. Josat and Dorian started plucking as many fruits as they could carry on their backs. Luckily, Josat had brought candles that rested inside lanterns, which helped them with the picking. They had filled their cassocks to near capacity when Josat spotted a big bunch of large Jimjam fruits hanging from a branch near the edge of the mountain. It was too big a prize to resist, so Dorian held the lantern, whilst Josat climbed on the limb and began cutting the scrumptious Jimjams from their resting place.

For whatever reason, Josat happened to glance downwards and noticed a strange apparition of a figure tucked behind a rock. It looked like a Garnio to him, as he could just make out its shape in the fading light. Josat called out to his brother, asking him to bring the other lantern. With the help of the two lanterns, he had enough light to clearly see a Garnio sound asleep.

On noticing the footprints nearby, Josat and Dorian knew that a party of people had been climbing the track. After long deliberations, they felt that the party must have abandoned the Garnio. As they did not recognise this Garnio to be a resident of Tremlite, they figured that he must be from Scaysborough. Observing the tracks, they were certain that a mix of beings were amongst the group – some Fallons, Garnios, Nipoos, Trehwells, and Etruscans. Though due to the large number of footprints they were unsure of how many creatures were in the party, it looked as though they had been circling the spot where the Garnio was lying.

Believing that the group had abandoned the poor sleeping Garnio, Josat and Dorian refuelled their beliefs that Scaysborough folk were indeed cruel, selfish, and mean, just like their father had reported. *Why else would they leave this poor little Garnio behind without any covering or care? It's not like they couldn't move this rock,* figured Josat, who was not aware that having wings restricted a Fallon's strength, no matter how much of it they had. Josat and Dorian put both their shoulders on the rock and pushed and pushed, they strained every muscle, pushed with their shoulders and their calves, slipped backwards and pushed and pushed. It didn't budge. 'Stubborn ' said Dorian and beckoned to his brother to try another way. They turned around and now placed their backs firmly onto the rock and pushed backward. Their feet and calves strained as they pushed backwards, the rock responded with a tiny movement towards the edge of the path. They now encouraged pushed and pushed even harder, their calves and leg muscles bulging with the strain,the rock caved and moved slowly but surely until it creaked into submission, lost its balance and obediently dropped off the edge. Josat and Dorian watched in satisfaction as it bounced down the cliff all the way to the bottom of the valley.

For some reason, the stone made little noise as it made its way down. It's probably because it hit tufts of grass repeatedly, which softened the sound. If only Dorian and Josat had known that Barnio was indeed cared for and a warm blanket lay nearby. It had become buried underneath a pile of leaves which had blown off the hapless Barnio with an unexpected gush of wind. It was further unsettled by some curious Bolbroks (possum-like creatures), which had come across the piece of cloth. They had smelt it, tasted it, and, on finding that it was not edible, tossed it aside. Of course, the brothers didn't know that Barnio, the Garnio, was a much-loved member of the group from Scaysborough. Josat and Dorian gently picked up the sleeping Garnio, carrying him carefully back to their camp and settled into a troubled sleep.

Chapter 8

Barnio Awakes

*Those who speak don't know those whom
they know don't speak.*

Josat and Dorian could not sleep well at all that night. So, around two am, they decided to leave camp and head home so that they could arrive around mid morning. They were concerned that the treacherous Scaysborough band might come in the night and steal their Jimjam or harm the Garnio whom they had found abandoned. Josat and Dorian had heard many tales of the Scaysborough folk's cruelty and did not wish to be on the receiving end of their treachery. They both knew too well of the time when the freshwater lakes at Tremlite turned salty overnight, causing immense damage as most of the fish in the lake died and water in Tremlite became scarce.

The town was on the brink of complete collapse when one Etruscan named Evarb arranged for the lake to be siphoned and sifted through a special substance that removed the salt. The limited number of fish that could be rescued were placed in a holding tank. Once filtered, the water was pumped back into the lake and the surviving fish were released in it. A ban on fishing in the lake was placed for two years, until the fish were able to regain their numbers.

The Tremlite folk were overcome with a lot of anger and

anguish about this incident; it was widely believed that some Scaysborough folks had entered their territory overnight and emptied salt sacks into the lake. Someone had discovered small footprints near the lake; scientists believed they were more likely a child's footprint. Nevertheless, it was attributed to be the footprints of someone from Scaysborough. It was this tale that made Josat and Dorian shudder at the treachery and wanton destruction of the Scaysborough residents, which gave them extra impetus to set out for home early, placing themselves at a safe distance from the rogues at Scaysborough. If only they knew how similar an event had occurred in the lake at Scaysborough and how the Tremlite folk were thought to be the culprits!

Josat was running down a rugged mountain path when the first light penetrated the forest leaves, lingering on Barnio's cheek long enough for him to wake up with a jolt of fear. Barnio, now completely roused from his sleepy state, could feel the weighty hands around his legs and arms, as he was moving up and down, flumping and flopping around. Absolutely unamused at his undignified treatment, Barnio began berating whom he thought was the culprit at large – someone whom he knew had the same strength in his arms and firmness of body.

'Zaphod! Put me down immediately, immediately, immediately,' shouted the indignant Barnio. Almost as soon as he said it, Barnio suddenly realised that it could not be Zaphod who was carrying him, as he could not feel the bulbous edges of his wings situated near his collarbone.

Barnio shrieked out in alarm, as he now realised that he was being carried by an unknown captor. Josat stopped abruptly, taking a look at Barnio with such compassion and care that Barnio somehow knew instantly that he was safe, and he relaxed his body somewhat. He could now see that he was being carried in a makeshift hammock-type structure that had hitched him to his carrier's back. Hearing the commotion, Dorian stopped alongside his brother and gazed at Barnio with such kindness and concern that Barnio felt even more relaxed. Barnio however did not take to being carried and clearly requested the strangers to kindly put him down. Josat gently untied the cloth that was holding Barnio, with Dorian assisted him in gently lowering their unknown charge, the Garnio, to the ground.

'Haito beterd, haito beterd,' said Barnio, which was a well-known Garnio greeting.

'Jenta Jonty,' replied Josat and Dorian in unison, something that they did often, oddly enough. 'Jenta Jonty' was a well-known Fallon reply.

'My name is Barnio, Barnio. How is it that I came to be on your shoulders,your shoulders?' enquired Barnio, tilting his head sideways with a curious stare, his eyes as wide as saucers.

Quickly and excitedly, Dorian and Josat recounted how they found Barnio and considered that he had been abandoned by the fiends of Scaysborough. Barnio remembered the blockage on the road and enquired if they had seen his friends, whom he was accompanying on their journey to discover the Lurkin. It was at this point that the brothers remembered that they had not introduced themselves; as this was a cordial procedure, it was initiated with much haste.

'My name is Jorian,' they both blurted out together. Dorian and Josat said it such unison that it was heard as Jorian. In an attempt to clarify, they repeated their names several times – in unison every time. Barnio, becoming frustrated, suggested that they go one at a time. Dorian and Josat attempted to do so, but they ended up speaking simultaneously again. Barnio, becoming thoroughly agitated at this point, pointed to Dorian, gesturing him to go first. This way worked well, and Barnio finally got to know his presumed captors' names.

Dorian and Josat told Barnio all that they knew about the

Lurkin, which was a mythical creature according to them. Barnio gasped and froze in fear as they told him that they were Tremlites. Although, the gentleness of his two strong companions melted his fear somehow, and he became decidedly more curious than afraid. The brothers gave Barnio some of their collected Jimjam to eat, which solidified his respect for his two newly made friends, as he heartily devoured the delicious bounty at hand. With a lot of confusion in mind, Barnio listened to Dorian and Josat's account of how their families and others in Tremlite had suffered at the hands of the cruel Scaysborough folk.

He reiterated his confusion to the pair with his counter tales about the Tremlites' dastardly deeds to his companions in Scaysborough. His instincts told him that his companions would not have abandoned him, though he did agree with his new Fallon friends that he could not be sure with 100 percent clarity. Garnio's are curious by nature, which is why Barnio agreed to go with Josat and Dorian to Tremlite town. However, before that, he wanted to check for himself if his friends had indeed deserted him. Dorian and Josat agreed to wait for Barnio whilst he checked, as they both were aware of the speed that Garnios could travel. They knew it would be minutes, not hours, before he returned. Barnio sped like light to the place where he was left the evening prior. He was easily able to follow the rather heavily trodden tracks made by Dorian and Josat earlier that morn. In the blink of an eye, Barnio found himself at the ledge, which was the last thing remembered from the previous day. Curiously, the large boulder was nowhere to be seen. He nudged closer to the edge and peered down to find the boulder somewhat hidden at the bottom of the gully, resting at the banks of a brook. Barnio remembered a big hullaballoo, which his group had engaged in, about not being able to move the rock, but he couldn't remember anything that happened afterwards.

A small seed of doubt grew in Barnio's mind, about why indeed did his companions leave him. He scoured the ground around him, but he could see no trace whatsoever of anyone anywhere. No signs of struggle or problems of any kind were left behind. He called out his friends' names – Gallon, Perina, Truscott, Zaphod, Nadoo, and Nomad. He listened intently for any sounds but only heard the echoes of his own voice reverberating in the gully. Did they really abandon him? Could there really be such treachery in Scaysborough as Josat and Dorian described?

Barnio recollected a time when Zaphod had refused to share some crayfish he had found with him, even though Barnio had willingly shared a bucket of berries with him the day prior. 'Harrumph,' began Barnio, 'Harrumph, Harrumpth, and Harrumpth.' Barnio had picked up the habit of harrumphing from Nadoo; it was a sign of his displeasure. The seed of doubt was becoming bigger in Barnio's mind. He was perplexed and angry at the same time, which lead to more harrumphing from him. Barnio then sped back to his rescuers, Josat and Dorian. He arrived in no time but took longer than usual, as his heart was heavy with a new-found sorrow.

'You were right; there is no sign of my friends at all. Not at all, not at all, Thank you for your care, your care,' bowed Barnio. 'I am very happy to travel, to travel with you to Tremlite, Tremlite.'

Josat and Dorian, nodded to gesture their understanding, gathered their things, and the triad began their journey to Tremlite town.

Chapter 9

The Group Parts Ways

The journey with oneself is the pathway to knowledge.

Back at camp, Perina, Truscott, Zaphod, Nadoo, and Nomad were sitting in a circle, feeling utterly forlorn. All of them appeared to be in harmony in terms of their dark thoughts and innate sadness regarding their current situation. Only Heffla seemed to be busying himself about the campsite, preparing to gather his beloved Jimjams.

While picking up the sciors (a tool used to cut the Jimjams off the trees), Heffla noticed the sombre group before him and felt that he might be able to offer some advice, as he had much knowledge about the mountains and paths of the forests. It was then that Heffla himself sat down and pondered the situation, drawing in the sand with a stick, muttering to himself, crossing things out. Zaphod heard these scratchings, which made him curious about Heffla's actions. Just then, Heffla broke the silence by sharing his opinion, with the mellow group, about the best way to find their friend, which he had formulated after much deliberations. Heffla requested the entire party to gather around his drawings. He then began to articulate his ideas.

'I feel that the best way to find your friend, Barnio, is for you to split up and take different paths to the Tremlite camp. Barnio could be along any one of these tracks.' Heffla pointed to the map, whilst the team gathered around him with animated interest.

'We are very fortunate to have Heffla stumble across us on our journey. His knowledge of the area is vast. We are very grateful for your valuable advice, Heffla,' Zaphod stated on behalf of his friends.

'Each path is not without its own peril,' warned Heffla, pointing to the five detailed maps that he had drawn on the hardened earth. Path number one traversed through a dense forest named Binto; it had vines and shrubs that sometimes grew over its path and had to be cleared with a knife or axe. The second path required crossing the Jinku River, for which one had to be sure that the tide was low, otherwise the stream could be too turbulent for someone to swim or wade through. Number three wound around Minju Mountain, which was a steep and windy road that became quite rocky and difficult to climb at the summit. The fourth descended down a valley; its bottom was dark, cold, and slippery, making the ascent harrowing, as one needed to find footing in the muddy path. This leaves the final path number 5 which traverses around a large lake named Lake Doli, It was the longest, but considered the easiest, of the five routes to traverse. The only difficulty in this path was a small climb up a rocky incline towards the end, which was also worryingly close to the edge of Tremlite town. Heffla advised that the group should expect up to five days to make their trek to meet in the Town Square of Tremlite. Heffla advised the Town Square was safe and where other outsiders met to sell their wares. Thus the group of travellers would not come under any suspicion as they would be considered traders from other lands.

Gallon lead the discussion with positive refrain, as was his usual manner. He focused on the pros and cons of each path, stroking his beard, and thought purposefully when discussing each option. He felt that the Fallons should take the most difficult paths, as their wings could make the journey easier should they encounter peril. Nadoo was given what the group thought was the easiest path – the one around the lake. This was agreed upon, though Nadoo, possibly having a premonition about her forthcoming ordeal, complained loudly about her lot, as it was the longest walk, feeling that she might run out of food due to the long time required to traverse the path.

Nadoo was offered the other paths, but on looking at the possible perils of the other four ones, she settled with the path through the lake and discussed how she could best utilise her supplies during her walk around the lake. Heffla assisted in convincing Nadoo by telling her that the path, though long and winding, did not involve much climbing and would be perfect for her delicate legs. Nadoo blushed and agreed at once with Heffla. No one made a comment, but a few grins were exchanged, as her legs were as thick and sturdy as tree trunks. Nipoos were always worried about food, and Nadoo was no exception. Rarely did she go one hour without eating some tasty morsel, which were generally cooked and carried by her.

Truscott, considered the bravest and strongest member of the group, would take the path over Minju Mountain. It was considered that his strong legs and sturdy body would help him climb the mountain when the path became the steepest. He was known for his rock-climbing skills, which would definitely come in handy according to Heffla. Heffla confessed that he himself rarely took this path due to its steep incline, even though there was a particularly tasty berry named Marja that grew on the top of the mountain. Forgetting their mission for a moment, hearing about a new delicious berry, which Heffla described to be sweeter than honey and as juicy as water, Nadoo implored Truscott to pluck some for her on his way. Perina quickly reminded Nadoo about the task at hand – finding their friend Barnio. Nadoo ashamedly bowed her head but still secretly wished for a taste of the berry and did not give up the hope of receiving some.

Zaphod would take the track through the Binto forest, as he was the most experienced one in the jungle and had the best knowledge about the food available there.

'Your wings will be of very little use over there,' warned Heffla, as the forest was very dense and the track was overgrown in some parts. 'If Barnio was along the track, you would not be able to see him in case you flew above.' However, Zaphod was very happy about the path allocated to him and was keen to begin his journey, as he loved stretching his body, climbing up hills, and challenging his strength – not to mention the joys of finding edible treasures amongst the foliage and vines.

Perina was chosen for the path through the Jinko River. Prior to her metamorphosis, she held the record as the strongest swimmer in Scaysborough. Perina had won many swimming competitions at the local carnivals and county fairs. It was Perina's love for swimming that had deterred her from growing wings at a younger age. But eventually, Zaphod's flying agility and antics enticed her to leave her swimming behind and take to the air. Perina was still able to swim, though her wings had slowed her down considerably. Despite this, Perina could still outswim many of the unwinged residents of Scaysborough. Perina was delighted with the path assigned to her and was keen to swim across the banks of the Jinko, plunging into its welcoming depths. She would then need to climb Binku, which was a smaller and less travelled mountain adjacent to the Minju Mountain, and cross the summit to meet the others at its foothills near Tremlite.

This left Nomad with the winding, at times perilous, track through the steep Vindu Valley and its slippery slopes. Nomad was well accustomed to steep rocky climbs, as he had been brought up in the Volty Valley of Scaysborough. He and his brothers used to race and scale the steep wall that surrounded his home situated at the bottom of the valley. He did this with grace and ease; actually Nomad did everything with grace and ease, which was befitting of his title as the leader of the Trehwells. Nomad however hid his royal identity from the townspeople in Scaysborough, as he hated the attention. Even though no one knew him as a king, he had a princely manner about him, which he had been taught by his father and his predecessors. He was trained in diplomacy and appropriate etiquettes, though he preferred to be alone, so that he could behave like a child, abandoning all graces. He had great dexterity, capable of grasping rocks with his hands and feet with equal grip. Even Nomad was happy with his choice and couldn't wait to enjoy his path – free and unencumbered.

Well, that leaves Gallon. 'What about him?' – you may as well ask, dear reader! Gallon had decided to swiftly head back to Scaysborough for gathering extra support, as it was equally important to have additional forces backing the group when they did enter Tremlite. In case Barnio was not found before that, along the five chosen paths, they would need to look for him in Tremlite. His plan was to summon the council of the wise with the view of gathering another band of Scaysborough folk, which would take the most direct route to Tremlite. He hoped that, with this group on the sixth path around the bottom of the mountain, he would reach Tremlite a few days after them and would be at their disposal, to assist them if need be. Naturally, there was a fair bit of discussion about this choice. Nadoo, in particular, was upset as she felt that Gallon had got it easy. Though after much deliberation, it was agreed that Gallon's wisdom would be required for gathering the perfect band of Scaysborough folk and talking to the council of elders regarding their predicament, which would help them utilise their collective wisdom for assisting the party's perilous quest.

'Why can't we all go back to Scaysborough?' inquired Nadoo,

but her suggestion was immediately put down, as the aim was to find Barnio as quickly as possible. He had now been missing for almost 24 hours, and the group needed to try and find him as soon they possibly could. But still, Nadoo harrumphed and harrumphed some more, somehow trusting Gallon less and less. Zaphod considered Nadoo's proposal and also went away holding a tiny bit of a grudge against Gallon. Something was wafting around. Discontent was entering the group; it was like the Lurkin himself was whispering in the wind, wafting into the minds of willing receivers.

CHAPTER 10

THE JOURNEY BEGINS

No matter which path you choose,
let the journey be a lesson learnt.

The band divided the food and sleeping equipment equally, they just had enough for each to last five days. This was largely due to Nadoo being in charge of food supplies she always overpacked food so this coupled with Barnio's supply meant they could just manage a five day journey. 'We must also look out for fruit on our paths,' advised Gallon, 'to add to our supplies'. Nadoo was the first and only one to complain about her fear of running out of food and that. She loudly announced that she did not have enough Jimjam cakes. But, in reality Nadoo would never have felt she had enough, even if she had the entire lot! So, with a lot of huffing and puffing, and only after making everyone show their portions to her, she eventually concluded that she had received a fair share. In complete fairness however as she had been given the easiest path she should have received a little less though not one was willing to have this discussion with her and all food was packed in their cassocks.

Heffla, now keen to leave the party as he was not used to company for long, bid them well and hastily got back to his own endeavours. He was eager to regain the solitude and solace in his oneness, as that was when he was most content.

After eating their evening meal, the party retired to their own tents, though each slept fitfully in troubled slumber – each concerned about their own particular path and the unknown obstacles therein – all except Truscott. Truscott went to bed with the firm belief that he would be able to get through the tasks assigned to him and whatever he required would be provided. He would always think like this, rationally, and never appeared to be troubled, shining and smiling contentedly wherever he went.

However, Gallon was disturbed in his sleep not by his thoughts but by a sound of something creeping around. He thought he heard a twig break under a foot. He strained his ears immensely to determine what may be outside his tent. In a few moments, he heard the cry of a Truon tangled in a branch of a nearby tree. Feeling comforted by this explanation, he settled into a peaceful sleep once again. But, if he had investigated further, the curious eyes of a young Trehwell might have been discovered!

The entire group woke up with the sun rising and stoically started preparing for the trip. Even Nadoo did not grumble or complain; she just ate her breakfast and steadfastly packed her belongings, ready for her solo trip. Nadoo even tried to change the sombre ambience by singing a song of courage and victory, which was extremely popular in Scaysborough. It went like this…

If we all stand together, we can give it a chance
If we all band together, we will strengthen our stance
If we all walk together across this great land
We will meet every mountain and trouble at hand
We can solve every problem, even one that's nigh
And will dance on return with victory on our side

Everyone at camp sang this song with great delight, and before long, everyone was packed and ready for the daunting task ahead. They all stood in a circle and wished each other well. Each of them had their map for their journey and knew where they would meet up near the mountain. They all sang the song as they departed, singing in unison, until each was alone with their own voice, and complete silence fell.

Chapter 11

Perina's Quest

Don't lose yourself; stay present and focused wherever you are.

Perina was chosen for the path over the Jinku River, which she would have to cross before climbing up the Binku Mountain to meet her comrades at the Tremlite camp. The group felt that this path would be most suitable for Perina, as her wings would come in handy crossing the river in case swimming across the river was not possible. Heffla had said the path had less trees and obstacles, which would allow her to fly unhindered. This was important as her flying skills were still quite amateur when compared to Zaphod – the other flying Fallon.

Heffla recommended that Perina should fly up, instead of climb, the small but quite steep Binku mountain on the other side of the lake, which he considered a very laborious task. However, the energy spent when flying is still quite debilitating; flapping the large and, at times, cumbersome wings could sap a Fallon's energy quickly, which meant that they could only fly short distances – this was the reason many Fallons chose not to metamorphose. You might be wondering why do any of them metamorphose at all, right? But, if you asked those that do, they would say that that the joy of flying even a small distance was such a jubilant and exhilarating experience that one forgot any difficulties that the wings posed at all.

It was this joy and the freedom found in soaring in the air, as spruiked by Zaphod, which finally convinced Perina to go through the metamorphosis. Perina's journey to Jinku river began quite peacefully; she wandered through the bushes, admiring the many and varied plants. She stopped often, smelling the flowers, admiring the butterflies and insects buzzing and crawling throughout the lush vegetation that she was meandering through. A shiver passed through her and she was ashamed of the joy she was feeling, she admonished herself as if it was some dishonour to Barnio. She became vexed with her conflicted emotions and shivered at the thought of the Lurkin and what she would do if she encountered this being on her path. This thoughts however were only fleeting, as the joy and beauty of her surrounding captivated her, delighting her thoroughly as she walked through the forest.

Seemingly only a few hours along the trail, Perina caught a glimpse of the magnificent Jinku River. Spurred on by it's turquoise beauty, she hurried through the path to a clearing where she could look out to the whole of sparkling river that gently flowed through scattered and lapped the forest's edge. She marvelled at the majestic sight. It seems very safe and beautiful she thought to herself, why then were the elders so afraid of these territories she pondered. The water however seemed to call her to it, diamonds of light danced across the surface beckoning her to join them. It was so inviting that she momentarily forgot her mission of finding Barnio and decided to go for a swim, taking full advantage of the crystal clear stream before her. Perina swam in the crystalline water, losing herself to the pleasure of the coolness against her body. Swimming through the bubbling waters, delighting in the majesty that surrounded her, She felt exhilarated and energised. After swimming awhile, she noticed that she had to drag her wings,which were becoming heavier and heavier with each stroke. Had Perina had more experience with her newly formed wings she would have known that water would soak into its spidery web,creating extra weight which in effect would prevent her from flying any great distance.

As the weight of her wings interrupted her joy from swimming her thoughts turned to the Scaysborough community, wondering who Gallon would bring along with him to meet them at the foothills of the mountain. She thought fondly of Gallon and always felt somewhat comforted when he was near.

Perina now felt a little guilty about the time she had spent idly swimming,instead of searching for Barnio. This she chastened herself should be at the forefront of her mind a prompt that spurred her to launch herself out of the water.

As she crept out of the water, she felt the full weight of her sloppy wet wings. She dried herself off the best that she could and sat in the sun hoping that would them out and lighten her burden somewhat Flying will be a lot harder she speculated, better get some energy then and she promptly prepared her midday meal. After having her lunch, she looked at the distance ahead that she needed to cover. As the sun was progressively moving towards the west, she decided that she would fly above the river instead of walking up the winding steep path. Perina assumed that she would be able to get enough clearance from the trees and be able to reach the summit of Minju Mountain by sunset. She thought her wings were decidedly drier and flexed them a little to dislodge any remaining drips.

As she stood she noted that there were a few trees she would need to carefully maneuver past, though she felt relatively certain that she would be able to pull off this feat. Time now pressured her to get going. Perina packed up her equipment, placed her cassock on her back, and readied herself for the flight. Despite the drying in the sun the weight of her wings were still considerably more, she shrugged and thought well I think it will still work. Perina was fortuitously assisted by a mountain breeze, which helped her catapult herself to a nearby tree's height. She flapped her wings quite furiously to gain extra height, eventually propelling herself just above the canopy of the trees.

Flying however was quite cumbersome, due to the weight of her still water-soaked wings along with the cassock that was packed to the brim with food and camping equipment. Nevertheless, she managed to create a momentum by repetitively and earnestly flapping her wings, eventually being able to soar without a great deal of effort. Again, being inexperienced, she got lost in the joy of flight, beginning to swoop up and down in perilous delight. A memory of Zaphod's voice interrupted her, reminding her about his warning regarding flying delirium – where one could get caught up in the pleasure of flying, forgetting about the surroundings. Precisely at that moment, she was jolted with a large crash, excruciating pain, a sense of falling haplessly, being tossed like a feather in the breeze, this way and that, and finally her body thudded to a halt at the stump of a tree.

For the initial few moments, she felt dazed and disorientated, covered in branches and leaves of the tree that she fell through. Acute pain shot through her body, like a hot knife, and she was horrified to see that her right wing had twisted and was partially severed from her body. Perina let out a doleful piercing cry of pain, quick to realise that she was in quite a perilous position. She began sobbing at the stupidity of her actions, feeling that she was a disappointment for Zaphod who had tried to warn her about the follies and dangers of flying. Now she also remembered that wet wings were a pitfall when flying and that it was not safe to fly until they were completely dried out. Perina was overcome with pain and self-pity, feeling that she had failed the group, especially Barnio, whom she had no hope of finding any more. She again let out a mournful cry, beginning to sob profusely, feeling absolutely crestfallen.

Chapter 12

Danio to the Rescue

*Be your own knight in shining armour, as you are
the only one who knows what you need to be saved
from and how to be saved.*

It was the initial shriek that first alerted Danio that something
other than him was in the forest. In a nearby cave, Danio was
searching for a phosphorus substance that glowed in the dark.
He was well versed with the forest and knew of all the glories it
possessed.

Danio was a Trehwell only nine years of age, but he had the
bravery and stoic wisdom that many adult Trehwells could never
attain. He was earnest, living and breathing the virtues of the
forest's surrounds. Danio was the neglected child of Wilmsea and
Jardjon, both Trehwells, who lived in a small forest community
called Badon situated on the other side of Binku Mountain in a
tiny hidden valley that even Heffla didn't know about.

Badon evolved into a community, as aimless travellers, either
from Scaysborough or Tremlite town, stumbled upon the place.
They all had one common theme of their being – jaded from
everyday life, feeling that life had not treated them fairly. Their
shared perception was that others got more than them, and no
matter how hard they tried, things always went wrong for them.
In a way, such a supposition seemed to be true always in their

case. A wheel would fall off their wagon, and they would say, 'So typical. This always happens,' and abandon the wagon in the street, leaving their wares to spoil in the sun.

However, if they would look at things differently, they would notice that it was only a stick caught in the spoke which stopped their wagon and that there was a patch of delicious berries growing next to their wheel. This way, they would have the opportunity to collect more fruit to sell in the market! They however rarely looked for anything good around them, focusing instead on the lack and unfairness, as if drawn by a magnet. If they looked ahead and saw a dead tree, they would say to themselves – *oh look! Everything is dead and dying*. Although, if they would cast their eyes around, they would see the fields of flowers and fruits growing around. These misery-loving folk somehow found their way to Badon, where everyone agreed that it was there miserable lot to be poor and unhappy.

Badon yielded a fruit named Gogo growing in abundance around the town, which Danio's father, Jardjon, had learnt to turn into wine. He had discovered this by mistake, as he had picked a lot of berries and left them in a bucket outside his billop whilst he slept. It was a particularly rainy night, and in the morning, he had found that the berries had become swollen and inedible. Typical, he would have said, *'This always happens to me, now I will have to pick some more.'* But, he had left the berries rotting for a week and noticed some bubbles emerging at the top. On smelling the bubbling brew, he discovered that it somehow smelt sweet. He scooped up some and tasted it to find that it was strangely appealing and drank a few cups. Noticing how his troubles seemed to melt away on drinking the brew, he continued to drink it until he was unconscious. Jardjon woke the next day with a splitting headache. However, it disappeared after a while, and he had found himself strangely drawn more and more to the brew. He had therefore made some more and offered it to the other wretched residents of Badon. All of them soon found the wine to alleviate their troubles, allowing them to forget their misery for a while. So, they demanded Jardjon to keep up the supply, and they drank the substance heavily. Over time, they got used to drinking this wine, whiling away their time drinking, dancing, and not doing much else.

I guess, in some respects, they were happier than before, though the town was in much decrepitude. The residents of Badon did not do much other than sleep, eat a little, and drink. Whilst they were drinking, they didn't complain at least. They went through life playing instruments, singing, dancing, and drinking. Danio was born in this community, but his parents and most other residents were never sober enough to look after him. So, he busied himself the best he could. He loved experimenting and exploring in the forest, learning from life itself through trial and error. His father, Jardjon, had opened a tavern, so that he could serve the copious amounts of Gogo wine that the residents of Badon demanded. He and Danio's mother, Wilmsea, spent all their time serving Gogo wine, whilst drinking from the brew herself. It was not uncommon to find both Wilmsea and Jardjon asleep in the corners of the tavern in the morning, a drink balanced precariously in their hands, whilst they snored, snuffled, and slumbered snuggly. Jardjon however had developed an equilibrium with Gogo wine. He could live with it and live without it. Wilmsea however totally became addicted. She could not go a day without drinking and drink she did every single day. Gogo wine was the thing she thought of and reached for in the morning, drinking it steadily throughout the day and early morning before she succumbed to an unconscious state of being.

Danio was the only child in the community and was considered a miracle by the townsfolks, only when they were sober enough to remember him of course. Gogo seemed to affect a person's ability to conceive children, and Danio was an anomaly, treasured by an older couple, Jyno and Shona, who drank very little and enjoyed caring for the waif child. Jyno and Shona looked out for Danio, who began to rely on their care and assistance as he grew up.

As Danio had no daily routine or expectations, he spent his days touring the wilderness, discovering the wonders therein. He was often gone for days at a stretch and could easily fend for himself, being adept in bushcraft. It was during one such overnight expedition when he heard a loud piercing shriek, followed by muffled sobbing from a distance. I Wonder if it could have something to do with the party of explorers whom he had crept past the other night, he thought to himself. Curiosity spurred him on to try and find out who and what was crying, he scurried deftly through the dense undergrowth to seek out the object in distress.

Slashing and smashing his way through the forest,suddenly he was confronted by the wide eyes of despair. Perina shrieked again, startled by the young Trehwell. She stared at this strange apparition a Trehwell child wearing a yellow robe,dotted with slight tears and yellow hanging threads. She had not seen this colour attire before and thought he may be a small assailant from Tremlite. Danio quickly reassured her that he was there to help, not harm. After hearing his kind assurances, Perina relaxed somewhat, wondering what help, if any, could this young Trehwell provide her. Danio of course had many questions for Perina and, upon learning that she came from Scaysborough, discussed how he had visited the place many times under the blanket of night.

Perina was surprised to hear that he knew about Scaysborough; she was even more surprised when he told her he was not from but had been to Tremlite and could find not much difference between the inhabitants of both towns. Perina however, being gripped in pain, asked about the quickest route to Tremlite, so that she could meet with her friends. Though young in years, Danio was wise enough to know that, in her condition, the trip to Tremlite would be an impossible task. Danio was bold enough to suggest that she follow him to the town of Badon, which they would reach by nightfall, and he could get his friends, Jyno and Shona, to look at her injuries. 'Badon. Never heard of it,' she exclaimed somewhat intrigued. Whilst narrating his ideas, Danio tore some cloth from his cape and gently tied it around Perina's chest to keep her wing from flopping around, causing greater damage.

Perina was surprised by how someone so young could be so wise. If only she knew how many times Danio had to bandage and care for the wounds that his stumbling drunk parents had sustained, she would have then realised why he became so adept as a caregiver. Danio assisted Perina along their path by supporting her waist whilst they walked, hobbling up the mountain and over a large cave, through a wood into a tiny little village located in a valley, which was alive with music. Danio took Perina to his elderly carers, Jyno and Shona who had drunk some wine already, but were lucid enough to meet and greet Perina, find her a place to rest, and tend to her wounds. But, just as she was settling in, Jardjon, Danio's father burst into the room. He was grinning from ear to ear and was sporting a large jug of wine in his hand.

'There you are my little larrikin,' Jardjon said, casting his eyes on Danio. 'I was wondering where you were.' Truth is, he had not seen Danio for days, nor was he ever sober enough to actually care or look for him. However, Jardjon had seen Perina hobbling into town and was quick to enlist a new client for his wine.

Jardjon, poised with a jug of wine and a goblet in his hand, greeted Perina with great fervour and candour. He set about charming and enticing her to join him and his wife at the tavern to enjoy their brew. Perina, though considerably tired, wounded and ready to retire, was persuaded by the charismatic Jardjon.

'Don't worry about your wound and fatigue. This wine will help both,' he said, pouring her a glass. Perina obligingly took the glass from Jardjon, readily swigging down the brew, thoroughly delighted by its mellow sweet taste. Somehow, after drinking only one glass, she felt less pain and, as Jardjon had said, was not as tired as before. 'You will need more than one,' grinned Jardjon. 'Follow me.'

'No,' implored Danio, 'your wing needs attending to'.

'It needs stitching at once' added Shona.

'Oh that little scratch' Jardjon cooed. 'Nothing that cant wait to morning.'

Perina who already felt better from the effects of the brew was keen to take more. So, against advice from Jyno, Shona and the small but wise Danio's, she soon found herself stumbling alongside Jardjon who was steering her towards his establishment. On reaching the crowded tavern, Perina was given another goblet of wine and, before long, was ready for a refill. She found herself tapping her toes, singing and drinking, forgetting all about Barnio, her broken wing, Danio, Zaphod, and all her comrades. Life was merry, merry, merry, or was it?

Danio felt thoroughly forlorn; he crept into the tavern himself and peeped through the window, witnessing Perina being drawn into the stupefied charade of the tavern, watching helplessly as she with the other townsfolk of Badon stumbled into the night with raunchy gusto. Danio sighed as he watched Perina slowly collapse into a drunken slumber. He loitered into the woods, deciding to stay within the solace of the forest's bosom. Genuinely concerned about Perina, he feared that, in her stupefied state, her wing might become more infected, putting her life at great risk. He vowed to return to the Tavern in daylight and check on his new-found friend.

CHAPTER 13

ZAPHOD'S QUEST

*Strength is knowing that you are strong
and not having to prove it to anyone.*

Zaphod stepped eagerly into Binto forest, which was the path chosen for him. It was perhaps the densest and most overgrown path according to Heffla, and the group thought that Zaphod's, strength, courage, and valour would be most suited for this wild terrain. Zaphod loved testing his strength and agility, relishing the feeling of being alone with his own devices and wisdom.

As the jungle was extremely dense, Zaphod had no use of his wings, which suddenly felt heavy, drooping behind his shoulders unused. He contemplated how easy it would be to soar above in the sky, but the dense canopy of trees and treacherous craggy peaks of the mountain made it unsafe to pursue the journey by air. Zaphod then invested all his energy into clearing the overgrown path before him, scouring for any sign of the pre-used trail that was obscured by the forest overgrowth.

It was painstakingly hard work, but every time Zaphod found himself grumbling, he thought of Barnio and his cheeky mischievous face, which helped him find new vigour and resolve to surge ahead, hoping to find his missing friend soon. Zaphod recalled the races that he would have with Barnio. Barnio would shriek with delight and set off at the speed of light to the finishing point. Barnio, who was known to be impatient, would huff and puff at the finishing line, where there was no one to witness his victory. He would then run back along the track to find Zaphod and taunt him about his glorious win.

Zaphod however, aware of his friend's impatience, used to hide behind a tree or a bush, in order to avoid Barnio's gaze. Then, when he neared the victory post and could see Barnio buzzing around looking for him to gloat to, Zaphod would leap from his hiding place and run across the finish line, exclaiming his victory. Barnio, who did not have any witnesses to him finishing the race earlier, would huff and puff about the ruse, making Zaphod laugh heavily at the flummoxed Garnio.

Zaphod and Barnio however never held any ill will, and they both would laugh heartily about the race and the outcome. Zaphod often carried the exhausted Barnio back to Scaysborough after the race, as he would end up exhausting himself by all that running. Caught up in his thoughts, Zaphod failed to notice the steep ravine right next to him. The jungle had become so dense that he stopped to draw his knife from its sheath on his belt to cut some of the vines in his path. As he moved his weight towards an intrusive large vine, a rock gave away under his foot, causing him to lose balance and fall helplessly down the steep incline.

Zaphod rumbled and tumbled down the slope, before coming to an opportune abrupt halt on a short ledge that was protected by a large fallen log. Zaphod, thoroughly shaken and bloodied, looked up to see how far down he had slipped and found that it was about 50 metres – not too far from the west side of the river Jinku. He wondered if Perina would be anywhere near, on the other side of the bank.

Zaphod knew he had been incredibly lucky; a few scraggly trees had slowed his tumble, or else he would have rolled off the rocky ledge and slammed into the rapids of Jinku. While considering his luck, he noticed a large piece of what looked like a piece of cloth flapping in the breeze. The pain and realisation flooded through his being, as he became aware of a large tear in his wing. Zaphod then began cursing his luck, instantly aware that the tear was too large to be repaired and he would need to get his wings amputated.

The pain throbbed through his body, and as he was attempting to get some supplies from his cassock, he noticed a large gaping wound on his leg, which was now screaming for attention. Zaphod quickly tore a spare shirt and wrapped it around his leg. He tied his wing to his body to keep it secure and perused his situation. He understood that he was in great peril, as the climb up or down the ravine would be equally treacherous. Considering his limited strength and growing gnawing pain, he decided to go down the ravine, instead of going up, which was completely off his path though the easiest to traverse.

The dwindling light offered him no choice other than to set off on the journey at haste. Zaphod's strength was put to the test, as he tightly held onto the footholds and painstakingly scaled the rocky surface to reach the banks of Jinku. On one occasion, Zaphod was hanging from a crevice by the tips of his fingers, as the rock at his feet gave away and crashed to the depths below. With all the strength and dexterity he could command, he managed to swing his sore and bruised body to another foothold and continue the craggy climb down the rock face.

Thankfully, he made it to the platform next to the river Jinku and set up camp, attending to his wounds. Zaphod, now exhausted and in pain, ate his meal solemnly, trying to think of a plan to get out of where he now was, so that he could meet his friends in Tremlite. If only Zaphod had not been so tired, he might have caught sight of the shining unfriendly eyes that were staring out of a crack in an overhanging rock nearby. Noticing nothing unsettling, Zaphod lay on top of his mattock, as he had no strength left to even make his tent, and fell into a deep and disturbed sleep.

If he had been in his usual state of alertness, he would have awoken to the clambering of a band of Trehwells creeping towards him. But, his body was too bruised and battered for that. He dozed solidly, whilst a mass of creeping creatures encircled him, gazing at him with their wide eyes. The sound that finally awoke him was the maniacal shrieking of a piercing voice, 'Friend or foe; friend or foe.' Zaphod, who thought he was waking up from a dream, slowly squinted his eyes in the dark, trying to comprehend his predicament. Zaphod tried to rise from his be though instantly noted that his is hands were tied behind him and his feet bound together. The pain of his torn wing throbbed and Zaphod noted he was on his side,with his torn wing neatly tucked up, completely covered by a large rope net that was drawn at the top with a larger rope. His eyes began adjusting to the darkness he saw the shining eyes and shadowy figures of w of approximately six Trehwells excitedly discussing him, Before he could make any further sense of the scene, a Trehwell, noticing he was awake,rushed over,, and sprayed some slimy substance on his face, which instantly sent him back to an oblivious state of unconsciousness.

CHAPTER 14

NADOO'S STUMBLING

Heroes and heroines come in all shapes and sizes.

Had her comrades had more time to consider the journey ahead, they would have surely not allowed Nadoo to go unaided. Whilst they deemed her journey to be the easiest path, if they had any idea about her fate, they would have certainly sent her back home to Scaysborough instead. Nadoo was an older Heffla, skilled and accomplished in her own right, though nearing the end of her adventurous days. Her body was lending itself more and more to a subdued lifestyle. But, Nadoo was a stubborn Heffla, and anyone who would have tried to talk her out of going on this adventure would have been severely dismissed in the most ungenerous of tones.

Some of the Scaysborough folk considered Nadoo to be haughty and ill mannered, but those who knew her well admired her greatly for her forthright honesty. It was this manner that had greatly helped her friend, Gida, to win first prize for her Jimjam tarts at the Scaysborough fair. When her friend had begun testing the recipe, it was Nadoo who was always honest in her appraisal, regardless of how harshly they were announced – 'Yuck! 'Too floury,' 'too sweet,' 'too doughy,' 'start again,' 'terrible,' until one day, when Gida presented Nadoo with her umpteenth tart, and Nadoo announced that they were delicious.

Gida promptly enrolled herself in the cake baking contest at the fair and won the first prize !

Nadoo's cakes came second, but she did not hold a grudge. Plus, her friend had given her all the tarts she had made with the quip, 'After all, it was your taste that created them.' Nadoo always triumphed; not only did she come second, but she also got to eat all of the spoils from the first prize-winner. Nadoo loved scrumptious things and ate at every opportunity she got – hence, her rather quite large girth. It was these tarts that Nadoo was thinking of when she sat down to eat a rather early lunch not far from the beginning of her path.

After settling down on a fallen log, Nadoo looked ahead to find a nice easy track winding around the bottom of Minju Mountain alongside the large, expansive Doli lake. Quite pleased with herself, she began to think more fondly of Gallon, who had chosen this easy path for her, hoping he would remember to bring back a lot of supplies with him, especially some delicious Jimjam cakes. Nadoo was thinking of Barnio as well, half expecting him to pop out of nowhere and steal one of her cakes as he had done plenty of times in the past.

It had become a big joke between the two; he would laugh and laugh as the unexpecting Nadoo would have the Jimjam cake snatched out of her hands just when she was anticipating her first bite. Though angry initially, Nadoo would calm down, as he never played the joke twice, allowing her to eat the rest of the plentiful supplies she always seemed to have. This was the reason Nadoo always packed several cakes when she went anywhere, as she secretly delighted in how much Barnio loved her cooking. Nadoo was about to treat herself to another cake when something glittering on the ground nearby caught her eye. She stooped down and saw a shimmering rock engraved with gems sparkling with a rainbow shine.

Nadoo was mesmerised by this gems-studded rock as its

colours danced in the sunshine. She began to wonder about its worth, imagining a necklace of the stones hanging around her neck for everyone to adore. Thinking of the jeweller in Scaysborough, she began to unearth the rock, so that she could place it in her cassock. If only she wasn't so preoccupied with the fortune, she might have noticed the large flying Truon speeding up from behind her, who took the opportunity to scoop up the unattended basket by its handle with its large and bulbous beak. It rang out a call in delight and soared up to the highest tree, settling in a branch, beginning to devour all that was within the cake container.

The call of the Truon distracted Nadoo's focus from her glittering find, and she turned just in time to see her basket sailing upwards to the tree. She placed the rainbow jewel in her coat pocket and attempted, though in vain, to run after the escaping Truon. She ran and ran as quickly as her small, rather stocky, legs could carry her. After a short time however, she knew that she would never be able to recover her basket from the tree on the lofty ledge. Even though she didn't run far, she was panting and panting, so she stood still to catch her breath. After recovering her breath, she looked around to see that she had run off her track and that she could not remember her way back. She spun round and round, but saw no signs of trodden grass; every blade had sprung back quickly, and there was no visible evidence of where she had been.

She could however make out a glimpse of blue, which she reckoned was the lake Doli. Nadoo advanced towards the blue that was flickering through the path and soon came upon the still and calm banks of Doli Lake. By this time, night was looming large, so she decided to bunker in for the night and search for her previous path in the morning. Nadoo was adept at making do with whatever little resources she had, so she cleverly set upon making a bed of grass, gathering some large leaves to cover her girth whilst sleeping. Though she could not possibly be hungry, as she had eaten one fourth of her rations already, she was convinced that she was starving and that she was having hunger pains. If anything at all, the pains stemmed from her overreacting to the situation, but Nadoo was almost sweating with the fear of never being able to eat Jimjam cakes again.

Never in her whole life had Nadoo spent a night without having dinner. Nadoo felt utterly sorry for herself and forgot about Barnio and his plight entirely. Instead, she was fixated on food, and when she finally went to sleep, she dreamt of Scaysborough's baking day and the fair. She was of course the tasting judge and was running about from tent to tent, sampling all the delicious confectionary. If only she knew what was in store for her, she would have wished even more that the dream was indeed real.

CHAPTER 15

NOMAD'S CLIMB

*Don't preoccupy yourself with the destination
and forget to enjoy the journey.*

Trehwells, as discussed previously, are natural climbers, who originally inhabited cliff faces high up in the mountains. Some families continue to live on the mountaintops; they made their homes within caves with windows and doors on the outside. Some are said to have many, many rooms that honeycomb inside the mountain itself. But now, most Trehwells live in Scaysborough town in white little cottages with grass roofs and chimneys.

Nomad seemed to be nonplussed about his chosen path through Vindu Valley. Heffla had warned Nomad about the craggy cliff faces along the path, which most travellers would find daunting to say the least! Nomad was however well accustomed to such pathways; it was in his blood, and he took to it in his stride. The first cliff he was confronted with appeared to be an effortless climb for him, as he stealthily mounted up one crevice to another, rock to rock. Nomad even hummed to himself as he carried on his journey onward and upward, enjoying the exhilaration of the climb.

In seemingly no time at all, he was on top of the ridgeway that looked down upon Vindu Valley. Nomad had not stopped or rested even once until he had reached the top, blissfully unaware of the fact that he had been climbing for so long. He had not stopped at all, and now that he had reached the summit, he could see that evening was nearly upon him. Just as he was about to get his cassock off his back and roll out his tent to set up camp, he saw a strange sight on the river bank below. He strained his eyes to see what the object was, and though the light was fading, he was sure it was Nadoo sleeping in a clearing on the path below!

She should not be there, he thought, *her path did not follow the river.* He also wondered why she had not put up her tent. He considered calling out to her. But, on remembering how unpleasant and spiteful she was when woken from her sleep, he decided against it. *It was a mild night, and she probably did not feel like she needed the covering of a tent,* he reasoned to himself.

I will call out to her in the morning, he thought, knowing that he would arise well before she would. He then chose a peaceful spot on the ridgeway to camp for the night. He ate dinner from his supplies and settled down to enjoy a well-earnt sleep. Sleep came swiftly to him, though he had a strange dream. He dreamt that his brother was calling out to him, asking him to hide as a great danger was approaching. Nomad woke up with a start, and though he was not really that superstitious, he decided to move his mattock out of his tent and hide under a rocky ledge nearby, in case the Lurkin was nearby and the dream was a premonition.

After settling down under the ledge, he peeped out of the craggy nook to take a look at Nadoo, to check her safety. Nadoo was still sound asleep and was snoring; even though he was miles above her, he could hear her snorts and sniffles. Once again, just when he was about to shut his eyes, he saw a figure come out from between the rocks behind Nadoo, followed by another one, and another one, and another one. Nomad's eyes widened when he saw that a band of Trehwells were surrounding Nadoo. He did not think, he knew, this band, as they looked familiar to him. But, he could not make out their faces very well because of the distance and poor light. However, from the clothes that they were wearing, he was able to identify them as a gang of Vingoos.

Vingoos were a band of Trehwells that had left Scaysborough a long time ago. According to folklore, these Trehwells did not like living with Garnios, Fallons, Nipoos, or Etruscans and decided to live in caves like their forefathers. It was said that they were not statesmen and mostly preferred to live lawlessly, robbing and raiding when they needed supplies. Vingoos were believed to inhabit somewhere between Scaysborough and Tremlite, but no one really knew there exact whereabouts, as they kept to themselves and could have been anywhere deep within a mountain.

Nomad was extremely concerned, watching helplessly as they surrounded the unsuspecting Nadoo. When one of the Trehwells poked Nadoo in her slumber, she automatically began screaming and cursing, 'Flippity Flop, how dare you wake me up, you ding dong dangoodle!' She then began flinging rocks, dirt, and anything she could find at her assailants, not particularly because she felt threatened, but more due to the fact that she hated, hated, hated to be woken up! Having finished her tirade, she became alert, staring wide-eyed, as she looked up at six Trehwells, none of whom she knew.

She was instantly gripped with fear and began stammering and apologising, whilst walking backwards towards the river. She shoved her hands inside her pockets, as they were cold and clammy; however, to her great relief, she felt some Jimjam cakes. Unbeknownst to her, Truscott had placed them in her pockets, knowing that she would never be satisfied with the food she was given and would naturally be looking for more cakes. Nadoo quickly offered this delicious treat to her attackers; luckily she had exactly six.

'So-so-sorry,' she stammered. 'I don't ta-take to be wo-woken up as you... as you have seen. M-my name is Na-Nadoo. Ple-please accept these ca-cakes.'

The Trehwells, who had never seen such fine food, readily accepted the cakes and gobbled them down. Nadoo explained to them that she was looking for a friend and that she would be out of their territory in no time, apologising for trespassing if that is what she had done. The Trehwells, being suspicious, sprayed something on Nadoo's face, and she promptly fell unconscious. They quickly wrapped Nadoo in a net and tied up the end. They then fastened the end to a long thick stick and carried her away. Nadoo was swinging from side to side, as they carried her, like a pendulum swinging from a thread in the wind. Nomad watched in silence, quickly and stealthily following their trail, perched atop the ridgeway. They finally placed Nadoo down with such a bump that she came to her senses for an instant; In the fraction of a moment when her eyes were open, she saw Zaphod tied inside a net next to her and felt somewhat relieved and alarmed at the same time. But, a split second later, she fell back into a stupor and saw no more.

Nomad spotted Zaphod almost at the same time as Nadoo did. He noted that he was in the same tied-up predicament as Nadoo; and they were both placed on a clearing in front of a rock face with six cave entrances. He watched as the six Trehwells danced around them, singing a song that went like this...

Who are they?
What they do?
What are they here for?
Who are you?

They chanted this over and over again.

'They are spies,' cried one.

'Thieves!' another exclaimed.

'No, they are lawmen in disguise,' one piped up.

'Maybe they are looking for a friend as the fat one told us,' another added. 'She did seem friendly, and the cakes were delicious,' he furthered.

'Maybe they want to join us,' one of them reckoned, and so it went on, until the oldest in the group hushed them and said, 'Let us wait until morning and find out from them when we wake up.' The others begrudgingly agreed, and one by one they retired to their home inside the caves.

Chapter 16

Nomad Revealed

Everyone has a story one needs to stop and listen.
Much may be learnt that way.

After watching this spectacle from the ridge top, Nomad realised that he had met this group before a long time ago. He remembered that, after sharing their philosophy with him, they had tried to lure him to move out of Scaysborough, and band with them in the woods. Nomad had tried to reason with them at the time, advising them that secluding themselves would not make them any happier or richer and that Nipoos, Etruscans, Fallons and Garnios, whilst different, had their own strengths and abilities. He told them he believed that when together, all types of creatures enriched the lives of all. Nomad would have liked a second audience with this band, so that he could try and convince them about the virtues of collaborative living with other beings, but their hearts were full of hatred, and they just refused to listen.

Nomad waited patiently until he could hear the snores of the Trehwells in their caves and decided to make his way down to his captive friends. Slowly and stealthily, he made his way down the cliff, step by step, inch by inch, making sure his foot did not land on any twig or leaf, which would make a noise and disturb the captors. He finally made it to a platform of the rock just above where Nadoo and Zaphod lay sleeping, entangled in nets. As there were no footholds between the rock's platform and the ground where they lay, he had no choice but to jump down in between his unconscious friends.

Although he tried to be as quiet as possible, when he landed, he made a thud that shuddered through the ground. This stirred the sleeping captives Nadoo and Zaphod, who were mumbling and turning in their drug-induced sleep. They however did not wake up, and no movement was detected from the caves of the assailants either. Nomad stood like a statue till all was completely quiet, after which he quietly made his way to where his friends lay. Passing his hand through the net, he placed it over Nadoo's mouth, gently shaking her awake. She woke up wide-eyed and, from Nomad's stern gaze, understood that she shouldn't make a single sound. Instantly conscious of her predicament, she motioned towards Zaphod, who was now rousing from his sleep.

Nomad quickly moved to Zaphod, who upon seeing Nomad bolted upright. Nomad placed his fingers to his mouth immediately, asking him not to make a sound, and Zaphod nodded in agreement. Zaphod and Nadoo watched helplessly as Nomad crept over and started undoing both of their nets until they were released from its bounds.

Nadoo could see that Zaphod was injured when she noticed the way he moved out of his net, limping and clutching his wing. Nadoo set into action by rewrapping his wing as best she could, promising to do more when they were safe. Nomad motioned them to follow him, and they obeyed willingly. They were making good ground, heading for the cliff in order to climb up its walls and reach safety, but just before they arrived at the stone, Nadoo tripped over a large log that she had not seen and began cursing and swearing, without even thinking of the grave danger they were in.

'Hushhhh,' cautioned Nomad, but in vain. As quick as a

heartbeat, the six Trehwells came running towards them and surrounded them in no time.

Nadoo, Zaphod, and Nomad looked at each other in horror and huddled together helplessly with their backs to one another. Morning was beginning to break, its light shining through the mountains. This was when the oldest of the six Trehwells, Gonza, experienced a moment of recognition.

'All hail the king of Trehwells,' exclaimed Gonza, looking at the other five with the expectation that they would follow suit. They first looked incredulously at Gonza, but one by one, they also recognised Nomad, and all of them saluted him as their king.

Zaphod and Nadoo were shocked, as they had no idea that their friend was considered to be a King! He had never told them, nor did he have any haughty manner about him. Nadoo face turned red, remembering the times she had teased him, poked him, and robbed him of his food. He had always taken her antics in good humour and depicted great tolerance. Zaphod also thought of the times he had jostled with Nomad and mocked his strength, tipping him over in playful battle.

The Trehwells bowed again and apologised for their actions, expressing that they had no idea that Zaphod and Nadoo were his friends and that they meant them no harm. Nadoo, who could not help herself, harrumphed and harrumphed some more at this, as she felt that they had been rough and mishandled her in a less than appropriate manner.

'They ate my cakes! They ate my cakes too!' she blurted out, but Nomad silenced her when Gonza told him that she had willingly given them as gifts.

Nomad introduced the six to Zaphod and Nadoo, one by one, 'This is Gonza, Hely, Trival, Jansto, Pento, and Chinto.' Nomad had a great memory when it came to names, and he took great pride in knowing all the Trehwells of the land. He was named 'King of the Trehwells' as his forefathers held the line to kingship. Nomad however did not actively take on the title of the 'Trehwell King of Scaysborough' as there already was an elected governing body called the council of the wise, which included representatives of the Etruscans, Nipoos, Trehwells, Fallons, and Garnios. Of course, the six Trehwells present all thought that Nomad should rule the entire land, but as they always found him to be reasonable and wise, they accepted his decision not to do so.

It was true that the six Trehwells meant Zaphod and Nadoo no harm; they had only made them unconscious so that they could find out what they actually wanted. The six Trehwells were also concerned about the Lurkin and thought that Zaphod and Nadoo might be working for him.

All of them lived in the caves and survived by hunting and gathering. It was Chinto who had found the small black berries that rendered people unconscious, though it was all by accident. He had gone out in the forest one day to collect berries and fruits when he came upon a small bush that he had not seen before. It had small jagged leaves and grew tiny black berries. Being an avid lover of berries, he had picked one of the largest ones he could find and popped it inside his mouth. He found it to be quite tart and bitter, but before he could move his jaw muscles to spit it out, he fell asleep. After he gained consciousness, Chinto had collected more berries and experimented with them by mixing them with water and making a spray.

He found this to be more useful than he considered. On one occasion, when he was again out in the wilderness collecting berries, he had accidentally stumbled upon a bear that was heading for the same Jimjam bush as he was. The bear, appearing to be furious to have a Trehwell heading for the same bounty of fruit, stormed towards Chinto, flashing its large ferocious teeth. Luckily, Chinto was carrying some spray with him and promptly sprayed it on the bear's face. The bear fell to the ground and began snoring in its sleep. What a lucky escape! When Chinto told the rest about his near-death experience, all of them had decided to carry this spray with them, which is why they had it when they stumbled upon Zaphod and Nadoo.

After introducing everyone, Nomad told the band of six all about their adventures and their quest to find Barnio. Gonza was the first to offer his help in finding Barnio and hunting down the Lurkin. The other Trehwells swiftly followed suit and enlisted their support as well. Thus, the six bandit Trehwells, Gonza, Hely, Trival, Jansto, Pento, and Chinto, readied their supplies and attended to Zaphod's wounds to prepare for the trip to Tremlite. Nadoo was not impressed by the fact that the six were joining them; she felt they were outlaws. But, she softened down when Jansto showed her a huge Jimjam tree nearby, and she collected so many of the fruit that it took three of the Trehwells to carry it back to camp.

CHAPTER 17

TRUSCOTT'S TRIUMPH

Expect the answer to every problem; expect every
need to be filled; expect abundance at every level.

Truscott was perhaps the most steadfast, strong, and sturdy one of the group. He was also dependable, reliable, honest, and loyal. Truscott was happy that he was assigned to what everyone considered as the most difficult path – the track over the steep Minju Mountain, which Heffla had warned was nearly impassable.

Truscott was so caring that he had snuck some of his Jimjam cakes into Nadoo's pockets, knowing how much she loved them and how hungry she became. He knew he would find some wild fruit on the way, being ever mindful to watch out for such treats upon his path. The funny thing was that the more Truscott gave, the more he received. It had not been long into his journey when Truscott stumbled upon a Jimjam tree full of ripened fruit. He laughed heartily and filled his cassock to the brim with this delicious fruit, after savouring a few to ensure they were ripe.

He could hardly wait to meet up with his friends and share these tasty treats that he knew Nadoo in particular would be delighted to see. Truscott looked at the mountainous path ahead, and instead of noticing the steep incline and craggy outcrops, he glanced lovingly at his surrounds and welcomed the sights into his being. 'Well, here we go big fellow,' he said, smiling as though he was befriending the mountain itself. A warm, calm breeze fluttered around Truscott, as if the mountain was responding to his friendly address and beckoning him towards itself.

Truscott gently set upon the climb to the summit; he neither looked up nor down, he just kept stepping forward. It was as though the rocks themselves rose to his feet, carrying him upward. He only looked in front of him to marvel at what was before him, knowing that his step would always find a foothold. This attitude of Truscott was perhaps the reason he always seemed to succeed wherever he went, discovering the most amazing treasures and delicious delights along the way. He would then disperse his treasures among his ever-grateful kin who would bestow upon him the best of their wares in return. Joyous, abundant, and triumphant is how you would describe his life!

Truscott was focusing on finding his friend Barnio safe and well as he climbed, imagining their reunion and the celebrations they would have when Barnio was found. He imagined the trees at the top of the mountain were reaching out to support him and pull him up, in his minds eye, the trees energies were surrounding him and propelling him onward and upward. Laughing at the joy he was experiencing in doing this he gave thanks to the mighty trees, and as if in the blink of an eye, he found himself atop Minju Mountain. Elation swept through his body when he witnessed the panoramic view at the top and revelled at the sight. He noticed a small patch of smoke at a distance, which was clouding one valley, creating a friendly ambience. Truscott wondered which happy folk lived within that township and wished them peace and joy. Camp was set up at the top of the mountain near a stream cascading down a rocky outcrop. The clear water bubbled downstream and tasted of honey, just as Heffla had described. He was already beaming with delight when lo and behold, he found a Marja Berry Tree in full bloom. Despite his cassock being full of Jimjams, he somehow managed to stuff several of those juicy delights in his bag,for Nadoo as he promised and ate a few himself before retiring for the night.

Truscott smiled and beamed, giving thanks to the providers of all. He sat up for a while and sent loving thoughts to all, especially his friends, before drifting off into a blissful slumber. It was always like this for Truscott!

Chapter 18

Perina's Fall from Grace

*Do not let go of your wise mind, as your body
without guidance is like a flower without a stem –
left to the mercy of the wind of desires.*

Although he had left Perina at the tavern with his father, Danio
had resolved that he would not allow her to suffer the same fate
as his parents. He had endeavoured his entire life to convince his
parents to leave the tavern and discover the beauty of the forest
he loved so much. His parents would often vow that they would
do so and spend some time with him and even have a picnic
down the river. Danio would always have a leap in his step and
joy in his heart when they made such promises. But alas, every
time the morning of the day they were meant to go came, Danio
would arrive at the tavern to collect them and find them to be
unconscious from drinking the night before. He would busy
himself and pack a picnic basket, then shake and shake them to
stir them from their stupor, but never to any avail.

Danio came to live with Jyno and Shona when he was around
two years of age. He was at the tavern with his parents, who
were caught up in song and drink as per usual,so, they hardly
took notice of Danio sitting in the corner, playing with his
blocks alone. Danio saw the door ajar and the shiny blue
water of the lake beckoning him. He tottered out of the door

unnoticed, ambling his way down a rocky path to the river's bank. Precariously balanced on a rock, he was bending forward to touch the shiny wet substance sparkling in the fading light. This was when the old man Jyno, who happened to live nearby, glanced out his window and saw the little toddler about to plunge into the turbulent waters. He shrieked out to stop him, leaping from his chair and yelling for his wife Shona to come quickly. Fortuitously, despite being old and frail, Shona managed to sprint to the river's bank and pluck Danio from the tantalising liquid, only moments before which he would have surely been carried away.

Jyno and Shona took the wriggling Danio straight to Danio's parents, Wilmsea and Jardjon. The old couple was furious at the neglect his parents had shown and hoped to shake them from their stupor. Danio's parents however, instead of showing extreme concern, laughed and laughed, while carrying on with their dancing and drinking, as though nothing at all had happened. This was when Jyno and Shona decided that Danio should stay with them and put forth this idea to Wilmsea and Jardjon, aware of the fact that his parents rarely left the tavern and were unable to pay attention to Danio's needs more often than not. Danio's mother, Wilmsea, and father, Jardjon, jumped at the idea, as they did love Danio and knew in their hearts that he would be much better cared for by the old couple. Wilmsea and Jardjon packed up Danio's scant belongings and promised to visit him often, but they rarely did so. Danio was not angry with his parents, knowing that the wine had a hold over them, and this way, at least they were always happy and laughing when he did see him. Jyno and Shona cared very much for Danio and nurtured his need to explore, delighting in his agility and aptitude of the wilderness. Jyno had taught him how to swim, and Shona taught him about bush food and the way to cook. At only nine years of age, Danio had become the most knowledgeable person in regards to the forests that surrounded the village. Danio would visit his parents regularly but had learnt to ignore their promises of spending more time with him, having lost any hope that they would stop drinking. Danio however was not entirely unhappy; he joyfully meandered around the countryside all by himself on most days, enjoying nature in all of its glory.

Today however, Danio was not being able to enjoy his time trekking up a mountainous path. He had woken up before dawn and was walking on the cobbled pathway to his parents' tavern to rescue Perina. He was not relishing trying to collect her in her in a incapacitated state knowing that his parents would attempt to persuade Perina to continue her drunken revelry as soon as she was conscious. Danio was worried about her wounds as they could easily get infected if she was lying in the quagmire of spilt drinks and expelled ale that dwelt on the Tavern floor. He was pretty sure that if he collected her before she drunk another glass, she would find her wisdom again and avoid being forever captured by the spell of wine.

Danio knew that Perina's sober ambition was to rescue her friend Barnio, whom she had forgotten all about it seemed. His carer's Jyno and Shona, had agreed to provide treatment and support for Perina at their home until she came back to her health From his experience with his parents, Danio had learnt that just after a night's sleep, prior to waking and drinking again, there was a very short period of time when he could talk to his parents and they would respond with a sober, rational mind.

Once, when he was about seven years old, Jardjon and Wilmsea had not sipped on a drink all day. They both were nauseous from an illness that was going around town. They had come back to their senses completely and yearned for their son. Full of remorse, they ran to Jyno and Shona's home, telling them that they would stop drinking and reclaim Danio's custody. Jyno and Shona however were suspicious that this would not last and asserted that they would return Danio to their care only if were sober for a month.

Jardjon and Wilmsea genuinely intended to stay sober and closed the tavern for the evening. The townsfolk however kept knocking on the door, ceaselessly pestering them to return to their trade. One Trehwell was even said to be crying on the doorstep, lamenting the loss of the wine that he called the blood of the earth. Finally, Wilmsea and Jardjon, unable to stand the fuss any longer, opened the doors for one drink and one drink only. But, they of course could not stop at one drink, nor could any other townsfolk, and soon the drinking, dancing, and merriment resumed, and Wilmsea and Jardjon once again forgot about their son. Danio's parents appeared to become clumsier and dumber as the years passed.

Danio reached the tavern just before daybreak and crept into the darkened Tavern. His mother and father were slumped against each other's backs, supporting one another's body like bookends. They were sitting with their legs stretched out in front of them; their heads were tilted with their tongues hanging out their mouths, snoring like thundering horses. His father had his chalong (banjo-like instrument) resting on his lap, cradled like a baby in his arms. Perina lay hunched in the middle of room on a rug with her good wing spread over her body. She was snoring as well, but she sounded more like some cicadas in the forest; it was a cheerful chirpy sound.

Danio wished to wake Perina, not his parents, as he knew that if they woke up, they would entice Perina with another drink, and all would be lost. Danio crept over to Perina and whispered into her ear exposed slightly through her matted hair, 'Sppss, sppppsss, spppppsssss.' Perina stirred immediately, instinctively grabbing her mug and extending her arm to have it filled.

'Noooo, nooooo,' whispered Danio. 'It is time to meet Jyno and Shona again. You really like them,' he purred to Perina in an attempt to lure her from her sleep.

Perina was not fully awake and, in her stupor, thought that this offer would lead to further merriment and wine. So, with her glass in hand, she eagerly stumbled down her way to Jyno and Shona's cottage, supported by Danio. She kept wanting to burst into a song, and Danio kept hushing and shushing her the whole way. The elderly couple, waiting for their arrival, were appalled to see Perina's wretched state, as she stood grinning before them with her glass in hand. She was dirty and exuded an obnoxious odour. They could also see that her wounded wing was oozing blood and muck. They shook their heads in dismay and began to tend to her with loving arms.

CHAPTER 19

PERINA RISES AGAIN

Inner knowledge is always ready to be consulted.

Jyno and Shona carried Perina to the bathroom; once there, Jyno left Shona to coax the clambering and stammering Perina into a bath where she could clean her to a sparkling pre-tavern state. Perina stumbled in and out of consciousness, though she appeared to be able to move when directed by Shona to get out of the bath and put on clean clothes, after which she trudged with Shona by her side onto a warm and inviting bed. With Jyno's help, Shona supported Perina to sit up and gave her a cup of herbal brew that Jyno had concocted to make Perina fully unconscious, so that they could fully assess the damage endured by her wing. Perina readily gulped the brew down, despite the peaty taste, thinking that it was more wine. Once the cup was empty, they lowered her on her side, and Perina dozed off into a deep sleep straight away. This allowed Jyno and Shona to scrutinise the seeping wound on her wing. The elderly couple were known in the village to be the best at treating the sick and ailing. They were quite competent at curing injuries and had acquired many instruments to assist them in this over the years. Danio would bring them the herbs that they asked for, which they would ground up to make various lotions and potions for healing purposes.

They carefully inspected the wing, and it was not good news. The wing was so damaged that it was irreparable. It was hanging loosely from her body, torn and tattered, much worse than when had she arrived in n Badon the night before. They concluded that, whilst she was in the tavern, she must have stumbled and fell many times, as the wing was now dangling from her body by a small amount of sinew. If it was attended too before she went to the Tavern, they might have been able to save it, but now, it was beyond repair. They readied themselves to operate, whilst giving time for the herbal brew to make Perina completely unconscious. Once they were certain that the anaesthetic effect of their herbal brew had knocked Perina out, they amputated her wounded wing deftly and swiftly and stitched up the cut they had made on her body. They smeared the stitched slit with ointments and bandaged it, leaving the other wing untouched, wrapping it over her whilst she slept.

They decided to keep Perina in this state for two nights days to give her wound time to heal. Hence, they sent Danio off to collect the extra herbs they needed to do so. Danio readily agreed, as he loved collecting herbs and knew exactly where to find them. They decided to let Perina work out what she wanted to do after she gained consciousness – did she want to have the other wing amputated or leave it be? They would find out only after she awoke. They knew of other Fallons who had lost their wings, some of whom kept the other one, finding it come in handy for wrapping themselves or fanning themselves in summer when it was hot. Others chose to amputate both, so that they had more balance and less weight to carry around.

The second day's rays rose from the earth, and it was time for Perina to wake up. They stopped giving Perina the herbal brew, and hours later, they noticed her nose twitch, then another twitch; her legs wriggled; her fingers began poking out from under the sheets, and then she slowly opened her eyes. Initially, she was bewildered about where she was and gasped with wide eyes, but the ambiance and warmth of the cottage, paired with the gently eyes of Jyno and Shona, helped her relax somewhat, and the memories came flooding back to her.

'I have to find Barnio and the others,' she said, abruptly sitting upright on the bed. She had a dull headache, and just as she began to lift herself out of bed, Danio burst into the room, hearing her talk. Perina immediately recognised the child who had saved her. A bolt of urgency surged through her. 'What day is it?' 'Where are we?' 'I need to leave for Tremlite now, how far is it? I must meet them by day five,' she shot all the questions and statement at once leaving no time for reply.

Danio however was focused on her wing and replied only with, 'We couldn't save it,' he mumbled, looking at Perina forlornly. Perina instantly reached for her injured wing, finding nothing but a bandaged stub. Jyno and Shona jumped at explanations, but Perina was in shock and began to cry profusely. She kept sobbing and sobbing, somehow recollecting the memories of herself drinking wine and stumbling over many times at the tavern. She felt so embarrassed and ashamed, she could hardly look at her caregivers for fear of reproach. The elderly couple however looked at her lovingly, trying to sooth her by telling her that it was all right. Perina was so remorseful about her drunken escapade. Shona and Jyno, shook their heads it understanding. 'It takes hold of you,' stated Jyno shaking his head.

'That it does indeed,' added Shona in agreeance. They boasted about the heroic Danio rescuing her from her near-demise in the tavern. Perina held him in even higher esteem – a miracle child, she called him – so young yet so wise.

'How will I ever be able to repay you all?' queried Perina who was ever so grateful to all three of her new friends. She vowed silently to never to drink again and to somehow repay her hosts for their loving kindness. ' I have to leave tomorrow if I have any chance to, get back on the path and meet my friends at Tremlite,' stated an emphatic Perina.

'Will you not want the other wing off, first?' questioned Shona. Startled by the notion, Perina shot her a confused look.

'Well, I have not had time to think of that,' she responded rather curtly, as the question brought her back to the shock of her reality. 'No time for that now,' she barked, though upon looking at the startled faces of her healers faces she softened and spoke again. This time more gently as she was aware of the great care and effort Jyno and Shona had taken to mend her thus far. 'I will consider that on my journey and seek attention should I need it back at Scaysborough,' she pronounced with a swallow, trying to be brave. ' Is it possible to get there in one day?' she queried.

'With a shortcut in mind, it just might be,' replied a grinning Danio, who was suddenly proud of his knowledge of the lands.

Jyno and Shona pleaded with her to convalesce for a few more days though Perina had a very stubborn streak and refused with such tenacity that they shook their head and held up their hands in defeat. 'If you could just point me in the direction of the track,' she continued, 'I will be on my way in the morning.' Though Jyno and Shona felt frustrated at her decision they consoled themselves with the fact that Pernaat least took the medicines they offered for her to administer on her trek.

The road to Tremlite was unknown to Perina who wished for, though dared not ask Danio to show her the way, feeling that she had bothered him enough. Unbeknownst to her however, Danio was planning and preparing for the journey. He was excited about the prospect of going to Tremlite as well as to find and meet Barnio, whom Perina had spoken much about. Jyno and Shona were advised by him about his intentions, who were not entirely happy about his scheme, though also knew that they would not be able to stop him even if they had tried to. Despite him being young in years,her was old in wisdom. They had a lot of confidence in his abilities and knew that he would support Perina well.

Perina crabbed when she walked and had to accustom herself to hold her wing in a certain way that allowed her to balance herself and walk straight. It was rather cumbersome though there was little time for her to preoccupy herself with her bodily concerns as finding a map to Tremlite was on the forefront of her mind.

'Danio can I bother you to draw a map of the path to Tremlite?' Perina asked politely.

'A map I will not supply,' replied a cheeky Danio, though before Perina's face descended into a furrowed brow he quickly added, 'I will instead be your guide,' and he bowed with all the elegance a nine year old could offer. Perina turned towards Jyno and Shona who were nodding in agreeance. She shrieked with delight and awkwardly drew Danio towards her with her one functioning wing to give him a hug. It was at this moment that Perina almost toppled due to the shift of weight though somehow managed to steady herself enough to squeeze Danio roughly to which he protested and shimmied out of her clumsy grasp. He was not really used to hugs and found them a bit suffocating.

The night came quickly and Perina slept soundly whimpering at times in her sleep. She dreamt of flying and soaring high, feeling exalted then landing in a pile of mud and being unable to get up. The dream vanished from her thoughts when she awoke and the only thing on her mind was finding her way to Tremlite and to find Barnio. The Lurkin now was secondary in her and for that matter all the parties minds, Barnio was first on their list. After eating a hearty breakfast, set out by Jyno and created by Shona, Danio and Perina were packed and on their way. Perina waved a teary goodbye to Shona and Jyno, whose kindness she swore never to forget.

Chapter 20

Perina's Journey to Her Friends

Your looks are not the sign of your beauty; it is how you behave and act that is beautiful to others.

Before Perina and Danio set upon their journey, Perina managed to convince Danio to say goodbye to his parents, Wilmsea and Jardjon. Danio tried to talk her out of this, saying it was a futile exercise, as they would probably not be awake or, in case they were, wouldn't be in their senses enough to remember their visit. Perina however pursued the topic till Danio reluctantly agreed. He really just wanted to be on his way and understood that by agreeing with Perina, he would consequently be hastening the time of departure.

Perina wished to inform Wilmsea and Jardjon that their son was accompanying her and wanted to get their consent. It was around ten in the morning when Perina knocked loudly on their door several times, before hearing a commotion of knocks, groans, and yawns, followed by an audible plod, plod, plod to the front door. Wilmsea opened the door and greeted Perina with a large toothless grin, pulling her to give her a large warm hug. Perina winced, as her wing's wound was still raw, and groaned a little. Wilmsea look bewildered for a while, then a foggy memory crept in about Perina's broken wing.

'I am so-sorry,' Wilmsea stammered. 'I for-forgot all ab-about tha-that. Ohhh… it's gone now! What a sh-shame,' Wilmsea slurred, motioning to the missing wing on her left side.

Perina nodded, getting the stench of the fruit wine, and observed Wilmsea's unsteady gait back to the kitchen.

'Come in, come in.' Wilmsea motioned. She kicked Jardjon's leg with quite some force, as he was sitting motionless with his back against the wall and his legs outstretched. 'We have company,' she announced to the stirring Jardjon, who was now rubbing his leg where she had kicked him whilst returning somewhat to his senses.

'Hello, hello,' Jardjon said in a friendly manner, managing to pick himself up from the floor, dusting his body. 'Who do we have here! Why it is our brilliant son and his friend, Perina. Welcome, welcome. Come, sit down.' Jardjon got up to his feet and went to fetch a clay pot resting on the table, beginning to fill the aromatic liquor into some nearby mugs. 'Let's drink to your health,' he said, passing a cup over to Perina.

Remembering the glorious taste and the effect this wine had, almost without thinking, Perina took the cup to her lips.

'Stoppppp! Barnio! Remember!' Danio shrieked with all the effort he could muster.

Perina got so startled on hearing his shrill holler as well as the mention of her friend that the cup slipped from her hand and crashed to the floor with the sweet velvet liquid spilling all over the stone floors. She turned around to see Danio eyes squinting at her with fury, staring at her, holding up his cassock and walking stick, shaking them a little at her. Perina came back to her senses, completely shocked to see the effect the offer of the liquor had on her and how quick she was to forget her promise never to drink.

The task at hand once again became her priority, so she swiftly got to the business of telling Danio's parents about her journey to Tremlite to find her friends and their son's offer to accompany her. In an apparent moment of true affection, Jardjon patted his son's head and granted full permission for him to accompany Perina.

'Danio knows the forest and its paths better than anyone else in town. He is a good lad, and despite his parents, he will make an excellent Trehwell one day,' Jardjon expressed affectionately.

'Whatever Danio chooses is fine by me,' Wilmsea said, nodding in agreement with her husband. Then, she staggered over to the bottle and poured herself a large cup. 'Cheers to Danio and Perina!' she exclaimed.

Jardjon was quick to join her, and as Perina and Danio stepped outside of the tavern, they heard Jardjon pick up his chalong, starting to play a lively tune. *It won't be long before that tavern becomes full of drinkers and dancers once again,* thought Perina, as she picked up her pace and began walking in earnest towards Tremlite lead by her gallant scout, Danio.

Chapter 21

Gallon Reaches Scaysborough

*When fear is your master, even a peaceful
world is a dangerous place.*

Gallon had reached Scaysborough in what was a relatively uneventful trip; the only issue that occurred, which delayed him for a while, was a most unfortunate accident with an extremely tiny creature. On the first day after leaving his friends, he made good time, reaching the rock where Barnio had vanished. Still curious, he walked around this site to see if he could uncover any other information that could have assisted him in finding his friend. He did find some orange thread, which he thought was curious. Deep in thought about this, he reached into his cassock and pulled out a Jimjam cake that he had packed for the journey. He was so curious about the thread that he did not even take a look at the cake before placing it in his mouth. If he had done so, he would have noticed that a rather large Dacon (a wasp-like insect) had settled on top of it. As Gallon advanced the cake towards his mouth, the wasp, being rather alarmed at the thought of getting munched down, promptly flew to Gallon's face and stung him on his rather large and bulbous nose with all its might.

Utterly shocked by the sudden sharp sting of pain, Gallon leaped up, yelping and screaming out loud. As he did so, he flung his arms about, which lead him to lose the piece of thread that he was so interested in.

'Dash and balderdash!' exclaimed Gallon, jumping about in pain. He noticed the Dacon sitting on a nearby branch and knew instantly that this was his assailant. The Dacon, obviously very happy with himself, was preening its wings with its tiny mouth, looking very content indeed. Gallon was so furious, he reached up to slap the Dacon, but Dacons are very, very smart creatures, and on seeing Gallon, it leapt up, buzzing away in a flurry.

Gallon's nose swelled up in pain to the size of an orange. It was throbbing so much that, after eating his lunch, Gallon had to walk, instead of running, for several hours. The pain eventually subsided, and Gallon vowed never to take his mind off things again. Eventually, his nose also became smaller, though it remained larger than usual for the next five days at the very least.

The rest of the trip went well, and Gallon reached Scaysborough one day and eight hours after he had separated from his friends. It was late in the evening when he arrived, and Scaysborough was quiet, settled in a slumbering peace. Not wanting to disturb the townsfolk, Gallon decided to rest his eyes on a tuft of grass in the large field at the centre of the town, so that he could wake up feeling refreshed and summon the assistance that he required.

Gallon settled into a deep slumber, as his body was more tired than he had anticipated. He slept through daybreak, well into mid-morning. Imagine his surprise when he was woken up by a village farmer named Gando, who was rapaciously chasing one of his scuttling Chonju (a chook-like bird), which had escaped from the coop when the farmer was feeding it. The chortling of the Chonju running at full speed along with the huffs and puffs of the farmer sprinting with all his might trying to reach for the flapping bird woke Gallon up in a state of fervent fright.

Gallon sprang to his feet, quickly taking stock of the situation before him. He reached out in the nick of time and grabbed the startled bird by its feet, much to the thanks of the panting farmer. Gallon recognised the man at once and greeted him warmly, reaching out for a handshake. The disconcerted farmer however withdrew himself, as he did not recognise Gallon with his swollen nose. Feeling confused as he had forgot that his nose was bloated, Gallon began talking to Gando, inquiring about his health and his farm. Gando intently observed the face of the man who seemed to know him; on finally recognising the somewhat disfigured Gallon, Gando acknowledged him with a warm handshake.

'What happened to you?' Gando enquired. Gallon quickly updated his friend about his nasal woes and then informed him about Barnio and his other friends' plight, exclaiming that they need to call a town meeting for a matter of utmost urgency. After returning the Chonju to its cage to hatch more delicious eggs along with its companions, Gando and Gallon briskly walked into the town to summon the council of the wise and arrange an urgent meeting.

CHAPTER 22

NADOO AND FRIENDS DEPART TO TREMLITE

Shining bright is our birthright.

Nomad, Zaphod, and Nadoo spent some time with the band of Trehwells, recovering from the exhaustion of their previous plights and preparing for the journey ahead. Zaphod had to have his wounded wing amputated; the Trehwells made use of their potion to render him unconscious, as Nadoo and Nomad decisively removed the wing and stitched up his wound as best as they could. The operation went smoothly, but they decided to stay in the Trehwell camp for at least another two nights for l for Zaphod's wounds to heal somewhat, so that they could all journey together. The Trehwell band knew of a shortcut and felt that Nomad, Zaphod and Nadoo would still be able to meet up at Tremlite square by day five as planned.

Nadoo busied herself during this time, collecting acorns and other grains that grew around the camp, teaching the Trehwells to grind them to flour, so that she could bake her delicious Jimjam tartlets and cakes. Nadoo was so happy to be baking again and found the Trehwells to be such good sous chefs that she almost forgot about finding Barnio and rejoining her other friends.

The Trehwells, Hely and Trival however could not stand

Nadoo's constant demands and rebukes for long. 'No, not like that you oafs,' she would scream at them, whist they attempted to grind the acorns. 'Faster. Quicker,' she would yell at them. Unable to handle the ever-growing demands of Nadoo, Hely and Trival stepped back from adhering to her ceaseless commands and spent time planning for the upcoming journey with Zaphod and Nomad.

However, Gonza, Jansto, Chinto, and Pento were so enchanted by Nadoo's tasty cakes that they were willing to endure the cutting comments and derides made by her to learn the secrets of her trade. Fuelled by their youth and creativity, they tried new fruits and tastes, becoming better cooks than Nadoo herself. Nadoo however would just harrumph when they gave her their scrumptious dishes to taste and shrugged, saying that they were all right. She secretly loved their cakes and was excited by their enthusiasm but did not want to publicly acknowledge this, as it would potentially entail giving up her reputation as the best cook in Scaysborough.

Nadoo was getting used to the Trehwells, especially her apprentices Gonza, Jansto, Chinto, and Pento, finding that they were a lively, helpful, and funny lot. Nadoo had learnt that behind the Trehwells' scary and gruff exterior were gentle, kind, caring beings who were just confused and thoroughly misunderstood. The Trehwells greatly enjoyed her delicious delights, happy to be bossed about grinding the flour and fetching berries for her. Nadoo was preparing for the journey, making sure that the troop would not run out of food, especially not her!

The Trehwells themselves were also benefiting from spending so much time with Nadoo and Zaphod, learning that Nipoos and Fallons were actually not that different from them; they were now considering going back to Scaysborough and living with all the different groups of creatures once again.

Zaphod's wing was still healing and had been wrapped with

special herbs that Gonza had gathered to help him recover faster. Zaphod had to get used to having only one wing, which he had learnt to maneouvre in such a way that he could balance his weight and walk properly. At this stage, he was unsure whether to amputate the other wing as well, deciding to wait until he had safely settled back in Scaysborough in order to fully assess this option. If only he had known that Perina was also in the exact same state, except that he had his right wing removed whereas she had her left one amputated. What a pair indeed!

Zaphod however was able to use the stub of his severed wing, becoming quite adept in using it, along with his other one, to pick up things. He got better and better with practice and, before long, was able to complete quite intricate tasks, such as putting on his shoes and tying his laces. Zaphod healed quite quickly, and as the week's end neared, he felt that he was fit and ready to depart. Upon hearing this, the group packed their cassocks, including the many cakes baked by Nadoo and her four apprentices, and prepared themselves for the climb up the mountain to reach Tremlite.

They set off the next morning and walked steadfastly without stopping, reaching Tremlite by nightfall. All in the group were enthralled by the sparkling city that was candling the looming night. They were wary upon entering this jewelled horizon though were tired and weary and found a large flat area which was suitable for them to set up camp. They were chuffed that they made it by day 5 and if they had a bit more energy would have celebrated their success. Little did they know they were right in the middle of Tremlite Town, which is exactly where the Town Square is. The flat area was actually the market place, so fortuitous. Nadoo, who was starving, supported by her new found Kitchen hands made a sumptuous meal for them all to eat. Being exhausted they retired not long after eating. Tentatively one by one they entered the land of nod interrupted by dreams of the new exciting city they would be exploring tomorrow. Except for Zaphod who kept watch over the fire until his concerns of finding his friend Barnio and re-uniting with Perina gave way to the peace of the night which lulled him into slumber and gentle dreams. Nadoo's dreams were dominated by new and exotic foods that may be found in this glistening town and of course to find her friends, especially Barnio. Although if they had of known they would not have camped in the middle of town though it proved to be the most provident spot, as you will soon find out!

CHAPTER 23

BARNIO IN TREMLITE

Stand by your morals and on your ground;
do not be swayed by those around you.

Barnio had arrived in Tremlite with his new friends Josat and Dorian not long before night fell. He became closer and closer to them on their journey to Tremlite, as along the way, they disclosed more about their personal life by recounting the tales of their various escapades and journeys. Barnio felt more and more comfortable with them, beginning to regard them as his close friends. However, upon arriving in Tremlite, Barnio was unprepared for the alien landscape. Unlike Scaysborough, where cosy cottages with thatched roofs are nested in green hamlets alongside winding creeks, Tremlite glistened in the fading light like stars blinking in the moonshine. Tremlite was a vast city that he had never seen before. There were white steep buildings clustered together, like a beehive, with creatures bustling and bumbling around preparing for the ensuing night. In the hills surrounding Tremlite, other smaller homes existed, which were more like the ones he was used to seeing in Scaysborough, but Barnio had not visited those areas as yet.

Dorian and Josat were great hosts and eagerly showed Barnio around Tremlite town before the light faded away completely. Dorian and Josat's homes were next to each other and were clearly identified by their own handprints. They only had to place their hands on their door, and it opened into their haven automatically. Dorian arranged for Barnio to sleep in a spare bed that he had, as Josat was a regular visitor to his home. Barnio slept well in Dorian's home, despite it being such a strange environment. He totally trusted his new friends and was able to sleep soundly and undisturbed.

Barnio awoke at first light, delighted to feel the lovely warmth of his surroundings and hear the hum of Dorian singing. He crept out to find Dorian tending to a pot of simmering tea heating over a carefully arranged fire in the hearth of the kitchen. Dorian noticed the creeping Barnio and welcomed him with a 'Hi Ho, old pal.' Josat was sitting at the table next to the fire, waiting expectantly for a cup of sugared tea.

'Greetings Barnio!' exclaimed Josat, 'I trust you slept well. Today, Dorian and I would like to show you around Tremlite in the daylight.'

Barnio, who had quite forgotten where he was, somewhat shrieked out in horror. 'Don't you… don't' you know that tha-that's where the Lu-lu-lurkin lives? He has en-enslaved the Tre-Tre-Tremlites, and they do-do his na-nasty ser-service f-for him,' stuttered a rather nervous Barnio.

Just as he finished speaking these words, he noticed the bewilderment on the faces of his new-found friends. Barnio also noticed Josat and Dorian's eyes shining with a pure innocence that was suggestive of a soul of the purest kind. Barnio regretted his rant instantly and shook his head, saying, 'I am sorry, but that is what I have been told. I know this is not true of you both.'

Josat and Dorian only laughed, shaking their heads. Josat addressed Barnio's claims, telling him that the Tremlites were blameless and that he and Dorian had been told that it was the Scaysborough people who were known to be murderous. He recollected the tale of the salted lake and dying fish, believing that the Scaysborough folk had poisoned their lake deliberately. Barnio was very confused and expressed that he had never heard such nonsense. He asserted that the Scaysborough people would never do such a thing. Josat and Dorian also appeared to be confused, but they let the topic go and offered to show Barnio around their town again, so that he could witness the friendly folk that lived in Tremlite for himself. Barnio, although nervous, was very curious and finally agreed to their offer. They ate a hearty breakfast and several cups of tea, after which the trio left from their home and went down the winding hill to the heart of Tremlite – the sparkling city town.

Barnio was amazed at the ornately carved buildings that seemed to reach up to the sky. He also was extremely impressed at the care and pride the townsfolk appeared to show for their town; the paths had been swept, the windows cleaned, and flowers bloomed in pots on windowsills. Everywhere he went in Tremlite, he was greeted with smiles and friendliness. Josat and Dorian introduced him to the beings they knew as their friend. He did not meet any unkind words or acts of intolerance, only friendship and acceptance. People in Tremlite thought he was lucky to escape from Scaysborough, as they believed that the people there were hateful and nasty. Barnio was also beginning to doubt his comrades' purity. Why did they leave him? Was it some bizarre, callous joke? Did they return home, leaving him behind? He would certainly let them know how hateful their behaviour was when he would meet them the next time. He was feeling that he might not include them in his friends' circle in the future, owing to their disappointing and perplexing behaviour.

The more Barnio saw Tremlite town, the more enchanted he was with it. He thoroughly admired its abundant beauty and charm. He could not find any reason for alarm and did not feel unsafe at all. Barnio began to disbelieve that the Lurkin even existed. He was keen to return to Scaysborough and tell everyone about the things he had seen and witnessed in Tremlite, to rebuff the perceptions that the Scaysborough folk had regarding Tremlite town. He decided that he would return to Scaysborough in a few days' time and tell all the creatures he met about his travels in Tremlite. Barnio was also very sure that he would return to Tremlite, as he felt very much at home there, captivated by its beauty.

CHAPTER 24

SCAYSBOROUGH PLANS AN ARMY

The hardest enemy to defeat is the animal that lives within.

The council of the wise had gathered, taking their place in large carved chairs with arms that resembled a lion's claws. The chairs were positioned in a circle, so that the members could easily see and converse with one another. Gallon, also a member of the council, was standing in the middle of the group, gravely discussing the situation as he knew it.

'Barnio is missing and considered to be captured by a Tremlite under the spell of the Lurkin, perhaps,' recounted Gallon. 'The rest of the original party, Perina, Truscott, Zaphod, Nadoo, and Nomad are taking different paths to Tremlite to search for Barnio.' Gallon briefly discussed how Heffla assisted the group in determining the pathways; several of the members nodded with affection, acquainted with the friendly loner, Heffla, who traversed around the land.

'The aim of the solo journeys is to cover all ground between the camp where Barnio went missing up and the foothills of Tremlite, in the hope of finding Barnio along the way. The party's aim is to reunite in the outskirts of Tremlite,' continued Gallon. It was at this point that Gallon stressed on his level of concern for each member of the party's welfare, as they would potentially be arriving alone in Tremlite and be at the mercy of the ill-reputed townsfolk there. The elders pondered this perilous situation, and due to the urgency of the matter at hand, they unanimously agreed to take the unprecedented step of gathering a battalion to rescue their friends, using brute force if necessary.

The town prepared for an eminent battle with Tremlite, and over 1,000 Scaysborough folk volunteered to join the posse. There was much to do to train this mob, as well as pack supplies and strategically plan for the attack. The council of the wise had given the commanders one week to prepare for departure. Scaysborough's townsfolk busied themselves in preparation for the foreboding clash with Tremlite town. A solemn air descended over the town, as the residents were dismayed and forlorn at the unhappy events that were unfolding. Gallon helped wherever he could, hoping and praying that his friends would be safe until the army reached them.

Chapter 25

Truscott Arrives in Tremlite

Old friends are like fine jewellery that has been locked away. They may not always be in sight, but they are always cherished and, when found again, loved with the same passion.

Truscott awoke from his mountainous perch, feeling refreshed and energised from his deep and tranquil sleep. Meditation under the morning sun,was his habit giving thanks for the bounty before him. Breakfast was a bounty of berries that he found growing along the bank which imbued him with the desire to hum in gratitude. He continued his journey down the summit on the other side of the mountain towards Tremlite town. Truscott was full of wonder and curiosity about what Tremlite town was like and was excited to meet the people who lived within. Everything would always be all right wherever he was. 'Expect all your needs to be met, expect abundance on every level, and expect answers to all your questions' was Truscott's motto. Happy is how people saw him, he never went without anything that he desired; he had no enemies and never expected to find any.

In his heart of hearts however, he had an unfulfilled desire for a life partner. He often meditated expressing a desire for companionship a person with whom he could share his passions, his trials, as well as the mundane tasks of living. He wrote a list of the characteristics in a partner that he desired and carefully checked the list to ensure he himself had all those characteristics. If, for example, he wanted honesty in his partner then he himself should be honest. This was how he knew the law of attraction to operate. Birds of a feather flock together. The list he created was read by himself over and over: *My partner is honest, kind,has healthy habits,is fit, loves meditation and spiritual pursuits and has a beautiful heart.* A soul mate was what he had in mind and he often longed for the fruition of his desires to occur.

Just as sure footed as before he journeyed effortlessly towards to his destination, enjoying the sights along the track. Before he knew it, he could make out the faint outlines of the buildings from what must have been Tremlite town at a distance.

Truscott was in awe of Tremlite as he saw the town unfold before him. He was dazzled by the glittering tall buildings that were ornate and seemed to reach the sun beyond the mountains. There was a jewelled lake glistening in the sun on the outskirts of the city, which had an abundance of large inviting benches for the Tremlite folk to sit on, nestled under leafy boughs of shady trees that were encircling the lake. Truscott took full advantage of these comforting and beckoning chairs, sitting down contentedly on one rock, taking in all the glory that laid before him. By chance, a fisherman from Tremlite meandered to the lake from the direction opposite Truscott's and as though drawn to the same spot, promptly sat down beside him, ready to fish for his evening meal. The fisherman's name was Gastod, a Fallon like Truscott, who had also not wished to grow wings.

'Well, hello there,' Truscott said, introducing himself. 'Very pleased to meet you. I am visiting from Scaysborough and looking for my friends actually.' Despite being initially wary of someone from Scaysborough, after staring at Truscott's face for a moment, Gastod somehow knew that Truscott was kind and trustworthy. He responded by introducing himself, and in no time, the pair were conversing together like old friends, even though they had only just met. Truscott told Gastod about his journey to find his friend Barnio and his need to find the other members of their party of six, who were also looking for him. Due to his easy trek, Truscott had arrived in Tremlite on day three of his journey, and he would not be meeting his friends at the Square until day five. He relayed this information to his new companion and enquired as to whether Gastod may have seen his friends who also may have arrived early.

Gastod did not know anything at all about his friends, nor had he had sightings of them; he was a simple Fallon who kept to himself, primarily taking pleasure in fishing and pottering around his home. He took so well to Truscott that he offered him lodgings at his home until he found his friends.

Gastod forgo his fishing for the moment and lead Truscott to his home, winding up a nearby path on the side of a mountain until they reached a golden staircase that led to a dazzling shiny white building glimmering with purple light. The home was small and humble but clean, bright, and beautifully furnished with tapestry-covered chairs, sturdy timber tables, and a beautiful large comfortable lounge. Gastod was keen to get back to his fishing and requested Truscott to help himself to anything he needed. He thanked his new friend for his kindness, which he vowed to repay somehow. The rest of the afternoon was spent walking around the city, encountering exhilaration at every step as he discovered all the fantastic wonders found in the shimmering city. Tremlite folk to him appeared to be extremely friendly with a good sense of humour; he greeted the beings as he met them, and they replied with heartfelt cheer. He felt at home in Tremlite and did not find any cause to be alarmed or frightened. Peace reigned here as it did for him at home in Scaysborough.

Truscott kept an eye out for Barnio and his friends as he wandered through Tremlite, which was quite a large city with many streets that wove their way around its hilly terrain. He repeated this routine day after day, and before you knew it, day five had rolled around. Besides wandering around Tremlite and discovering its virtues, he also helped Gastod fix his fishing nets, cook food, clean the house, as well as fetch berries and fruit from the nearby forests. Truscott woke up feeling peaceful and refreshed as usual; he was thoroughly enjoying his time in Tremlite and was quickly becoming very good friends with Gastod. However, he had not given up his quest to find his friends and decided to take a moment to meditate on what to do next about his mission. He sat comfortably on a chair, quietening his mind, and immersed himself into a relaxed state of being. After around 20 minutes of being in this delightful state of euphoria, a flash of light appeared to spark from the corner of Truscott's eye. Truscott emerged from his trance and peered over to the window whence the dancing light was parading. On doing so, he saw a glass prism on the windowsill, which was sparkling in the morning light, and as he looked beyond the prism, out of the window, at the market below, he saw the silhouette of a familiar face. He rushed steadfastly over to the window and could see that it was unmistakably his friend Barnio purchasing some toffee from a vendor below. Truscott bolted out of Gastod's house, running at full speed down the winding lane towards the market, shouting Barnio's name. But Barnio, in typical Garnio fashion, was unaware that Truscott was nearing and, after collecting his treasured toffee, disappeared into the depths of the city like the wistful wind.

Truscott laughed and smiled, realising that Barnio was safe and well. He vowed to come to this market tomorrow, as he knew Barnio well enough to know that he found toffee and sweets to be irresistible and would hurry back to buy more. Truscott wondered who according to him loved sweets more – Barnio or Nadoo? Suddenly, as soon as he turned around, he ran right into her.

'Harrumph, harrumph,' exclaimed Nadoo. 'Watch where you're going, you clumsy...' she began, as she steadied herself from the collision, dusting off her clothes. When she raised her head to continue the deluge of anger, she recognised the culprit. 'Truscott!' she screamed, and before she could say anything else, she was swept up into his arms, as he effortlessly scooped her from the ground and hugged her in delight. 'Put me down, you big oaf,' scolded Nadoo, though she was secretly thrilled by his spontaneous display of affection.

Zaphod and Nomad were nearby and, on hearing the commotion, ran over to greet their friend with exuberant happiness. The band of Trehwells accompanying the trio were introduced to Truscott, who cordially greeted them.

'At your service,' Gonza, Hely, Trival, Jansto, Pento and Chinto chimed together. 'A friend of the Trehwell king is a friend of ours.'

'The Trehwell King?' questioned a puzzled Truscott.

Nadoo wasted no time in telling Truscott all about Nomad and his hidden kingship. The friends spent the afternoon recounting the details of their journeys to one another. They were exhilarated to hear from Truscott that he had sighted Barnio. Nadoo jumped up at the news, breaking into a small dance and clapping her hands. They all wondered aloud about how Perina and Gallon were faring.

They talked well into the evening and had created a fire that could be seen far from a distance. As dusk crept along the horizon, a familiar song was heard ever so faintly like a whispering on the wind.

'I love to go wandering along the mountain track, and as I do, I love to sing with a cassock on my back. La de di, La de da, La de de, La de ha ha ha ha ha ha!'

Zaphod was the first to identify the singer. 'That is Perina!' he exclaimed. The group looked expectantly in the direction from where the tune was coming. 'We used to sing that song together,' continued Zaphod, 'I would recognise that voice anywhere.' Zaphod jolted up and began running towards the sound's direction. The evening was darkening, so the voice was the only clue to Perina's whereabouts. Zaphod ran and ran, trying to trace the sound of the song and its singer. He however came to an abrupt halt as the singing ceased. Unsure what to do, he waited, hoping to catch a glimpse of Perina or hear some other sound like approaching footsteps. He bent down to the ground to place his ear on the path, in an attempt to hear if any sound was being made.

As Zaphod suspected, it was Perina whom he could hear at a distance; she and Danio were nearing Tremlite, and to steady her nerves, Perina began singing, nearing the feared Tremlite town. She could see the outline of the city in the fading light. Feeling weary and in pain from her travels, she stopped singing and took some time to catch her breath.

Danio could also see the lights of Tremlite in the distance and encouraged Perina to keep going, 'It won't be long now,' Danio assured her, with all the wisdom that his nine years on this land had given him. 'You can make it,' he said, trying to motivate her. 'I know of a camping site near the lake; we will be there in no time.'

Upon hearing the encouragement of her small friend, Perina gulped down her fear of what to expect and, to steady her nerves, began singing again – this time with full gusto. 'La de di, La de da, a cassock on my back.'

Thrilled by the sound of Perina singing again, Zaphod could finally make out some shape at a distance in the inky background. He moved towards them and, before long, could be sure that it was Perina's silhouette, but he noted that only one wing was visible. He could also see a small figure trotting next to her and wondered who it was. *Could it be Barnio?* He ran towards the pair as fast as his strong legs could carry him.

Perina shivered with fear as she noted a figure storming towards her in the darkness of the night. Her fear turned to ecstasy when she heard a familiar voice calling her name.

'Perina, Perina!'

'Zaphod?' Perina questioned, and in the matter of a split second, she fully realised that it was indeed him, as he ambled up to her and held her tightly around the waist, raising her into the air.

'My wing, my wing,' she cautioned, as pain ran though her body. She flinched and turned her head to the side, noting that one of Zaphod's wings was bandaged heavily.

'Please forgive me,' Zaphod apologised, gently placing Perina back on the ground.

'No problem at all,' Perina said. 'It looks like we share the same affliction.'

They hugged as best they could with their injuries, embracing one another for what seemed like eternity, until Danio, who was now starting to feel uncomfortable and forgotten, coughed out loud and cleared his throat.

'I am so sorry!' exclaimed Perina. 'Zaphod, this is my hero, Danio. It's a long story, but not only did Danio save me twice, he has also led me all this the way to Tremlite town.'

Upon hearing this, Zaphod scooped Danio up and placed him squarely on his shoulders. 'Then he will receive the treatment a hero deserves,' he exclaimed flinching. It did cause pain to his shoulder though he grimaced through it knowing he could at least make it to the campfire. As darkness deepened, Zaphod, with Danio perched on his shoulders, and Perina, walking close by his side, staggered their way back from the darkness to the fire beckoning in the distance. In no time at all, they were reunited with their entire posse of friends. Well, almost all – only Gallon and Barnio were missing from the pack now.

CHAPTER 26

THE GROUP CAMP TOGETHER

Wisdom of one can move mounds; wisdom of two can move piles; wisdom of a whole bunch can move mountains.

Despite her lost wing, Perina looked well and was smothered with affections by her friends who greeted her all at once with extreme delight around the campfire. Danio stood back in proud silence, as he was exhilarated by the result of Perina coming back safely to her friends. Perina, who managed to pull herself out of the caring clutches of her friends, introduced Danio as her hero, quickly recounting her perilous tales of injury, drunkenness, and escape. The group congratulated Danio one by one, ruffling his hair and shaking his hand profusely. Danio did not like to be in the spotlight and was uncomfortable being called a hero. After all, he was just helping out wherever he could and doing nothing out of the ordinary, according to his considerations. He liked the solitude of the wilderness, and when Perina's friends settled back down to sit by the fire, he seized the opportunity, winked at Perina, and escaped back along the track whence he came.

Perina knew that Danio was an accomplished bushman, even though he was still a child, and respected his wish to return to the company of his own choice. She therefore did not protest when he left, explaining his need for quietude and his amazing bush skills to the group.

'He will starve for sure,' Nadoo moaned, unconvinced by the explanation. She was worried that Danio would not have enough to eat.

Perina reassured Nadoo, who was always thinking of filling one's stomach, telling her about Danio's ability to find and gather the best food the bush had to offer.

'It's a pity he ran off in that case. He would have been useful around here,' Nadoo lamented.

Perina agreed and would have liked to give him a better farewell she was more than grateful for all that he had done for her and vowed to visit him again in the future.

The group decided to camp together in that spot for the night, as it was close to the shop that they hoped Barnio would revisit the next day. They chatted and chatted well into the night, telling and retelling their tales and their delight at being in Tremlite. All of them had nothing but good experiences to discuss, which certainly surprised Perina. Perina and Zaphod laughed at how similar their injuries were. Zaphod was hopeful that his wing would recover, though he knew that it was unlikely. Perina would need to adjust to her situation and possibly take the decision of having the other wing removed. The group was very happy to be reunited; they also enjoyed the company of their new-found Trehwell friends.

'Nomad's a king?' Perina was heard exclaiming, when Nadoo recounted her ordeal in the bush. Perina was amazed at how cordial Nadoo was with her once-upon-a-time captors. But Gonza, Hely, Trival, Jansto, Pento, and Chinto kept apologising many times over for their actions although they had been completely forgiven by Nadoo and Zaphod. After all, they tended to Zaphod's wounds and followed Nadoo's cooking instructions to the T, eventually becoming better cooks than her! Although no one would tell her that, as they knew how upset she would get.

The group was keen to tell the others in Scaysborough about the greatness of Tremlite town and the good-hearted people it housed. Tremlite also had a mix of Etruscans, Fallons, Nipoos, Trehwells, and Garnios, who lived together and cooperated well. No one had seen or heard about anything like a Lurkin, and they discussed whether the Lurkin even existed. They debated whether the Lurkin was a made-up myth or just existed in people's minds, as they could not see any evidence of ill will or dark doings in Tremlite town. Nadoo, realising that it was very late as her stomach had already began rumbling for breakfast, said that they should all settle down to sleep. Even though they were excited about the prospect of finding Barnio tomorrow when he would return to the market to buy his sweets, they gave way to slumber quite readily, one by one. Perina was the last one to dose off, wondering where he little friend, Danio, had settled for the night. She wished him well in her thoughts and curled up next to Zaphod, falling into a content slumber.

Where was Danio, you may ask, right? Danio did not travel very far from the group at all. He was quite happy to become unencumbered again, but he thought he would stay nearby and explore Tremlite himself. *It is so big and bright,* he thought to himself, and there was much to discover in this magnificent town. Settling down on his mattock, Danio searched for the iridescent clay in his cassock, which he had packed carefully. The clay was very useful at night, as it glowed brightly, radiating some light. He settled down to sleep, looking forward to the adventures he would encounter the following day, as the hoots of the owls and songs of the larks soothed him into a steady dream.

CHAPTER 27

BARNIO IS FOUND

In stillness there is clarity, sit still and all will be discovered.

Barnio skipped out of the house in the morning after having a hearty breakfast with Dorian and Josat. He had decided to leave for Scaysborough the next day to find out what had happened with his friends and to return home in order to talk about the delights of Tremlite town. Barnio had been told that there was a shop near the toffee stall which sold Jim Jam. He was keen on stocking up with such delights for his trip home. Dorian and Josat insisted they accompanied him to the outskirts of Scaysborough, and it was useless for Barnio to protest since they were determined to see him safely home. Barnio tried to encourage them to go to Scaysborough and stay with him for a while, meet his friends, and hang out there. But Dorian and Josat were both sceptical that Scaysborough would be safe and friendly as Barnio had described.

Barnio was planning what to pack and which path to take for his journey home, these thoughts were so preoccupying that he failed to see the bodies sleeping soundly around a smoking ember of a fire. Therefore, as he hurried along in full gusto he ploughed right into an unsuspecting snoozer and tripped head over heels. He landed on his stomach with his nose just centimetres away from an orange ember in the blackened remains of the fire.

Jumping to his feet, he dusted himself off. As he lifted his head up and turned his eyes to the causation of his tumble, he became stupefied with disbelief at the recognition of the now-stirring bodies. The campfire surrounds were scattered with the bounty of his friends and others whom he did not know. 'Well, well, well… What have we got here. What have we here?' bellowed Barnio in his loudest voice to spur on his friends to their wakeful state.

Barnio was unsure about whether to be angry or be happy. 'My friends who left me alone, alone, without a friend, without a home, a home,' he screamed. Barnio loved to rhyme whenever he could. 'Along a ledge from which I could fall, yes fall, with no friend around, no one, no one at all,at all!' he added further. His friends were slowly waking up, trying to comprehend what was happening. Nadoo, however, was the first to spring up to her feet. She ran over to Barnio and picked him up with both his arms, squeezing him so tight that he was struggling to breathe. 'Barnio, Barnio, Barnio!' she screamed with delight. The others jumped to their feet one by one, and Barnio was squeezed and prodded several times before being released. His friends danced around him. What a spectacle it was! Many Tremlite residents were looking with surprise at the fun and merriment that was taking place right in the middle of the market.

Barnio, who was still trying to come to terms with what was happening, broke away from their embraces. He then repeated his poem with a deliberate stare of hostility and with a loud and menacing voice: 'My friends, my friends, who left me alone, alone without a friend, without a home. Left me on a ledge from which I could fall, yes fall, with no one around, no one at all, at all!' He changed the words slightly this time to enhance the dramatic affect. He was in such as state of flux that he was angry and delighted at the same time. He felt that his friends had betrayed him. But seeing them with their sparkling eyes and their eager and friendly gestures, he was also inexplicably excited to see them.

They all answered him at once. 'We didn't! It wasn't like that… We did try… I went looking for you!' But the explanations came out in such a disorganised jumble and frenzy of words that Truscott had to raise his hand and silence everyone. Truscott then calmly and mindfully told the tale of what had happened on the path when Barnio fell asleep, and how they had to leave him there since they had no way of delivering him up the steep incline while he was asleep. He recounted how shocked they were upon not finding him there the next morning they, and how all of them took their own paths to find him. Barnio softened after hearing Truscott's explanation. He could see from the earnest way in which Truscott was speaking that he was telling the truth.

A teary-eyed Barnio apologised for thinking ill of his friends, and he hugged them. He was introduced to the six Trehwells: Gonza, Hely, Trival, Jansto, Pento, and Chinto. 'At your service,' they bowed and chimed together, 'A friend of Nomad, the Trehwell king, is a friend of ours.' 'Nomad is a king?' Barnio questioned and shook his head in wonder at what he just heard. He, however, did not have much time to fathom this news as, one by one, each of his friends recounted their own journeys to him.

Barnio was saddened to see Zaphod and Perina's injuries, and was he hoping to meet Perina's hero, Danio, to whom she was so indebted. When Barnio heard about Nadoo's journey, he could see that she had faced quite a challenging time. However, he could not help but think of the funny side of her having to give up her Jim Jam cakes to the Trehwells and being carried inside a cocoon-shaped net. He tried not to laugh, but he couldn't help but let out a few smirks, which promptly was addressed by Nadoo with a few harrumphs and a swift hit to his head. Nadoo, however, only slapped him lightly. She too was now amused by her own doings, but she did not let anyone else know of this. She went and busied herself stoking up the fire to prepare some Jim Jam cakes and tea for breakfast. Nadoo always had some food on hand, and today, she had just enough for everyone in the group. She was always thinking about filling up stomachs –hers and then everyone else's – she always planned ahead for food.

'Some Marja berries, too,' said Truscott who had quickly returned to his cassock to collect as he remembering his promise to her. A delighted Nadoo stared at him in disbelief and sampled the heart shaped berry. It was a taste from Heaven and Nadoo was taken aback from its sweet delight.

'Divine,' she bowed to Truscott and placed the remainder in a bowl for all to enjoy. She was careful to place the seeds in her pocket. 'I need to plant one of these trees,' she said to no-one and everyone. Those who had tasted the fare nodded in agreement and spurred the others to try.

At breakfast, after the journeys of the different people had been recounted several times, the focus of discussion turned to Gallon. He was the only one who had been missing from the group. So, everyone started to voice their concerns since they knew Gallon was possibly rallying troops believing still, that Barnio, had been taken captive by the Tremlite folk and may be in peril. He was not privy to the what they were all seeing, that the Tremlite folk were friendly, caring, and not at all nasty – They were as loving, kind, and peace-loving as the Scaysborough folk. Maybe both Towns could find the Lurkin together motioned Barnio. They all nodded heads together. The talk in the group soon shifted to what might be occurring at Scaysborough, and if the council of the wise had already summoned an army. They all were now in fear of what trouble could be approaching Tremlite.

Barnio urged the group to finish their breakfast quickly, and he wanted to discuss the situation with his new friends, Josat and Dorian. He was sure that they would have some ideas as to how the imminent conflict between the towns could be avoided. All of them hurriedly ate their cakes, drank their tea, stamped out the fire, and just like a line of ants, they traversed the winding, climbing streets to the steeple tower where Josat and Dorian lived. They almost lost Nadoo along the way as they passed by the most glorious cake shop. She was so enchanted by the delicious aromas floating in the air that she became bewitched and could not move from the window front, staring at the samples that lay inside. Luckily, Truscott, who saw her plight, reached for some Marja berries in his pocket and offered them to her. The smell of the fresh berries aroused Nadoo from her delirium, and she joined back in line with plodding her way with the party to the steeple tower. 'Why do they have to live so high!' complained Nadoo as she marched up step after step after step. It certainly was a long way up.

After a long and winding hike, they reached Dorian's house. A surprised Dorian opened the door to find Barnio with a trail of his friends. Barnio quickly explained the situation to him, and Dorian wondered aloud as to how he would fit all these people inside. Fortunately, Josat was inside, and he recommended that they open the adjoining door between their apartments which they rarely used. This worked like magic – The door was slid open, and the room suddenly became more spacious, so much so that all of them fit inside comfortably. The twelve were introduced, and the concerns about Gallon and a possible army heading towards Tremlite was raised. Josat and Dorian felt that they needed to consult the elders of Tremlite town at the earliest. Dorian even requested Truscott to join them, and he cordially obliged. So, Josat, Dorian, and Truscott hurriedly left the group and ran towards the governing circle to alert the elders and seek advice.

Chapter 28

The Meeting of the Elders in Tremlite

The wise are gathered, and from this hue,
the ways of the future will ensue.

These were the words that were written above the large meeting hall in Tremlite. Dorian and Josat knocked loudly on the door with a big brass knocker, which had the shape of a lion's head. The huge door was inched open, and a wizened, hunched elder named Chenou, who was an Etruscan, greeted them. Chenou was dressed in a black robe and had a black cord tied around his waist. He had long white hair and a beard so long that it reached his belly. Chenou cordially invited these strangers in and asked them to sit. The hall was large and grand; the space could fill thousands of people – perhaps even the whole town. The hall was built of large granite stones, which were ornately carved with images of local flora. It had a cathedral-like ceiling that loomed over 0-feet high and was covered with glass panels, which allowed light to stream down in prism-like form to the circle of chairs in the middle of the room. Truscott was awestruck at the splendour of the majestic premises. He was delighted in taking a seat and enjoyed the glory around him. Dorian informed Chenou of the reason for their visit and the urgency of the situation at hand. It was with grave concern that Chenou heralded the trio to remain seated, while he summoned the panel of the wise.

Chenou struck a huge gong that was perched on a large ornately carved shelf attached to a nearby wall. The gong chimed out a beautiful haunting sound which reverberated around the room for several minutes, resounding until it ebbed out to a stately silence. The silence was broken by a distinct shuffling. One-by-one, the council men arrived in the room through the arched doorways that were situated at the side of the building. Each of them wore the same black robe as Chenou, and they glided across the room to the circle of the chairs. They cordially greeted the three in a procession by holding their hands together in front of their chests, as if praying, and directly looking into their eyes and holding their gaze. Once satisfied, they seated themselves down on the big high red chairs, where the trio had already settled.

There were thirteen elders in all, a mixture of the wisest Etruscans, Fallons, Nipoos, and Garnios who lived in Tremlite. They listened intently to the tales of their Scaysborough visitors. Truscott narrated the whole tale of Scaysborough's plan to find out more information about the Lurkin, their lost friend, and the trials of what had occurred on their path to Tremlite. Truscott spoke clearly and purposefully. He did not distort any facts, only recounting what he knew to be the truth. The thirteen elders nodded in unison when Truscott was done with his narration. They asked for a short adjournment to the meeting so that they could consider the information and conclude a plan of action.

For what seemed like an eternity, Truscott, Dorian, and Josat waited silently in forlorn hope for a peaceful outcome. Eventually, the posse of thirteen elders came through the locked room to return to their high red chairs and settled themselves to prepare for the solemn task at hand. The spokesman for the elders, Isotar, who was another, Etruscan, began the delivery of their plans: 'We have been aware for quite some time now about the tales about the Lurkin. Our reports have this creature to be living in Scaysborough, and it is apparent that it may not exist at all, and that both towns have a wrong view of what is occurring. However, if your friend Gallon speaks of such things upon returning to Scaysborough and is blaming the Tremlite folk for the presumed snatching of your friend, Barnio, then we fear that a vengeance-seeking party may be heading to our doorsteps.' He paused and bowed his head in an emotional state of decline. He breathed deeply, straightened his shoulders, and regained his composure. 'Our aim,' he continued, 'is for peace, though we must be ready to defend our town if that becomes our need. We are, therefore, calling for an army of as many Tremlite folk that can be amassed to stand ready for the ensuing invasion of Scaysborough.' Dorian, Josat, and Truscott all gasped at this news.

Being able to comprehend their distress, Isotar went on, 'It is our hope that we have the opportunity to diffuse the situation prior to war and make friends and allies with Scaysborough. If the Scaysborough folk are as loyal, wise, and commanding of respect as Truscott who sits before us, then we will have no hesitation in welcoming the Scaysborough folk into our territory. We elders request that your friend Barnio, who we know is a Garnio and can travel swiftly, make his way to find his group before sunset tonight. We realise that Barnio will not be able to resist sleep on nightfall, which is the case with all Garnios, we will, therefore, send with him a trained Truon (a lark-like bird) who will fly back into the evening and report the words spoken by Barnio about his discoveries. There must be no haste, and Barnio must leave within the hour as by all accounts of events Scaysborough folk may be very near, and war may be imminent. We have to avoid this. So, set Barnio on the trail at once. Tell him to meet us here when he is ready, and we will release the Truon to journey with him.'

Josat, Dorian, and Truscott bowed to the elders and quickly made their way out of the hall, running at full speed towards Dorian's home, where Barnio was waiting expectantly with the others for the outcome. Bells were heard ringing throughout the town, and criers in the street were calling all the willing participants to prepare for a battle. There was commotion on every corner, and Dorian, Truscott, and Josat hurdled forward, diving left and right to avoid residents of Tremlite who were milling about readying for war. Truscott was the first to arrive, and he pushed open the door to find a startled group waiting nervously before him. Josat and Dorian were not far behind, and all of them were struggling to catch their breath and carry out the elders' plan. Truscott bent over and drew a long breath, steadying his nerves. When he was calm, he looked Barnio clearly in the eye and bespoke of the urgency that was required of him, needing him to leave and find Gallon and the Scaysborough army.

Barnio understood what he needed to do and was alarmed since it was already afternoon. As if reading Barnio's mind, Truscott delivered the news of him travelling with a trained Truon who would fly back and repeat the news to the elders. Barnio gathered a few things, while Nadoo fussed around him about giving him cakes to place in his cassock, straightening his shirt, and rustling his hair. Josat and Dorian intervened and pulled him to one side in order to instruct him with regard to possible tracks and pathways that the troops might be on. But, as time was of the essence, Barnio knew that he must cease all activity around him and depart. So, he exclaimed loudly, 'Enough, enough! I must be on my way. There is nothing else that you need to say.' He really loved to express himself with a rhyme whenever he could. All of those who were present smiled and nodded in agreement. The group of friends gathered around Barnio and wished him a safe journey. 'This is beginning to become a habit,' quipped Zaphod,

'You taking off like that on your own.' Barnio laughed at the joke, and in a flash of hurry, he departed to the elders so that the Truon could be released with him.

In almost an instance, Barnio arrived at the door of the hall of the Tremlite elders, marvelling in its glory. Isotar was keeping a lookout for Barnio's arrival, and he swiftly opened the door and greeted the Garnio. 'So, you must be the Garnio whom we were expecting,' boomed Isotar to Barnio. They introduced themselves, and Barnio was led to the elders table and greeted by them. A Truon was preening its feathers in a woven cage on the table, and it also greet Barnio with a 'Hello!' Barnio was amazed. He had never seen a talking Truon before. Seeing that Barnio was befuddled, Isotar told him that the Truon was trained to say the last thing that was spoken to it and repeat it whenever asked. Isotar even went on to demonstrate what he just said. He looked at the bird and said, 'The time for peace is now.' He then took the Truon out of its cage and allowed it to fly around. He motioned him over to the table, and the Truon perched on a stand nearby. 'Speak,' commanded Isotar. The Truon obediently replied, 'Warrk…the time for peace is now, warrk, wark!' The Truon was given a small treat of a Jim Jam seed, and it ate it contentedly.

Barnio was advised by Isotar that the Truon, when commanded, would follow Barnio and return at nightfall to retell what was said last to him. He was told to make sure that he made eye contact with the bird before he spoke. Barnio nodded his understanding of what was to be done and was asked to repeat them to Isotar. When Isotar was convinced that Barnio had understood his task, he advised him to make haste and have a safe journey. Isotar commanded the Truon to follow Barnio by pointing at Barnio and motioning it forward. The Truon, understanding its task, flew from his perch and hovered above Barnio. Isotar was content that all was in hand, and he advised

Barnio to leave forthwith. Barnio, without any hesitation, set off at a dazzling speed, leaving the Truon in his wake flapping furiously to try and keep up.

Chapter 29

Barnio Finds Gallon

Let your passion be for the truth
as the truth stands the test of time

Barnio furiously ran from one track to the other with the hapless Truon fluttering on his tail, determined not to lose sight of his target. Barnio continued going hither to wither, criss-crossing over the countryside in an attempt to find Gallon and whoever that may be with him. Unbeknownst to Barnio, Gallon was cautiously leading the thousand-strong troop through the back-tracks and under-clearings to avoid being sighted. Gallon had bumped into Heffla again on his way to Tremlite and had managed to persuade Heffla to lead the army. That is the reason why they were able to make such progress undetected. Heffla knew the country and its every nook and cranny, and was, thus, able to know instinctively where the large mob should traverse so that they would be camouflaged by the landscape.

Barnio continued his hapless search, his worry increasing with the moving of sun towards the horizon. Barnio would ordinarily make sure that he was tucked up in bed at this time of the day to settle in for his impending sleep as the sun set in the horizon. But he now sped with extra vigour. Just as his hopes to find Gallon were fading, he heard a rumbling noise and a large crack. He instantly stopped still. The poor Truon, which was following him, nearly crashed into a tree as it was unprepared for the sudden stop. Barnio later learnt that the crack that he heard was Heffla, who was clearing a large branch of a tree to allow the troop to follow through. Heffla was leading Gallon and the army to a campsite on the outskirts of Tremlite, very near to where Barnio was standing, to rest for the night.

Barnio took off in a whirl in the direction of where the noises came from with the Truon following close behind. Heffla saw an object moving towards him at great speed, and he motioned Gallon and the troops to stay put under the canopy of the forest. Barnio saw Heffla and steadied to stop at his feet. He had not met Heffla before, but he quickly introduced himself as Barnio and told of his need to speak with Gallon. He asked Heffla whether he knew him or had seen him. Heffla remembered that Gallon and his friends were looking for Barnio. So, he called out to Gallon to come from cover and meet the Garnio. When Gallon emerged from the clearing, he could not believe his eyes as he met the wide-eyed Barnio. The two dear friends raced to embrace each other. Barnio quickly told Gallon about meeting his other friends in Tremlite, but he was distracted from explaining any further since the Truon squawked nearby from a treetop. When Barnio turned to see what the fuss was about, he noted that the sun was just about to set. He inadvertently looked directly at the bird and cried out, 'Oh no! It is too late…' Even before he could finish his sentence and talk any further to Gallon, he promptly fell asleep.

The Truon, on command of this eye contact from Barnio, remembered his last sentence and flew off immediately to return to the great hall of the elders in the hope of receiving a tasty treat for remembering and repeating the words.

Gallon was relieved at finding his friend. But he was disturbed by the last words that were uttered by Barnio, prior to him falling asleep. 'Oh no! It is too late.' To Gallon, this seemed to imply a sense of urgency, and he felt that Barnio was urging him to act immediately. Gallon quickly instructed the troops of the plan to attack tonight in order to rescue his friends whom he presumed were in grave danger. If Gallon had not been so preoccupied with the solemn and urgent task at hand, he would have noticed the small figure of a boy crouching in the undergrowth, listening to every word and watching every movement. It was Danio who had been wandering around Tremlite and knew everything that was occurring. Danio had been in the village when Perina and her friends met Barnio. He knew where Josat and Dorian lived, and he knew that the Tremlites were preparing for battle.

Danio had been on his way home to retreat to safety when he stumbled upon Barnio whistling through the forest. Danio followed Barnio's trail and watched him as he met Gallon, listening to the events unfolding. Even though Danio was only nine years of age, he understood the gravity of what was about to happen. He knew that a war was brewing and that it would been caused due to a misunderstanding. Both Scaysborough and Tremlite folk were similar in nature, and neither of the two towns liked war. Danio knew this much since he had spent time in both towns, undetected. Danio, though trembling inwardly at the idea, decided that instead of retreating to his own safety, he would command all the courage at his disposal and try with all his might to stop the war. With this resolve, he set off running as fast as he could back to Tremlite town to warn Perina and the others about what was about to unfold.

CHAPTER 30

THE TRUON SPEAKS

Listen carefully, seek the whole truth
as one uttering is only one part of the whole.

The Truon flapped onto its perch at the Great Hall approximately one hour after sunset. It was visibly exhausted, and the elders let the poor creature refresh itself with water and preen its feathers until it looked like it was in a more relaxed state. Isotar looked squarely at the bird and said in a loud and commanding voice, 'Speak.' 'Oh no! It is too late,' squawked the bird and looked around expectantly for its treat. The treat was given by clammy and solemn hands. The elders looked miserable and interpreted the last words spoken by Barnio to mean that the war was inevitable. It was with long and forlorn faces that the elders gathered the troop leaders and announced the news. 'We must leave at once to the clearings at the bottom of the mountain to protect the village,' spoke one commander. The others agreed, and without further discussion, the troops gathered and marched in unison out of town to the foothills and the clearings below to protect Tremlite from an impending invasion by the people of Scaysborough.

Meanwhile, when Josat, Dorian, Perina, Zaphod, Truscott, Nadoo, Nomad, and the six other Trehwells heard of the news about the last words spoken by Barnio and the troops leaving for an impending war, they fervently began their own discussions since they refused to believe that the war could not be stopped. They valiantly tried to come up with some solutions to prevent the slaughter of good people from both the towns and helplessly racked their brains for ideas. It was during this brainstorming of ideas that a small knock – rap, tap tap – was heard on the door. 'Who could it be at this time?' exclaimed Dorian, who ran over and cautiously opened the door. At first, he did not see anyone since Danio's head was not visible at his height.

'Greetings!' beckoned a voice from below, and Dorian was astonished to see a small boy at his doorstep.

'What is it, lad?' questioned Dorian.

'I am here to see Perina,' came the reply.

Dorian gulped, as he was not used to meeting and talking to strangers.

Upon hearing her name, Perina ran over to find Danio at the doorstep. She scooped him up in her arms with delight. 'We have to stop the war,' squeaked Danio in earnest, and he relayed what he saw in the forest.

'Ahh! That makes sense,' exclaimed Truscott, who now knew that Barnio was speaking of the fading light and that the 'It is too late' was uttered because he knew of his impending sleep. If only he had not looked at the bird directly. But Truscott knew that there was no point in going over things that could not be changed. He put his mind to what they could do to prevent the war that was about to take place. They needed to alert the leaders to the mistake and prevent bloodshed.

Danio knew very well the clearing at the foothills, where the troops were headed. He had spent a few days there himself, exploring the bush and surroundings. He predicted that the Tremlite troops would gather on one side of the lake and that the Scaysborough troops would be on the other. The attacks would happen from the sides. They needed to get to the lake and preach wisdom to both sides and alert them of the errors in their reasoning.

The mood was broody and just when they thought things could not get any darker a large thunder clap was heard emitting from the darkened skies. Lightening next and then a heavy downpour of rain. The inclement weather only served to heighten the tensions developing in the soldiers. Frustration rose,soldiers on both sides started to bang on their shields with their swords. Soldiers grimaced their faces and clenched their teeth to make them seem more fierce and frighten their enemy. Muscles were tensioned and swords held high ready for the command that they knew was coming.

'We need something to gain their attention,' Nomad declared loudly through the din of the storm and the thudding of the shields. The others now drenched with rain nodded in agreement.,Danio, in a flash of inspiration, produced the iridescent clay from his pocket which was indeed surprisingly bright. 'That should get their attention,' he roared in his loudest voice. Nomad beamed and slapped young Danio on the back, appreciating his quick thinking. Nomad, not knowing his own strength, nearly winded the poor lad. But Danio recovered quickly, and the group waste no time in hurrying to the clearing, following Danio's lead since he was the only one who knew a shortcut.

Nadoo tried to keep up but was straggling from behind. Truscott decided to keep an eye on her and steadied her along the way until she, along with all the others, made it to the end of the path. They all came to the clearing and noted that the troops were gathered on both sides of the lake as Danio had suggested they would. The lake was large, the night was dark and the rain was relentless. Visibility was now so poor they now were doubtful that both the troops would see the glowing clay as an alert for them to stop their fight. 'If we could get to the middle of the lake somehow, we would be visible,' Truscott suggested. Zaphod suddenly came up with an idea. But, in truth, he had been thinking about the possibility of flying this way with Perina prior to this in his private thoughts. Zaphod enquired whether Perina thought that if they stood together and wrapped their good hands around each other, whether they would be able to fly with their wings and carry Danio and his fluorescent clay on their backs.

Perina, remembering what happened last time she flew with wet wings was initially reluctant. Though upon casting her eyes around and seeing the gravity of the situation, she nodded towards Zaphod and through gritted teeth agreed to the challenge. They had no time to practice and began somewhat confusedly to try and get a rhythm of flight. Truscott, seeing their awkwardness, suggested that they flap to a count to begin with until they got the motion right. Zaphod and Perina nodded in agreement to his suggestion and stood together, entwining their good hands around each other. Danio climbed onto their backs and placed his hands around both their necks. Perina and Zaphod released their good wings and began flapping slowly as they counted 'one-two, one-two' until they had a steady rhythm. It was one of the Trehwells, Jansto, who noted that the troops on the Tremlite side had their arrows ready and were making moves to meet the Scaysborough troop in battle. Nadoo saw what Jansto was pointing at and instinctively knew that it was her who had to stop the troops from firing arrows somehow, until Zaphod and Perina reached their destination.

She did what she hoped would arouse the shooters from their bows and started to sing! Most people did not know that Nadoo was a powerful and strong singer with a hauntingly beautiful voice. She practiced singing in the depths of the Scaysborough woods while gathering fruits, and not many townsfolk had heard her operatic pitches. Nadoo stood on a rock near the lake and pierced the dark broody sky with her melodious tones. Her pitch and note were perfect, and the night seemed to shiver with delight at the sound of her booming voice.

Her sound rose above the heavy sound of the falling rain, transfixing the soldiers on both sides of the banks. The voice was so pure and angelic that the troops somehow knew that this could not be treachery and relaxed their steely stance. They craned their necks and listened intently to fathom a meaning behind this musical phenonomen. The words were not distinguishable thought he notes, the notes were pure delight.

Perina and Zaphod in the meantime had made great progress in counting whilst rhythmically flapping their wings together then finally falling into a harmony that allowed them to fly and climb high into the night sky. Danio was perched on their back, holding out the fluorescent clay in his outstretched hand as a beacon of light interrupting the blackness of the night. The rain subsided to more of an irritating drizzle allowing Perina and Zaphod to fly a little easier, arriving in the to the middle of the lake and perching themselves on an massive obtruding rock. The troops were looking to the lake and its surrounds for the source of the song. One soldier noted the small glowing light pointing to it. Soon all eyes were transfixed on the tiny translucent glow that was shining on the back of the two Fallons whom appeared to be as one in the distance. When Nadoo saw that the gaze of the troops had turned towards Danio, she faded her singing to a quiet and tranquil melody. The rain itself softened and now drizzled down to no more than a slight pitter patter. At that subdued moment, Danio, with the wisdom of all his nine years, began to speak in the loudest voice that he could muster. As the lake was in the middle of a valley, his voice echoed and was heard quite clearly all around. The rain now had completely stopped and the clouds gave way to the night sky allowing the seven moons to offer some illumination to the scene.

'Put down your weapons! You have no quarrel with each other,' began Danio, 'Scaysborough and Tremlite towns are like rice and wheat. They are both wholesome, and both have potential for rot or for growth. Yes, you are different towns… though what you have in common far outweighs any difference that may be apparent. I have heard from both the townships about the treacherous Lurkin, and the influences that he has in each town. Even though I am young enough to believe in fairy stories, I know with utmost certainty that there is no Lurkin. Each and every being has the capability of doing good and not-so-good deeds. One common story is that the Scaysborough folk put salt in this very lake. The Scaysborough folk blame the Tremlites for poisoning their lake in the same way. I, however, know that neither is to blame. It is Truons on their journey to feed their young who are the culprits.'

Perina and her friends were amazed beyond belief at this point since they had not heard Danio talk of such things. They were astounded by his wisdom and confidence. Danio continued, 'My parents are drunkards, and I have been raised by these lakes and mountains. I have drunk from its waters and have been nursed by the warmth of the forests. I have befriended the animals and watched their every move. This is how I know of the Truons' habits. This is how it occurs. Just after the fish in the lake spawn and leave their eggs on the reeds, huge masses of Truons fly past on their journey south, to care for their young, after fishing in the oceans beyond the hills. They have mouths full of sea fish to feed their hatchlings, and they need water on the way back to their chicks to hydrate themselves for their journey home. They, therefore, swoop down for the water in the lakes. In doing so, some of the salty water they are carrying in their beaks are released from their mouths.

'I have seen the fish in the lake squirm and die when the volume of salt from these masses of Truons becomes too much for them. The fish, however, become tasty delights for the bears, who creep out of the forest to partake of the bounty of fish. The lake replenishes itself well since the eggs of the fish enjoy the benefits of the enriched nutrients from the salt and hatch just after the monsoonal rains have filled them again with fresh pure water. So, you see,' he continued, 'there is no Lurkin. It is nature working in it miraculous and, at times, mysterious ways.'

The crowd was amazed at the knowledge and wisdom of such a small boy. Gallon could see from the shores that it was Perina and Zaphod who were carrying the child, and he motioned his troops to lay down their weapons. The Tremlite leaders, were a little more suspicious however as it was the first time they had met any of these Scaysborough creatures. Though in the pursuit of peace the Leader's followed Gallon's actions, and they too advised their troops to place their weapons on the ground. Just as the sun was rising from the sky, a huge flock of Truons flew past and scooped down to the water below, partaking of the cooling liquid and leaving behind salty remnants of the fish they held in their beaks to feed their young. It seemed as if it was magic. As denoted by Danio, the fish flapped at the shores attempting to escape their salty environment.

'Well, we cannot let the bears eat all these,' cried out one commander, 'Let's all fetch these up and make a feast of them.' Hungry soldiers set to their task and grabbed the flapping fish from the shores. Tentatively, the Scaysborough soldiers began to talk with the Tremlite hoards. Before long, they were eating, laughing, sharing stories, and becoming friends. Barnio had woken up by that time. Fearing the worst, he raced towards the sound of this commotion. He breathed a heavy sigh of relief upon encountering the townsfolk from both Tremlite and Scaysborough talking as if they were old friends.

Nadoo and Danio were picked up by the six Trehwell friends of Nomad, who joined their hands and made a makeshift throne for them to sit on while they were being hailed as the hero and heroine of the day. Nadoo was harrumphing and demanding to be put down since she wanted to have a share in all the feasting. Danio was also complaining since he didn't think of himself as a hero and was not used to such fuss. The Trehwells, however, were too busy rejoicing to hear them, and they carried them around like that until almost everyone had congratulated the pair.

Upon finally placing them down, Nadoo beamed with pride and began singing a song which she had made up on the spot there. This was another hidden talent that Nadoo had. And before you knew it, everyone else sang it too.

> *If we all pull together, you know that we can.*
> *We can meet every milestone and work every plan,*
> *We can all pull together with all of our might,*
> *We can solve every problem and put matters right!*
>
> *We are a small planet really, just hurdling in space,*
> *But are diverse in life matters, culture, and race.*
> *We can't let that divide us like we know that it can,*
> *We have to put that behind us and start a new plan!*
>
> *If we all put together...*

And, so it went on...

Whilst the merriment was contagious and all soldiers seemed to partake in the song There was dissention. Not everyone sung with vigour some mouthed the words and whispers were overheard. 'What sort of magic is that, the boy just talks about the fish and presto Truons arrive!'

'This too could be the work of the Lurkin. The boy may be the Devil's spawn.'

'They just don't look trustworthy to me those Scaysborough folk, I think it's their beady eyes.'

'What is this Town, Tremlite? The lights, the buildings, do

they think they are gods themselves? Not to be trusted, I say.'

These sentiments were swallowed by many with the very fish they ate which led to uneasy guts and forced smiles. Though others ate heartily and were pleased to put The Lurkin to rest and entertain the thoughts of peace between the two cities. The Lurkin however did not rest, it continued living between the cracks of wisdom and ignorance, perpetuated by myths in unguarded minds. Subdued, perhaps, well at least until the next gathering of the Towns, and that dear reader is a whole other story…

PART 2

PERINA'S JOURNEY

This part is dedicated to those who are venturing to make peace with themselves and those whom they come into contact with. We are all fragile beings on the planet all trying to live the happiest life we can. Those who come from suffering often continue to walk in this valley only causing more misery to themselves and continuing its path of destruction. It is when we tap into our higher selves we can act with love and light instead of anger and hate. Spend time every day meditating and quietening our mind. It is here that we will find the sweet solace of nirvana that can influence our every action. Spread love seeds and watch them grow and blossom one human at a time, then one family, then one community, then one state, then one country, then one world.

CHAPTER 1

ZAPHOD PROPOSES.

*Unconditional love is like the blood that runs
through us all. It makes us truly live and doesn't
change even with the questions of life answered.*

Perina spiralled to the ground. The wind soared through her body and her wing was flapping aimlessly at her side. The trees, which were initially quite small in the distance, were growing bigger and bigger as she dropped further and further down towards the green fields below. Perina, shocked, rallied her senses and in the precious seconds before she came to a thud on the ground, recounted how she became in this predicament. She had been out flying with Zaphod practicing for the upcoming Fallon flight competition at the sister city fair, which was occurring in two months' time.

Perina and Zaphod had been practising for weeks and had mastered some aerial swoops and dives hoping to win the first prize. Perina and Zaphod were in the middle of a full 360-degree swoop, which required them to place their bodies together so they faced each other. Unbeknown to Perina, Zaphod had been practicing for this exact moment to ask for Perina's hand in marriage. Zaphod, on cue, produced a large and shiny ring from his free hand and tenderly asked Perina to marry him. Perina was taken aback with surprise. Delighted, she began to say yes whilst at the same time reached instinctively for the ring and in the process unwittingly uncoupled herself from Zaphod's side and like a large sack of Jim Jam began plummeting to the ground. So, her yes came out as, 'yyyyyyyyyyyyyahhhhhhhhhhhhhhhh.'

Perina panicked and stretched her neck to the side to see what had become of Zaphod. He was plummeting in the same helpless state as her. Zaphod being heavier was slightly lower than she in the sky. He quickly took stock of the situation and knew he only had one chance to survive. With all the strength he could muster, he stretched out his good wing, calling for Perina to do the same. Perina was able to hear his muffled voice through the wind and obediently, with all of her might stretched out her wing as best she could. In an attempt to get nearer to Perina Zaphod mustered all his strength to move his wing with one huge upward motion. He had some success and was able to grab and hold on to Perina's leg. This action made Perina unstable and her whole body flapped around wildly in the sky. She grabbed out for Zaphod's body as her arm flailed around until she was able to anchor herself to his torso with her hand. She then shimmied her body down until she was able to grab Zaphod firmly around his waist. Once this was achieved, Zaphod and Perina's wings were able to operate together again. They now facing downward could see that they were now were only seconds away from a crash landing. They locked eyes and with all of their energy they thrust their wings together upward to rise into the air.

They continued this action until they managed to climb to a safe distance from the ground. Perina glanced at Zaphod and was about to apologise when Zaphod himself apologised.

'I am sorry Perina, I thought this would be a memorable way to propose.'

'Well,' Perina replied, 'It certainly was that.' And then she added, 'In case you are wondering, the answer is yes.'

'Let's land,' said Zaphod and the pair flew down to the field below, their wings beating in perfect harmony with a perfect and effortless landing.

'That was amazing!' called out Nadoo who had, unbeknown to Zaphod and Perina, watched the whole display from the ground. 'You will definitely win the first prize with that amazing show,' clucked Nadoo. 'I particularly liked the part when you fell and recoupled, that was incredible, very impressive show indeed.'

Nadoo was keen to continue on her way, so she did not add any further comments to the dumbfounded pair who, if she bothered to notice, were looking at her in complete astonishment. Nadoo was preparing for the fair and was completely pre-occupied with her own thoughts about her entries. She was frantically collecting Jim Jam fruit for her famous pies and cakes and had recipes and techniques running through her head, so did not feel like chatting further. She was about to part when she added, Oh I also saw this fall from the sky and promptly gave Zaphod a ring, I think it came from you she added. As Nadoo was busy, she did not think any further about the ring and what it could mean and continued on her path waving goodbye.

Zaphod and Perina shook their heads and laughed helplessly about all that had happened and embraced for what seemed like an eternal moment.

'Well,' Perina finally said, 'It looks like there is going to be a wedding.'

'Yes,' Zaphod said, 'And it looks like we also have a brilliant act for the Sky show.'

'Oh no, don't you dare think that we could do that again.'

'We could carry a parachute each in case of issues, we could start higher in the sky,' he said. Perina just smiled and let him continue, as she was deliriously happy and would probably agree to anything he said right now. There was going to be a wedding!

CHAPTER 2

SCAYSBOROUGH AND TREMLITE ARE UNITED

One is strong, two are stronger but cities combined have power beyond imagination.

It had been almost one year since Scaysborough and Tremlite became sister cities. The council of the elders in Scaysborough and the Council of the wise in Tremlite now had meetings every three months where they discussed matters of trade, pooling of resources and collating of rules and regulations so that the two communities could live more effectively together. The townships also arranged for a yearly fair which was to be held in its inaugural year in Scaysborough, then the alternative year in Tremlit. This was aimed at producing further comradeship and trust between the two large communities.

So far, there appeared to be a lot of enthusiasm and excitement about this event and persons in both cities were buzzing with preparation for the events listed.

There was to be a baking competition, a flying competition, a race for the Garnio's, a strength competition, a chook show, a cow show and many other fair events. Judges were to be appointed from both cities for all the events to avoid any suspicions of preferential scoring.

Scaysborough and Tremlite had different cooking styles, dress styles and home and decorations styles, so the show was also an opportunity to explore and encourage cultural diversity. This is why Nadoo in particular was trying her utmost best to perfect her tarts as she had herself tried the pastries in Tremlite and they were astonishingly delicious. Nadoo was extremely fearful that she would not take the number 1 prize for her cooking; she had always achieved that accolade in the solo Scaysborough Shows.

What happened to the others you may well ask. Nomad was not at all interested in the fair as now that everyone knew he was the king of the Trehwells, he had decided to take up residence in the old Trehwell castle which preoccupied all his time and thoughts. The Trehwell Castle was an old glorious building that his grandfather had once lived in. The castle had been neglected for many years as Gallons' own father Godean was the first to refuse his crown, preferring to build a Billop in town and to live as a farmer. Godean did not have the desire to lead the race of Trehwells nor did he have the interest, skills or dedication to renovate a Castle for which he had no intention to live in. He chose to leave it to its own disrepair and mentioned little to Nomad about his royal heritage, hoping that it would dissolve into its own ebb of nothingness.

Nomad's decision to take up the Castle was not a selfish one. The Vingoo tribe of Gonza, Hely, Trival, Jansto, Pento and Chinto had ventured back to Scaysborough with Nomad after the nearly missed skirmish at Tremlite. Nomad, knowing that they would need housing, approached the six to assist him in the task of restoring the Trehwell castle to its former glory. They obliged and offered their service to repair and beautify the decrepit old building back to its former glorious state. Gonza, Hely, Tival, Jasto, Pento and Chinot would all be given large and ambient rooms in the revamped palace and they, in turn, would clean, cook and maintain the gardens as payment for their free accommodations.

Truscott, upon returning to Scaysborough, kept a low profile. He tended to his home and garden and was enjoying the peace of the comradeship between the Tremlite and Scaysborough, marvelling in the new found serenity for all. He spent his days in quite reflective meditation and had developed a new peaceful exercise that drew him further into a state of sublimity. He continued to enjoy life, and life continued to enjoy him.

Garnio, whom in some ways had caused all the fuss, had happily returned to Scaysborough he kept in frequent contact with Josat and Dorian whom he regularly visited in Tremlite. Truth be known, it was the delicious toffees that could be bought in Tremlite Markets which spurred the visits though he thoroughly enjoyed Josat and Dorian's company. Josat and Dorian also visited Barnio, regularly staying with him in Scaysborough whenever they collected the famous JimJam fruit from the nearby mountain path. Garnio delighted in his new friends, whom were also forming meaningful relationships with Perina, Zaphod, Nadoo, Gallon, Truscott and Nomad.

Gallon, who had pious intentions always, had returned to duties in the Council of the elders. Gallon had felt refreshed and wiser from the happenings between Tremlite and Scaysborough and the learning that it created. Now that the Lurkin had been dissolved from existence in his mind, Gallon regularly consulted those who studied nature. He then formulated decisions based on varying input from those observations to ensure that informed decisions were made by the elders. Peaceful relations between the Tremlite and Scaysborough were observed by him and Gallon presumed that the looming fair would bring everyone even closer together.

Gallon was not the only person in the village to envisage this, most in the townships of both Scaysborough and Tremlite all were in agreement that this fair would allow for more interactions and more discovery. They would all be shocked if they could have predicted what was to occur at the fair.

153

CHAPTER 3

THE WEDDING PLANS

All that glitters is not gold.
All that is gold does not glitter.

Nadoo was preparing Jimjam for her delicious tarts when she all of a sudden remembered something.

'Did I give a ring to Zaphod?' she asked herself. 'A ring to Zaphod, Zaphod, what the hey—does this mean Zaphod and Perina are getting married!' She screamed this so loud that Barnio who was walking nearby, heard the statement and fled to the commotion, demanding to know if this was the truth. 'I—I gave him the ring myself,' stammered Nadoo as she faced the perplexed Garnio. Barnio wasted no time in racing to the Person-In-Question with Nadoo plodding steadfastly behind.

'Is it true?' demanded Barnio, 'Are you getting married to Zaphod?' queried the bulging eyed Barnio.

'Yes. Yes, it is true. We are getting married,' said an excited Perina. Nadoo by this time was close enough to have had this verified and picked up the flailing Perina and swung her around so many times that she was giddy when she finally placed her down. The three joined hands and were dancing in merriment.

The groom has asked the bride
To stand always by his side
Now we will sing and dance

Celebrating their romance
Until the day is neigh

They sang this song, dancing in circles until they were interrupted by a curious Zaphod who had stopped by to see his betrothed. He was forthrightly grabbed by Nadoo and entangled into the circle and he himself was also caught up in the vortex of motion, dancing and dancing until they all became quite exhausted.

'Fang Dangle, we have to prepare for a fair and a wedding, maybe we could have them together!' shouted an exuberant Nadoo. In her mind, she was just doing that, thinking of what food and cakes to prepare, some for the fair some for the wedding.

'Whhoooa, Whoooa,' Zaphod said in a determined voice. 'One thing at a time. We will have the wedding well after the fair as there is already too much to do before that.'

'Yes, I agree!' said Perina. 'I think we should wait until at least a few weeks after the fair.'

'A few weeks.' Zaphod rolled his eyes at this comment, thinking months would be the better idea, though upon seeing the excitement and delight etched on Perina's face, he nodded his head in a somewhat concerned grimace.

'I also want to invite Danio, I would like him to be a flower boy,' she continued.

Zaphod smiled at this notion and added 'I know he is only a child, though I feel due to his manly behaviour he should be exalted to the man of honour at our Wedding.'

'I agree totally,' Perina replied staring at Zaphod with adoring eyes. 'I wanted to visit him anyway to see how he is going, so I will plan a trip soon and give him a personal invite. Though I don't want to go alone,' she said, looking squarely at Nadoo with imploring eyes.

'Well, it is eight weeks to the fair so I could spare some time,' piped up Nadoo, who was always keen to see new places and find new and exciting foods. Perina was delighted that Nadoo would travel with her. Perina did not admit to anyone that she did not know with exact certainty how to get to Badon. Yes, she had travelled with Danio though she was experiencing a lot of pain at the time so was not as observant as she would have liked. She would be glad of the help of Nadoo to assist her to find the right path and provide her with good company to boot. Nadoo who is a very organised Heffla, would never have agreed to this journey had she known about Perina's lack of real knowledge of how to get there. The exuberance of the moment failed to shine a light on practical issues for the journey so they lay firmly hidden in a back recess of their minds.

'Wonderful,' exclaimed Zaphod, 'that will give me the time I need to finish our Billop for you to move into once we are married.'

'I will help you build,' said Garnio. 'I would like to learn these skills myself,' he added.

'Then it is set,' Perina concluded. 'Nadoo and I will set off tomorrow and we will be back in plenty of time for training for the fair.'

'I will go home and get the provisions ready,' said Nadoo and was thankful that she had baked so much to test for the fair that they would have an abundant supply of food. If only she knew what was in store for her, she would not have offered her service—or at least would have thought much more about the preparations for the journey ahead.

Perina and Zaphod settled for the 11th day of the 11th month for their wedding date. That was exactly in 11 week's time.

'Perfect,' they clucked together. The Fair was being held on the 9th the 9th month of the thus they had three weeks after the fair to get their wedding ready and eight weeks until the fair. Busy, busy, busy but excitably so, especially if you were deliriously in love, which is what afflicted both Perina and Zaphod. Had they not been so obstructed by love, they may have planned better for the wedding and ensured that Perina had exactly the right path mapped out for her to visit Badon. Though, as they say, love is often blind.

Nadoo was on her way home when she bumped into the Trehwells, Hely and Trival, who were foraging for wood in the forest to complete some repairs to Nomad's castle. Nadoo and the Trehwells acknowledged each other and exchanged small pleasantries. Hely and Trival were wary of Nadoo as they had not forgotten her rebukes and demanding behaviour at their camp. Though, to be polite, Hely enquired of her plans for baking for the fair. Nadoo had advised them of her respite from her cooking due to her plans of accompanying Perina to Badon to invite Danio to their wedding. Hely and Trival, the most restless of the band of six Trehwells, became excited about the idea of travelling to new lands. They asked Nadoo if they could have a word to each other and out of Nadoo's earshot they discussed the idea of heading to Badon with Nadoo and Perina.

They tossed up their commitment to restoring Nomad's castle, though argued that the other four would be enough to complete this task. They would like to see Danio again, whom they both liked and felt that Badon may be close enough to their old Mountain home that they could also stop their and revisit their camp along the way. The excitement of new lands won out and they rejoined Nadoo, offering to accompany her and Perina to Badon.

Nadoo who quickly assessed that she would need to share the provisions, harrumphed a bit at first, though after she went through all her current cakes, breads and tarts in her mind's eye, she felt she still would have enough to accommodate the extra mouths and promptly accepted their offer. Nadoo was not overly fond of Hely and Trival as they were poor apprentices when she was trying to teach them baking skills though she knew that they were strong and amenable and would offer Perina and herself extra protection in case they come across any Noonan (Cheetah like animal) or Gangio's (rather like a wolverine) on the way. Nadoo could not be bothered to walk back and tell Perina of their extra company as she was already planning food for the journey and did not feel it of any real importance. She arranged for the Trehwells to meet at Perina's Billop at dawn to begin their journey, which Perina estimated would take two days. Off she went to pack, as tomorrow was a start of a new adventure and a new journey.

CHAPTER 4

THE JOURNEY TO BADON

By failing to prepare, you are preparing to fail.

Hely and Trival arrived at Perina's Billop prior to the sun coming up. They liked to be prepared and were keen to begin the journey. There was no sign of movement in Perina's abode, and Nadoo was nowhere to be seen. They waited a few patient minutes, but when the silence continued, Hely banged loudly on Perina's door. There was a sound of snoring then a startled scuffle and then the sound of shuffling feet towards the door.

'Oh, come in Nadoo, I thought you would not be awake until at least ten so I thought I would sleep in too.' You can imagine her surprise when instead of her rather short stout friend two large Trehwells lumbered themselves inside her door. A rather startled Perina grabbed at her nightclothes and stared at them in wide eyed bewilderment.

Trival quickly recounted the tale of yester evening where they met Nadoo and offered to accompany her and Perina to Badon. Perina agreed to this and was rather quite relieved to have such competent and strong companions. It was at this moment that Perina revealed to Trival and Hely that she only had a strong hunch about where the road to Badon was. She explained that as she previously journeyed along the path over Jinku River to Binku Mountain on her previous quest to find her missing friend Garnio. It was upon this path that she fell and where Danio collected and assisted her in her wounded state to his town of Badon. Hely and Trival were not happy about this revelation and were seriously considering backing out of the trip altogether when a rather grumpy and dishevelled Nadoo arrived with delicious food in tow.

Nadoo, as you know, is incredibly grumpy in the mornings and was not happy to be up before the sun. Perina was astonished to see Nadoo this early and predicted that she would have to collect Nadoo from her home around mid morning.

'Harumphhh, Harummph,' began Nadoo, 'the morning is bleak, who gets up at this time, ridiculous, ridiculous.' She began and spread the table with food to eat. No one dared speak to Nadoo as they know from previous encounters when she was in this type of mood she was easily tempered into a stamping rage. Perina quickly got dressed to join in on the morning feast. Thus Perina, Hely and Trival, along with Nadoo, began eating the delicious and sumptuous fare in front of them. Hely and Trival were so taken by the fine food that they forgot about Perina's ill prepared plans and after eating had finished and all had contented bellies the four gathered all the supplies in mattocks and set off in the same direction as they did almost one year ago to find the path to Badon. Nadoo was still not in an agreeable mood, so the four walked in silence for quite some time so as not to stir her into an angry tirade. They continued in and continued in that mode until they came to a familiar turn on the path ahead.

Perina was at the head of the four and excitedly pointed to the place where they had lost Barnio. Nadoo, who had by now come to terms with her wakened state and was somewhat friendlier, agreed with Perina that this was indeed the fork in the road where they were met with a huge boulder. The four gazed down into the gully to see this large rock at the base of the incline.

Hely and Trival marvelled at the strength of Dorian and Josat, whom they all now knew were responsible for levering the large rock to the edge of the mountain so that it could fall to its resting place in the valley below. The path ahead was now clear and they quickly reached the place where they previously camped and plotted their individual paths to find the then missing Barnio.

'I am pretty sure the path to Badon will be easy to find on the road I took along Jinku river,' said Perina. Nadoo was quick to pick up on the indiscretion, "Pretty sure" What do you mean?' demanded Nadoo. It was then that Hely and Trival were reminded of their own concerns and joined in on the questioning.

'We don't want a repeat performance of your previous adventures,' began Trival.

Hely joined in with a, 'You had better be dammed sure as we will not put ourselves at risk for your unprepared folly.'

'Don't worry, don't worry,' Perina crooned. 'I will no doubt know it as soon as I see it, I was travelling rather slow, if you remember with my damaged wing so I will remember the way!' She nominated rather cajolingly. Perina, however, remembered that she had not really taken much notice of the path trod as Danio was assisting her the whole time and as she was in so much pain, she had her head down most of the way. Perina decided to keep this information to herself as she could see the others were already alarmed. 'It is an easy path' I remember that,' she lied.

'We can camp along the Jinku River and take the path to Badon the next day. We will be there by lunch time tomorrow,' she added cheerfully. The mention of food cheered Nadoo somewhat and Hely and Trival just shrugged and said together. 'Well, we are this far now, no use turning back.' They smiled as these friends often did this.

'I just hope you are right,' added Trival, raising his eyebrow and tensing his jaw. Trival was the moodier of the two friends and held grudges. He was already nursing and old grudge with

Nadoo and Perina could easily slip into his list of persons to avoid. He was definitely starting to regret his decision to come, though he still was quite curious about Badon and would like to visit the town.

Perina fumbled her way along the track trying to hide her unease about the certainty of the path that lead to Badon. At times she wished she could control her impulsive nature which often got her into trouble. A crossroad presented itself in the path and Perina could not hide her dumbfounded look to the others. 'Well' barked Nadoo with her arms folded, Trival, noticing her hesitation tensed his neck and shoulders and was about to launch into a rant when she noticed a gnarly Jim Jam tree in the distance. 'It is this way,' she pointed, 'I remember that tree.' It was unusually gnarled and the berries were more purple that pink, which thankfully stuck in her mind.

'The clearing is not too far now!' shouted a jubilant Perina, grateful that some memories of her previous trip had came back to her. Nadoo, Trival and Hely followed somewhat relieved though continued to harbor doubt about Perina's ability to lead the trek. The group marched on without a stop, finally arriving at the clearing mid afternoon. The sun was sparkling on the water and the banks were green and lush. The spot looked so inviting that they decided to set up camp, have an early dinner and settle down for the evening.

The group was in pretty good spirits despite an earlier dispute with Nadoo. This came about when Nadoo wanted to stop for lunch. The other three, whom were still satisfied after their hearty breakfast, wanted to push on to make it to their chosen camp. Nadoo fussed, pleaded, begged and harrumphed to get her way. The three however joined forces against her and were adamant on their wish to continue. Perina pointed out that democratically it was 3:1 and Nadoo, realising she was beaten, reluctantly agreed to continue on to camp. Nadoo, however, still somewhat disenchanted about not getting her way, complained along the way saying she was starving—though if she was really honest with herself, she did not have any hunger pains. Soon enough the beauty of the bush, the pretty darting birds and the iridescent forest flowers commanded her attention and distracted her from her fixation on her stomach. The four continued on the path somewhat contentedly and now having reached the camping spot, set up their mattocks and Nadoo quickly and deftly prepared food. Perina was fixated on the sparkling water, it was like the water had mesmerised her, she remembered the coolness and sweetness of its depths and without much thinking dived in clothes and all. The splash startled the others though seeing Perina splashing about enjoying themself, they smiled and continued with their task of setting up camp.

Perina felt like a fish in the waves and she dived and swam and jumped up and down in and out of the water, relishing its velvet coolness on her skin. She was careful to keep her wing tucked to her side and then to totally immerse herself in the joy of the moment she rolled over onto her back and floated, allowing the stream to caress her body and for her to relax totally in the watery bed. She closed her eyes and enjoyed the rolling and lolling and her body gently being carried by the stream, with the water lapping at her sides and her face. If only the others were not detained by their tent setting, they would have noticed Perina gradually moving towards a bend in the river where followed a rapid in the stream which fell sharply to a pool of water below.

All other parties were oblivious to the plight that was befalling Perina, as they were steadfastly engrossed in setting up camp activities. It was a brightly coloured butterfly who raised the alarm. The small creature was billowing around the river banks looking for a succulent flower with a stamen full of nectar. It saw the brightly coloured attire of Perina's dress as she floated nearer and nearer to the falling stream. Unperturbed about her pending demise, it was instead curious about the bright colours and flew towards her to take a closer look. The butterfly needed to taste the colours with its long spiral tongue, so it landed briefly on Perina's dress and attempted to find some sweet liquid. As it placed its tongue on her red garment, it was instantly disillusioned by the acrid taste of the cloth and fluttered on its way. It was this fluttering that awoke Perina from her dulcet state of rest and she arced her head up to see what was tickling her belly. As she did this, she saw the beautiful insect flying towards the bank and almost instantly saw from the corner of her eye the water cascading downwards. She hastily sat up and managed to place her wet wing around a rock just as her body gave way to gravity and dropped down the steep incline, flailing against the rocky edges of the waterfall. She cried out as best she could.

'Ahhhhgghhh, help, help!' Whilst the rapid water falling was blocking her cries from its own thunderous noise a faint,' Help, Help' was heard by Nadoo in the distance. She had very good hearing which is part of the reason why she hated getting up early as she was often distracted during the night by pesky Bulbroks, Truons or other creatures of the night. She turned to the sound of the noise and saw nothing untoward. Perina had floated around the corner of the river and was unseen by Nadoo in her position.

Trival had also heard this feint cry for help and motioned to Hely to walk with him to find the noise.

'Where is Perina?' questioned Nadoo and with this statement spoken they all now ran towards the cries for help. It was Hely who reached the bend first and saw Perina's wing firmly clasped around a rock with her head and body obscured by the cliff face of the waterfall. He ran as near to the rock as he could and could make out Perina's head and body being tossed and trampled by the tirade of water. She was calling for help in between the gulps of water streaming down her face.

He called out to her to alert that help had come and she managed to tilt her head upwards to see Trival's face etched with concern. By this time, Hely and Nadoo had caught up to Trival and saw at once Perina's predicament. Nadoo was quietly wondering why all this drama always occurred to Perina and how lucky they were to have Hely and Trival with them. She herself would not have had any clue about how to assist Perina in this dire state of affairs. Trival and Hely quickly exchanged ideas and between them, they promptly came up with a plan of rescue. In the meantime, Perina's wing was sore and tired and her body was being battered and bruised against the rocks. She did not know how much longer she could hold on to the slippery rock though she thought of Zaphod and their upcoming wedding and was determined to hang on to see his warm and smiling being again.

With renewed vigour, she clung to the rock with all of her might. Trival then stood as close as he could to the rock that her wing was wrapped around and Hely edged behind him in the rapids of the river just before it streamed over the rocky ledge. He held Hely's arm tightly and with the other reached over the ledge to attempt to get hold of Perina's body and assist her to the safety of the edge. This was extremely dangerous as he had to bend down to scoop his large hand around her waist and hoist her up onto the ledge. He attempted a few times and almost lost his footing, meaning that he also had the possibility of succumbing to the watery grave below.

Perina now was getting desperate and with large pleading eyes looked up towards Hely. Hely, now seeing the gravity with increased determination he deftly swung his arm towards Perina and this time succeeded in planting it firmly around her waist he then twisted his body towards Trival and leaned heavily on his outstretched arm to gain momentum to pull Perina to the top. Trival began sliding towards the stream with the extra weight pulling on him. Nadoo took swift action and grabbed firm hold of Hely's leg on the bank and pulled backwards with the strength of the three together they managed a large pull and Perina emerged on the top and was able to get her legs over the ledge and hobble to the bank.

Trival made it back to the ledge and both Hely and Nadoo found themselves tumbled on top of each other as Perina and Trival let go they fell backward onto the bank.

'Get off me, you clumsy oaf!' bellowed Nadoo, though she instantly was ashamed of her outburst and hugged both Trival and Hely commending them on their efforts. Perina was ashen faced and bleeding from superficial cuts and scratches she received from the jagged rocks. She hugged and thanked the three for their exceptional effort. Perina was ashamed that she allowed the delightful state of the water to lure her into an unconscious state of delirium that prevented her from seeing the dangers around. She now was aware of her own frailties of character, which made her a burden to herself and others. With this new awareness, she hung her head crying and apologising.

They all walked back to camp and Nadoo tended to Perina's wounds.

'It could have been a lot worse,' she clucked as she washed and dried Perina's scratches with a cloth that she had packed.

'Yes,' Perina concurred. 'I know that sincerely. I vow from this day not to do anything that will put me or anyone else at risk.'

'Harumphh,' stated Nadoo, who was all too used to Perina's predicaments. The four ate well at the camp fire and settled down for the evening retiring to their tents for a well-earned rest. Just before they all had retreated fully into their honeycombed abode's Perina was jolted by a memory she had whilst trapped in the stream.

'I saw the track to Badon!' she blurted. 'I noticed it at the bottom of the waterfall.' She was hoping this new revelation would calm her somewhat testy companions, whom she could sense were inwardly gritting their teeth and falling out of favour with her. 'This must have been where I fell the first time on this track,' she added rather carelessly. Whilst they all were happy that the track had been found, they each retired with their own anxious thoughts about how ill prepared Perina was to ask them to travel with her. On top of this, they also were very concerned about how they were going to traverse the steep ridge to the bottom of the waterfall where the path to Badon commenced.

'What was I thinking to come along,' muttered Nadoo as she imagined herself safe in her Billop in Scaysborough baking new treats and warming her feet by the fire. Trival and Hely were having similar thoughts though, as they all had come this far they felt that they could manage to find a way to the track below. They all ate their supper with subdued disdain and retired in to their individual mattocks to nurse their grave thoughts. Perina slept fitfully and was awoken by a nightmare that a large dark cloud enveloped her body and stopped her from communicating to everyone.

Chapter 5

Badon revisited.

Mountains have an end to their heights.
Valleys have an end to their depths.
There is always an end.

Badon was not the same place that Perina had left. It had fallen even further into disrepair due to the introduction of an entirely new concoction that Jargon and Wilmsea had added to the tavern's list of beverages. The new concoction was called Dream cloud and the whole town of Badon lived for this new brew. Even Jyno and Shona, Danio's carers, were at the Tavern far more often than they previously frequented to replenish their beings with this foul though intoxicating liquor.

Townsfolk of Badon were now slaves to Wilmsea and Jargon due to their dependence on the Dream Cloud brew and they now ran the whole town due to this dependence. Dream Cloud came about by accident and the most unlikely of Badon's residence brought it to light. It was Danio! Danio was out on one of his usual adventures in the many meandering forest trails surrounding Badon town.

On this day Danio was wandering in the forest without a care when he abruptly stumbled over a log and found himself face first on the forest floor. He brushed himself off though as he was levelling himself and relieving his clothes of dust and debris, he glanced down and noticed some rather small white berries that he had never seen before growing on the other side of the log from where he tripped. He picked a handful and curiously stared at them. They were translucent white and inside you could just make out a small black seed in the centre.

Curiosity got the better of him and he plucked one from the stem of the shrub, broke it in two and smelt the flesh which smelled of peach and strawberries. Next he rubbed the broken fruit on the back of his hand to see if he had any adverse reaction. None was noted so he repeated this to the wrists, he was taught this method by his carer Shona who knew the bush fruits well. She had advised Danio if he used this method and his skin did not respond with a rash then it was ok to eat. Danio, having put the fruit through its paces, tentatively placed one in his mouth. He spat it out directly as the fruit was sour beyond imagination, having an acrid taste like rotting apple. He washed his mouth in a nearby stream though the foul taste permeated his tastebuds for a long time after.

Even though he felt they were inedible, he collected a large pile in some cloth he had and tied the cloth to a stick to carry them back home. He would ask Jyno and Shona if they knew of the fruit as it may be of some medicinal value. He then set off back to his home to his carers, full of curiosity about his new found fruit. He was strangely a little light headed and at times felt unstable on his feet. He however had been out all day and felt the symptoms he was having was due to tiredness, so he picked up his pace and hurried home.

Jyno and Shona were not at home when he arrived, they had presumable gone to his parent's tavern which they did from time to time. Danio was unusually tired and he lay down to rest in front of a fire he made and before you could say, 'Cook a chook,' he was fast asleep. Danio had the most amazing and memorable dreams that night, he dreamt he was flying along the ridge tops of the nearby mountain ranges and found dancing Bulboks, who were not their usual brown, they were purple, red and one even had yellow spots. The were smiling, laughing and eating the strange white fruit that he found that day. Danio slept longer and deeper than usual and when Jyno and Shona arrived home from the tavern, they found a usually energetic Danio in a deep though agitated sleep. They could see his eyes fluttering wildly in his sleep state and was tossing and turning in his sleep. They did not want to disturb him in this state, believing him to have a fever so they covered him with a knitted blanket wandered off to bed themselves.

In the morning, a rare occasion happened. Danio's father Jardjon, in a moment of fatherly duty, went to visit his son Danio at his carers home. This was very unusual for Jardjon as he rarely was lucid enough in the mornings to even consider what could be happening to his son though in the night Jardjon had a dream himself and in the dream Danio was calling to his father from the other side of the town river. In between himself and Danio was a river full of swarming snakes. Danio was reaching out for his father to assist him across this sea of reptiles. Danio was seen holding something out for his father, a small round object that was radiating light. Jardjon reached out for his son's hand though instead of assisting Danio, he snatched the shining light and ran back to the tavern, turning his back on the now wailing Danio. Jardjon awoke at this point sweating. He found his hand in the firm shape of a fist, as if he was carrying the treasured object that he collected in his dream. He thought of waking Wilmsea to tell her of the dream. He walked through the tavern to find Wilmsea snoring, slumped over in a corner with a half a cup of Gogo in her hand. He shrugged and set about clearing the tavern of its empty mugs and sweeping the floors ready for the next evening.

He was still fixated on the dream trying to understand its

meaning when he thought of visiting Danio to see whether he could make anything of it. He knew the wisdom of his son, which was beyond that of any elder in the community. He fathomed that Wilsmea would sleep a few hours more, so he set off and Shona's small thatched Billop, which was nestled next to the river down the lane. He remembered that Jyno and Shona were drinking at his tavern the previous night, though they were cautious drinkers and he remembered them leaving early in the evening, so he felt that they would be awake to receive him in this early morn. In any case, he fathomed to himself, Danio definitely would be awake if he Jargon knew anything about his son it was that he was up with the birds and asleep with the cows. He was musing this fact when he arrived at his destination and knocked loudly on Jyno and Shona's door.

Jargon listened out for the familiar sound of Shona bustling towards the door with her long key in her hand, but the house was quiet and still. He peered through the window and saw his son lying next to the hearth with a blanket over his dormant body and no others around. Jargon was genuinely concerned for his son. He knew where Jyno and Shona hid their spare key as they had told him the location in case a situation like the very one before him occurred.

Jargon claimed the black squiggly key from its resting place under a nearby rock and gently placed the key in the lock. The door creaked slightly and he crept over to where Danio lay, bending down to feel the head of his son which was a little warm, he noted his son was breathing heavily and fast asleep. It was probably best to let him sleep, he mused and visit on another occasion. He turned to walk from this sleepy cabin when he noted a large amount of some strange white berries spilling from a neatly tied cloth that was lying next to Danio on the hard wooden floor.

Jargon was very curious about these berries as the Gogo berries proved very beneficial for him as it was now his livelihood and the main drink at the tavern so he scooped up all these unusual fruits that had been neatly tied by his son into a pack hoping they had a similar effect to Gogo and headed out of the door. The door banged loudly behind him, which stirred Danio a little, though he now had a banging headache, which he wanted to avoid and fell swiftly back to the inky depths of sleep. Jargon returned to the Tavern with a spring in his step and a song in his heart. Maybe this was the glistening thing he grabbed from his son in his dream. He felt it was an omen of good fortune and could not wait to try the berries for himself.

Jargon was not a bad man. He really did think fondly of his son. He remembered his own childhood on his way back home; his father Gondon had been an alchemist and was always in his dispensary making brews and concocting ointments for the town's ailments. His father was often in his den of bottles until early in the morning. He was always fixated on refining and creating better and better remedies for people's illnesses. The priority for him to treat was his wife Narmil, who was in a state of unconsciousness. It had been like that with his mother after he was born she suffered an infection which rendered her in this state of nothingness. Jargon's father was always forcing some concoction into Narmil's lips with the hope of recovery. Nothing worked and his mother eventually succumbed to her plight and slipped away into the next world.

This appeared to make Gondon more vigorous in his endeavours to create medicine and Jargon, not unlike Danio, was left to his own defences learning from life and the bush and relying on townsfolk to steer him in the right direction and offer him a meal or two. Jargon thought perhaps this was why he was not an affectionate man; he had not had this experience himself and his armour of toughness was just that protection from dreaming that love that he most longed for would ever reach him. When he met Danio's mother Wilmsea, she was herself a free spirit whom herself, was spawned from uncaring and unjust parents whom she had learned to hate. It was this hate that protected her from caring about others just in the same way as her husband, she really was spuriously jealous of those that were born with a tender touch around their bodies.

Jargon arrived home and set to work straight away in determining what the fruit was all about. He tested their poison in the same way that Danio did, rubbing the fruit on his body. Nil rash or other burning was felt so Jargon felt validated that the fruit was edible so gamely he took a whole fruit and despite the initial sour and acrid taste he chewed it slowly and found that the taste warmed on him. He then looked at his hands and found that they were spiralling in front of him, warped and thin. He looked at the cupboard in front of him and it smiled and greeted him in a garbled tone, everywhere he looked he saw fun and joviality and he laughed and laughed and went on a cosmic ride of discovery, sailing above the town whilst riding a wave of a golden stream in a moving staircase into the sky.

It was Wilmsea that disturbed his delirium by poking at him as she awoke from her slumped state of sleep, she yawned, looked around and saw that Jargon in the opposite corner of the room writhing on the floor with his hands outstretched grabbing for invisible objects, laughing.

'What on Badon's grounds,' she started, when Jargon interrupted her—

'They are beautiful they are beautiful,' he said and kept reaching for the invisible objects, laughing. Wilmsea looked harder now. What he could be talking about, there were no signs that he had drunk some Gogo wine. What could be causing his strange state of being? She looked beyond his sitting body and noticed a large pile and some scattered white berries next to him.

Wilmsea took Jardjon by the shoulders and shook him, staring in his eyes until he returned her gaze.

Once attention was gained, she looked hard and square at Jardjon and asked him directly, 'Is this what you ate?

'Yes, they are marvellous,' he said. 'You should try them,' he added, and promptly began grabbing for imagined objects. Wilmsea, who was always willing to try anything once nibbled one of the berries cautiously. She almost spat it out as the initial taste was quite sour, though the more you chewed the sweeter it seemed. Wilmsea was herself taken to an altered state and in her mind, she was being heralded up a vertical stream that was orange in colour. She saw small Bulbroks playing instruments and flowers dancing in the sun.

'Lola, lolah,' she said, as she climbed a wave of purple water.

Jardjon overheard her comment and in a somewhat sobered tone he said, 'That is what we will call it Lola berry.' He had a momentarily lucid thought about collecting the seeds and growing more of this fruit. 'This will increase our business tenfold.' he giggled, though the thought came and went and Jardjon was taken again to a land of dreams with purple skies and golden music piping in the sky.

CHAPTER 6

DANIO BECOMES FURIOUS

*If you use substances, you may find
the substance is using you.*

Danio woke by the fire. His banging headache, kept banging and felt quite ill in his stomach. He was trying to place together what had occurred the previous evening. Jyno and Shona were already awake and Shona was bustling in the kitchen preparing pancakes for breakfast.

'Ah, there you are,' she clucked, 'You had quite a fever, we let you sleep where you fell,' she added. Danio looked curiously at the bustling Shona. 'Could have been those berries you brought home,' she commented, 'Don't know what you've done with them now though, I hope you didn't eat them all or you may suffer more.' Danio remembered the strange white berries he collected yesterday. 'Never seen them myself before,' she went on, oblivious to Danio's quizzical looks.

'I didn't eat them,' he countered, 'In fact, I only tasted one. Surely that would not have given me this headache?' he questioned. 'I brought them home so you could look at them, they may be good for some ailments!' he added. He looked at where he left the large pile tied up in the cloth and they were nowhere to be found. He shot Shona an accusatory look as Shona liked things tidy and was always on the guard for things not in their place.

'Don't look at me,' said Shona. 'Twer'nt me that touched them, never seen them myself or I probably would have put them in the pantry, she added. Truth is Shona drank more Gogo that she usually would have so was not on the look out for strewn objects the night prior due to his thwarted state of being.

'Very strange, indeed,' Danio said, though as he said this, he noted that the spare key was lying carelessly on the table nearby. 'Why is this here?' Danio enquired as Jyno and Shona always placed it back in his hideout as he did.

'Not I,' both Jyno and Shona chimed together. The only other persons who knew about the key was Danio's parents. Jyno and Shona had arranged for the key to be hidden outside, mainly for Wilmsea and Jardjon to let themselves in and leave clothes and food for Danio when they were not at home. Wilmsea and Jardjon did this from time to time, though with no real regularity. Shona often had to make the pilgrimage to the tavern when Danio needed more shoes, clothing or food. This occurred when the couple were unable to forage for food due to their ailments that their aging state delivered. Danio was certain that his father had come around and taken the berries. He was known to be very curious and often tried to make ales out of other berries in the forest. Danio could not imagine what made his father visit in the first place. It was curious indeed he rarely came over and even rarer was a morning visit. Danio shook his head at the thought of his father trying to brew the white berries as he remembered the bitter taste of the fruit. Danio vowed to visit his father this very day to see if he had anything to do with the missing fruit.

Danio rested until the afternoon which was unlike him. He would usually be communing with nature and rarely back home until early evening today however if he had not had the desire to solve the puzzle about the missing fruit he would happily stay curled up on the lounge. Though the dwindling light heralded him to journey to the Tavern. There was little time before it was in full swing and his parents would be unable to be communicated with.

Hastening he took a shortcut through a clearing which delved him deep into the forest. Danio loved the space of the forest and to walk amongst the welcoming trees which opened their bows widely creating shade and space for the many bulbrooks bulbongs, birds and other creatures that squirreled around.

Danio was in his element and for the rest of the afternoon, he forgot all about his father and the berries and delighted in the glory of his surrounds. He became distracted on his quest, as the forest had many items of wonder. Danio was particularly captivated by a small colourful spider, which he named a rainbow spider. It was a tiny little spider with black legs which was largely unnoticeable until it reared on its hind legs and protruded it body from its torso backwards to display a colourful underbelly which it swung from side to side like a pendulum in an attempt to attract a mate. Danio was entranced by this majestic display and waited long enough to find the spider successfully attracting a larger and plainer female who succumbed to the rainbow spider's advances after which she promptly ate him.

Danio, horrified by this cruel fate, set back upon the path to Badon's centre to his parent's tavern being somewhat unnerved about the spider's demise. He reached the Tavern somewhat later than he expected and found a drone of townsfolk making their way up towards the door. Danio sped up and overtook the dilapidated bunch whom grunted acknowledgement to him. Danio who was in a rather annoyed mood, chose to ignore them and spurred on past them barely looking their way. This was very unlike Danio, whom usually gave everyone the time of day and would endure their ignorant comments and senseless talk with patience and kindness, but today he found himself in an unusually foul mood. He arrived at the Tavern to find his father furiously stirring a concoction on a stove in the Kitchen. He glanced up as he heard the noise of the door slam behind Danio.

'Hello, Son,' Jardjon said with good humour as he continued stirring. Danio saw in an instant what Jardjon was brewing as he saw a portion of the small white fruit that he had picked the day before next to Jardjon on the bench, the rest presumably was in the pot.

Jardjon looked worse than he usually would at this time of the day. His skin had a greyish look to it, his eyes were red and cloudy and his skin was noticeable sweaty. Jardjon noted Danio's accusing eyes and quickly added. 'Oh, yes I found those berries you picked, very interesting affect, don't you think? I am brewing them up for sale, pretty sure they will grow from seed. Why don't you try some? Your mother loves it.' Danio darted his eyes around the room to see his mother squatting on her haunches laughing and grabbing at unknown entities.

'The moonbeams are dancing with the moths,' she chuckled, 'and the river is pink with sparkles,' Wilmsea then began laughing and laughing and rolled around the floor in a hysterical fashion with her hands clasped around her face crying, 'Lola, lola, lola,' in between hyena like noises.

'We are calling it Lola berry,' Jardjon said, 'and the brew we are making we will be called Dream Cloud,' he exclaimed clapping his son on the shoulder. 'It is very powerful medicine,' said Jardjon, whilst stirring. 'You only need a little. This should last some time.' He shot Danio a quizzical look, 'What providence that you have come, Danio. It will take some time to grow more, would you mind going to collect another basket for us?' said Jardjon in a hopeful tone. 'We wouldn't want to run out.'

Danio' face went red. He balled his hands into fists and he was shaking in the most intense rage that his small body could muster. It was not only that his father had taken the berries from his person and was now making another potion of despair, which would further entrap the townsfolk into and addictive lifestyle.

It also wasn't that he actually had the audacity to ask him to collect more. It was the years of betrayal and neglect that Danio was exposed to all his life that gathered like a storm in his soul and he with a tornado like fury and the strength of a locomotive ran towards his father and collided into him with such impact that Jardjon was knocked to the ground. Danio whose body was tensed like that of a boxer who was about to place the winning punch, raised his flexed arm and was just about to hit his father with all his might when his hand he had in the air was grabbed in flight and wrestled to the side of his body by an unknown though strong-armed assailant. Danio looked up and saw Jeone, one of the Townsfolk, an Etruscan brute who by this time had entered the premises and was keen for some Gogo ale. Jeone was strong armed and Danio was no match for his strength.

Jeone barked at Danio, 'Get off your father you little punk,' and Danio turned to stare at him with eyes that were full of disgust and hatred.

Jardjon picked himself up rather unsteadily from the floor and dusted himself off. His attention was drawn to the brew off that was bubbling on the stove. Once satisfied that the brew was in no danger of burning, he turned his gaze to his now captive son.

'Let him go.' Motioned Jardjon to his friend Jeone. Jeone reluctantly loosened his grip, though stood in between Danio and his father to fend off any further violent attempts by Danio.

Danio knowing that he was no match for the bulky Jeone, was exasperated and had no words to say. He simply stared at his father, shook his head in complete dismay and turned and ran from the Tavern with the energy of the storm still brewing inside. White knuckled and red in the face he ran like lightening, running aimlessly and forcefully, spurred on by emotions he had little experience with; anger and hatred. He kept running out of town into the forest onward, onward and onward, running, running, running until after many, many, miles and when daylight was turning into night finally his pent up energy was expelled and he fell in a heap in a dark corner of the forest. His body curled tightly into a tense ball, he cradled his feet with him arms and cried whilst rocking his body to and fro up and down up and down. Crying, wailing, crying and howling until his tears were all spent he then stared into nothingness he fell into a state of a black and depressive void. *Why did I succumb to violence?* He was furious about his actions and blamed himself entirely for finding the so named 'Lola' berries. Somehow he imagined that all the problems in the town of Badon were due to him which fed his self-hatred to an inconsolable state of being. The Lola berries, he reasoned would undoubtedly have an adverse affect on the already struggling town of Badon and he feared it would render all the inhabitants completely useless.

Danio was overburdened and helpless to override what was happening in Badon town. He stood up and walked ahead, not focusing on anything, one foot after another. His lips were pursed tightly and self-loathing was stamped in the lines of his forehead. In this state of total self-annihilation, he aimlessly propelled himself forward in the forest, taking no care in avoiding the biting needles of plants. It was as if he was deliberately inflicting pain on his being, which once succeeded, drove him further into self-hatred and loathing. He did not bother to look ahead, just moved forward determined to forge deeper and deeper into a cobweb of dank and spiky bushes. A place had he been in his logical state of being he would have avoided all together.

He continued further and further into this abyss of jagged forest until his feet met with a rubbery tangle of roots. The roots tensioned and stretched under his weight which gave rise to fear in Danio's body, this fear snapped Danio out of his disassociated state of being and in an instant, he recognised that a cavernous hole lurked beneath the tangled roots which were likely to collapse under his weight. Instincts took over and he gingerly attempted to back himself off the unstable setting. The roots however disentangled which sent him tumbling helplessly down to an unknown depth. His body flailed from side to side, like a lifeless doll bumping r from rocky outcrops on the sides of the hole and onto other jutting obstructions on the perimeters of the cavern. He continued sailing from side to side, rock outcrop to rock outcrop until he thudded to a unforgiving stop where his battered, limp and lifeless body rested in a heap.

CHAPTER 7

THE ROCKY PATH TO BADON

Do not follow where the path may lead. Divine the future by living it as you would have it now!

Back on the path to Badon the travellers four all woke up in a state of trepidation about their journey forward. Trival and Hely, who were the first to wake, conversed in whispered grave tones prior to joining the others for breakfast. They were considering leaving Nadoo and Perina to their adventures and return to Scaysborough. Trival reasoned that they did not owe either Nadoo or Perina anything, and they could easily return to live with Nomad and the other Trehwells in the castle. Trival regretted his desire to see new lands and was sinking into despair about what the upcoming day would bring. Trival felt that Perina was totally unprepared for the trip and was not someone they could trust and rely upon. Hely listened to Trival intensely and agreed on all he had to say. Hely, however, was keen to see Badon as he had not completely fitted in at Scaysborough. He did not feel at peace there. Hely and Trival were becoming firmer friends and they came to a compromise; they would continue this journey for one day more and if they did not reach Badon by the next night, they would return to Scaysborough.

Nadoo was having similar conversations with herself. She was now having fractured feelings towards her friend Perina.

She began noticing her frailties and was less enamoured by her friendship. Nadoo also felt that if there were any other issues in the journey to Badon that she, herself, would not continue any further on the path and return to Scaysborough. No one related their concerns to Perina and instead sat and ate breakfast in the same gritted silence as the night before. Perina was lost in her own thoughts. She felt very embarrassed about her unpreparedness and was regretting her haste to make this journey. Perina could sense her fellow travellers' disdain and knew that any wrong decision by her now would completely destroy any flicker of trust they had.

Hely decided to walk over to the waterfall to see how difficult the track below would be and was curiously delighted to see that a steep, though relatively easy, path to navigate appeared to be carved out along the edge of the cavernous rocks. He felt a little lighter in spirit and quickly related this to the others at camp.

'See,' Perina said, 'we'll be in Badon in no time at all and If I remember rightly, it will only take a few hours and we will be there.' She said in a forced cheery tone. Perina felt anything but cheery. She knew too well that she had put her friends at risk and overestimated her memory of how to get to Badon. She only hoped that the path was easy as she too was beginning to think they all should return to Scaysborough too

'Humph,' started Nadoo in an accusatory manner, though said no more as she was nursing too many ill thoughts and decided to keep herself in check.

The path down the edge of the waterfall was oddly shiny. It somehow gave the impression that the rocks were polished and used quite regularly. It was steep, though winded down the hillside in a manageable fashion. Nadoo could only think about how hard it would be to climb up on the way home and began grumbling and humphing. Perina was the leader of the four, with Hely and Trival not far behind. They could all hear Nadoo decompensating into a grumpy state and they, not wanting to be the brunt of her wrath, hurried down the path and left her to plod along in her disgruntled mire.

And then it happened! No one actually saw it happen nor did they forsee it, but it did and Perina, Trival and Hely were none the wiser until they reached Badon. What happened, you may ask? This: Once Perina, Hely and Trival reached the bottom of the waterfall, they could see the larger path to Badon in front of them. They huddled together to wait for Nadoo so they could take the path together. Nadoo was heard cursing and stumbling down the path. Her mood had not improved which sent waves of anxiety the three who would be subject to her bad mood and wrath.

As Nadoo neared, Perina shouted out to her, 'The path is down here' She yelled. She then yelled again, 'Do you want us to wait for you?' These words carried up the path and were heard faintly by the clambering Nadoo. Nadoo was not in the mood for company and was deliberately keeping space from them.

'Not at all,' Nadoo yelled in her loudest voice to ensure they left her be. 'I will be alright.' She furthered in the same bellowing tone.

'If you're sure you're alright,' said Perina in a voice to match Nadoo's tone. Her words echoed over a tree branch and the wind took them through the leaves of its branches and Nadoo heard a stifled, 'Go to the right.'

'Ok,' yelled Nadoo, 'I will take my time. See you all in Badon.' And with that, Perina, Trival and Hely delightedly scooted up the path knowing that Nadoo wanted the solace of her own company and they would be free from her grouchiness. Perina, unaware of the mistaken message, had no concerns for her friend as the path was straight and well kept. Soon the trio relaxed and began to enjoy their journey, noticing the hanging forests of tangled vines and beautiful flowers which provided a haven of nourishment for the plentiful butterflies. Perina was becoming joyous in her venture and gladdened that she would soon see her young and faithful friend Danio. Trival and Hely were also in better spirits as the surrounding country reminded them of their previous home in their caves so they felt somehow nourished in this familiar territory. They began conversations about Badon in hopeful anticipation and curiousity about what to expect.

Nadoo, however, had not improved her mood. She made it to the bottom of the rocky incline and as she was still in no mood to talk to the others, deliberately sat on a rock to enjoy the sun and to put further time between them. Nadoo was used to time by herself and now was realising that she was happier in her solitary life. This is when she picked berries, sang songs, and entertained thoughts of new culinary delights. Nadoo did like company on occasion and enjoyed watching the delight of others, especially when they ate her fare. But time by herself fed the essence of her soul.

Nadoo waited on a rock and ate one of the cakes that she'd packed for the journey. This cheered her somewhat and she then looked around for the track that Perina had cautioned her about. 'Keep to the right,' she remembered hearing. Nadoo's mood declined as she perused her surroundings. Straight to the left was a large clear path and to the right a track that looked like a goat like creature had scraped through it. It did not appear very worn and there was a great deal of overhang from the quite sprawling trees and shrubs.

'Typical, Typical,' she fumed to herself. 'Harummph. Harumph, Harumph.' Nadoo was not amused and wished that Perina was close by so she could unload herself of all the negative thoughts and aim them directly at Perina.

It was this rather charged angry energy that propelled Nadoo forward on the higgledy-piggledy path that rose and fell onwards and upwards. If Nadoo had not been in such a squalid state of mind, she may have thought twice about the path she took and noticed the craggy hills curiously moving in the distance. Nadoo, however, was like a rocket filled with fuel which was spurning her on in a fast and furious pace. She did not stop to reason and did not even consider for one minute that she was actually going on a path was in the exact opposite direction to Badon.

Chapter 8

Badon at last

To change a world, you must begin with a village.
To change a village, you must begin with a family.
To change a family, you must begin with yourself.
To change yourself, you must look within.

Perina arrived at Badon almost unaware that she arrived. She had been enjoying the track so much and her head was full of ideas about planning her wedding to Zaphod that it was in a euphoric state that she stumbled upon the outskirts of the town. She waited for Trival and Hely, who were not far behind her.

Perina's wish was to visit Jyno and Shona's home first in the hope that she would find Danio there. Trival and Hely wanted to walk around the township and attend the famous tavern to see for themselves the perils within. Perina cautioned them against trying any brews and they departed with the understanding that Perina would meet them there in a few hours, where they would consider accommodation options for the evening. Perina was hoping that Jyno and Shona would offer them all a bed for the night.

Perina set off down the familiar path towards the river to the people whom offered her such good care on her last visit. Memories flooded back to her, their gentleness tending to her wounds and giving her broths which aided her recovery. In this sentimental mood she decided there and then to invite Jyno and Shona to the wedding as well. Zaphod would not mind, she reasoned with herself and it was the least that she could do!

It was not long before she was in front of the cobblestone path to the wooden cottage that housed Jyno, Shona and, she hoped, Danio. She walked joyously towards the door past the tended flower gardens that were cordoned off with tree branches painted white resting on other white painted forked branches firmly embedded in the ground. The flowers were out in numbers; they provided a Kaleidoscope of colours which brightened her mood and camouflaged the decay of the timber that lay beyond in the structure of the house.

Perina grasped the door knocker and rapped three times. The house appeared silent and Perina could not hear any murmurings from inside. She rapped again this time with more force so that the knocks were louder, she did this several times and again listened keenly for sounds within.

She was not disappointed this time and heard the murmurings of Shona calling out to Jyno, 'The door, someone is knocking Jyno.' Perina then heard a sniffling and a snuffle which was Jyno opening and shutting his mouth making a sucking sound with his tongue as he emerged to a bewildered state of wakening.

Jyno who was failing in his hearing called back to Shona, 'I didn't knock anything.'

'No,' she countered, 'The *door*, the door.' Upon hearing this, Perina promptly knocked another three times.

'Oh! I am coming, I am coming,' Jyno exclaimed both to the knocker at the door and his wife and creaked himself out of his chair and hobbled to the door buttoning his pants at the same time. He always unbuttoned his pants to rest after lunch when his burgeoning belly gave rise to discomfort as it tensioned against his canvas trousers.

He had managed to place his attire back in its position of

modesty when he opened the door. He was astounded to see a smiling and healthy Perina and stood back stammering, 'It P—P— P—,' he exclaimed she tried to remember and pronounce her name when Shona, who was becoming inpatient by now, rushed to the door and was also taken aback.

Shona, however, was quicker to remember names than her husband exclaimed, 'Perina, what a surprise! We had not expected a visit from you.' Shona gushed and fussed around Perina, checking her healed wing that they tended to and spinning her around to see the full healthiness of her now beaming body. Perina quickly informed them of her impending marriage and of their invitation. Shona was charged with enthusiasm and promptly picked Perina up in a fit of delight and spun her around by the waist.

Jyno noticed the giddiness on Perina's face and said, 'Put her down woman.'

Shona, too delighted to rebuff Jyno in such a gruff manner, saw herself that Perina was getting giddy and stopped the spinning until her legs became settled in one spot. Perina wobbled and corrected herself so she stood firmly upright and straightened her ruffled clothing. Beaming with excitement, she asked the whereabouts of Danio so that he too could be a part of the merriment at hand.

The voicing of Danio's name had a profound and sobering effect on Shona and Jyno. Both now looked concerned and they quickly informed Perina of the berries that Danio had found and the actions of Danio's father naming the berries Lola berries and concocting them into a brew called Dream Cloud. They also spoke of their worries that he had not returned home since early this morning and they had been informed by residents that he had attempted to assault his father in the Tavern. Perina now shared the same forlorn look of disbelief as Jyno and Shona. All three knew this was totally out of character of the peace-loving

Danio and were at a loss to understand what could have incited him to such actions.

Perina advised that she wished to go to the Tavern to find out more and hopefully find out where Danio was. Shona was very concerned about Perina going to the Tavern, warning her she had heard that Dream Cloud brew was more intoxicating than the Gojo ale that she was previously addicted to. Perina reassured them somewhat taken aback, that she would never succumb to the addiction of Gogo wine again and would be back within the hour with news. Jyno and Shona offered their hospitality and advised they would make up a room for her to stay. Perina told them of her fellow travellers and whilst apprehensive at first to house unknown guests upon learning they were fellow Trehwell's like themselves, they quickly offered to make up some beds in their living area for the extra guests.

Perina hurried determinedly along the path to the Tavern. This time she noticed her surroundings less and was indifferent to the fields, homes and flowers along the way.

She was consumed with concern for her friend Danio and almost brushed right past Trival and Hely, who were in avid conversations with Danio's father Jardjon on the porch of the pub. Nodding to them all she edged her way into the conversing trio.

'Look who it is,' said Jardjon who instantly was reminded of Perina's last visit to town and the profits he made from her. He licked his lips and puffed up his mouth and motioned Perina towards the bar. Perina had a memory of the pleasant tasting wine and a vivid picture arose in her mind of her tapping her toes, smiling and laughing with a drink in her hand. She wanted to grasp the wine that was offered to her, but her now healed wing twinged with pain and she recoiled wondering how she could've even contemplated a sip.

'Oh, I see,' cajoled Jardjon, 'No Gogo wine for you. You have heard about the Lola fruit that Danio found and want to try our Dream Cloud Brew. Jardjon had already learnt that only a tiny amount of boiled up Lola berry juice was needed to be added to drinks for effect. He could see that the pot on the stove would bring him much business and profits. He was keen for Perina to try the brew, he was always keen for more customers.

'No, not at all,' the rather shaky Perina replied.

'I have asked your friends to work at the bar,' said a rather sulky Jardjon who was not used to non-purchasing customers. 'They do not want to try the brews either,' he said. 'Funny lot, you people from Scaysborough. What can I help you with?'

Perina now shot a bewildered look at Hely and Trival after hearing they were going to be employed at the Tavern. They immediately removed themselves from the conversation and leaned back on a nearby wall to discuss their new future. 'I—I—I was wanting to know where Danio was,' stammered Perina.

'I expect he is gathering more Lola berries as we speak,' lied Danio's father. 'We had a fight earlier. He would not let me know where he found them and does not want to share profits with me,' Jardjon folded his spindly arms over his chest. 'They have a wonderful effect and are completely safe, otherwise why would Danio be so keen to get more?' questioned Jardjon in a matter a fact tone.

Perina could not imagine Danio wanting to claim profits. Who has he become? she wondered. It was compelling, however, to think that Danio might be hoping to help those in the Tavern with a wonderous new brew. Perina, now full of curiosity asked Jardjon if she could try this for herself to help her understand his unusual behaviour. Jardjon could not pour the drink quickly enough and smirked as he watched Perina savour the drink and become entombed within its hallucinogenic effect. Perina felt she was sailing on a sea of rainbows. She trailed her hands along an imaginary river and watched as bulbrooks danced on cushions of purple grass and drank wine under the jewelled sun.

Trival and Hely watched in astonishment as Perina became nonsensical, muttering to herself and swinging her body around in a jerky fashion appearing to avoid invisible objects. They had accepted jobs at the tavern, cleaning tables and creating order when guests become troublesome. They were offered lodgings as well. Trival and Hely felt no obligations to Perina and left her to her ramblings taking their Mattocks and belongings to their rooms and returned to get instructions from their new boss about their duties. He instructed them to guard the room which served as a greenhouse and laboratory where his wife Wilmsea was busily collecting the Lola Berries tiny black seeds, then painstakingly spreading them out one by one on some moistened bracken with the hope of them sprouting and producing more shrubs that fruit this hallucinogenic magic.

They dutifully followed orders and stationed themselves outside the heavily curtained room, only seeing a dim light beyond the curtains and the shadow of Wilmsea, who appeared to be pacing up and down the room. Wilmsea *was* pacing! There was only a handful of Lola berries left and she now knew without any doubt that there would be a lapse in time before her new plants struck and bore fruit. She was not only worried about the profits of the tavern she was also worried about her own addiction. Whenever she stopped taking Dream Cloud Brew, she shook, feeling ill and became more agitated than she usually was. The only cure for this unwanted state was more Dream Cloud brew, which renewed her feeling of exaltation and carried her to a land of fantasy and fun. She was further troubled that Danio had refused to get more and was quite violent to his father. When she was in a sober state, she could see how she had neglected her son and hated herself for it.

These feelings of self-hatred were another reason why she relied heavily on Gogo wine or Dream Cloud brews. The substances took her mind on a journey away from her past mistakes and regrets to a trouble-free land of make believe. Little did she realise the more that she turned away from her problems and failed to repair them, the bigger they become and the more they grew. The distance between her son and her grew further and further. Her life was becoming a wasted nothingness, a whimsical dance of despair.

Wilmsea sweated and her fingers trembled. The effects of the Dream Cloud brew were wearing off. She needed to come up with a solution to extend the capacity of the berries to not only feed her addiction but to supply a growing number of patrons whom had already tasted and like her, relied upon the brew. In desperation, she grabbed all the stems and leaves of the plant that had been attached to the berries her son had picked. Without any testing to see if the substance was toxic, she began adding the leaves to a new experimental Dream Cloud concoction. With the hope it would extend their already supply and carry the Tavern through until the seeds matured into plants.

It was an ill prepared plan, created under the effect of a drug that made users lose their capacity for rational thought. It had failure written all over it, though Wimsea only laughed as she sipped a tiny sip of the Dream Cloud Brew that Jardjon had poured her earlier. The goony grin that followed illuminated the lunacy that was behind this plan.

Back in the Tavern, Perina was in an altered state of consciousness and imagined that Danio had found something that would give peace and joy to the world. She imagined him climbing multi-coloured mountains placing Lola berries in his back pack smiling and excited. If only she knew that he was in exactly the opposite state of being. Perina continued to accept Dream Cloud brew from the smiling Jardjon, unaware that this substance was slowly rewiring pathways in her brain that was damaging her ability to make decisions and altering her awareness of the world. A musician had been employed by Jardjon, to sing and play a lute, Jardjon was very keen to increase his clientele and sales so thought a singer would do both. The singer Johan, an aged bearded Trehwell, wore a pointed felt hat with feather and ragged clothes. He settled himself by a corner and began to play. The song he delivered to the audience was scribed by Jardjon to improve sales and dependence on his brand new drug. Rohan was encouraged to also participate in taking Dream Cloud brew though in a very small dose, this allowed him to remain conscious though still be alert enough to sing. Johan begun singing and playing in a drawling robotic tone.

Oh Dream cloud, please come hurry to minimise my scream
Oh Dream cloud, you bring back colours to my
disambiguated dream
Silky clouds of rainbows, purple skies and velvet rains
Oh Dream cloud, you have mastered the answer to my pain
All the time I am your servant, I have everything to gain.

Jardjon chuckled under his breath. The song and the effects of the drug were working.

'Perina looks hooked as well, very good for profits!' he exclaimed. At the same time, a rather small framed Truon bird with a large bulbous beak was resting on a post outside the tavern. The bird, as if sensing the atrocities before him, felt urged by an unknown force and lifted himself from his roost and went on a determined flight to Scaysborough to send a message to a resident there whom was in deep, meditative state.

The Truon who are renowned for copying noises kept repeating in a loud screeching tone, 'Perina is hooked, Perina is hooked, scrawc scrawc!' It was in this manner that the bird sailed the gentle offshore wind that blew directly to a large and well-made timber verandah.

Chapter 9

Zaphod fears for Perina

Better work and greater effort are achieved under
a spirit of approval than a spirit of criticism.

Truscott had awoken to the news that Perina and Nadoo, along with Trival, and Hely had journeyed to Badon to give Danio an invitation to her and Zaphod's wedding.

It was Zaphod himself who re-iterated this news and Truscott chuckled t the thought of them in their travels and only could imagine some of the adventures they may be having.

Zaphod sought Truscott's help in completing his Billop for Perina and himself to live in after the wedding. Barnio was assisting Zaphod, though did not have the strength needed to lift the heavy beams and rafters to hold the roof and walls and place heavy support posts in place.

Truscott was happy to oblige and together with Zaphod's help, the posts were stood and beams placed with seemingly little effort. Before each lift, Truscott breathed deeply into his body and used the strength of his core and thighs to distribute the weight in his body and to lift with ease. He orchestrated Zaphod to do the same, and they lifted with synchrony and without any hiccups.

Barnio was darting around this way and that excitedly watching the process and without need exclaiming things like,

'Be careful of the post, don't drop it, bend your knees.' Instead of getting angry at these superfluous commands of care purported constantly by Barnio, Truscott laughed and wondered how it would be inside Barnio's body always moving and worrying.

'Perfect, yes perfect!' pronounced Barnio in a manner that suggested that he somehow needed credit for orchestrating the success. This time Truscott and Zaphod burst out laughing and gently ruffled Barnio's hair in a gesture of good will.

'I have been perplexed, perplexed,' offered Barnio. Barnio's mind was whirring due to a rise in stress hormones that was fed by him imagining disasters about Nadoo and Perina's trip. He had questions in his mind about how Perina knew the way to Badon. 'Well, Perina fell upon the track, upon the track along Jinku, Jinku River and that Danio, Danio had discovered her and led her to Badon, to Badon

'Yes,' said Zaphod

'Well then, then,' continued the animated Barnio, 'How would she know where the track, the track started to Badon, to Badon from the track, the track to Jinku to Jinku River, River? She fell, fell upon it and didn't walk, didn't walk there!' And with the raise of his eyebrows, he punctuated a stop in talking and both Zaphod and Truscott stood still and poised, reflecting on what he was saying. It was sometimes exhausting listening to Barnio who was as most Garnio's in the habit of repeating things.

'I have always admired the strength in Perina. She will just get up and do things.' Zaphod nibbled on his lip. 'Though at times she does not think things through and may have gone ill prepared for the journey' he admitted.

'When is she due back?' questioned Truscott.

'She said she would be back in plenty of time to practice for the fair, so I would imagine at the end of the week?' offered Zaphod. But his voice was now worried.

'Best not to be worried unless we know there is something to be solved,' advised Truscott picking up on Zaphod's rising concern. 'I will go home for lunch and come back to discuss when and if we need to follow and check on the four travellers.'

With that, Truscott turned and left steadfastly walking back to his cabin, striding with ease and certainty. Zaphod however could not take Truscott's heed and he absentmindedly drew his fingers in the dirt and now started to worry in earnest about Perina's travels and what could occur when she reaches Badon given that she become so intoxicated last time that she did not care for herself and lost her wing due to infection. Zaphod now had his head in his hands and was weeping.

'Don't worry, don't worry,' buzzed Barnio in excited tones, though Barnio himself could not stop worrying and the contagion effect of despair soon found Barnio slumped alongside Zaphod with his head in his hands in the same exact same manner.

Truscott arrived home and changed into loose and comfortable clothing. He ate a modest lunch and used his awareness to savour every mouthful of what he considered a delicious, though very humble, cheese sandwich and a glass of water.

Now content, he settled into a comfortable position in a high-backed timber chair that had a comfortable seat made from woven straw. He placed his hands in his lap and closed his eyes drifting into a delicious state of awareness that allowed his higher consciousness' to be open to universal wisdom that offered itself to persons in such a state. The colour purple was seen by his closed eyes, which was something peculiar to him. A calm wider force,wafted ideas of peaceful solutions to any issues he may have, as well as comforted any emotions that may be emerging. He stayed in this state for 10-15 minutes, though it appeared time stood still. It always amazed him how much time could lapse in these moments of bliss.

Truscott emerged from this state in a manner of knowing and was guided by an instinctual force to go outside. He went outside and felt the warm embrace of the afternoon sun on his skin and the gentle breeze that tussled his well-kept hair. Closing his eyes again he succumbed to the beauty of the sensation, relishing the caresses of the wind and the warm light of the sun. He then opened his eyes to see a rather straggly Turon bird watching him with some curiosity with a turned head.

'Oh, hello,' beamed Truscott, 'why have you come for a visit?' he added warmly.

'Perina is hooked, Perina is hooked. Squawk Squawk, Squawk!' repeated the parrot. And with that message delivered he returned to the sky and was observed by Truscott to veer his wings in the direction of Tremlite, the now sister city of Scaysborough.

'Curious,' said Truscott, though in exclaiming this word he knew it was not curious at all, it was a message delivered by the ancients of time to alert him that Perina was in trouble and that help was needed. He hastened back to Zaphod and Barnio to find them both still seated, with their heads on their hands in full despair. 'Hum hum,' exclaimed Truscott which woke both of them from their troubled stupor. Truscott recounted his meditation and the visit from the Truon straight after. When Truscott repeated what the bird had said, Barnio went into a flap of worry.

'I knew it, I knew it,' he repeated over and over, 'silly, silly silly,' he scolded to no one in particular. Zaphod however had an unexpected reaction and he lifted up a large boulder and flung it with fury. It collided into one off the new fence posts he'd laid yesterday, which promptly cracked under the explosive collision.

'Calm is needed,' commanded Truscott in an authoritative tone. 'We have no use of imaginings and anger right now. What we do need is to prepare for a journey to Badon, let's hope we can find the right route and we can see for ourselves what is happening for Perina and offer any assistance needed.' Zaphod fought the urge to damage more property. He could reason that he was angry with himself for agreeing for Perina to go off in such an ill-prepared journey. He also was very concerned and worried for her, which was frustrating as he could not offer any immediate help. He pined to see her again and the news she may be in danger was intolerable. Barnio sensed the despair of his friend and, ignoring his own sorrows, he offered to run up the mountain and back with Zaphod to help his burn off his emotional energy and help him regain his rational thought. Truscott beamed with delight at Barnio's insight and the pair took off on the rather steep track to Mount Vusis and back. As Barnio could travel the speed of light as all Garnio's could he ran and zig zagged up the mountain to keep in sight of Zaphod who appeared was running at full pace up the jagged track spurred on with emotional energy. Barnio noted a slowing of pace and a more relaxed look on Zaphod's face as he continued, and by the time they had reached the top and he was pacing himself on the way down.

Zaphod turned and smiled to his friend and said, 'We will find her it will all be ok.' And it was with this attitude that he met with Truscott again at his house and engaged in animated discussion about the journey ahead.

The trio agreed to leave the next morning which gave them the evening to pack and the night to be well rested prior to the embark the next day. It was late in the afternoon and Barnio, like all Garnios, automatically shut down at sunset which signalled a deep catatonic sleep state. No one wanted a repeat of the last adventure where he went missing after this occurred. Barnio mused that he would find that exciting though they all knew he was joking. Barnio was used to Nadoo doing the food packing and was wondering out loud what they could possibly take. Truscott, in awe of serendipitous moments, exclaimed with gusto that he had just finished packing his larder with more cheese and bread than he usually did and that he could provide enough food for them all.

Now that it was all set, the trio returned to their individual homes to sleep and to awake refreshed for the next day. Truscott was the only one to rest well. Once he placed his head on his pillow, he easily fell into slumber. Truscott had mastered the art of shutting down thoughts that were not helpful to him prior to sleep. He did this by completing a progressive relaxation tensing his muscles then relaxing them and soothing his psyche by saying peaceful soothing things. These were statements such as, I am Ok, I will solve any problem tomorrow, I will awake refreshed and renewed, I am so grateful for my life etc. Barnio and Zaphod however had not mastered this art and both had difficulties resting their thoughts of concern which kept them awake long and disturbed their dreams introducing nightmares and terror which fuelled there sense of foreboding.

Chapter 10

Nadoo meets a Vindervay

Every action is either an act for love or a call for love

Nadoo was becoming grumpier by the minute. The track was becoming narrower and narrower and she had to look hard for where she had could actually place her foot next. Unbeknown to her, she was actually following a Bullbong path. A Bullbong was a creature that resembled a Kangaroo. It had a large thudding tail, though unlike the Kangaroo it has a rather large and round floppy nose. A local Bullbong had forged this faint path that Nadoo was walking on to get from its home in the craggy rock caves to the banks of the Jinku river. Nadoo was soon to become fully aware of this. She was frantically trying to follow the scratchy path in the dense bush and her total focus was fully on the ground. She was having grave concerns about her predicament when she was alerted to a loud thud, thud, which was the sound of the Bullbong's tail flailing on the earth as it jumped.

She lifted her head from her focus on the ground to find the cause of the sound when she came face to face with a large male Bullbong and let out a rather loud and high-pitched scream that bounced back to her in an echo from the craggy rock face that was in the near distance The Bullbong was as shocked as she was and bounded in huge bounds as far away from her as it could get. This is when Nadoo fully understood that she was lost. The path she had been following led to a jaggy grey rock face that sported triangular jagged entries which from where she was standing, she surmised they could be caves. With some fear and trepidation, she forged through the remainder of the path to come to an endless wall of jagged stone that reached to the sky, unclimbable and formidable. She leant up against the face and cried forlornly to herself, disbelieving that she could be in such a predicament.

As she did so, she was jolted into shock when the wall moved behind her and she heard a voice that was both cranky and bewildering.

'Goodness, woman what are you doing? Get off me. Get off me, I am no leaning post!' The voice boomed. Nadoo almost feinted at this point and mustered enough strength in he panicked state to turn to see who or what was responsible for this rant.

She stared dumbfounded at a small statured thick bodied grey creature with two stubby hands and two stubby legs with an acutely pointed triangular head. His whole body resembled that of the craggy granite rock face now directly in front of her and she had to squint to keep her focus on him as he seemed to blend right into the rocks behind him. 'Stop staring, stop staring,' he spat out. 'Explain yourself. Explain yourself,' he commanded rather abruptly.

Nadoo, who was not used to such demands, became irked and with all the ire she could muster, she placed her hands on her hips and looked him squarely in the face.

'I think the explaining is yours to do,' she said and they leaned into each other with pursed lips and determination.

'Enough. Enough,' a voice called out and astonishingly, Nadoo saw one creature after another peeling themselves away from the rock face and stand in a circle around her. They all had similar features of the first, and Nadoo quickly took her hands off her hips and dropped to the ground in horror.

The owner of the new voice, sensing Nadoo's fear, was more placating.

'Vick the Vindervay at your service,' he announced and bowed his triangular thick skinned craggy body at her.

'Oh, a Vindervay!' Nadoo exclaimed. She had heard of such creatures, though firmly believed that they were only of make believe told to children. She unwittingly said all of the above out loud, which gave fuel to more insults from the first Vindervay she saw.

'Not real, not real,' he menaced. 'Outrageous talk'

'Gorrow, calm down,' said Vick. 'I am sorry about him,' said Vick. 'We were just about to prepare for supper when you bumped into us and he was very much looking forward to his dinner. I am afraid any delays with supper send him into a fury.' Nadoo nodded in recognition and she remembered all the times she was driven to anger when people interrupted her meal time.

The news of food excited Nadoo greatly and she just remembered she had not eaten for at least four hours, and immediately her stomach growled in anticipation.

Vick seemed kindly and she calmed herself somewhat and questioned the rock man in front of her, 'So you are friendly folk then?' questioned Nadoo, who remembered the childhood stories of Vindervay's stealing children and fattening them up for dinner.

'Very friendly. You are probably thinking of tales that we eat children. Of course we don't. A Trehwell whom was concerned about his children's wanderings made up that tale to scare him into staying at home. This is why we hide out in the mountains away from persons who wish us harm,' said Vick.

'Tell us why you are here then,' interrupted a still grumpy Gorrow. Nadoo told all the 15 Vindervays in the circle around her the whole tale of Perina,

The wedding, the journey to Badon and her now being lost in the bush. 'No worries' said Vick.

'Gorrow knows the way to Badon, don't you Gorrow? He stumbled upon the town recently and he would be happy to escort you there.'

'Happy?' questioned Gorrow, 'I don't think so.'

'Of course you will,' commanded Vick, who happened to be the leader of the clan. 'There will be no further discussion. He will take you there tomorrow but for now you must eat with us and we will arrange a lodging for you for tonight.'

Gorrow glared at Nadoo who glared just as menacingly back. They both followed the other Vindervays to a large heavy wooden table and the band worked together in stocking the table with breads, cakes, cheeses, and berries. Nadoo and Gorrow were first to eat and they hurriedly filled their screaming bellies. Then a strange thing happened; the fuller they were, the friendlier they got to each other. Gorrow began chatting about the life in the caves and told Nadoo of the Jim Jam tree nearby and the delicious fruits it had. Nadoo remembering a cake she still had left in her bag foraged around to find it and presented it promptly to Gorrow, who gobbled it up and complimented her on her fine cooking. They chatted for hours whilst the stars and moon danced around the sky enjoying each others company as well as finding out they both love to sing. An astonished Vick looked over at the pair and shook his head in wonder remembering how agitated they were towards each other only hours earlier.

As the Vindervays turned into their caves one by one, Nadoo realised that she didn't feel tired at all and that she could stay up all night. This was a strange sensation, as she felt light and airy and as content as a cow full of hay. Nadoo however, remembered her need to get well rested for her walk to Badon tomorrow and was growing excited at the prospect of journeying with Gorrow the next morn. Nadoo reluctantly excused herself from discussions with Gorrow and bade him goodnight. Gorrow, visibly disappointed by the news, bowed before wishing her magical dreams, then he turned and sprang light-footed to his cavernous abode.

Her cave lodgings were surprisingly delightful. There was a comfortable bed made from timber. On top, lay a straw mattress decorated by a hand sewn quilt with cleverly stitched bouquets of bright flowers scattered all over the cover. There was a warm quilted mat on the floor and an armchair made from cowhide that was soft and sturdy. Nadoo was not long to sleep. Once her head hit the pillow she had a content of spirit that she had not felt before. Soundly asleep and snoring loudly, she had a wonderful dream of a wedding and woke up with a start when she saw it was her not Perina in a wedding dress and the groom was Gorrow not Zaphod. She chuckled and drifted back into a restful slumber.

Gorrow felt strangely enchanted by Nadoo's company; a feeling he had not entertained before. Perplexed, he drifted off into a peaceful slumber, luckily just before Nadoo began heavily snoring in her cave next to his and he is his sleep state was oblivious to the tractor sounds emanating from her mouth.

CHAPTER 11

DANIO IS FOUND

Divine the future by living it as you would have it now!

Danio felt a dull ache. Disorientated and confused, he fumbled around in the darkness of his surrounds and memories of falling, bouncing and thudding down a dank, seemingly endless tunnel came flooding back into his mind. He now was fully aware and back into a state of consciousness. He fumbled in the darkness to find his fluorescent clay, which he always kept on hand. He brought it out from the darkness of his pocket and he could see clearly his entombed chamber of roots, rocks, and dirt.

He placed the clay on a rock nearby and surveyed himself for any damage. Remarkably he was covered in scratches and bumps, his left foreleg in particular was very sore though on trialling moving all his body parts he was pleasantly surprised to find nothing broken at all.

He had a rather large egg-shaped lump on his forehead, though he did not discover that until sometime later. He felt lucky to be alive and the fall appeared to shock him into realising what was really important. In this sounder state of mind, he knew he could not be blamed for his father's ill use of the berries he founded and that if he used his mind and evoked the help of others, he may be able to stop the decay in Badon and shut his father's tavern down.

He forgave himself for the anger he tried to deliver to his father, understanding that pent-up emotions of a neglected childhood and now betrayal by his father was the cause of his valve to burst and the steam of the pressured emotions burst into being. Danio was not proud of himself, though chose to forgive himself and learn from the experience.

He looked intently at his surrounds and was not encouraged by what he saw. He could see that the tangled mess of roots he fell through was a good 20 or more metres up. The walls of the upright tunnel he was in was partly shale rock with some dirt and roots higgledy-piggledy scattered amongst the 180-degree incline. Danio saw little opportunities for foot and handholds for climbing upwards, but was hopeful that morning light would uncover more. Danio himself had not been in this part of the forest before due to its dense and spiky foliage. He knew it was no use shouting to the void as far as he knew there were no inhabitants for miles and miles. Barely visible beyond the matt of roots and leaves he could make out glimpses of the sky which was darkening. No other choice was available but to sleep in this confine for the night and spend his dwindling energy tomorrow in plotting a path of footholds and finger holds to get him out of his miserable hold.

Unbeknown to Danio, the tunnel in which he was trapped had an adjoining tunnel that led to the caves of the Vindervay. He was not able to see it in the dwindling light as the entrance was hidden behind a large boulder that was casting a shadow over the entrance. He managed to sleep as a state of exhaustion overcome him. His body, though not fatally wounded, had many bruises, scratches and bumps and all his remaining energy was utilised by his cellular repairs. He slept long and hard, and nothing but darkness entered his dreams.

Cannily enough, Garrow was planning to head to Badon not far from where Danio now lay. He had stumbled upon the very tunnel that led to Danios now dungeon, he however found another one to the left of where Danio lay and would be taking this exit, which led him to a clearing out the back of Badon not far from the river.

Garrow woke in a less euphoric state as hunger entered his bones and darkened his mood. Nadoo herself was more sour when she awoke and was scouring her room in the cave for any treats that may have been left for her. To her dismay there was none and she 'Harrumphed and Harrumphed,' getting dressed and packing her things in a sulky, bullish manner. Her mood lifted somewhat when she headed outside to find other Vindervays preparing breakfast and packing some supplies for her and Garrow for her journey. She raced to the table and in very poor manners, began gobbling down what ever she could. In the corner of her eye, she saw Garrow doing exactly the same and she smiled slightly as she envisioned what she must look like to him.

Garrow was too focused on his food to notice the arrival of Nadoo at breakfast but after his seventh piece of toast and his fifth bowl of berries, he felt decidedly full and put his head up to see Nadoo waving at him across the rather large table.

'Oh, good morning, I trust you slept well,' smiled Garrow.

Nadoo blushed and started with, 'Yes, but I had the most amusing dream.' She quickly changed the conversation when he enquired to what it was about. 'Oh, nothing really,' she stammered, 'I am ready when you are.' In truth Nadoo was far from ready. She didn't really want to go back out on the bush, she was incredibly angry with Perina whom she blamed fully for her current predicament. She remembers Perina calling ' Go to the right' and now she was extremely angry thinking that she deliberately tricked Nadoo. Nadoo however did want to get back to Scaysborough for the fair and would have preferred Garrow taking her home but she dare not ask and she did want to speak her mind to Perina, let her know how her nonchalant attitude placed Nadoo in peril.

Nadoo tensed with anger as she imagined dressing Perina down for her contemptuous behaviour. Her body softened, however, when she witnessed Garrow load both his pack and hers onto his shoulders. He spoke gently to her about the journey ahead. His gallant and chivalrous actions melted her mood into admiration. She looked into his eyes and blushed as he smiled at her. Nadoo was not used to such attention and she promptly turned her head, stammering that they should get going.

It was a warm and sunny day and the track around the tall grey mountain turned suddenly into an open forest. This path was filled with Jim Jam trees and they stopped often to pick and eat this treasured fruit.

'I could just about live here,' Nadoo murmured.

Garrow raised his eyebrows at this and said, 'It certainly is a great spot.' They journeyed onward and Nadoo burst into song. Her voice was melodious, her notes were on key and she filled the valley before her with the harp like sounds of the song. She was stunned when she was joined in voice by a deep and booming baritone, she looked over and they sang together in complete harmony and joy.

> *'The day is loved*
> *The mood is great*
> *Let us take time to celebrate*
> *Our bodies are strong*
> *Our minds are wise*
> *No-one or nothing, do we despise.'*

It was this noise that awakened the sleeping Danio, who was not too far away in a dank and dark hole nearby. Danio strained his ears to hear an angelic melody that was in the near distance. The song was so beautiful that for a minute it was more important to hear the sounds emanating than to consider the implication of people being so near to him who may be able to assist him out. He was carried away when he remembered he had heard that voice before. His memory of being at the lake at Tremlite and the song that had stopped the troops in their tracks; it was Nadoo.

'Nadoo! Nadoo!' Danio bellowed in his loudest voice. Despite his best intentions, his voice in the background sounded merely like a chirping cricket and did not pierce the singing which was in full force. Nadoo and Garrow continued this way on sprightly feet, singing and smiling until they came to an entrance of a cave.

'I hope you are not fearful in tunnels,' challenged Garrow.

'No. Not at all,' lied Nadoo. She wanted to make a good impression on Garrow.

He led her into a path and if she was not so full of fear, she may have heard her voice being called in the distance.

Garrow stormed ahead in the tunnel until Nadoo who could not feign her bravery any longer whelped like a hurt animal and stood very still. Garrow turned to see a huddled Nadoo whom seemed gripped with fear.'I thought you said you were not afraid in tunnels ' he said with soothing concern, ' Don't worry I will walk with you and with that he held out his large and rather soft hand for her to hold. Garrow's hand instantly soothed her and she was relieved, she relaxed knowing that she was in good stead and that it when she heard it.

'Nadoooo, Nadooo,' a faint squeak was heard in the distance. Nadoo motioned Garrow to stop by holding out her hand like a stop sign and put her finger to her mouth to signal to him to be quiet. Garrow complied and he like her heard a feint cry in the distance, 'Nadoo, Nadoo,' it continued like that in a moaning type fashion that reminded Garrow of a calf looking for its mother.

'What in the name of Scaysborough Town could that be?' She exclaimed with intrigue. Though feint, it sounded like a younger person, though she could not make it out. Garrow and Nadoo journeyed further along the Tunnel, following the sounds until they stopped. They listened intently, though no more sounds came. Little did they know that Danio was so exhausted and had such little energy that he had petered out and he could not make a sound at all. Danio's battered body was more damaged than he thought whilst most was bruising, his organs were also bruised and battered and all his energy was aimed at repair.

Nadoo immediately began shouting in her loudest voice. Her voice boomed in the chamber and Garrow himself had to put his hands over his ears to dull the intrusion of noise.

'Who is it? I am here!' she shouted. Danio could hear her booming voice and tried his hardest to reply.

He only squeaked out his name, 'Danio,' his pitch was high and was Garrow who heard and interpreted it.

'I think he said it is Danio.'

Nadoo was very perplexed, 'Danio? Keep squeaking. Keep squeaking,' she shouted, having some indication by his tone that he was injured. Danio upon hearing the command squeaked and squeaked until Garrow could pinpoint the direction that his warbled voice was coming from.

'I think he is in the tunnel to our right,' he said and quickly informed her of how this path meanders to a dead end that posses a large shaft that reaches to the ground. 'It is a narrow track that is long,' said Garrow. 'I will need to travel this alone,' he continued. Nadoo nodded even before he finished the sentence. Not even the soft and manly hand of Garrow would not be able to entice her to enter the small and pokey tunnel. She shuddered at the very thought. They hugged to say goodbye and were both a bit taken back of their spontaneous offer of affection to each other. A quizzical look was exchanged by the pair, and Garrow hurried along the unwelcoming tunnel in the direction of the fading squeak.

By the time Garrow had reached the end, the squeak was barely audible. In the darkness of the confine, he almost did not see the crumpled body of a child that lay in the corner. A slight squeak emitted from his mouth, Garrow replied reassuring him of his safety as inched his way towards the small flaccid body. Danio was alert enough to make out this strange apparition and stared at Garrow with eyes as wide as dinner plates. He had never seen a Vindervay.

'Don't worry. I am not going to eat you.' This made Danio's eyes widen further. Unlike Nadoo, he had not heard any stories about Vindervays and hearing the words, 'I won't eat you,'made his broken body shiver. Garrow, seeing the terror in his eyes reassured him that he was a friend of Nadoo's and gently started singing the song that he and Nadoo were singing together. This relaxed Danio, as he felt that a voice as beautiful as Garrow's could not mean him any harm. Garrow scooped Danio up in his arms and carried him carefully back along the tunnel to the waiting Nadoo.

As he emerged from the tunnel with Danio's crumpled and body in his arms, Nadoo gasped.

'It's ok, its ok, he is just sleeping,' reassured Garrow, 'but he certainly needs tending to his body is battered and bruised all over.' Nadoo could see purple and black bruises all over his legs and arms and one huge egg-shaped lump smack bang in the middle of his forehead. He was in no state to answer the barrage of questions that Nadoo had in store for him so she saved them up for when he got better.

Nadoo picked both packs up and placed them on her back whilst Garrow carried the unconscious Danio. Danio's arms and legs swung helplessly backwards and forwards in rhythm with Garrow's steps. They forged on throughout the tunnel until it came to a clearing near a river. Nadoo remembered Perina telling her all about the river near where Danio lived. She also recalled Perina telling her in great detail about Jyno and Shona's house and the immaculate garden out the front. She could see such a house ahead of them and hurried Garrow to the spot where it nestled on the top bank of the river.

Nadoo and Garrow walked up the path and used the knocker on the door to alert the residents within of their coming. Jyno and Shona were now wide awake and expecting Perina to return, so hurriedly opened the door to gasp loudly at the party before them. Jyno and Shona saw at once the condition of Danio and motioned them inside, staring at Garrow.

'I don't eat people,' he offered which saw an increase of alarm on their face. He turned to Nadoo and whispered I have to stop saying that.' She smiled, though quickly introduced herself as Perina's friend and introduced Garrow as a Vindervay.

'A vinda—what?' exclaimed Shona, though he did not stop for an explanation.

'Bring him in here,' she motioned and Garrow followed Shona. They entered room a small room and upon her instruction, he laid Danio gently outstretched on the bed within.

Shona wasted no time in removing his clothing and barking instructions to Jyno, 'Get this ointment, get this bandage,' and he obliged, running backwards and forwards handing her all the items she needed. She swiftly and deftly tended to Danio's wounds, cleaned, and dressed him and offered him tiny spoonfuls of broth. Danio was in a delirious state, though he could feel the familiarity of his bed and the soothing hands of Shona and he fell into a healing sleep.

'Let's leave him now,' commanded Shona and you can both tell me the adventures that got you here. As they did this, Jyno made tea for them all and they ate and talked and rested. Shona told Nadoo that she was expecting Perina home at any time from the tavern and said that she was also expecting some Trehwells she knew.

'Trival and Hely,' Nadoo offered.

'Yes, Perina mentioned she was travelling with two Trehwells, Trival and Hely, that was it. She said they may need a bed for a few days, though I've not seen a hair of them!' Shona replied. 'Look, as the beds are now made up, you folks can have them. I will make up some more if the Trehwells arrive. You can wait up for Perina or go to bed up to you,' Shona said nonchalantly, and with that, she retreated to her chambers to sleep. Jyno swiftly followed, leaving Nadoo and Garrow by themselves.

Nadoo decided that she would wait up for Perina to return. Garrow, who succumbing to Nadoo's gritty charm said he would keep her company. They nestled together on the lounge and talked about this and that and nothing at all. Beyond the window and into the night the seven moons were settling high into the middle of the sky. Nadoo was enchanted by the ambience of the evening and moved slightly towards Garrow feigning discomfort as the reason for the premeditated move. As she turned to draw closer to Garrow she noted the moons positions, and with a sigh said, 'Oh dear it is very late now.' Garrow nodded and was preparing himself to catch Nadoo in an embrace as she huddled towards him.

Nadoo however jumped to her feet to scrutinise the skies closer, she contemplated going to the Tavern to check on Perina, though as she stood her calves responded with throbbing pain from so much walking ans Nadoo still angry with Perina, spluttered out. 'Why should I worry about her? She didn't as much care for me.' Garrow shot her a quizzical look. 'Too late to wait up or check on Perina now,' she stated matter-of-factly. 'Best to hop to bed and follow up in the morning,' she added.

Nadoo bid her goodnight to Garrow, who surprised her by standing up, drawing her close to him and kissing her on the lips. Nadoo was taken aback though at the same time exalted in a state of bliss and kissed him back, lingering in his arms, revelling in contentment. A cough heard from upstairs brought them back to surrounds, and they lowered their eyes and reluctantly separated and settled into their beds. They settled into a blissful sleep. Romance entered both their dreams and they were heard by the upstairs residents to be giggling, laughing and snoring at the same time.

Chapter 12

Truscott, Zaphod and Barnio go to Badon

Real strength is mastery of mind, not muscles

Truscott awoke early, refreshed from his night's sleep. He set about getting dressed and checking the bags that he packed the previous evening for the journey ahead.

He sat in a chair near his kitchen window and feeling the early rays of sunlight gently caress his face, he meditated in reverence of all that he was and all that he had. He always started his day in a meditation of gratefulness which focused his mind on all that he had and all that he knew would be delivered unto him.

He'd learnt early on that focusing on lack only brought more of it. He remembered as a child desiring a red hula hoop. This was a toy that a lot of the village children had and spent hours whirling the circular hoop around their bellies, arms, and legs. His parents were very kind, though quite poor. His father had a farm with a few chooks and cows and his mother tended to the house and made cheese and bread. The family ate well and were comfortable, though had no leftover money for toys that could be bought in the marketplace.

Truscott, however, was very keen to have a hula hoop of his own. To entertain himself, he spent the whole day visualising himself twirling and playing with a red hula hoop. As if by magic, a neighbour's grandparents were visiting the home next door the very same afternoon. They were very kind and generous persons and had given treats to Truscott's family before. Truscott remembered delicious cakes, sweet honeycomb pastries with custard and bags full of berries.

On this day, however, the gifts delivered to the family were not edible. The kindly octogenarian called out to Truscott's mother over the fence to hand her three hula hoops for her children.

'I was buying some in the market for my grandchildren and I thought of your three youngsters,' she explained. His mother thanked the woman very much, knowing how much her sons would love them. She called Truscott and his two brothers and handed out the gifts. A green hula hoop, a blue hula hoop, and lastly a red hula hoop. Naturally, Truscott called out for the red one which he readily received. Truscott was wide eyed and astonished as the very thing he was concentrating on had came to him, as if by magic.

He somehow knew in his conscious from that day forward that he could expect his every need to be met, to expect the answers to every problem and to expect abundance on every level. A habit of meditating in the morning evolved, he practiced quietening his mind and thinking of things he needed as well as the things he was grateful for. Other benefits he found for meditation was when n he had a problem to solve. By meditating on a problem he was able to reach into his higher being of awareness and to be open to higher conscious solutions. It was probably the contentment he gained from such daily practice that stopped any desires for him to metamorphose and grow wings like other Fallons. Truscott was delighted in his being the way he was and had no need to fly, he loved treading on the earth and feeling its solidness under his feet.

Truscott did not boast or talk of his practice, though if anyone was interested or asked him about it, he would advise them. A few other people in Scaysborough also meditated and practiced gratefulness and could be seen like Truscott to walk assuredly and talk kindly to those that met them. Truscott also completed a series of body movements after meditation and before breakfast. The moves were taught to him by a friend, Nomad the wise, Trehwell king in Scaysborough. He told Truscott that the movements were centuries old and helped energy circulate through ones bodies to keep them strong and supple. Truscott added this moving meditation to his daily routine and he had never suffered from any aches or ailments of any kind.

Refreshed from his meditation, he felt compelled to place one further item in his backpack for his journey. It was a small elf like figure that Perina had made him as a gift. He always loved the figure, it was a little elf-like man grey in colour, it had a misshaped head and a pointy hat. The figure was sitting in a leg crossed position and had a long beard and outstretched hands. Perina, at the time, was making pottery figures and she made it for Truscott as she often saw him sitting and meditating and she thought of him as a wizard. He carefully wrapped the figure in cloths, and was a little perplexed about the desire that urged him to include this object though as it came to him in meditation. He knew there must be a reason and found a safe place in his burgeoning pack.

He said goodbye to his beautiful home and walked to Zaphod's house, where they'd pre-arranged to meet. Barnio was already waiting outside and appeared happy to see Truscott walking steadfastly towards him.

'Hurry, hurry.' No time to be wasted. We must set off at once,' hastened Barnio darting this way and that. Barnio was always like this, keen and quick. Truscott let out a hearty laugh in seeing his friend in such a frenzied state.

'Relax, Barnio. You will burn yourself out,' called out Truscott as he neared the gate.

'No time for relaxing, no time for relaxing,' repeated Barnio, 'Perina, needs our help, our help,' Barnio continued.

Upon reaching Barnio, Truscott took his head in his hands and held his head gently. 'It will be ok, Barnio.'

Barnio calmed a little as he felt the soothing warmth of Truscott's strong hands. 'Zaphod is inside,' Barnio added. Truscott walked inside to find Zaphod sitting forlorn in his chair.

'I never should have let her go. I should have thought it through better, this is my fault,' lamented Zaphod.

Truscott approached Zaphod and placed both his hands on his face as he had done to Barnio. 'It is not your fault Zaphod. Perina is Perina, and she does what she wants. Nothing you could have said would have stopped her. She has Nadoo, Trival and Hely with her. Do not blame yourself.' Truscott said this with such earnest and honest intention that Zaphod melted into Truscott's touch and relaxed coming to his senses. Barnio too, relaxed somewhat more himself.

'Let's go then,' said a rather more subdued Barnio and with that Zaphod picked up his pack and the trio headed off to an unknown path in an unknown town. They discussed the journey ahead of them on the way. 'We know that Perina took the path along Jinku river and we know she fell and then Danio assisted her to the township of Badon.

'It is finding the track between Jinku River and Badon that's the problem as Perina is the only one who knew that,' said Barnio in a very matter of fact tone. Truscott, who always knew that they would find it, was just about to offer this statement when who should appear over the horizon but their very good friend, Heffla.

Truscott beamed at seeing Heffla, and the three all exchanged glances of pure delight. They waved frantically at him in the distance, which almost made Heffla take another path. Heffla had seen all type of treachery and tricks on his travels and knew well indeed a feign of someone needing help could very well turn to them robbing him. Best to avoid whoever or whatever this is about he mused. Heading to an alternative route he paused for a second look. He squinted and stared,the figures were drawing closer and he was just about to flee when he recognised the silhouette of Truscott's large stately body. Sighing with relief his angst turned to joy, and he scurried towards them keen to meet up with these old acquaintances. The trio also picked up their pace and in no time at all, the four were in contact.

'Haito, Beterd,' called out Barnio, which is the usual Garnio greeting.

'Jenta Jonty!' exclaimed Zaphod and Truscott in unison in usual, Fallon fashion. 'Greetings friends and travellers' returned Heffla in a genuine and hearty voice.

'Where might you all be heading this time?' questioned Heffla in a curious tone. It was Barnio who had not met Heffla before, who recounted all the happenings since their last journey. Barnio was so excited in his speech that Heffla had to ask him to slow down on more than one occasion. After several minutes, he had not even got to the point of them looking for Perina and so was abruptly interrupted by Zaphod. Zaphod quite sternly said to Barnio that he would take it from there and told of how Perina had traversed to Badon to invite Danio to his and her upcoming wedding and that they were now fearful for her safety. They told him they knew she was going to take the same track that she took when Danio escorted her from her fall near the Jinku River.

Truscott added the story about the message he had received from the Truon, 'Perina is hooked.'

Heffla, stroking his beard with one hand whilst the other was planted on his cheek, said repeatedly. 'I see, I see.' He stood in contemplative silence for a few minutes, stroking, stroking, thinking, thinking. Barnio was keen to interrupt his silence and was about to speak, though a stern glance from Zaphod told him not to do it. Stroking continued, Barnio could hardly contain his frustration, zigzagging this way and that when finally the silence broke.

'Ok,' Heffla announced. 'The track to Badon must be the one at the base of the waterfall at Jinku River. I know of it, though I have never taken it myself,' added Heffla.

'That sounds right,' said Zaphod. 'Perina discussed hearing a waterfall in the background when she took the track to Badon.'

'As for your concerns for Perina, I have heard that there is some substance being offered to persons in Badon that sends people bonkers at the Tavern there. This the very reason I don't want to visit the place myself,' Heffla offered candidly.

'No. Perina would never have anything at the Tavern after what happened last time,' Zaphod said crossing his arms with indignation. Though as the words left his mouth he was reminded of the sometimes impulsive actions of his soon to be wife and could actually visualise her saying, 'I will try anything once,' and then tossing down some vile mixture to see of its affect.

'Let's not jump to any conclusions, and let's be on our way,' offered Truscott, trying to calm the now brooding Zaphod. After getting more directions and advice from Heffla, they bid him farewell and soon found the path to Jinku Mountain.

As the day was more than half over now, they trekked with earnest only stopping briefly to eat. As they hastened down the path he noted the sun was retreating on the horizon. They could just see the glimmer of the majestic which quickened their steps to behold the grandeur unfolding. Around the next corner the majestic river revealed itself. Truscott revelled in the earthy wet smell of the river surrounds. Zaphod and Barnio were also taken aback from the glorious sparkly wonderland of The Jinku bending down to drink of its cool and refreshing bounty. They decided to camp the evening before taking the next part of the journey. Barnio, in true Garnio fashion, retreated to his tent just before the sun set to embrace his automated snooze. Zaphod, who was still restless and concerned for Perina, went for a short flight In the fading light. He wanted to use the opportunity to retrace Perina's movements and, in doing so, feel more connected to her. In flight, he could see the waterfall below their campsite and could make out the signs of a track to the right of their base. This must be the track to Badon, Zaphod thought to himself and somewhat more satisfied, flew back to camp, arriving just in time for the sun to slip beyond the hillside and the night to take its kettle black form.

Zaphod laid down to sleep, though his thoughts were consumed with Perina and he imagined her with him alongside him for ever. He would never let her out of his sight again he promised to himself over and over again. He continued like this until his body gave way to sleep and Perina filled his life with dreams of her

If Truscott could have heard Zaphod's thoughts, he would caution his friend to be careful for what he wished for as it may very well come true. The trio slept well, as the backdrop of the waterfall in the distance lulled them and kept them in a comfortable and pleasant sleep.

CHAPTER 13

PERINA'S PERIL

The ultimate measurement is not how we conduct ourselves in times of comfort, but how we conduct ourselves in times of challenge.

The light gently rose over the horizon in Badon Town, gently creeping across the fields and sleepy Billop homes, extending itself further up the cobble paths, climbing up the hill into the tavern window and rested gently upon the unconscious but smiling Perina.

Perina had not left the Tavern for one day and one night. Her world was now full of fanciful colours, imaginary creatures and flights of fancy. She had not drunk anything beyond the dream cloud brew since entering the Tavern. She had not eaten either and unbeknown to her, this was having a devastating effect on her body. Her body and brain was dehydrated worsening her ability to think rationally, her muscles and organs were drawing on stored fat in her body to operate their functions and if they could talk, they would be screaming out for proper nutrition and water so that it could stop the self-cannibalising process and restore and replenish her body again.

Perina, however, was oblivious to her demise. She stirred slightly when the sun caressed her face and flickered her eyes to a semi open state. She was greeted by a smiling Jardjon, who upon seeing her wake, was keen to offer her some more Dream Cloud brew. Perina, with a drooling grin, was about to accept when Wilmsea stormed in like a torrent of wind.

'Stop that at once,' Wilmsea barked. Jardjon, startled by the interruption, almost dropped the jug of brew in his hands. He quickly corrected the toppling jug, knowing the value of its contents and stared at his wife, who was spitting with fury. 'This is the very last jug,' she screamed with such gusto that far away, a sleeping Nadoo was awoken in an unfamiliar bed.

Wilmsea was spurned by the over overwhelming physical pain that was now brewing in her body. She grabbed the jug from Jardjon and straight from this vessel, promptly gulped down almost all the contents. Jardjon,stared in astonishment at Wilsmea who had the look of a bulging eyed Bulbrook caught in a snare. Upon taking the brew, she transformed back into the wife he knew and could talk sanely about the situation. Wilmsea was not taken into a magical state by the brew it merely stopped her physical pain and cravings. Jardjon, himself had stopped using Dream Cloud as the last time he drank the delusive brew, he saw images of monsters, large dark monsters with large pointed tails and large sharp teeth. He remembered crawling into a ball rocking and lashing out at his invisible foes. As his mind became more coherent he vowed never to place himself in this self propelled hell and from then on only used Gogo wine. He briefly pondered about the affects the brew may be having on all concerned when another problem interrupted his thinking.

'There is not much left' Wilmsea stated somewhat matter-of-factly. They had served the brew all day and throughout the night, never stopping once to check on the vat's level. Wilsmea quickly told Jardjon of the diminished supply of berries and that she had added the leaves and stems to the few she had left to add to the vat. Jardjon ' You added the leaves and stems already' He questioned. 'Did,you assess the toxicity by rubbing them on your hands to see if a rash occurred?' he continued somewhat worried.

'Nothing wrong with them,' she replied, 'they are from the same shrub' Wilmsea retorted and appealed to him to try it on Perina, who was now coming more to her senses and was complaining of aches and pains. Perina's moans increased and her body shook violently. Jardjon looked around in desperation at what when Wilmsea taking matters into her own hands gathered some of the newly concocted brew and offered it to her. Jardjon watched helplessly with wide eyes observing the scene unfolding before him. Perina accepted the liquid from Wilmsea's shaking hands and grimaced with disgust at the taste. Perina's body slumped immediately and she flopped to an unresponsive state on the ground.

Jardjon raced over and felt her neck to see if there was a pulse, he could feel a feint throbbing of the vein and decided to leave her rest. Trival and Hely were assigned by him to guard the door of the tavern.

'Do not let anyone enter,' he commanded them. They bowed their heads in unison and stood steadfast at each side of the door with their hands folded in front of them. Jardjon was definitely worried about anyone seeing Perina in the state she was in which would be bad for business, but he was also concerned about his customers who would soon be trailing up the winding path to the Tavern expecting Dream Cloud brew and he was worried about how they would react when they learnt there was none to be had. Jardjon was only too aware of the addictive effect of the substance and how ii affects persons demeanours when there was none to be had. If they behave like his wife Wilmsea did, he could imagine bedlam and he himself was beginning to think he should head for the hills.

With his guards in place, he hoped that and they would hold the ghouls out the front before they became as wild and uncontrollable as Wilmsea herself a few minutes earlier. Wilmsea and Jardjon decided to wait and see the outcome of Perina before giving the brew to the wider township and sat down to discuss further options should this not have a favourable outcome. Unbeknown to them, Perina was now fighting for her life. Her body was already poorly but now was also responding to a toxic substance trying to rid it from her cells. With no replenishment of water, her body was atrophying and her usually pink plump skin was now shrivelling, wrinkling and becoming an unhealthy grey in colour. Her breathing was shallow and if Wilmsea and Jardjon were not in such animated discussion about their dwindled supply of dream cloud brew and how to deal with the soon to appear regular customers, they would have heard an odd gargling sound coming from Perina's extinguishing body.

As Jardjon feared his usual clients were lining up to be let in, they too were aching for more Dream Cloud to extinguish their bodies ailments. Trival and Hely had to shout out in their loudest voices in an attempt to quell the crowd who were not used to having the Tavern shut. They began to panic at the thought that their needs would not be met and began complaining, shouting. 'We need it now! Let us in, Move out of the way,' the crowd began to chant. The mob was in danger of becoming completely unhinged and violence to gain entry was a real threat. Trival and Hely looked at each other and shrugged shoulders.

'Don't worry it will open soon,' Trival shouted as loud as he could above the din.

'Remain calm,' shouted Hely also using his loudest voice. The crowd softened a little with the hope of an imminent opening and kept their discontent to a lower grumble. 'Safe for now,' murmured Hely to Trival though they both exchanged worried looks. Very worried. Both had huge misgivings about their newly found jobs. It appeared a brouhaha was brewing a rather large and untidy brouhaha.

Nadoo was startled by a shouting noise that was coming from afar but loud enough to interrupt the most heavenly dream she was having about a wedding with so much food and merriment and again, it was her wearing the bride's dress. She sat up at once and harrumphed out loud.

'What in the world was that?' She quickly took in her surroundings and saw that Gorrow was twitching in his sleep and slowly awakening as well. Shona was already up and in the Kitchen preparing breakfast.

'I heard it too,' said Shona as she nodded to her awakened guest.

'Oh, good morning,' said Nadoo.

'I think it came from up the Tavern way,' continued Shona not replying to the conventional morning greeting

'The Tavern?' queried Nadoo, 'I guess Perina didn't come back,' she added.

'No I have not seen or heard anything at all about her. Pity though, she came all this was to see Danio and he is here now.'

'Oh yes how is he?'

'He is sleeping soundly,' answered Shona. 'I have tended to him during the night and given him broth, he will recover soon I am sure.' Shona continued as she pounded some dough.

'I think I'd better go at once to the Tavern' stated Nadoo, If Perina has not come home I need to check on things there.'

'I'll come sunshine,' grinned a smiling Gorrow who now was fully awake and stroking his long grey beard. Then, something amazing happened. For the first time in Nadoo's, and for that matter Gorrow's, life they didn't even think about breakfast. They looked kindly at each other and seemed totally content, even with their grumbling stomachs. They quickly dressed themselves and were out the door as fast as their legs could carry them. They smiled at each other, instinctively Gorrow reached out his hand towards hers and she obligingly placed her chubby small hands in his and they almost danced up the hill to the Tavern beguiled by love and strengthened by the joy it brought swinging their arms this way and that until they caught sight of the porch of the Tavern. Nadoo was astounded to see Trival and Hely stone faced with their arms crossed over their chests, standing with a formidable terse expression on their faces. Beyond them was a crowd of Badon folk milling about on the verandah, they looked poorly, some were bent over holding there stomachs, some were holding on the railings. They were sweating, shaking and all were very, very angry. Nadoo and Gorrow gave each other a concerned look, Nadoo pointed towards Trival and Hely and they maneouvered their way through the tense crowd until they cam face to face with them.

'Whats all this then?' asked Nadoo with widened eyes.

'Well hello to you too,' retorted Hely, offended by her non cordial behaviour.

'Well I never,' started Nadoo, riled by the memory of being left to her own devices and being told to go on the wrong path. She momentarily forgot about the maddening crowd and gave them a dressing down. 'Thanks a lot for leaving me. You brutes have no idea what happened and how—' she remembered had she not gone on the wrong path, she may not be now holding Garrow's hand and she softened slightly. 'Well, anyway, where is Perina? I will give her a piece of my mind,' said Nadoo,, now with more pepper in her tone.

'She is inside,' offered Trival, though Hely just looked at her with annoyance.

'We told you which path to take,' he said sulkily, taking offence to Nadoo referring to him as a brute.

'You said go to the right,' she spat with all the ire she could muster.

'Never did!' he spat back. 'The last thing Perina called to you was, 'Are you all right?' You might want your hearing checked, you old goat!'

Well, that was enough to send Nadoo into a rage and clenched her fists into a ball and was about to launch herself at him when Garrow slightly coughed and raised an eyebrow. She at once came to her senses and sheepingly looked at Garrow, dropped her shoulders and fists, shrugged and shook herself slightly 'A misunderstanding then,' she offered in a much calmer, softer voice.

'Yeah, that would be about it,' agreed Trival.

'Who is the rock?' questioned Hely in a menacing voice.

'Garrow the Vindervay at your service,' offered Garrow in an unusually considerate tone. If he had not been under the spell of love, he may have joined Nadoo in flying into the increasingly obnoxious Hely.

'Vinder*what?*' sneered Hely.

Just when Garrow was about to spit something back, Nadoo harrumphed and said surprisingly calmly, 'We can have full introductions later but now we must enquire as to where Perina is.'

'She's in there,' replied Hely as he pointed to inside the cabin, 'been drunk for days,' he added with a viperish tone.

Nadoo sank a little upon hearing the news and commanded, 'Let me in there at once.'

'No can do,' sneered a recalcitrant Hely, pushing his nose close to her face.

'And why can't you?' Nadoo demanded.

'Bosses orders, we work for Jardjon now,' stated Trival trying to diffuse the unpleasant scene.

'Yeah, bosses orders,' added Hely smugly.

'What time does it open?' enquired Garrow seeing that they were determined to maintain a fortress until opening.

'Usually at ten,' lied Trival, who didn't really know the hours of the Tavern or why they had it shut. Garrow looked at the crowd around him who were now engaged in tense talk. He overheard conversations which were aimed at forcing an entry to the building, alarmed he questioned Hely and Tival. 'Do you think you can hold these lot back until then?'

'Come back at 10!' Trival ordered standing firm with his hands folded. Hely backed him up by taking the same stance.

'We have this covered,' added Hely smugly. Nadoo looked at Garrow and shrugged and they both turned to walk back to Shona and Jyno's cottage. Garrow shook his head harbouring huge doubts about their ability to hold back the restless mob outside.

'Maybe we can have breakfast after all,' said Nadoo trying to make some good of the situation Upon hearing this Garrow's belly started to growl in agreement. 'We will be back at ten,' yelled Nadoo. Burdened by the unpleasant encounter, Nadoo and Garrow walked in silence, appeased only of the thoughts of their awaiting breakfast.

Jyno was now awake and joined Shona at the table, enjoying breakfast, when Nadoo and Shona returned knocking at their door.

'Just come in,' called Shona, who was surprised to see Nadoo and Garrow back so soon and without Perina to boot. Shona and Jyno were dumbfounded when Nadoo and Garrow recounted their events.

'Very strange indeed,' mused Shona, 'Jardjon has always opened his door for early customers and we've never heard of it being shut until 10 before…Very strange,' she repeated.

Soon their minds were focused on the spread before them, homemade crusty bread, jam, cheese and a large bowl of Nadoo's favourite fruit Jimjams. They ate heartedly until there feasting was interrupted by a slight whimper coming from Danio's room. The four swept themselves up and with food and crumbs spilling from their mouths, they raced to his room. Upon seeing them, he smiled weakly and nodded with large thankful eyes, then promptly fell straight back to sleep.

'This is a good sign,' said Shona, with a sigh and they all returned to their feast, delighted that Danio appeared to be convalescing well. They ate and drank warm tea until the clock gonged 10 times, signalling opening of the Tavern and the collecting of Perina.

'We will be off then,' stated Nadoo, and with that her and Gorrow trotted back down the now familiar path to the Tavern. In better spirits now due to their full bellies and the signs of Danio's recovery, they walked hand in hand taking in all the delights along the way. They stopped to smell flowers in the fields, pointed to unusual trees in the distance and swung their arms in joyous unison until they caught sight of the unruly crowd at the Tavern.

They saw that even more townsfolk had gathered out the front, possibly now 50 or more. It was apparent that the situation had worsened, some now looked extremely ill and were holding their bellies with their hands writhing around in pain on the ground. Those who remained upright were shouting with red faces at the now stone faced and terse-lipped Hely and Trival who were seen beyond the crowd. Nadoo and Garrow pushed and shoved their way to the entrance, only to find the door still shut firmly and Hely and Trival were asking people to return to their homes until further notice.

'Further notice?!' shouted members of the crowd.

'I want Dream Cloud now!' shouted another.

Someone else in the crowd joined him and soon half the crowd were chanting ' Dream Cloud now, Dream Cloud now!'

'Where is Perina?' Questioned Nadoo.

'Still inside,' answered Trival with his arms crossed.

'Can't you just let me in?' Nadoo cajoled in her sweetest voice she could muster.

'No one in, no one out. Bosses' orders,' replied Trival in a robotic tone.

'Nadoo,' whispered Garrow, taking her arm and moving her to a quieter spot on the rowdy verandah. 'I think I can get you in.'

Nadoo eyed her rather short and stout companion up and down and said in a disbelieving tone, 'Oh you can, can you?'

'Yes' he said grinning with a nod with convincing fervour I can change to match my surroundings, this is what defines me as a Vindervay.'

'You can w—what?' stammered Nadoo. Garrow who was sensing Nadoo's scepticism promptly changed into a Nippoo creature like her. When Nadoo saw Garrow in this guise, she almost feinted and lent back to steady herself on the verandah post.

'Why you are…' She wanted to say good looking, though she didn't want to offend him by mentioning this as she'd fallen in love with the stony triangular shaped man.

Noting her admiration, blushed a little and interrupted her before she could complete her sentence. 'This is actually how I would ordinarily look had I not made home in the caves. I guess me and the villagers there had gotten so used to using the grey stone camouflage that we never changed back.'

'Oh my,' said an enamoured Nadoo.

She quickly came to her senses when someone in the crowd shouted rather loudly,'Let's ram the door!' Cheers could be heard in the crowd and some ran off presumable others to get the tools necessary. Gorrow suggested that Nadoo distract Hely and Trival whilst he camouflaged himself on the door and creaked it open so that she could slide in.

Nadoo nodded and racked her brain about what she could possibly distract them with. She unwittingly put her hands in her pocket and shook her head when she felt something shiny and hard in her right hand. As she drew it out she was delighted to find the rainbow rock that she had discovered in the river not too far from where Trival and Hely used to live. An idea came to her and she quickly conspired with Garrow about her plan. Despite all the drama at hand she could not help feeling delighted when she looked upon the shiny gem in her clutches.

In execution of their plan they casually walked up to Trival and Hely and started some small chit chat. Trival and Hely were a bit annoyed as they were also watching the crowd and its movements. Nadoo however kept talking, this time with even more charm and compassion. Nadoo was enquiring about their new abode, talking about her cooking and the upcoming fair in Scaysborough. Due to her friendly manner Trival and Hely relaxed somewhat, even unfolding their hands, Nadoo took this opportunity to pull out the beautiful rainbow rock she had entombed in her pocket since their last adventure.

Trival and Hely who like Nadoo had never seen anything so beautiful leant in to her to see its sparkly colours. It glittered in the sunshine and the light revealed shades of red, blue, and green as Nadoo twisted it and turned it for full affect. Garrow, seeing his chance, slipped behind the large torsoed Trehwells and stood flat against the door and metamorphosed himself to match the red and yellow striped paint on the door. He stood still as a statue and watched Nadoo engage Hely and Trival further.

'Hely and Trival,' she crooned, 'I must apologise for my previous behaviour. I want to offer you this rock to beg of your forgiveness. Hely and Trival bowed in unison and gladly received this amazing treasure. They handled the rock themselves, fascinated by its changing colours and did not notice when Nadoo tiptoed behind them and as quietly as she could. Garrow who was now camouflaged so well that Nadoo had to squint to find him against the door his beaming eyes of success the only give away. They shot each other chuffed glances and Garrow gently turned the handle of the door, ever so softly, holding his breath and grimacing with every feint squeak Once fully turned he began opening the door fraction by fraction, Hely and Trival still dumbfounded by the rock were turning it this way and that and talking to each other about the prisms of light.

The door was finally eased open enough for their stout little bodies to push through sideways and slip into the Tavern. Garrow, carefully pulling the door shut behind them. It shuddered a little with a small thud until resting on the frame. Nadoo and Garrow braced themselves, fearful they may be discovered.

Nothing occurred and upon hearing the now roaring crowd outside they knowingly felt that Hely and Trival had much more to deal and were still oblivious to their trickery.

They slumped with relief though this was short-lived as they looked up to meet the stares and wide eyes of Wilmsea and Jardjon who were surprised by the two Nippoos, one who was yellow and red striped like their door. Garrow, seeing their shock, realised he had not yet reversed his camouflage and quickly did so. Wilmsea and Jardjon rubbed their eyes in disbelief. Panic rose in them and they were just about to shout out to the guards when Nadoo heard a guttural sound and turned her head to where it was emanating and saw the huddled heap that was her friend Perina.

'Perina!' she shrieked. Wilmsea and Jardjon were themselves shocked to see the dishevelled appearance of their once healthy customer. They, like Nadoo and Garrow, made haste to run over to her. Perina was huddled in a ball, her skin was grey and loose over her body, her mouth was open and a guttural sound was emanating from her mouth.

'Gaugle, gaugle, gaugle' was the insensible sounds. Nadoo tried to gently shake her and talk to her, she even sung to her in the hope she would rouse though nothing she tried could penetrate her deeply cannoned unconscious state. Perina's state was desperate indeed. Fuelled by helplessness, Nadoo was infused with intense rage which she promptly fired at the publicans.

'How could you do this? This is the second time that Perina has almost expired at your very hands. For what it is worth, your son too is hanging on the edge of living, very poorly indeed, not that you would care,' she spat. These words and news of her son Danio in such a condition jolted Wilmsea from her usual state of cold indifference.

She stared wide eyed at Jardjon and lamented, 'What have we done, what have we done.' Jardjon reached for the jug of the now known to be poisonous Dream Cloud brew and promptly poured it down the sink.

'No more Lola or Dream Cloud,' he commanded Wilmsea who hung her head in shame and nodded.

'We must go to Danio,' Wilmsea said.

'You have more problems than that right now,' exclaimed Garrow, whose attention was drawn to the increasingly noisy crowd outside. By the discussions that were shouted in loud tones behind the door, it was obvious that the crowd had returned and were counting down ready to ram open the door. Jardjon, who had dealt with a few crowd unrests over his time in the Tavern quickly came up with a plan.

'Ok, open the door,' he commanded to Trival and Hely whom standing on the other side were ready to run themselves, as they strong as they were, they knew they would be no match indeed for the crowd and large hammering post readily approaching. Relieved to hear that command and just seconds before the large tree trunk slammed with intensity into the door, they opened the door wide. The log and the crowd, still running, spilled into the Tavern, rolling, bumping and falling all over each other and their surroundings until they and the large log came to an abrupt stop at the far end of the room.

The crowd wasted no time in collecting themselves from the

ground and demanding with verocity the dream cloud brew.

Over the din, Jardjon jumped up on the counter of the bar and announced in his largest voice, ' Free Gogo wine for all. Free Gogo wine for all.' A contagion of confused looks occurred throughout the Tavern. No folks in Badon had ever been offered free drinks before by Jardjon. Even though they came for Dream Cloud brew no one could refuse a free drink and they clambered to the bar accepting their free brew. One led to another and another and soon they forgot all about Dream Cloud and began revelling in the effect of Gogo wine.

'It will be a long day,' lamented Wilmsea who was frantically washing glasses to keep up with the demand. The plan worked, and the crowd was subdued.

Hely and Trival were swept along with the crowd inside and were themselves about to line up for the free Gogo wine when a higher-pitched sound of alarmed crying interrupted the rapacious din. Hely and Trival turned to where the noise emanated and saw Nadoo and Garrow huddled over the obviously seriously ill Perina. Trival was unaware of the trick that Nadoo played on them was still chuffed by the generous gift of the rainbow rock bestowed by her, so when he saw her wailing and struggling with Garrow to lift the limp and lifeless body of Perina he ran over to help.

Nadoo readily accepted his help and explained they wanted to take Perina to Shona as they knew she was good with herbs and if anyone in Badon could heal Perina, it would be her. Hely also agreed to assist and Trival and looked at his boss Jardjon for approval of leave. Jardjon nodded and despairingly watched as he watched the grey tangle of a mess that was Perina being carried caringly by his new guards.

'This is why we will never sell Dream Cloud again!' He stated loudly with an authoritative voice for anyone who would listen. A few wide-eyed patrons watched and nodded in agreeance.

Nadoo and Garrow, attended to Perina as best they could to prevent her limp hanging arms from coming into contact with the rocky path as they flayed from left to right as Trival and Hely carried her down the cobbled pathway to the little thatched Billop of Jyno and Shona.

By the time they reached the cottage, Perina's gargled moans were more audible. She had a foamy white substance emitting from the sides of her mouth, her eyes were shut tight and her unkempt, matted hair strung over her face like a craggy frame. Trival and Hely reached the cottage and barged their way indoors with no any announcement, startling Shona who was sweeping cobwebs behind the very door.

'Who the heavens might you be?' She started with an ire that befitted the rude interruption of her cleaning. Before the intruders could reply, she gasped as she recognised who they were carrying. She scrutinised the remnants of the Perina she knew. She looked many years older than she was and her face and mouth were hardened and tense with lines etched around her forehead. Her body was grey and lifeless and the foamy substance that was emanating from her mouth sent shivers down Shona's body.

She shook her head with despair, 'This is bad, this is very, very bad,' she murmured out loud. Soft though audible enough for Nadoo to hear as she and Garrow stumbled in behind them. There is no time to lose, 'Jyno! Jyno!' she bellowed, calling out to her husband so that she could bark commands. 'Put her in that bed,' she instructed Trival and Hely who obeyed willingly and placed her gently on a small wooden bed with a quilted cover with hand stitched birds on it. 'Out! Out!' she bellowed, 'Where is Jyno?'

'Right here,' he said and he stretched his neck inside the room as the Trehwells pushed past him in retreat.'Good luck,' they offered in unison, though no one replied or noticed as they left the room and made their way back to the Tavern to complete their work shift.

All eyes and concerns were for Perina,Nadoo and Garrow, comforted each other and watched helplessly as Jyno raced to and fro from the guest room with towels, lotions and potions in what seemed like an endless stream of mixtures, balms and tinctures. Taking order after order from Shona who was desperately trying to revive her failing patient.

A small cough was heard from Danio's room and Nadoo raced in to see Danio stirring from his stillness of days, 'What time is it?' he asked, believing that he had just woken from a sleep the night before. Nadoo raced to his bed and hugged him so hard that Garrow voiced his concerns of her crushing the poor lad. Garrow was right to be concerned, as Danio still bore many bruises over his battered body. Danio winced in pain and noticed his body was purple and black, scratched and scarred. 'What happened?' he questioned with complete bewilderment. Nadoo had not sooner told him the when memories of him being inside a dark tunnel returned to him and he stared at Nadoo and Garrow with wide and thankful eyes.

'The Vindervay,' nodded Danio, 'I am so hungry I might eat you,' he countered joking memory of Garrow pronouncing he doesn't eat people when they first met. Whilst this ordinarily would make Nadoo and Garrow laugh, they could not hide their concerned faces. 'What is wrong?' questioned Danio with a quizzical stare.

'Let me get you some food first,' offered Nadoo, who wanted to see how Perina was before burdening the convalescing Danio any further and went to the kitchen to prepare him some food. Nadoo could hear fervent worried conversations in the guest room where Shona and Jyno were tending to Perina.

She had to concentrate to get some food on a plate for Danio as she was trembling with concern for her friend. She managed to get some fruit, broth and bread for Danio and re-entered the room. Upon seeing Nadoo enter, Danio attempted to pull his body upright to a seated position. He felt every muscle in his body ache and strain as he lifted himself up. A sharp pain shot through his thigh causing him to gasp. He quickly retreated, lying down again. Nadoo spoon fed Danio, cupping her hand under his head and bringing it upright a little as he painstakingly ate morsels of food. After eating a small amount, he motioned her to stop, which she obligingly did. 'I think I need to sleep more now,' he said and in no time he drifted back off to sleep. Nadoo was grateful that Danio did not have enough energy to pursue the reason for her and Garrow's concern,s as she felt that all Danio's efforts should be applied to healing his own body before he cared for anyone else. She retreated into the lounge area and waited with Garrow straining to hear any signs of progression with Perina. Watching, waiting and being patient was all they could do right now so they settled in to anxious state of wait.

CHAPTER 14

ZAPHOD MEETS PERINA

*Better to have climbed the peaks and fallen, better to have
reached the crags with bleeding feet, better to have watched
loves embers burning out, better by far, better by very far.*

Zaphod was the first to wake in the campsite from a fitful sleep.
His first thoughts were consumed with fear in regards to Perina.
He was imagining her being 'hooked' on some substance as the
Truon bird exclaimed or possibly hooked up on some cliff face
or another type of peril. Being too anxious to eat, he arose and
packed up all his belongings, readying to start on the journey. In
his mind he was mapping out the track down the mountain they
would take to reach the path to Badon.

Impatient now to get moving, he deliberately made as much
noise as he could in the hope they would stir. He thudded his
pack down, coughed, threw rocks in the water, though nothing
appeared to disturb their slumber. As frustration rose, he noticed
that the sun had just begun to appear, meaning that Barnio
would not be able to wake until it rose a bit further diffused some
irritation. His energies now turned to Truscott. If he could get
Truscott into action he felt that they could all get going as soon
as Barnio woke. Zaphod noted a Truon bird in a tree above and
gathered a rock and threw it in the bird's direction. As intended,
the bird let out an almighty screech and took flight, squawking

in an indignant fashion. This evoked the desired result, and Truscott was noted to stir in his cassock. Zaphod wasted no time in running over to him.

'Awake, are you?' he exclaimed 'That bird, I wonder what alarmed it,' said Zaphod in a tenuous tone.

'I wonder myself!' exclaimed Truscott, who upon scanning the campsite found all of Zaphod's things packed up and Zaphod pacing backwards and forwards. The sun was now high enough for Barnio to open his eyes and noted Zaphod and Truscott exchanging words. He jumped to his feet and raced over to his companions to hear what the conversations were about.

By the time Barnio arrived, Zaphod was exclaiming rather loudly, 'Ok time to hit the road let's get on our way!'

Truscott spoke next, 'Zaphod, I understand your desire to check on Perina as soon as practical, though you will not do her any service if you arrive fatigued and malnourished. Let us sit and eat before we begin and I invite you both to meditate with me.'

At this, Zaphod protested immediately, 'No time for that, just time wasting,We can eat bread on the road,let's just get going.'

At this point, Barnio piped up. 'Let's just relax a bit and eat. We will get on the road in a jiffy.' Zaphod nodded, acknowledging his friend and defeat at the same time. Zaphod sighed and sat cross-legged on the ground, looking helpless and harried.

'Perfect position,' Truscott beamed and sat alongside him in the same way. Zaphod moaned and shook his head. Truscott, seeing how forlorn his friend was, tenderly said, 'This will help you. Just try.' Zaphod, too exhausted with anxiety, sighed heavily and nodded. 'You too Barnio,' Truscott commanded.

'Not a chance.' Barnio grimaced and took off like light down the river banks.

'Just you and me then,' Truscott said. Zaphod sighed again and shrugged.

'Ok,' Truscott started. 'Make yourself comfortable. Tense up your body like you are frozen and then imagine that you are in the sun and you are slowly, slowly melting, slowly, slowly melting until your body is a fluid pool. Zaphod followed the instructions and felt his body relax. 'Good. Now imagine all the tension streaming out of your body leaving your body completely relaxed,' Truscott continued. 'All your body is working in complete and perfect harmony. Notice any thoughts come and go and notice that you are noticing them. Let your thoughts come and go and place you attention on your breath. Zaphod as he followed Truscott's instructions felt the storm and tempest of his mind calm into a gently wind. Zaphod observed his breath rolling in and out and became lost in the silence within. He began to see colours swirling and felt a sense of peace emanating through his body. Calmness took over, time stopped and worries appeared to vanish in the wind. Feelings of joy and peace emananted. In this reverent state of being, he felt that all is ok and will be ok. Time appeared to stand still and for the first time in a long while he enjoyed the peace. Truscott gently continued, 'And when you are ready, wriggle your fingers and slowly open your eyes.' Zaphod slowly opened his eyes and the colours of the bush around him appeared more green and lush, the skies and river appeared more vivid in their blueness. More blue. Instantly he was in awe of his wonderful surroundings even noticing how beautiful the camp site was. He felt inclined to have a swim and smiled at Truscott and thanking him for the guided meditation.

Zaphod swam in the cool and clear water and delighted as he watched the butterflies flutter this way and that across the stream to the glorious flowers that adorned the river banks. He noted one settled on his chest and he felt connected to Perina, who he knew would have also delighted herself in this setting. By the time he felt immersed enough in the water, he found Truscott had packed up his belongings and prepared breakfast.

Barnio had also returned, zigzagging this way and that around camp.

'You would have really benefited from the meditation Barnio,' said Zaphod, whom was finding Barnio's antics a little unsettling.

'No time, no time,' said Barnio and sat down to eat. He grabbed food and devoured it as quickly as he could. Zaphod, like Truscott, ate slowly enjoying the texture and taste of the food whilst taking in the delightful surroundings.

'No wonder you collapse at night time,' mused Zaphod, nodding to Barnio. Barnio was in the middle of eating some fruit and stared at Zaphod indignantly.

'We will leave after breakfast,' announced Truscott they all agreed and in no time were packed ready and refreshed.

Zaphod felt calmer, and whilst he was still concerned for Perina, he somehow knew that worrying was not going to help her one bit. They made their way down to the path to Badon without any issues. Zaphod and Truscott were so calm and steadfast after their morning meditation it appeared to influence Barnio, who was walking alongside them without his usual zigzagging. It was like the calmness had a contagion affect, Barnio now felt a bit calmer and was a little curious about the meditation himself he may try this tomorrow he thought as he walked down the track one foot after another in a straight line.

They came to a small junction, though the path to the left was more worn and wider. Zaphod noted with curiosity that the other track to the right had been recently walked on. Some of the grass was trodden and bent and he wondered out loud where that may go to.

'Not sure,' said Truscott, who was also curious about who and whom had recently travelled that way. Truscott had an image of Nadoo flash across his mind. He smiled as he thought of her.

The rest of the journey was uneventful and the group mostly walked in solemn silence. The weirdest thing was that Barnio was walking slowly. He was matching the pace of Zaphod and Truscott and was seen noting the things around him trees, plants, and birds. Zaphod had never seen his friend behave in this calm manner and was just about to mention it to him when the road came to a clearing and small far away images of cottages were dotted in the distance.

'We made it!' shouted Zaphod Hugging his friends and throwing his hands high in the air. 'This must be Badon. I know Perina told me that Danio lives not far from the river with his carers Jyno and Shona in a small thatched cabin.' Zaphod was pleased with his memory of Perina's account. His arms were aching for her embrace. He imagined her joking and laughing and saying she was not hooked in or on anything at all, they would then be talking of their wedding and their plans for the flight competition in the Scaysborough fair. In this absent minded exuberant state, he narrowly missed walking into a tree when the path veered unexpectedly. A protruding branch brushed his cheek which halted him in his tracks and he let out a sigh of frustration.

'We are almost there' exclaimed,' Truscott who was noticing his friends' absent mindedness and eagerness to arrive.

'I'll shoot ahead,' said Barnio and took off, letting his next words trail behind, 'and find the house…'

Very soon after, Barnio returned with dust and small stones swirling around his lively feet. 'I think I found the house,' he said. 'It is not very far. Follow me!' and he took off again at lightning speed. Zaphod and Truscott shook their heads in unison and before they could say anything, a bashful Barnio returned. 'I guess I will have to walk slower,' he said sheepishly and they all laughed. Barnio slowed his pace and they walked to the home where Barnio had scouted as the one described by Perina.

In no time at all, they were on the verandah of this little home. Smoke was coming out of the chimney and Truscott was curious about what they may be cooking this mid-morning. Zaphod, who was first to the door, knocked with quick, deliberate, knocks in keen anticipation of seeing his beloved. The knocks were heard by Nadoo who was watching Shona furiously stirring a brew of potions to try to help the fading Perina.

'Who could that possibly be?' enquired Jyno.

'I expect it is Jardjon and Wilmsea and Jardjon I expect, they said that they would stop by and check on Danio,' Nadoo replied. 'I'll get it,' continued Nadoo noting that Jyno was seated. 'Save you the effort,' she added cheerfully and made her way to the door. The knocks were growing louder and Nadoo called, 'Alright, alright, keep your socks on.' She opened the door and was greeted by a wide eyed and astonished Zaphod.

'Jenta Jonty,' Zaphod said enthusiastically. Jenta Jonty is a Fallon greeting which is usually given in a more formal setting.

Zaphod was delighted to see Nadoo as he imagined Perina safe and well inside. He gave her a huge hug, lifting her high above his head, which is where she saw Barnio and Truscott behind him.

'Well, I never,' she started. Her delight quickly dissolved when she remembered the grave situation Perina was in. 'Please put me down, Zaphod,' Nadoo said in a calm and determined voice. This in itself was unsettling, as Nadoo would ordinarily be barking orders and harrumphing for him to put her down. He placed her down gently and looked into her eyes. She lowered her gaze in an attempt to gather her thoughts. How would she relay the news to Zaphod?

Zaphod followed her every move and could feel her trepidation. He could feel he anxiety of the morning rise up again in his body, he began to feel ill in his stomach, his hands were sweaty and his whole body was shaking slightly.

Looking Nadoo squarely in the face, he said, 'Where is Perina?'

Nadoo met his eyes and said, with tears in the corners of her eyes, 'She is ill, very very ill.'

Zaphod's gut seemed to twist inside,and his heart became heavy and still. 'Where is she?'

Nadoo looked at Shona who had walked over from the kitchen to see what all the commotions was about. She nodded to all the new guests and saw intuitively that the Fallon that Nadoo was talking to was Zaphod, Perina's betrothed.

Shona took control of the situation,nodded to Zaphod and said, 'Follow me.' Shona lead Zaphod to the room where Perina lay whilst Truscott and Barnio followed Nadoo to the lounge to meet a quite astonished Jyno.

'More visitors?' he exclaimed, perplexed. Nadoo introduced Jyno then turned her attentions to Garrow who was now by her side. The melting of her being and soft loving expressions gave away her feelings towards Garrow whom she reported was a Vindervay. 'A Vindervay!' Truscott exclaimed upon meeting Garrow.

'I don't eat people,' Garrow was heard to say. But his words flowed over Zaphod's head like wind in the leaves; his only concern was to see Perina and to see her now!

Shona stood in front of the door and faced Zaphod. 'She is very poorly, very very poorly.' Zaphod froze.

'What are you saying?'

'I am not sure,' she began, though Zaphod already had the door ajar before she could continue. He walked over to a shape in the bed. At first, he did not recognise the figure as Perina. She was grey and bent, and her face was sunken. Her cheeks seemed to be sucked into her mouth and her lips were pursed shut. Her eyes were sunken in her sockets and her eyelids were fastly shut and her body was cocooned in leaves of some type.

Zaphod shot an inquisitive look towards Shona. 'Her body has been poisoned with a drug,' Shona began. 'I am trying to draw the drug out with the leaves from the Colo tree which has absorbing properties.' Perina's body was heaving and her breath laboured and hard. She was quivering and moaning. Zaphod again shot a look at Shona who replied, 'She has been like this all morning since Nadoo found her in the Tavern. The Tavern had a new drug called Dream Cloud Brew made by a berry called the that Danio found.'

'Danio,' said Zaphod, finding a channel to leash the fury brewing inside him.

Shona, sensing Zaphod's deductions said, 'No, it was not his fault. Danio's father, Jardjon took them from him and named them the Lola Berries. They made people hallucinate,' Zaphod rose an eyebrow and hate stemmed from his eyes.

'No Zaphod!' Shona exclaimed, 'It is no use trying to blame anyone what is done is done. Let everyone learn from it. We need to focus on Perina.' Fury rose and fell in Zaphod's body and somehow the meditation of the morning helped to calm him for now and leave retribution on hold. Shona left Zaphod alone in the room and went back to her task of trying to brew a remedy. 'If only I had one of the Lola berries, I may be able to fashion a remedy,' she said to Nadoo and all the guests in the lounge room.

'What do they look like?' questioned Jyno.

'A little white berry. Or so I have heard,' replied a rather distracted Shona.

'Why, I swept one like that up a minute ago,' he replied jumping from his seat. 'It was under the lounge. I have no idea how it got there.' But before he could continue, Shona had run to the kitchen and tipped the garbage bin upside down, looking for the tiny fruit. Jardjon, Nadoo, Barnio, Truscott and Garrow were soon behind her and foraging through all the scraps. Barnio was stretching out fruit skins when a small white berry no bigger than a cranberry rolled out from the stretched skin.

'Could this be it?' he asked, holding up his prize.

Shona scooped it up and held it to the light. 'Why I believe it could be,' she said. 'I am sure that these were the ones that Danio had in his sack. To be sure I'll check if Danio is awake enough to identify them,' she said. Leaving the others to clear up the mess from the bin, she trod the familiar hallway to Danio's door. She knocked and went in at the same time. Danio was seen to stir in the bed. He opened his eyes at the sound of her entry and gave a warm smile.

'Thanks be!' Shona exclaimed as she witnessed Danio with life brewing in his body again. His cheeks were pinkish underneath the now yellowing bruises.

He lifted himself up on one elbow and whilst grimacing with pain said, 'I guess it is to you I am thankful; always a great nurse,' he said, with loving eyes. Shona smiled warmly. She thought of Danio as the son she never had.

'I will fetch you some food forthwith.' She beamed, delighted in his recovery. 'Though there are more pressing needs right now.' Danio's eyes were wide eyes. 'It is Perina,' she said, 'she is very poorly, very very poorly.' Shona hung her head in concern. Danio attempted to rise though his battered body responded in intense pain and he try as he might, his body refused to co-operate and he slumped back down.

'Perina?' Questions flooded his brain and his words jumbled up, 'Who is she with coming here for what?'

Shona recounted the visit the invitation to the wedding. 'Oh how wonderful!' Danio exclaimed when she mentioned this. She then went on to let him know about the Lola Berries and what Wilmsea had given Perina. Danio gasped, shocked into speechlessness. Anger rose in him like a thunderstorm, and he shuddered and shook. Shona looked on in horror at his state of rage and tried to subdue him.

'No use adding anger to your problems. What is done is done, we need to put all our energy into recovery, both hers and yours.' Danio relaxed at this point, knowing that in his condition he was useless to help anyone and conceded back under his bed covers. Shona then told him about the others now at the house Zaphod, Barnio and Truscott. Danio, shrieked with delight about seeing his comrades again and tried again to move his stubbornly disobedient body into a stand. Pain again interrupted this intention.

'I will send them in to visit,' stated Shona upon seeing his eagerness to greet his friends. 'One question, Danio,' Shona continued, 'Do you think that this is a berry that you collected that they now call Lola Berries?' Shona held the berry up to the light and Danio could see the translucent pearl-like tone.

'Yes,' he said as he memory of finding it revisited him. He could almost taste its acrid juice and feel the effect of its transfixing properties.

Alarmed that it was in the house, he blinked at Shona in astonishment. 'I am using it as a tincture to help remedy Perina's ailments,' she explained. 'I will return with food, just relax and get better. You know Perina would have wanted that too,' she added. Danio thought of the journeys that he and Perina had together. He knew he had little choice than to remain bedridden and convalesce as his body would not respond to commands of walking. He had to trust that Perina was in safe hands. If anyone could heal her it would be Shona. She was a wizard with herbs and medicines.

Zaphod remained in the room with Perina. He just held her, held her, held her. He held her until he didn't remain. He and her were linked by invisible embers. A warmth embraced them both and they were one. He held her transfixed and snuggled up next to her in the bed. He held her, held her, held her and drifted into a state of remembering, remembering her and remembering him. Together one, together one. He continued like this, trance-like until he fell into a slumber like state joined and harmonious with Perina at last. An energy moved like a figure eight around the pair, it moved and it moved and he held her and he held her.

The door opened and Shona walked over to the pair whom she believed were asleep. She gently prised open Perina's mouth slightly and poured a little of the herbal brew she had concocted with the Lola berry. Perina stirred a little and Shona noted that she swallowed this down. Perina settled back into the now seemingly blissful state.

'What love does,' Shona clucked and left the room. For the first time a glimmer of hope in regard to Perina's recovery nestled in Shona's heart. She tended to Danio as promised and fed him some broth that he readily ate. Truscott,and Barnio were then directed into Danio's room for a visit. They were both shocked to see his bruised and battered body and they embraced him as carefully as they could. Danio smiled and nodded at his trusted companions, however, still poorly, he fell back into a peaceful sleep whilst they were in the room unable to converse in much depth at all. Truscott and Barnio trailed Shona back to the lounge and discussed Danio and Perina's states of recovery. Shona advised all parties to leave the injured to rest and recovery.

'No more visitors yet!' she commanded. No sooner had she barked this command than she crumpled into her favourite chair to rest. The others, seeing her state of tiredness, carried themselves into the garden so that Shona could enjoy some silence. Truscott sat cross-legged on the grass and meditated on recovery and healing for Perina and Danio. He sat like this for hours whilst Nadoo, Garrown and Barnio discussed everything and nothing.

As the evening grew into shadows and then darkness, Shona busied herself making beds the best she could in the living area. They ate bread and cheese at the kitchen table. It was the best that Shona could come up with and the knowing guests relished the food however simple it was. Dinner conversations were subdued and thoughts were pre-occupied with the healing. Zaphod was still lying next to Perina and no one dared attempt to stir him from his post.

'He will come out when he is hungry,' stated Nadoo when the conversation pointed in Zaphod's direction. As Nadoo understood what hunger pangs will do, they certainly made her drop her attention and fulfill the desire for food.

Truscott however said he would check on him before retiring and he kept to his promise when all were fed and tired and one by one retreated to their makeshift camp in the lounge room floor. Truscott remembered the figurine that he took with him that Perina had fashioned. The clay figure of him meditating. He withdrew it from his carry bag and gently stole into the room where Perina and Zaphod lay. Truscott observed Perina whimpering and thrashing from side-to-side. Sweat dripped from her body. Zaphod was curled up next to her holding her transfixed and solid just holding her, not moving, not flinching just breathing in and out rhythmically.

Truscott placed the figurine that Perina had made into her hand. She responded in a fashion with a barely visible translucent energy passing through her face and going down her arm. Truscott noted this with wonder and concern. He had seen this type of energy before a person passed from the world into the new realm of existence. He noticed a hum of energy flowing between the curled up Truscott and Perina backwards forwards spiralling in a figure eight movement with each breath they both took, which now appeared to be in unison. Truscott stroked his beard and left the two to their destiny.

'All that could be done, is done,' he said and exited the room as stealthily and quietly as he had entered it. Truscott meditated on the best outcome for Perina and then entered a blissful slumber, letting the day fade away and make room for the adventures of tomorrow.

CHAPTER 15

PERINA'S NEW WORLD

Nature is the face of God, Nature is intimate,
Different face every day

Perina was moving. It was like she was flying again in a gentle breeze under a warm sun. She felt the most joy she had ever experienced and noted a warm hum surrounding her. What pleasure, what ecstasy. She was travelling towards light, that was sparkling and welcoming her, she was travelling towards it expectantly and with complete faith and trust in the purity of love.

Delightfully, she was travelling, pure joy, pure exuberance, luring her upwards and upwards. A warm object interrupted the journey. It was hard and had points and smoothness. It had caverns and mountaintops, her mind went back to a place in her memory. She was sitting on a mat with her hands covered in clay fashioning an object.

Remember, remember, a voice out of nowhere appeared to call out.

Remember what? Remember what? her mind replied to the nothingness.

The clay turned into something and she saw this in her mind's eye a wizard sitting. Truscott, she remembered and felt herself smile. She felt a presence next to her breathing rhythmically and purposefully, she felt her body being held her body she thought and then it happened, pain, fear, nausea she was back in her body, she felt sick, she felt ill, she remembered the tavern, she remembered the Lola drink, she remembered she remembered. She was sick, she was in pain, she was embarrassed she was guilty.

She was alongside Zaphod.

She was alongside Zaphod.

She stopped, remembered she felt safe and secure. All would be forgiven all would be ok. These feelings of safety, these feelings of 'ok' washed over her and she relaxed back into her feeble body and breathed rhythmically alongside her beloved. Breathing in and out, in and out, washed over with an energy that was rhythmically and reliably moving, moving, moving up down and around up down and around figure eight, figure eight. She relaxed and moved with it her and him her and him her and him then the absolute took over the knowing the reliable and she became him, he became her and peace was upon them. Well, for now at least.

CHAPTER 16

JARDJON AND WILMSEA CHANGE THEIR WAYS

Wisdom is the highest treasure of all.
It cannot be bought and it cannot be stolen.

Jardjon and Wilmsea were wiping glasses and stacking crates with the newly washed receptacles. Washing and drying was rote to the pair, who seemed to do it day in and day out. This time, however, each was in deep thought about the recent events of the day.

It was Jardjon who broke the silence, commenting through gritted teeth and shaking his head, 'No more Wilmsea, no more.'

Instead of the rebuke that he was expecting from his wife, she set down the towel in one hand and glass in another and said, 'I agree totally.' With that, she bent over with pain in her stomach. 'We were greedy,' she went on, 'I was greedy. I feel sick and sorry sick and sorry.' She was doubled over in pain now and crouched on the floor. 'I expect it is the Lola berry,' she said. 'It appears to take time to leave the body.

Jardjon had little sympathy for Wilmsea at present and was a little happy that she was suffering. Serves her right, he thought. Jardjon was used to Wilmsea suffering, lying in a corner of the bar unconscious, was her usual position at the end of the night, though he had never heard her discuss any wrongdoing in her antics. He looked down at her and her head was turned up towards him. 'I mean it,' she whimpered. She was overcome with guilt about poisoning Perina and could not even face herself with the shame that was swirling throughout her body. 'Contempt,' Wilmsea whispered.

'What?' said Jardjon, straining to hear.

'Contempt,' she repeated, louder glaring at Jardjon with her mouth pursed. 'I hate myself. I am a beggar, beyond a beggar. A worth for nothing, I should never have been born.' Wilmsea then began sobbing, sobbing, sobbing, sobbing. Picking up a glass in one hand and a tea towel in the other, drying the glass with wretched, skinny hands. Twisting and turning, twisting and turning, red teary eyes, blank stare. It was Jardjon that stopped the rote motion as he placed his hands on her shoulders. She looked up at him with large teary eyes.

'It will be ok. We will be ok, we can start over and we can make changes,' he said with a firm voice and a kind heart.

'Is it possible?' said Wilmsea.

'Everything is possible,' replied Jardjon, 'Everything is possible.'

'Let's start first thing in the morning,' said Wilmsea with a new found hope. She dried her eyes, placed the glass down on the counter and said to Jardjon, 'Let's go to bed now and first thing in the morning we will visit Perina. We must make amends and do all that is possible.'

'That we will,' said Jardjon.'As well as look in at our own little Tyke.'

'Oh!' Wilmsea gasped, 'My own flesh and blood. How could I forget about his plight?' Before she could begin to entertain more self-hatred.

Jardjon, held her hand and said, 'You have not been fully present anywhere of late. Go Go and Dreamcloudbrew took your awareness to a place of fantasy where compassion, truth, fairness, honesty do not dwell. How could you build a strong fortress of self from this place? It is the place where lies are planted, hatred sowed and ignorance watered which take root and grow into a tree of deception. But,' He squeezed her hand,

'It was me, who took the fruit from my own son while he was sleeping! I was the one who urged you to try it. I am beyond remorse. I began all this. I lied to Perina about Danio's endorsement of the brew, so she could try it, I got her hooked, I got your hooked. It is me who is reproachable!' Jardjon hung his head and sobbed into his hands.

For a long while the pair sat and sobbed into their hands with their heads up to their faces, hiding their eyes in shame. It was Wilsmea who began, 'We can now plant our own seeds, seeds of truth and love sowed with patience and watered with tolerance that grows each day with new awareness. This tree will take hold and eventually grow bigger higher and more magnificent. It will use the hardship, suffering and intolerance as manure and make its branches all encompassing. A new love, a new forest of hope to dwell in our town of Badon.'

'It's not too late then, all this time, all this time, doing things so very wrong?' Jardjon questioned with mournful eyes.

'It is never too late to change things. Do not mourn time lost but rejoice in time found,' Wilmsea replied. She was surprised herself by some of the things she was saying, it was like it was coming from a force beyond herself, a force of truth and love. She felt peace of heart. A thing she had not felt for a very very long time.

Jardjon and Wilmsea trod up the familiar stairs to their bedroom, though there was nothing familiar about their state of being, they were refreshed and renewed with a new heart and a new hope. They slept long and soundly and dreamt of a bustling happy Badon with smiles, love, and pretty kept gardens.

CHAPTER 17

WILMSEA AND JARDJON ATTEMPT REPARATION

Be the change you are trying to create!

Wilmsea was the first to wake; she woke with a peace in her heart. It was usually dread that fuelled her in the mornings and dread the thing that enticed her to take her first drink of Go Go. Though this morning dread was gone and peace reigned. In the past when circumstances prevented her from drinking in the morning it was not long before nausea and shaking of her body began. This time however she was determined to ride through the pain and suffering. She had to, she owed it to Perina, she reasoned. Perina could even be dead, she shuddered at the thought,and the familiar feeling of dread arose in her Instinctively her arm grabbed for the jug of her precious ale. Though the weight of its contents brought her back into her consciousness and she gingerly poured the contents down a nearby sink. With a sigh her reasoning began to contemplate that Perina may be ok too! And what of Danio? The thought of helping her son through his healing, reconnecting with him and attempting to make up for lost time gave her new vigour and strength. 'I will ride any urges through,' she pronounced determinedly out loud and busied herself to get dressed in aim to visit the two who were ailing. Then, Wilmsea did something that she had not ever done before: she made breakfast for herself and Jardjon.

Jardjon who woke to the smell of freshly baked muffins, came tumbling down the stairs rubbing his eyes with wonder. He saw Wilmsea smiling and humming as she pulled the baked goods from the oven with her dusty oven mitts.

'Whoa,' Jardjon said shaking his head.

'The new me,' said Wilmsea smiling. Wilmsea had cooked enough for their breakfast, as well as enough to feed the mob at Jyno and Shona's home. 'I expect they will be busy tending to Danio and Perina, so I made some for them as well.' She beamed.

Jardjon rubbed his eyes in disbelief, though quickly sat down to eat before the mirage disappeared. Though he found out soon enough it was no mirage at all. It was Wilmsea holding to her promise of change and her resolve to make up for all the no good of her past. Jardjon delighted in breakfast and told her so repeatedly. He looked nervously for signs of shaking which usually heralded her back to reaching for Go Go wine.

'Don't worry,' said Wilmsea noting his perusal, 'I will not respond to shaking. Keeping busy and eating are helping, so let's get on the road and visit Danio.' Jardjon wasted no time in getting dressed and ready and when he came back down the stairs Wilmsea was waiting for him basket laden with baked goods and a bunch of freshly picked grapes, 'Good for their convalescing as well as my own', she said as she picked a couple of the sweet juicy morsels and ate them to stem off a wave of nausea rising in her body. With that,they marched down the cobble stone path to their son's benefactors who housed him and of course the ailing Perina.

They reached the door of Jyno and Shona's home and made three determined raps on the door handle. Wilmsea and Jardjon had some nervousness about how they would be received, though held courage and a new found solemnness of care, spurred them on.

Jyno answered the door. 'Well, well the rats have come down the hill,' he spat out, with a bitterness that suited their actions. Wilmsea proffered her basket of goods and said

'This is for you and all your guests.'

'Laden with drugs, no doubt,' said Jyno in a dismissive tone.

'Not at all. That is a thing of my past,' stammered Wilmsea, who by now was starting to sweat and tremble as her body was calling for more of the toxins it was used to. 'I just want to pay a visit to my son and to Perina. I want to start mending my ways and paying my respects to the people I owe much.'

The sentiments were expressed with such conviction that Jyno dropped his jaw and contempt and looked at the pair standing before him. Their heads were down; they emanated humility and humbleness. He also noticed the familiar shakes and sweats in Wilmsea's body that came with someone denying themselves the very thing that could cure them and entrap them—in her case, Go Go wine and Dream Cloud Brew. He then understood that there must be some truth to her statement his scorn turned to hope that her character was strong enough to begin such a journey. His demeanour softened somewhat as his memory took him back to a time when his addictions overrode his life. The pain, remorse and suffering on the pairs faces, was familiar to him. His anger at the pair for the neglect of their son, entrapment of Townsfolk into addiction and the near death of Perina dissolved a fraction which allowed for a seed of hope of their change to grow inside him. Now feeling that he was a tiny bit hypocritical to judge them too harshly he buried his anger and still with some reluctance, nodded to them and held the door open for them to tread inside.

Shona was still sleeping after her exhaustive efforts of the day before, so Wilmsea's baskets of goods were welcomed by the mob of stirring and hungry guests. Wilmsea left Jardjon to distribute the baked goods whilst she sought permission to see Perina, whom she was most concerned for. Jyno pointed to the door where she lay.

'Her betrothed, Zaphod, is with her too,' he cautioned. 'She is very poorly so you shouldn't stay long,' he added. Wilmsea nodded and gently knocked on the door. No response or sound was heard, so she placed her ear to the door and thought she could hear a slight humming noise. A humming noise that was pulsating 'Hummmmm, mmmm, Hummmm, mmmm, Hummmm, mmmm.'

They were probably asleep, but she had the urge to check so that she could allay the fears in her heart that Perina may perish. She gently turned the handle and prised the door open slightly so she could peek into it. When horrors upon horrors, she saw something unimaginable and shrieked with complete terror, retreated and closed the door firmly behind her. The shriek woke up the remaining sleepers in the household, which brought everyone to the door with quizzical eyes.

'What is it, what is it?' everyone called out in a clamour of emotion. Shona herself had leapt up and was to the door before anyone else could make it.

Shona swiftly opened the door,f peered in and lamented, 'What in the world?' which had everyone else clambering to see what was so alarming.

Truscott remained firmly behind the throng and when they had all peeked and returned with bewilderment, he himself looked and observed what everyone else had seen. In the bed where Perina and Zaphod lay was a golden cocoon of translucent film that had texture like thick seaweed, with darker brown veins and arteries shooting all around it. Truscott shook his head in astonishment. 'It resembles the metamorphose that Fallon's use to grow wings, but both Zaphod and Perina have gone through this process,' Truscott said as he stroked his beard and pondered what this could possibly mean.

'I agree Truscott, but what the flying fairy is this about,' said Nadoo raising her eyebrows and slid closer to Garrow for comfort. Truscott noted the solace that Nadoo had gained from Garrow's loving arms and felt a stab of jealousy, he longed for such tenderness of touch. He was surprised by his yearnings and quickly placed his attention back to the scene before him. The cocoon hummed slightly and there was a swirling of movement that could be seen beneath the translucent skin, but nothing could be made out of what could be occurring.

'It is a wait and see thing,' said Shona, as she saw two unwelcome guests, Wilmsea and Jardjon. She gave them an icy nod.

'I am so, so sorry,' said Wilmsea who saw Shona's hostile glance. She dropped to her knees. Her whole body shook uncontrollably. 'It is all my fault, I will never sell wine or brew again.' Jardjon gave Wilmsea a funny stare. We never said anything about never, he thought to himself.

Shona melted a little with Wilmsea's laments as well as the obvious signs that she was suffering withdrawals and motioned her to the kitchen.

'I have some herbs that might help you,' she said and set to grinding some leaves together to let steep in a pot for drinking. The household all seated themselves in the lounge and made harried discussions about the state of Perina and Zaphod.

'Nought we can do but wait,' said Shona, who was seconded by Truscott. It was at this moment that a feeble voice was heard at the door.

'What is all this about?' squeaked Danio in an enquiring tone. He was walking ever so tenuously, holding his side and shuffling he feet best he could. Wilmsea jumped up and gave him her seat which was baffling to Danio, whose eyes were even wider now with questions.

'I will fetch you some muffins that Wilmsea made,' stated Jardjon which made Danio's eyes widen even further with astonishment. He could not remember a time his mother had actually cooked, let alone being here, rather than at the tavern. All the questions were brimming inside him though the most burning one came out.

'How is Perina faring?' he asked.

'There is a lot to be told,' said Truscott, 'Now, sit yourself down lad and all will be spoken' As he ate, they spoke, and fear and wonder moved up and down him like the waves crashing on the shore. Fear and wonder, fear and wonder.

'It is as it is meant to be,' added Truscott at the end of discussions. 'How could it be anything but that? All will be ok, all will be ok.' These words seemed to soothe all in the household and they settled into watching and waiting, watching the golden mass that was Perina and Zaphod swirl and hum, pulsate and flow, throb and move within its stationary post in the bedroom.

Wilmsea and Jardjon returned to their Tavern, though made daily trips with food baskets. Wilmsea's shaking subsided after one week thanks to the darkened brews that Wilmsea supplied to her upon each visit.

'Things are changing,' Wilmsea said to Shona, 'Things are changing.'

Wilmsea and Jardjon made a point to visit their son on each occasion and noted with joy that he was gaining strength each day. Danio was in awe of his parents' newfound character and was warming to them. On one occasion, Jardjon ruffled his son's hair and praised him and Danio, instead of his usual recoil from his parents' touch not only allowed it actually enjoyed it Wilmsea laughed at memories of Danio's antics as a baby in the days where she was less influenced by the demons of the brews.

So it went on like that, visiting, feeding, tending, caring until one day it happened. It was like a volcano of sound that alerted everyone.

CHAPTER 18

THE TAVERN RENEWED

*Happiness is not gained from the world around
you it is gained from the joy within despite how
the world treats you.'*

It was a clear beautiful morning. The skies were blue, the flowers were blooming. The bees were buzzing and the birds singing. Sun, joy and the smell of scented blossoms filled the air of the once gloomy town of Badon.

Wilmsea and Jadjon had re-opened the Tavern, though this time they limited Go Go wine to two glasses per person, per day. They added food to the menu and Wilsmea enjoyed her old passion of cooking. Each dish was served with a smile to the happy patrons. Nadoo offered her services of cooking, which added delicious cakes and deserts to the menu. Shona had supplied Wimsea with the herbal brew that assisted the detoxification of those once addicted and it was offered for free to any suffering patrons. Barnio would run to and fro with the medicine and give it to anyone that required this. It was a symbiotic relationship of greatness, he loved being useful and enjoyed the praise by the thankful receivers who were ever indebted.

Thanks to these efforts,people in Badon were healing. The residents were now tending to their home. Fences were fixed, houses painted and gardens weeded and tamed. People now smiled to each other and busied about their days with healthy bodies and appetites.

Danio was a regular visitor to the Tavern now, and he even helped out his parents by washing glasses and plates and sweeping floors. He was often overheard sharing a joke with and commending his mother for her culinary skills. Trival and Hely were not needed any further for security purposes and they found jobs around the town by townsfolks in great need of the two strong Trehwell's who were gaining notoriety as the strongest beings Badon had ever witnessed.

Trival and Hely were used to distrust when they lived in the outlawed Vingoo tribe, so they gained great satisfaction from the admiralty of the townsfolk who not only trusted them, they bestowed praise and admiration to them everywhere they went. All the residents of Badon were propelled by a vision for a healthy and happy town and busied themselves for this purpose. The townsfolk became like a hive of bees, buzzing this way and that with a certainty of purpose not only for themselves but for the collective whole of the Town.

This is how Badon was when the scream emerged. It was a howling, guttural scream that engulfed the township and made everyone stop in their tracks and look from whence the sound came. The stopping of the Town in itself was remarkable. It was like the world stood still, farmers poised in the field's, women still with dough in their hands dripping, carpenters with hammers poised. The howling continued worsening, pulsating, guttural screams, and then an exclamation that filled any gaps that pervaded in sound.

'AYYYYEAGHHHHAYYYEAGHAYYEAG,' it continued like thunder. 'AYYYYHEAGHAYYEAG, YYYEAGHHH HAYYYEAGHAYYEAG, YYYYEAGHHHHAYYYEAGHAY YEAG'

Townsfolk were running with hands over their ears, running

to where the sound was emanating from the Trehwells' Jyno and Shona's home. Jyno and Shona were themselves at home and had to run outside as the sound which was coming from where the remnants of Zaphod and Perina lay was too loud for them to sustain they ran to meet the flocking Township head on.

The wailing continued, 'AYYYEAGHHHH AYYYEAGHHHH AYYYEAGHHHHAYYYEAGHHHHAYYYEAGHHHH AYYYEAGHHHHAYYYEAGHHHHAYYYEAGHHHH AYYYEAGHHHH AYYYEAGHHHH AYYYEAGHHHH,'

It continued like a broken record, on and on and on. No one was able to sustain going nearer to the deafening noise and just when no one thought they could endure any more, it stopped. Abrupt, sharp it just stopped

CHAPTER 19

*Freedom of the heart, a luminous radiance
that shines on all.*

Panic ensued as the metamorphis concluded. There was light shining through a dark brown membrane and bodies were entrapped. Two bodies both fearful, confused, lost, despairing, struggling with all their tenure to escape. The screaming started and both screamed now in full terror. Well at least both tried to scream, only one managed to.

'AYYYEAGHHHHAYYYEAGHHHHAYYYEAGHHHH AYYYEAGHHHHAYYYEAGHHHHAYYYEAGHHHH AYYYEAGHHHHAYYYEAGHHHHAYYYEAGHHHH AYYYEAGHHHH AYYYEAGHHHH AYYYEAGHHHH.'

Screaming due to their entrapment, screaming due to their confusion, screaming due to their struggle to free themselves from their confinement and screaming because they were not alone! Though the screaming was loud and the struggle frantic, only one voice was heard and one body moving his body in struggle. Perina was the first to breathe as a memory returned to her, the memory of the oozing brown substance that was streaming over her and the voice that soothed her on that occasion.

'Remember to release the base of the structure.' It was Zaphod's voice in her memory of when she metamorphosed to gain wings. She was extremely confused and attempted to gasp out loud, though no words came. Her legs were commanded by her to move, though try as she may no movement came. Perina was aware that she was pressed hard up against another being. Could it be Zaphod? she wondered. Panic was beginning to rise in her though her body would not respond even to her fear, no response, no movement, just an internal scream. She of course could hear another scream so loud and piercing that she could hardly endure it.

'How could this be?' Zaphod attempted to speak though warbled in the oozing mire recognising the familiarity of his entombment. Zaphod had metamorphosed previously to develop his wings and he now was aligned to the fact that he was in a metamorphic process and began focusing his attention on trying to release the base structure.

Upon hearing Zaphod's familiar voice, Perina stopped trying to urge her body to struggle and relaxed. She was in safe hands, she thought, we will work it out.

It was then that Zaphod's last memory came to him. The memory was of him holding Perina, his whole body consumed with love for Perina and his heart engulfed with despair due to the condition that he saw her in.

'Perina?' Zaphod said tentatively, hoping beyond hope that she was now well and able to speak.

Perina tried to reply, 'Zaphod is that you with me?' she formulated in her thoughts to say out loud, though Perina again could not process them to her tongue to make sound and be heard, she only could lay there helpless, unable to speak to Zaphod.

Zaphod, whose main concern was to free himself from this entrapment, used his feet to push backwards and forwards in an attempt to dislodge the entwinement of the brown veined leather like covering the base.

All the time he was doing this his mind was consumed with

the condition of Perina, 'Are you ok?' he enquired of Perina. No response. Fear rose in him which drove adrenalin higher, he gave all the energy that his being could muster and kicked with such vigour that not only did he release the base of the cocoon he also dislodged the whole structure and promptly was released in a swoosh of brown thick liquid falling to the floor amongst the torn and tattered debris. He turned to see Perina on the floor and scooped her up in his arms to see her condition. It was at that moment Zaphod recognised two things in an instant.

The first that Perina seemed alive, had colour in her face and was breathing though was without any body tone and flopped in his arms like a jellyfish out of water. The second that Zaphod did not have arms as such, he now had two large, healthy, strong wings. His arms protruded from the bottom of his wings, his wings were folded tightly and firmly to his body.

'Perina, Perina, Perina,' he cried over and over and over, now observing Perina had no wings at all. She had two arms though, now both wings were gone. He held her and rocked her, crying while Perina helplessly flipped and flopped with his rocking, trying to reply trying to make a sound, trying to tense her muscles, trying to stop the motion though her body failed to respond again and again and again. Perina scanned her memory for how she became in this position. She remembered nausea and extreme pain and a journey to light, she remembered feeling the statue of Truscott she made and she remembered the presence of Zaphod.

If she could talk right now she would have asked Zaphod to let her be still, as the flipping and flopping around was making her feel nauseous. Zaphod looked at Perina and saw a strange look in her eye, a look that he had seen before when Perina was questioning his doings. He curiously and gently stopped rocking and saw a relaxing of her eyes to a more loving stare. He looked at her with love and compassion and they felt their worlds reuniting, peace falling on their hearts and breath and the hum of them connecting, remedying any previous hurt, pain or sadness. They stayed like this for a long time. Just breathing and relaxing.

A knock at the door broke the silence, a curious, feeble tap, tap, tap. Zaphod placed Perina down gently on the bed and stoically straightened himself up the best he could, brushing the oozing brown liquid off him with his winged arms and creaked open the door.

Chapter 20

Metamorphosis Again

Good souls are like lotus flowers, muddy water just runs off them. They are spotless.

Truscott was already on his way towards Jyno and Shona's home when the screaming stopped. He hastened forward with some apprehension about what the silence could mean. Nadoo was not far behind him, though was shaking and sweating full to the brim of fear about what had become of her friends. It was Perina in particular whose plight she was most concerned about. The last time she saw her she was at deaths gateway, engulfed by a cocoon. Barnio, sped up with to his friends and was dancing back and forwards saying, 'I can come, I can come,' though Truscott waved his keen friend away and said 'No please stay here Barnio,' knowing that the energy he was displaying may be off putting to something that could be making such estranged noises. Someone or something that may be struggling to understand who it was or where it was which was often the nature of the transformed.

Truscott walked steadfastly to the door of the Jyno and Shona's cottage and made his way to the bedroom where Perina and Zaphod last lay. Nadoo was right behind him and stood shaking, nervous about whom or what she may meet beyond the timber-framed door. There was no noise now heard a gentle silence imbued. Nadoo looked towards the panelled wooden door with knuckles white stretched and prepared to knock on the door. She glanced over to Truscott whom nodded his approval and Nadoo tapped lightly tap, tap, tap on the timber, tap tap tap quite gentle and full of trepidation. In what seemed minutes though was really only several seconds, the door in abeyance creaked slightly ajar and the familiar, though somewhat forlorn, face of Zaphod peered through to greet his friends.

Truscott was in Zaphod's vision as he swung the door open, he noticed worry etched into his brow.

'Your wing is now returned!' said Truscott. Truscott was immediately annoyed with himself for saying something so lame and obvious.

'Where is Perina?' piped up Nadoo, hoping to see her friend fully too.

Zaphod, hung his head and opened the door fully to reveal the source of his troubled eyes. Perina was slumped motionless, eyes open, laying on the bed. First observations indicated that her physical state of being was restored somewhat. Her colour was not grey and her skin had gone back to its usual peach complexion. Her face was more relaxed and she was breathing normally on the bed. Truscott and Nadoo moved closer to the bed where they could observe that Perina's wings were completely gone and her body now had gone back to the way that Fallons are prior to the metamorphic process of gaining wings. She also was breathing and lying uncannily still.

'Curious,' started Truscott. 'It looks like you gained a wing and Perina an arm.'

'She can't move or talk,' interjected Zaphod, 'What have I done?' he said, throwing his head downward in despair.

'You probably saved her life,' said Truscott who was again angry with himself for stating the obvious. He began stroking his beard, trying to comprehend what was before him.

Meanwhile, Nadoo was sitting beside Perina, holding her hand, talking to her about everything and nothing, waiting for a response, waiting for a sign. Perina stared ahead motionless, nothing moved, nothing murmured, nothing saw, nothing felt, nothing, nothing, nothing.

Perina however was screaming from the inside though her voice could not be engaged, *Can't you hear me? I am here! Why can't I move? Why can't my body obey me!* If her body could engage they would hearing her screaming at the top of her lungs though the signals that ordinarily flow from the brain to the body were not connected. Perina was alive and could hear, could see, though could not move or talk. Perina stared ahead as her friend talked at her. She wanted to agree, disagree and interject though she could not do anything. Perina closed her eyes and began to remember, remember the Tavern remember the Dream Cloud brew, remember feeling very ill. Could it be this, she thought, could it be this?

Now voices were yelling, Zaphod, Nadoo, yelling, 'She closed her eyes, is she still ok?' cried Zaphod, lamenting, crying, shaking her prodding her, Perina opened her eyes and it was Zaphod now staring into them.

Perina stared back. *I am ok, I am here,* she implored with her eyes, Zaphod stared back and seemed to know something.

'She is in there,' he said, 'I know she is in there.'

Truscott again stroked and pulled his beard and said, 'I am sure she is, Zaphod. We just need to work out how to find her.'

Chapter 21

The patient stagnates

Impatient ones will prod a bud and destroy a flower.
Patient ones allow flowers to open and enjoy their full glory

Time went on in Badon. Zaphod spent most of his time sitting alongside Perina, talking about this and that, the wedding, the fair that was looming, his new found wings and her being an ordinary Fallon. Perina heard all that he said, and she tried to respond, tried to relate though nothing, nothing, nothing, staring, staring, staring was all she could manage and she panicked often though no one seemed to notice.

Danio was healing well and he now came regularly to visit Perina. His parents were constant visitors at his house and Danio was experiencing loving care, which he was leaning into and enjoying. Badon continued to flourish as the effects of alcohol and drug dependency wore off, and other activities influenced peoples' desires. Many residents in Badon were mending their homes, growing crops, cooking food and generally looking healthier and happier. There were still some rogue residents that took to making their own alcoholic brews, though they kept to themselves and caused little trouble.

Danio's mother Wilmsea spoke with Danio about him returning to the Tavern to live, though Danio, as much as he relished his parents' newfound dignity, felt compelled to stay with his ageing carers Jyno and Shona. He also was committed to assisting them in the care of Perina, who still was showing no signs of movement. Danio and Zaphod took turns of feeding Perina painstakingly with small amounts of food. If she was given too much at a time, she would convulse so tiny amounts was all they could offer. Shona took care of Perina's body, bathing and cleaning her each day whilst Nadoo took control of cooking for her and grinding the food so that it was soft and lump free, which made her swallowing easier.

Time went on and the routine was the same: feed, clean and cook, feed, clean and cook, sit and talk, sit and talk. As time went on and the days became weeks, it was Truscott who discussed the need for movement. One late afternoon prior to the sun retiring and the party settling down for the evening, Truscott called for a discussion.

'Let us talk about our future plans and what path we should all take now.' Jyno and Shona nodded in agreement. They were both very welcoming hosts though they discussed together in the small hours on the morning how they wished to get back to their simple life without the added intrusions. Nadoo nodded too, for as loyal as she was to her friend Perina she had thoughts of the fair which was due to be held in a few weeks and she wanted to return to her home, her house and to show Vik around Scaysborough if he was willing to join her. It was only Zaphod who froze at this notion as he had not thought of leaving Perina, though at the same time felt helpless in her recovery.

Barnio was the first to speak. 'Go home, go home now, we can speak to Gallon and the elders in Scaysborough to see who may be able to help Perina there', Perina there'

'How can we leave Perina like this?' retorted Zaphod, with his eyes burning.

'We are all concerned for Perina,' interjected Truscott, 'and you must be feeling this intensely.'

Zaphod lowered his eyes and replied, 'Yes,' rather weakly, through swallowed tears welling throat.

'We have exhausted avenues of how to assist her and we would not be able to carry her in the state she is in back to Scaysborough,' said Truscott. 'We have also placed enough burden on our gracious hosts who cannot sustain our continued presence.'

Jyno and Shona lowered their heads and eyes and Jyno nodded slightly adding, 'We are feeling our age, you know. Though we will dedicate ourselves to take the best care of Perina until you return.'

'That is my word too!' chimed in Danio whose earnest voice brought a smile to their faces.

Truscott went on, 'We have no alternative than to return home and seek every advice and assistance with plan to return to heal Perina.

'Zaphod was planning to bring Perina home, he knew he would need to fashion a specialised cart that could meander over the bumpy tracks, with a pulley system that could assist when traversing over large rocks. He knew he would need to build these devices in Scaysborough as that was where specialised tools lay. A chair with wheels was needed so he could travel her around as well as ramps for the house for easier access These things and modification of him home had to happen so that he could bring his beloved home to their dwelling.

Frustrated at the necessity of him leaving Zaphod sobbed and held his hands in his head. He stood up purposely clenching his fists tight by his wings and walked from the house, thudding down the stairs.

Barnio was about to follow, but Truscott waved his hand for him to stop, knowing that Zaphod would need time to process his mixed emotions and heartache to make the best informed decision about his next actions. The party were homogenised with empathy and steered their eyes towards the window where

Zaphod was seen soaring high in the sky up and around, up and around flapping determinedly with long strokes of his wings, flying towards the shadows of the planets Trea and Binea until he looked as small as a moth circling in the distance. Nadoo also sobbing went outside to wait for him to land. She wished to console Zaphod. For the first time, Nadoo wished she too could fly too. She imagined she could take her pain with and wash it away in the wind.

Zaphod swirled and swirled. He knew he needed to go back to Scaysborough and prepare for his wife to be until she was cured. He could not help Perina any further than anyone was doing here. He had a fury and sorrow all mixed together, angry at Danio for finding the berry, angry at Jardjon and Wilmsea for marketing the substance. Angry for Perina's weakness for taking it. Angry with himself, soooo angry with himself, why did he let her go on her own? And so sad at her current state that he struggled for breath thinking about it.

He stopped in mid-air and began punching the air with his fists punching, punching and dropping like a lead weight. Dropping, dropping, losing grip on reality dropping, punching, crying then he heard a shriek, he heard it the whole town heard it.

He looked down to see Nadoo with her head craned upwards shrieking at the top of her voice, 'Nooooooooooo.' Zaphod saw this as well as an imagined image of Perina's eyes imploring him. Alerted now to his own danger,pulled out of his plummet, opening his wings hard and flapping with all his might to avoid the ground. Avoid the ground he did, and for those Townsfolk who were also witnessing this horrific sight sighed with relief. Zaphod, who now was only metres from the ground, came to a halt, lowering himself to rest next to Nadoo.

Nadoo stared at Zaphod. There was nothing she could say to remedy his pain. She just sat next to him and looked at his tear-stained face while he looked back at hers. Tears and pain mirrored in each other. They sat and stared and held hands, watching the planets and moons rise and the sun setting. The townsfolk dispersed and went back to their billops.

In Jyno and Shona's home, the party also sighed with relief when Zaphod safely landed As it was near sunset, Truscott wanted to clarify the decisions made before Barnio had to retire.

'We will leave tomorrow,' Truscott said.

Garrow who was also present added, 'If it is ok with everyone, I will join you.' Garrow had remained silent through the discussions as he did not feel it was his place to enter into any decision making. He was secretly delighted that the band was heading back to Scaysborough as he and Nadoo had conversed previously about her desire to show Garrow around her home town. They all nodded in unison and Barnio showed delight in this idea as he was imagining everyone's reaction to a Vindervay, a sight that no resident had seen before with his smirk about to formulate a word, he promptly fell asleep as the setting sun commanded.

Meanwhile, outside, Nadoo and Zaphod continued to sit quietly and with no spoken word. They sat knowingly, conversing with knowing nods between tortured faces that they had no choice but to agree to travel back to Scaysborough to find a cure for Perina. They walked solemnly inside the house together as the other party were readying to sleep.

'It's tomorrow we leave,' instructed Truscott as he saw the pair. They looked at him with heavy hearts and nodded. Nadoo sought the refuge of Garrow's arms and Zaphod sought the solace of Perina's company in her chamber to drink in her presence one last time before they were separated once more. Zaphod climbed on the bed next to her and spread his wings over her body and partially obscured her face. He hugged her tightly as he told her of the plans as she remained warm, but stiff and unmoving. Just the steady breath and beating of her heart.

Perina understood all that Zaphod said and if she could talk, she would have given him her total agreement. *Please take me home and find,* she tried to implore. She thought of nothing else but her and Zaphod running and laughing, being wed, being happy. She would have also asked him to remove his wing from her face as it was somewhat stifling. She laughed on the inside at this though Zaphod was unknowing, her world was her own. She slept with him next to her and dreamed of flying together again in the sun. If life permits, she thought, if life permits. Hope travelled through her body and flowed through her veins. This hope seemed to seep through Perina's pores of her skin and transfer into Zaphod's body, replacing anger and rage with hope, courage and valour.

He would succeed, he would succeed, he thought, as he entered the inky depths of sleep. He dreamt of returning with a cure for Perina and flying to Badon with it, scooping Perina her up in his arms as she drank the brew and awakened. Perina, then coming to life and her holding herself around his neck, kissing and conversing, healed and healthy. He woke in the morning with a smile and renewed vigour, it will come true, he thought, it will come true, he kissed Perina tenderly and vowed to return with a cure. She stared back and hope planted itself deep inside her.

The party, as discussed, left in the morning back to Scaysborough, back to adventures, tears and triumphs, back to discord, that would almost put Scaysborough and Tremlite Town on the brink of destruction... but that, of course, is another story.

PART 3

THE AWAKENING

This book is dedicated to the transient light beings of the future. The consciousness of humankind is growing and maturing. Future generations will be dwelling in the light and the world will be a beautiful place that shines bright in all directions. When we drop something in ourselves and live in the place of brilliance, we give permission in others to do the same. Act now, be now, love now.

Chapter 1

The Journey Home.

When you are inspired by some great purpose, your thoughts break their bonds and your mind transcends limitations.

The journey back to Scaysborough was uneventful. It was a sombre trek that saw for the most part everyone walking in silence. The only noise heard was the heavy thud of stoic feet motioning forward resigned to their unwelcome task of moving forward, having left their friend behind.

The one who laboured the most was Zaphod. Zaphod lumbered at the rear of the group, begrudging every step with gritted teeth. Even Barnio didn't speak nor fluttered just one step in front of the other.

Nadoo, like all the others, walked continuously all day without stopping or motioning for food. She heard the growl of her belly through a pang of hunger, she displaced her anger and upset at leaving her friend towards her stomach and dared it to utter another sound, it in complete abeyance made content with the remnants of an early breakfast and remained silent for the rest of the journey.

Garrow was the only person in the group that trod lighter and secretly enjoyed his surroundings. He had not known Perina in any great depth and of course was aware of the sorrow the others members felt due to her plight, though he was less encumbered grief and more enchanted by the new sights and delights along the forest path. Garrow stopped briefly at the junction of the pathway to his Vindaloo village and sighed with some longing for his familiar home.

Hearing his sigh, Nadoo could only manage to glance at him sideways. Too forlorn herself to offer him any comfort in words, she slightly squeezed his hand, unable to feel anything else than her own sorrow. Garrow accepted her heavy heart and gently took her hand and walked decidedly in the direction of his new future with the Nipoo chef. He tried to show no delight at the glorious water way in front of him shimmering in the sun and beckoning him to revel in its aqua depths.

Nadoo and the other members only glimpsed at the magical Jinku River where so much happened on both journeys. To remember and to mention would also bring back memories of Perina's mishaps, and they were already flooded with the pain and guilt of leaving her behind. They deliberately only noticed enough to get their footing along the rocks around the waterfall and lake to the higher ground of the winding track back to their beloved town. Onward they journeyed until they passed the rock where Barnio was lost. This monolithic structure now housed at the bottom of the mountain,however, did get the party to stop and remember. They almost all at once noticed the night was falling and they did not want a repeat of a disappearing Barnio.

No one wanted to camp, all hoping that their own home and surroundings would give them some respite and comfort from their tortuous grief. Zaphod suggested he carry the now flagging Barnio, who was steadily giving in to the lure of sleep as the light was extinguishing. Zaphod hoped that the extra demands of carrying Barnio would give him some reprieve from lamenting his decision to return without his betrothed. Barnio nodded and was swept up by Zaphod just as he was about to fall into sleep and Barnio was cradled under Zaphod's wing all the way back to Scaysborough. Zaphod refused any offers of assistance from others as the aches and pains arising from carrying this extra load in this rather awkward way did offer some solace to the sharpness of his emotional pain.

Truscott was grateful that the evening was littered with stars and that six of the seven moons in Scaysborough were out in full, shining a clear path for the weary travellers. They arrived in Scaysborough after midnight and all made their way back to the certainty and dependability of their own homes, which did indeed offer them some comfort from their burden of loss. Zaphod explained to the others that he would stay with Barnio in his own home, making the excuse to others that he didn't want Barnio to wake up unsettled. The truth however was that Zaphod felt that he would drown in the flooding emotions that he predicted would occur walking alone into his home. The enormity of his feelings scared him and he settled down to lie on the timber bench that lined Barnio's Kitchen. The hard discomfort of the timber diverted his need to release his screams of heartache and pain, Zaphod writhed on the bench clutching his body and muffling his sobs by burying his face under his wing, eventually through laborious anguish and physical tiredness he succumbed to sleep. A gentle hand and a brush of his hair played out in his dreams as he and Perina climbed the steep hill to the church where they were to be married. Zaphod for the first time in weeks, smiled in his sleep relieving the built-up pressure of sorrow in his subconscious mind.

Chapter 2

Scaysborough Enlivened

*A smile begins, it spreads to the eyes, a laugh rises up
the belly and bursts forth from your soul refreshing
and enlivening the spirit.*

When the troupe woke up in their respective abodes they were conscious of a bustling of activity around them. Posters were being hammered in trees, carts were being driven around town with produce and supplies, and people were chattering with excited voices.

Nadoo, who does not like to be woken, snarled viciously at the commotion, 'What the hey are those imbeciles—,' she started, when she noticed Garrow stirring from his sleep on a nearby lounge. She still wanted to portray her best nature for her newfound companion and attempted to reframe her annoyance in a more palatably. '—Oh, the Townfolk are up early today,' she corrected herself in her cheeriest voice that she could muster to try and camouflage her grumpy morning nature.

Garrow slowly emerged from his slumber, peeling his eyes open. He noticed a somewhat feigned attempt of happiness being displayed awkwardly on Nadoo's face and chuckled.

'Annoying, aren't they?' he quipped.

Relieved that she didn't need to keep up the pretence, Nadoo replied, 'Yes, it's not even 7.30am! I wonder what they are all so preoccupied with? She huffed and peeked out the window, noticing a freshly hung poster which displayed a colourful, cheerful poster heralding the Scaysborough and Tremlite Combined Town Fair that was being held in one week's time. Nadoo had completely forgotten about the fair and shivered, remembering Perina and Zaphod's plans for their aerial display.

Zaphod's wedding that was to be held three weeks after the fair on the 11th day of the 11th month. Nadoo decided not to bother her mind any further about Perina and turned to Garrow to advise him of the impending fair. The fair was an excellent diversion for her thoughts to ascend from fruitless despair.

She started clucking, 'I will need some more Jim Jam berries,' and started bustling around in the pantry. Garrow noticed the wall of 1st prize baking trophies which decorated the top shelf and sighed.

'I guess you will be entering the baking contest.' He grinned.

Nadoo embraced him. 'You bet. I will begin getting ingredients straight after breakfast,' she cooed. Nadoo had finally gotten her appetite back and in no time had a spread of delicious food that Garrow delightedly tucked into.

Garrow assisted Nadoo in cleaning and washing dishes, then Nadoo begun busying herself around the kitchen, flitting here and there, stocktaking her current supply of ingredients. 'Just Jim Jam berries' she decided, and looked hopefully at Garrow. He understood the look perfectly.

'If you tell me where to find them, I will happily collect some for you. I will be happy to look around Scaysborough on the way.'

'Of course, of course,' Nadoo replied absentmindedly, preoccupied with creating the most delicious Jim Jam cake and being awarded first prize of this New Fair competing with Tremlite bakers.

Nadoo gave Garrow painstaking instructions of where to find

the best tree and the shape and size of the berries expected. After hearing the directions and instructions several times, Garrow began backing out the door and nodding his head with a basket in his hand. He was almost out the door when he heard a loud, piercing scream.

'What the…'

'Arggghh, What the…Help …help… Nadoo is in danger,. help, help!' With that, he felt a heavy whack on his back. Nadoo rushed to the door to find her friend Gida with a carpet beater in her hand outstretched to deliver a second blow to Nadoo's perceived assailant.

'Stoooooooooooooooop!' Nadoo bellowed to a wide-eyed Gida. Garrow was nearby hunched over preparing himself for the next blow. Gida's arm was blocked by a quick reflexed Nadoo in mid-flight.

Gida with eyes as large as dinner plates looked sideways at Nadoo who promptly said, 'Let me introduce you to Garrow.'

'G—G—G—arrow?' Gida stumbled, 'Why, he is a…Vinder... Vindervay!'

'I don't eat people,' offered Garrow, who was still recovering from the shock of the attack.

Nadoo had been completely immersed in the upcoming fair and completely forgot how townsfolk may react to Garrow as a Vindervay. As no one had seen a Vindervay for generations, a legend had developed to stop young townsfolk from getting lost in the surrounding forests. The legend was that Vindervays lived in the far mountains, they could not be seen as they camouflaged themselves in the stone and would eat anyone that came near them. The only thing correct about the story was that they camouflaged themselves in the stone. Vindervays had decided to live amongst themselves, so moved out of townships to live in caves in the mountains.

'You may want to change into a more Nipoo look,' cautioned

Nadoo and Garrow immediately transformed into a rather good looking Nipoo which made Nadoo feel a little lightheaded. Nadoo turned to talk to her friend Gida, who had promptly feinted. Nadoo gently took her friend's head in her lap and gently shook her awake. Garrow, who now sported the look of a Nipoo, peered over Nadoo's shoulder as Gida regained consciousness. Gida looked at Nadoo and then looked at Garrow and shook her head.

'But I thought—but I thought—' she said. Nadoo took Gida by the hand and guided her into the house and sat her on a chair.

'Don't worry, Gida, I will explain everything. Garrow, I think you should stay as a Nipoo as you travel through Town until we can set everyone straight about Vindervay's.' Gida's bottom lip trembled at that word and Nadoo seeing her discomfort clucked, 'Don't worry they are meek as lambs.' Garrow shot her an indignant look as Nadoo motioned Garrow away and began a long conversation with Gida.

Sporting his new Nipoo image, Garrow walked determinedly into Town rubbing his back a little where he was whacked and chuckled to himself about Vindervay's reputation. If only they knew that Vindervay's are complete vegetarians and value peaceful relations with others, he thought. He walked through the meandering paths and neatly thatched houses with gaily planted flower beds and marvelled at the order and beauty of this little town nestled in the surrounding mountain,s one of which contained his home.

He was greeted by many friendly villagers whom stopped and chatted and were intrigued to know he was a friend of Nadoo. They all spoke fondly of Nadoo and lauded her cooking skills. Following Nadoo's specific directions, he found the Jim Jam tree as described by her quite easily and he took himself to task on selecting the roundest fruit that was bright pink, which indicated ripeness. He had not noticed the eyes of a curious and somewhat furious Bulbrook who was perched on a high branch of the Jim Jam Tree who was most perturbed by having some of the juiciest ripest fruit being removed from what he considered his tree. The Bulbrook now was becoming aggravated as he watched the berries one after one disappearing into a bucket until his tree was almost bare. His hairs raised notably on his back and he gnashed his teeth furiously, throwing his head backwards and forwards making a clicking sound with his teeth.

Bulbrook's are quite territorial animals and once nested in a tree like to think it is theirs alone. Most, however, are too fearful of Townsfolk to offer any resistance to those who pick fruit. But as this one felt his livelihood was threatened, he would try and conquer this thief. This Bulbrook snarled and spat and decided to secretly follow the intruder back to somehow recover this delicious bounty of berries. He scurried behind fences, hid behind bushes, snuck behind carts and barrows until he like Garrow were in the front yard of Nadoo's home. Lucky for the Bulbrook, there was a large tree in the front of Nadoo's yard. It was not a fruit tree but had beautiful pink flowers that Bulbrooks found edible. The Bulbrook climbed the tree unnoticed and from a branch peered determinedly through Nadoo's window to witness the curious events inside. If only Nadoo had thought to advise Garrow to always leave some Jim Jam fruit behind on trees for the native Bulbrooks, she would have avoided upsetting this persistent animal. The villagers of Scaysborough always ensured that they never stripped bushes or trees bare of fruit so that the wildlife would always have sustenance.

By the time Garrow arrived back to Nadoo's cottage, he found a relaxed Gida sitting next to Nadoo reminiscing about fairs and baking events. Gida wasted no time in greeting Garrow and apologised profusely for her previous untoward behaviour. Garrow dismissed her concerns whilst rubbing his tender back. 'Not too much damage,' he grinned. Nadoo was delighted in his pickings, being somewhat surprised about how many berries he had collected.

'Must have been a loaded tree,' she exclaimed, not even considering he had not left some for the wildlife. Gida, upon seeing this brimming basket of large and succulent berries, made excuses so that she could hurry away to find her own supplies. 'Oh, Gida,' Nadoo called out after her. 'Please don't reveal that Garrow is a Vindervay until we can talk to the elders, we don't want any more trouble.'

'Of course,' Gida replied, as she beat a hasty retreat. 'No worries.' Nadoo had decided that discussing Garrow's identity with the Elders would be best, as they could decide the best manner to alley any fears that Villagers may have. But for now Nadoo's focus was solely on winning the first prize. Garrow kindly offered to help and so the two focused and planned on delivering the winning entry.

Unbeknown to the pair, a large and increasingly flummoxed Bulbrook watched from his vantage point high in the tree branches in the garden. He was particularly transfixed on his delicious berries and watched each and every one going from the basket to the tap to big vats of unbeknown substance which only served to make the Bulbrook's animal instincts of survival more intense as his berries were being coveted away and this, this lack of berries for his own sustenance affected his very existence. He gnashed his teeth. He would get these back and he clucked and stretched, and kept his eyes fixated on his food source scurrying from one branch to the next pacing, pacing, waiting for an opportunity to pounce and retrieve the stolen goods.

CHAPTER 3

PERINA'S PLIGHT WORSENS

If we avoid our fears, they will control us.
If we face them, we will control them.

Perina remained unconscious and the strain of providing care to her was becoming quite burdensome for the ageing couple, Jyno and Shona. Wilmsea was now a constant visitor to their home providing fresh home-cooked meals for Perina. Danio was enjoying his mother's visits as this was the first time in his life he had witnessed his mother unaffected by any substance and being kind.

It was Wilmsea who could see the strain that Perina's constant care was having on Jyno and Shona and noted an emotion in herself that she had not felt in a very long time: compassion. Wilmsea, now unaffected by drugs and alcohol, was able to see suffering in others and had empathy. Prior to this, she was consumed with fuelling her drug habits and was callous and unemotional. She looked lovingly at Danio and regretted her poor mothering. She was extremely grateful to Jyno and Shona, who provided the care he needed when she abandoned his nurturing to her drug passion. Colours of pink were returning to Wilmsea's pallor, previously grey and gaunt, and her eyes were wide and glistening, moistened by the tears of remorse.

Wilmsea decided that she would offer to provide full care

for Perina,whom she knew was in this perilous condition due to her own rampant disregard for others. Wilmsea She posed an offer to Jyno and Shona without consulting her husband Jardjon. She knew intuitively that Jardjon would be more than happy to offer any assistance to any of his previous patrons as he was too remorseful about their Tavern, and the effects on all townsfolk, especially Perina. Wilmsea with soft compassion began, 'Jyno and Shona, I owe you my life and all that I have as you have without complaint raised my beautiful child with your own loving hands. He is the finest Trehwell the land could find and I owe this to you both. I cannot seek forgiveness from you as my sins as they are too great, though I can offer you some respite from your charge. I am to blame for her pitiful condition. Please allow me to care for Perina in our Tavern as I will set up a room for her and tend to her care.' Shona's eyebrows rose in triangles as alarm and suspicion flooded her due to her memories and dealings with the previously unreliable and untruthful Wilmsea.

Shona looked Wilmsea in the face with an indignant, scornful expression though softened immediately as she met the eyes of Wilmsea's which were glowing with love and compassion. Shona melted somewhat and Jyno interrupted the silence by saying.

'Well, I say girl, you will have your hands full!'

Danio was silently watching and listening to the discussion before him. He was moved by his mother's speech and like Shona, believed that she was earnest in the matter. With a newfound trust of his parents' care he said, 'I will come, mother to assist you in this task.' Shona Wilmsea knew that her and Jyno were unable to continue to pace of care needed and was happy that Danio would now have the opportunity to be cared and grow up with his kin and smiled with a knowing peace in her heart.

'It is settled then,' Wilmsea said.

'We will miss you young Danio,' Shona lamented and rose to

pinch his ear and hug him to her heart.

'Miss me? Why, I will be here every second day to visit! Don't think you can get off that easily,' he retorted.

'That would be right,' jested Jyno, 'just when I thought I would get to eat all of Shona's cakes by myself.' With that he grabbed Danio and hugged him tightly. 'Well, you better be off then,' said Jyno, trying to mask the lump in his throat and tears welling in his eyes.

Before you knew it, Danio's bags were packed, belongings collected and they, as well the unresponsive Perina's was carefully placed by four loving hands on a cart that Jyno and Shona had prepared. They had padded the hand drawn, small but sufficient timber cart with pillows for bedding for Perina's short but arduous journey to the Tavern.

Jyno and Danio, pulled the cart whilst Shona and Wilmsea pushed from behind, inch by inch and step by step they slowly and surely they edged their way to the Tavern. The Tavern was unrecognisable to Jyno and Wilmsea, who had not been there since Perina's decline. The place was freshly painted with big clay pots, flowers and plants dotting the verandah leading to the door of the establishment. It was clean and bright and overlooked the valley below.

'Why I never,' commented Jyno, ' This place is beautiful now.' Shona also astonished by the transformation nodded in agreement. It was still however with some trepidation that Shona opened the door to enter the Tavern as the memories of this notoriously troubled establishment and the despairing drunks within flooded back to her.

She creaked the door open and was delighted to be greeted by a feeling of light and happiness. There were no hapless drunks lining the walls and floors. Instead, they were clean with neat checked table clothed tables, each with four chairs placed under them. A menu placed was placed standing upright in the middle of each table and the walls were decorated with murals depicting beautiful gardens and peaceful scenes of nature.

The bar was painted brightly with a cheery yellow and a big sign hung above it that read, 'Strictly two Go Go juice's per adult which must be accompanied with food purchased.' Jardjon had not lost his ability to make money and this new enterprise proved lucrative. Jardjon, like Wilsmea, was committed to creating a peaceful and safe environment where no one was allowed or encouraged to become inebriated. The townsfolk had assimilated to this new structure and seemed to adapt to their new sober state. Smiles and friendly faces now were common in town and children were now a common topic of subject with a few couples already in the family way. Badon Town was certainly changing the very structure of its fabric.

Wilmsea called out to Jardjon to help her and no sooner than she called the rather tall and now good looking, Jardjon stepped outside wiping his hands on his apron, curious to see what Wilmsea would be wanting. Jardjon's yellow jowls and lines of despair had vanished. He now sported a smiling friendly demeanour and looked healthy with his tanned muscles protruding from his short-sleeved tunic He saw the party before him and knew almost at once what was about to occur.

'Danio and Perina are—' Wilmsea started.

Jardjon interrupted and said, 'We better get them inside then.' He, Danio, Jyno and Shona carefully lifted Perina through a corridor inside the Tavern to the living area,Wilmsea hurriedly prepared Perina's bed in a beautiful light sun filled room that opened up into the gardens outside. 'I was wondering what this room would be used for,' mumbled Jardjon as he settled Perina down in her new quarters. Wilmsea had been secretly preparing a room for both Perina and Danio as she had the heart felt desire to care for them both and to try and make amends for her past neglect of both of their care, Danio was shown to a room opposite Perina's that also opened up into the gardens outside and he noted that the room was carefully decorated with forest paintings. He shot his mother a glance of appreciation.

The party then retreated into the Tavern. The Tavern was littered with comfortable tables and chairs with the smell of delicious food wafting through the premise.

'Well, we best be going now,' offered Jyno who despite his feelings of sadness of Danio's absence was also somewhat elated from the freedom of the constant care to Perina and the cost that this was having on his and Shona's freedom and health.

'Not without a meal you won't!' bellowed Jardjon and busied himself in providing a meal everyone. Shona and Jyno attempted to protest, though Jardjon dismissed them with a wave of the hand and settled them to the best table in the place and soon surrounded them with a variety of delicious food. Jardjon placed a jug and glasses down firmly on the table and all eyes appeared to question him at once. 'Nothing but Jim Jam juice in there,' he smiled and all parties seemed to relax and drink the delicious, pure juice.

Lunch was joyous, though swift, as Wilmsea and Danio were keen to return to provide care to Perina and ensure she was comfortable. After a wonderfully satisfying meal Jyno and Shona said their goodbyes to Wilmsea, Jardjon and Danio.

They were somewhat unwilling to leave Danio, though were satisfied that true change had occurred with his parents and they were safe to relinquish their care of him back into the care of his parents. They trod solemnly but sure-footedly from the Tavern to the haven of their home by the river and to their new quieter life that befitted their dwindling twilight years.

Perina shuddered as the familiar surrounds of the Tavern unnerved her and she shook involuntarily, every cell now fearful of harm due to her memories of this previous decadent establishment. If Perina could talk, she would be screaming for help. She was uncertain still about Wilmsea's motives and terrified about being left in her hands. She was consoled by the fact that Danio was close by. Her shuddering stopped before it was noticed and she slipped into darkness that was cold and calm. Her eyes closed and breathing for now was all that she could muster.

Danio noticed the decline in Perina's condition, he saw her body was now limper and her eyes shut and sunken. He called to his mother and both she and his father came running into the room where Perina lay.

Wilmsea began wiping Perina's head and wiping her hands, 'Stay with us, its ok,' she crooned to Perina. Perina who had only heard these words before by Wilmsea as a treacherous method to get her to drink and take more drugs would have roiled from her touch if she had any command of her body. Perina was still unable to move or offer any resistance to the touch of what she considered a madwomen, and she slipped more into the respite of darkness, further into the protection of the abyss. Her breath now was shallow and her skin cooler to the touch.

'She is worsening!' exclaimed Wilmsea. 'We need to inform Zaphod at once!'

'I will go,' offered Danio without hesitation. Wilmsea and Jardjon had no choice than to accept his offer as they knew their son was able to navigate his way to Scaysborough and back safely, as they had heard of all his escapades.

'But you only just got here—' Wilmsea started though stopped. She knew there was no room for any self-pity, the priority was Perina's health. She looked imploringly at Danio, and countered her statement, 'But you must be on your way,' she said steeling herself.

Wilmsea prepared a pack of food and a mattock for him to sleep on. His father assisted with wrapping and the placing of items in his cassock. Danio was chuffed at their care and he shook his head slightly in admiration of his new situation. Wilmsea and Jardjon knew their son was able and could fend for himself on any journey, though it was not without heartache when they waved him on his way.

'He only just came back to us,' lamented Wilmsea as she watched her small but surefooted son shrink into the distance.

'I know,' replied Jardjon, 'We will have a lot of catching up to do when he returns, but it will be for good Wilmsea, for good,' he repeated and looked at her with earnest love and tenderness. 'We will make up for all our wrongdoing and Danio will come to know us in our new and reliable forms.' With that said, they embraced.

Wilmsea quickly untangled herself from his arms. 'I best tend to Perina,' she said and settled back down at Perina's side stroking her hair and head, hoping this would provide Perina with some sense of loving support. Little did she know that every touch by Wilmsea was sending rockets of fear throughout her body and sending her further into retreat of darkness. *Where is Zaphod and the others?* she thought, *Why have they left me? Am I dead?* she wondered and surrendered herself to nothingness.

Chapter 4

Truscott meets with the elders

Let peace be the prize that is striven for.
A prize that is claimed within.

Truscott woke with a sense of urgency. He was propelled with a desire to meet with the elders forthwith in regards to Perina's failing health. He ordinarily would have begun the day with quiet meditation and gentle stretches, though the urgency of Perina's health interrupted his normal quiet repose to one of decisive action. He dressed quickly and walked surefootedly in a hurried manner to the council of the elders to seek their wise council. He arrived at the council chambers and knocked purposefully on their large grey domed doors. The door was swiftly opened by Gallon, the Etruscan king.

'Jenta Jonty' they both exclaimed at once. Truscott wasted no time in informing Gallon of all that had occurred in Badon and the now perilous state of Perina's health. Gallon found it hard to contain his hard feelings about Wilmsea and Jardjon, whom he judged responsible for Perina's wellbeing. Truscott acknowledged Gallon's emotions and discussed how they have reclaimed themselves from addiction and are determined to stay on the path of healing, care, and kindness. Gallon softened somewhat, though still harboured some animosity towards the pair. He, however being one of the wise council, was glad of they were seeking restitution of themselves and could see the errors of their ways.

Gallon was the only councillor at the chambers due to the others being posted to the fairgrounds organising seating, camping and other necessities for the upcoming inaugural fair between Scayborough and Tremlite towns. He stroked his beard as he contemplated the situation.

Gallon finally offered the following, 'Perina's condition sounds like a state that no medic here has faced nor has the capacity to deal with. Recently, I met Heffla on a path in the forest. He told me of his recent meeting with a non-winged Fallon named Ashanti who talked to him about healing within the body using your own mindful meditations.' Heffla recounted how he discussed with her about his recurring headaches and that she sat with him in quiet repose and meditated on wellness. Heffla said he felt a peace of self he had not felt for a long time and that he noted his once throbbing head became still and the pain he felt melted away. Gallon continued, 'Heffla told me that Ashanti lived in Tremlite and stumbled upon her when he was out picking herbs and berries. He said that she reminded him of yourself as her manner was light and gentle as is yours.' Truscott blushed slightly at the compliment and could not hide his intrigue in regard to Ashanti.

'Yes, I thought that would interest you.' Gallon laughed kindly. ' I think you should go at once to Tremlite and seek her assistance.' Gallon somewhat ordered. Gallon, as if reading Truscott's mind said, 'I will go and counsel Zaphod. He is best to stay here as from what you told me, the pain in his heart is affecting his rational thought. I will keep him busy with building jobs around here and let him know of our plans to assist Perina,'

After saying their goodbyes, Truscott wasted no time in preparing for his journey to Tremlite. He sat crossed -egged in quiet meditation prior to his journey. He breathed and surrendered until white light drenched his body. In his mind's eye he saw the figure of a female Fallon with long white robes sitting in the same crossed-legged position as himself.

'Ashanti,' he said and she turned and looked at him and he saw himself. Truscott had never experienced such an apparition nor the joy that followed in that moment. He released himself from his meditative state and laughed out loud in pure ecstasy. 'How lucky am I?' he said and he knew that something amazing was about to happen. He gathered his belongings and set off on a now familiar road to Tremlite. He was fuelled by the joy of his meditation and he saw nothing but beauty as he embarked upon his path.

Truscott strode to his destination, taking in all of his environment along the way. He delighted in the cool smell of the fresh rain doused forest and the dank but delicious smell of the moss mingling with the rocks and earth. The enchantment of his surrounds made the journey effortless. He deliberately chose to experience the journey as a wonder and looked for the hidden treasures the forest path contained. He spotted many delightful flowers and fragrances, little animals scurrying and birds flying overhead. He was in such an exalted state of being that he almost missed the silhouette of a small hurrying Trehwell in the distance. Truscott followed the flight path of a Truon in the sky when he noticed a small familiar figure climbing down a rock face near the glistening Doli lake.

'Jenta Jonty,' Truscott called with the loudest call he could muster.

Danio stopped at once transfixed at the voice heard from the distance a recognisable voice, a friendly familiar voice. Danio scouted his memories and gleamed with joy.

'Truscott, Truscott. Is that you? Truscott?' Danio scanned his surroundings, craning his neck until he saw the small distant figure of a the trusted Fallon. They clambered to one another until they were caught up in a tangle of embrace.

'Always out adventuring,' said Truscott as he scuffed Danio's hair and ears.

'I could say the same about you,' retorted Danio cheekily. Before Truscott could enquire about where Danio was headed, Danio began. 'I have an urgent matter in regard to Perina. Her condition has worsened and I must inform Zaphod at once.' Danio's head hung low and heavy as he imparted this weighty news, and an update of all that had passed since they'd parted. Truscott's was unnerved somewhat to hear that Wilmsea was now caring for Perina, though was comforted by Danio's now complete trust for his mother. He wondered what Perina was making of this and if the move had some effect on the decline of her health. Truscott reported to Danio his plans of finding a healer in Tremlite to assist. They made plans for Danio to collect Zaphod and meet Truscott and the healer back at the Tavern in Badon.

'I will journey like the wind has full force behind me,' said Truscott.

'Ditto,' replied Danio and they both swept themselves away.

It was at nightfall that Truscott arrived in Tremlite. He settled himself to camp near the harbour. Seven of the seven moons were out and Truscott delighted in the warm light. He ate sparingly from his cassock and rolled out his mattock to sleep under the moonlit stars. Whilst concerned about Perina's decline, he knew that he would find her healer tomorrow and with that thought he promptly fell into a true and blissful sleep where the waves danced across the ocean and dolphins frolicked in its wake.

Chapter 5

Truscott meets Ashanti

To love who we are and to become what we are capable of becoming is a life fulfilled.

Ashanti awoke to a translucent golden glow that was steadily engulfing her bedroom. She could just make out the rippling of the water on the harbour as the dark pool of night relinquished its hold to the morning rays of light. The harbour was still slumbering in the glow with only a few night birds returning to their roost disturbing its slumber.

Ashanti smiled at the beauty before her and shuddered with appreciation and delight at the beautiful Town of Tremlite before her. She had decorated her room with crystals that she had found in the mountain surrounds, and they began twinkling in the echo of the dawn before her.

Ashanti had sewn a mat that she had placed next to her bed. She gave thanks to herself as she slid out of her warm comfort and gently walked to a chair that she had placed in the centre of the rug. The rug itself was shaped in a star and at each point were the six elements of life. Earth, Wood, Stone, Water, Fire and Air. Just about everything in Tremlite and beyond was made of these elements or they formed them somehow. Ashanti noticed in herself how her moods rose and fell with the moon like the tides of the ocean. We are all connected, she mused as she gently lowered her body to the chair and began meditating.

Ashanti practiced this every day. Meditation in the morning calmed her spirit and helped her focus for the day. She was a practicing healer and helped persons in the town regain their balance and health. To prepare herself for this salutary task, she liked to drop into this space of peace and calm. She knew she had reached a state of nirvana with her highest self when she became bathed in purple light. Ashanti knew that others who practiced meditations like this had other experiences. White light, blue light, our connections to our spirit self is as unique as each being is.

Ashanti had settled into a delightful shroud of purple and her spirit swirled effortlessly throughout her body. She smiled, enjoying the peace encircling her. She always said the same words: I am beautiful, I am strong, I am kind, I am healthy, I am bountiful, I place spirit first and I act as a vessel of wisdom for those who seek it. She liked to begin her day with these thoughts as it helped her remember her higher being and not succumb to human animal instinctual behaviour.

Ashanti was always astonished at how quickly time passed when she was in this state of ecstasy, humming in a glow of purple delight. When she felt filled, she eased her way back into the here and now and gently opened her eyes to the now emerging harbour becoming more visible through the ever-increasing strains of light. The sun was burgeoning on the horizon, about to emerge and give birth to the new day. Ashanti moved her chair with care and precision and began a series of exercises that moved the energy in her body to every extremity. This stretching and moving continued her meditation in motion which brought energy and healing to all parts of herself.

When Ashanti completed her movements, she saluted the sun with her hands together in prayer, closed her eyes, bowed her head and gently sighed. She was ready to begin her day. Ashanti opened her eyes and noticed a curious movement on the jetty. The sun was now easing its way upward, creating a now orange glow that made the sea glisten in tangerine tones. She noticed a figure on the foreshore moving in a similar dance like way that she does. She moved closer to the window for a better view and witnessed a male figure, possibly a Fallon seemingly in bliss, saluting the sun.

Curious, she thought, she did not know anyone apart from the elders in the hall of Tremlite who did these moves and no one wore such curious garments as the Fallon in the distant view. He appeared to have a long brown loose-fitting shirt that nestled over some baggy brown pants. He was barefoot and moved with grace and determination. He completed his moves bowing to the sun. Same as me, she thought and shook her head in bewilderment.

The Fallon completed his moves and, as if he sensed a presence watching, he turned and looked directly at the window where Ashanti was transfixed. He smiled and nodded at the now astonished Ashanti. She caught a glimpse of his eyes in now emerging sunlight and it took her breath away. She turned from his gaze as it seemed to move through her in a way that she had never experienced before. There was a knowing that was undeniable a connection that had collided with her so forcibly that it was like she was struck with lightening. She turned back and the figure waved to her. He seemed to notice the connection as well and like a magnet she was drawn downward to the harbour she sensed that to resist this urge would be like refuting her very existence.

She quickly dressed spurned on by curiosity and walked stealthily to the Fallon below to seek meaning from this phenomenal and unexpected experience. Their eyes met spontaneously like beacons shining in the curling mist of dawn. Both gasped and were drawn inexplicably together like magnets.

Ashanti blushed and looked away as the gaze from the most handsome Fallon she had ever seen, who seemed to reach right into her soul. This was an astonishing familiarity of soul connection that propelled them both into an embrace. No etiquette or code of formal greetings could interrupt the enchanted moment that's origin came from beyond the living world.

'Why?' they started together, 'Who?' again, announced simultaneously.

Truscott raised his hand to talk. 'Truscott, at your service,' he bowed.

'Ashanti,' he said her name at the same time as her.

'How do you know?' she said, tilting her head to one side.

'I have come to seek your assistance, with a very dear friend who is seriously ill,' Truscott replied regaining his sense of urgency. I believe you met Heffla?' he questioned and stated at the same. 'I knew it was you when I first met you in, a dream,' he added assuredly.

Ashanti tossed her hair in delight and replied, 'You had better fill me in. Please, follow me.' They left the harbourside and Ashanti swept Truscott up the stairs to the magical sanctuary of her room. Truscott was in awe of the similarities of furnishings and drawings that she had that adorned her small but compact apartment. He would have liked to have all the time in the world to chat and talk about their connections of being though that would have to wait. He instead sat as beckoned into a very comfortable chair and told the story of Perina and her current state to Ashanti who listened with great intent to every part of the detail.

'I can see your need,' offered Ashanti. 'Though I have just met you so am reluctant to follow you to an unknown town full of unknown people. I could possibly offer you some herbs to take and try?' she offered. Noting Ashanti's apprehension Truscott, launched into reasons for why she needed to come in person.

'Herbs have been given by a very experienced herbalist in Badon and so far none useful,' exclaimed Truscott, 'I have been advised that you cured Heffla of headaches by teaching him mindful meditation. I feel that this may be her only chance of healing,' he continued lowering his head. 'I understand your apprehension, though how can a meeting so pure be feared' he stated turning his head towards her to catch her glaze.

Ashanti was feeling rather compelled by Truscott to try to heal Perina. She took a moment to consider her options. Instinctively she felt safe around Truscott, though stories embedded in her upbringing about Scaysborough folk echoed in her mind. An internal struggle ensued, Truscott sensing this took her hand and looked gently in her eyes. 'I am safe, you will be safe with me, I will look after you.' Ashanti melted with his touch, her fears subsided somewhat. She took a deep breath turned her head to one side and matter of factly stated. 'We had better be off then.' Truscott sighed with relief and thanked her profusely. They grinned at each other, a rather soppy love filled grin. 'Lets get prepared,' ordered a now jubilant Ashanti.

A flurry of packing occurred and before long, Ashanti had closed the door to her unit making her way with him down to the harbour, where Truscott collected his belongings. Both now ready for the journey ahead, faced each other, both feeling a connection, a knowing, an irresistible need for proximity to each other, uncanny, it was like it was ordained, an undeniable rekindling of souls once parted and now re-joined. They laughed and reached for each other. Harmony flowed between them and with hands swinging they walked and talked deeply about how to best help Perina. Other discussions arose in regard to their sublime connection as they both intuitively knew that they could never again be parted from one another. It it was like they had found the other half of themselves they didn't even know was missing,and their souls were now complete.

CHAPTER 6

DANIO FINDS ZAPHOD

*To refuse the tumultuous climb of the journey would
be to miss out of the hidden knowledge and treasures
to be found on the other side.*

Danio found himself in the familiar fairground on the outskirts of Scaysborough. He noticed with interest that a fair was about to occur in the Town and that Tremlite folk would soon be arriving to join in on the combined celebration. Danio was enthralled by what the posters depicted: rides, events, and tasty treats. He would even imagine himself there if he didn't have a more urgent task at. Danio shook his head and laughed as he remembered the two Townships being on the brink of war. Now the Townships were celebrating their friendships by having a combined fair.

As he remembered, an older Trehwell called out to him, 'Say, aren't you that kid that spoke from the lake that night in Tremlite?' Danio turned to see an a curious looking Trehwell with a rather large and bulbous nose who in fact was one of the councillors who was responsible for organising the whole event.

'Yes, it is I Danio at your service,' he replied to the Trehwell whose name was Gustow. Gustow was surprised and delighted to see the young lad.

'I myself was in the trenches that night, awful business, and you my little one saved the day,' he stated with enthusiasm giving

Danio a rather large pat on his back.

'Are you coming to the fair?' he queried.

'I imagine not,' replied Danio, 'I have more pressing tasks,' he added.

'Pity,' said Gustow, 'I could arrange a spot for you to talk to the crowds—a sort of reminiscing of the past and tribute to the future sort of thing.'

'I am sorry, I must be off,' Danio said, edging away.

'It's a pity,' Gustow repeated, though by the time he had finished his sentence Danio, who had decided he had no time to waste was already walking into Town to find the cottage of Zaphod.

Gustow scratched his head and thought, how impatient youth are, and had a bit of a chuckle.

Barnio spotted Danio before Danio could even ask any Townsfolk for directions to Zaphod's cottage. Barnio had been flitting this way and that, getting equipment and supplies for Zaphod who was engaged in building stages and stairs to stages in the fairground. Zaphod had already completed most of the wagon to collect Perina and was waiting rather impatiently for the wheels that he had ordered from a local metal smith to be made. Gallon, as promised, had spoken to Zaphod about the needs of the council to erect new structures to cope with the large crowd of people arriving from Tremlite. Zaphod had agreed to help; being busy was a respite from his despair. Barnio offered to assist as well and became Zaphod's right hand man. Zaphod would bark orders and Barnio, always ready to assist, would grab the hammer, hold the nail, get the screwdriver whatever Zaphod needed. Barnio was on an errand commanded by Zaphod to collect some more screws from Council supplies when he encountered a familiar young Trehwell.

'Danio? Is that you?' he said, and promptly raced to Danio so quickly that Danio stumbled right on top of him.

'What the—' Danio began as he picked himself up from the dirt and brushed the thick crop of hair from his face.

'Why,' Barnio he said with joy. Barnio grabbed both his hands and twirled him around in a circle. 'Lovely to see you, lovely to see you,' Barnio continued. Danio was swept up in this joyous dance, though the constant swirling was making him dizzy and had to use every effort of his 9-year-old body to squirm out of his embrace.

'Great to see you too,' stammered Danio once he had released himself from Barnio's grip. 'It's just—' he started, though by this time Zaphod who had heard Barnio's singing had walked over to say hello to the lad as well. 'Zaphod…' Danio started though stopped as he blinked back tears. Danio did not know how to relay the message and looked down at his feet.

'Is it Perina?' Zaphod questioned his voice low and urgent. 'Is it? Is it?' He shook Danio's shoulder, as he could see that Danio was having a hard time telling him.

'Yes,' Danio said meekly. 'She is poorly and I ran to advise you at once,' added Danio leaning into Zaphod's body. Zaphod cupped Danio's hands in his hands and shook with tears.

'Is it bad then?'

'I expect it is,' offered Danio with all the directness the 10-year-old Trehwell could muster.

'I should never have left,' Zaphod snapped. 'Why did I leave? Barnio, why? I am a useless no good being, I can't do anything right! It is my fault that she has worsened my fault alone!' he announced with a bang of his fist on the nearby railing.

'It is your emotions,' Barnio replied solemnly, 'they are getting in the way. It is fault, not your fault, it just your emotions,' he continued.

'Argghhhhhhhhhhhhhhhhhhhhhhhhhhhhhhhhhhhh!' yelled Zaphod. 'My emotions, my emotions!' He wished he could contain them. The pain in his heart was so huge that he felt he may need medical attention. Zaphod was angry, no furious with himself, furious he let Perina go to Badon by herself, furious that he could not do anything to stop her drink or take drugs, furious that she did, furious that he would not be married in a few weeks as planned, angry for leaving, angry for being angry.' 'Argghhhhhhhhhhhhhhhhhhhhh,' he yelled again 'Arghhhhhhhhhhhhhhhhhhhh, Arghhhhhhhhhhhhhhhh,' and then threw his hammer as high and far as it would go. Nothing Barnio or Danio could have said or done would have stopped him. The hammer unbeknown to all landed squarely on the side of a pavilion that soon would house all the bakery items for judging. The collision of the hammer on the wall created a small jagged hole under the eaves that was undetectable from the outside.

Zaphod sat and pressed both hands over his face, sobbing, sobbing, sobbing.

'We best be off,' started Barnio and flitted backwards and forwards in front of his inconsolable friend. 'We best be off, be off,' he continued.

Zaphod looked at his friend through his despair and knew he was right. 'I will go with Danio,' Zaphod replied firmly to Barnio with a look that appeared full of self-hate and malice that seemed to caution Barnio to say nothing other than 'ok.'

Obediently and in line with expectations Barnio replied nervously with a simple 'OK.' Then as it was with Barnio he added 'I will help with the fair, help with the fair. Good luck, good luck.' And with that Barnio raced off propelled with nervous energy and a desire to be away from this uncomfortable emotion filled scene.

Barnio was truly concerned for Perina, though could see that the less people around Zaphod, the better, at least for right now. Zaphod was like a lit cracker that was about to explode. Danio would be a perfect companion he thought as the demeanour of this child would only serve to soothe Zaphod and keep the cracker from blowing.

Zaphod strode home to collect some belongings for the journey and soon reconnected with Danio, who was waiting by the fairground gate as promised. Danio had used the time wisely to eat some of the delicious food his mother had packed him and to rest his weary legs. He was happy to see that Zaphod appeared somewhat calmer and with the knowing of a small but wise heart, Danio knew that silence would be the best medicine for Zaphod right now. With a nod, he and Zaphod strode off. No words were spoken, one foot after another, both looking down at the path as if transfixed to the ground. It was that way they travelled all the way to Badon, solid, steady, eyes downcast. Few mumblings to set up camp, mechanically eating food, sleeping fitfully. Then back on the road one foot, one step, at a time.

CHAPTER 7

THE FAIR IS SIZZLING.

*If anger rises, let it fall. Let it fall for what you think
caused it may not be that at all.*

Streams of Tremlite Town folk were arriving at Scaysborough showground to set themselves up for the fair. It was the first time most Tremlite folk had left Tremlite surrounds and there was much talk and mutterings about the differences. Tremlite folks had the same mix of being as Scaysborough, there were Garnios, heading this way and that excitedly discussion whatever they could, flitting from one place to the next imparting their ideas to whomever came in their way.

'We are way faster,' one Scaysborough Garnio commented as he saw Barnio scooting around rather sluggishly. 'We will easily win the Garnio race, they haven't a chance.' He continued scoffing at Barnio who unbeknown to him was downtrodden with worry.

There were Trehwells, who stood tall, looking around and taking in their surrounds. 'I expect we should be on guard around the Scaysborough's. Commented a Tremlite Trehwell. 'They cant be trusted and look like they are aching for a fight.' He cautioned to another warningly.

There were Fallons, some in flight, some walking, taking in the new impressions that were before them. 'The fallons here are rather fat,' commented one Tremlite Fallon, 'we will easily wind the flying competition.'

'It's a wonder they can get off the ground at all,' sneered another.

The Etruscans, and the council of the wise who were heralded in at the rear, were the only ones who were not judging and taking digs at the differences that abound. They walked in rather cheerful authority, taking in the wonders of differences. And, of course,right at the very back there were some Nippoos; they waded in, with all of their stout dignity, sniffing the air for the smells of fruits and food, looking as always for some new tasty treat to satisfy their enormous appetite. Of course they were particularly scathing of the differences.

'You call that a cake?' commented one Tremlite Nipoo pointing to a Scayborough cake stand. 'They wont stand a change at the judging.' She smirked. Despite the small hostilities,there was also fun and excitement. Many Scaysborough folk lined the outside of the showground walls to greet the new arrivals and to see who these new folk were. The arrivals from Tremlite were noted to be wearing unusual clothes, long length flowing clothes that were sewn from shiny ornate material. Some were wearing scarves and headpieces and some wearing tall cone-shaped hats. Scaysborough folk wore less fancy and more practical attire, pants, shirts and dresses that were made of plain colours, mainly browns, greens and yellow.

There was much talk from residents from both towns about how different things were.

'Look at what they are wearing, don't they even work?' said one Trehwell from Scaysborough.

'Why are they wearing those rough clothes? Their bodies must itch with such course thread,' a Trehwell from Tremlite was overheard saying about a Trehwell from Scaysborough. It was not only the clothes that were being discussed.

'It is so flat and their homes are so small and square,' one Trehwell from Tremlite whispered. In Tremlite, the residents were used to the tall spiral towers that dotted Tremlite's hilly surrounds. These towers often had many levels and many rooms with vantage points to the nearby harbour where they relied on fish and sea creatures as their staple diet. They also relied on a few farms providing other fruits and necessities in the outlying meadows at the base of their hilly community. In Scaysborough it was flat and level and most who lived here were farmers. Folks worked hard and slept well. Scaysborough was fully of neatly painted thatched cottages, busy ovens baking many goods and busy farmers producing wheat, milk, eggs and other staples.

The presumed snobby demeanour of the Tremlite residents due to their flashy attire was noted by many from Scaysborough.

'Oh, look at the way they hold their heads up.'

'So grand, they think they are kings and queens.'

In truth, to keep your head piece or hat on your head you needed to remain in an upright position and over the years it led to a certain poise that was neither meant to be grand or pompous. Despite these differences, Scaysborough residents were warm and friendly enough, to their new arrivals and were quick to offer them drinks, directions or any other assistance they may need.

The council of elders from Scaysborough were also out to greet their distant neighbours and were delighted with the turn out for the fair. A feast was planned for the night and the fair itself would begin in two days, allowing for the travellers to settle in, place their goods for the judging and to prepare for the events ahead. There was much mingling laughter and joyous chatter.

A small hall stood at the beginning of the fairground to house the baked goods for judging, cakes, cookies and baked goods for the judging. It was here that the Tremlite bakers as well as the Scaysborough bakers began lining up to place their items for the judges to taste. The tasting would commence in the morning on the first day of the show and it was the judges themselves who co-ordinated which food went where and that the food was properly labelled with the cook identified. It was a tedious job as many of the bakers wished to explain to the judges how they crafted their cakes and what care they took in an attempt to impress them. Truth be known, the judges just wanted them labelled and set down so that they too could go out and join the frivolities outside.

Nadoo was one amongst the line up, and had her carefully crafted Jim Jam berry cakes, which she considered was her most delicious fare that she had created to date. She was very grateful for Garrow, whom she felt picked the juiciest berries in the land and she was still in awe at the bountiful supply he had managed. When it was her turn to place her wares on the bench, she attempted to engage a well-known but rather grumpy judge named Cashan about such things.

'You know, this fruit is the best I have ever seen and—' she was stopped abruptly. The Judge pointed her bony finger towards a table that had a large heading Cakes.

'Over there please!' she said with a yawn.

'Well I can see that, though you might want to know—' Again, she was stopped.

This time the Judge added, 'Place your name clearly on the placard in front.' She looked past Nadoo, at the next baker in line. 'Next!' she said.

'But—' Nadoo was ignored completely and Cashan the Judge barked similar instructions to the next in line with the same marked disinterest. 'Hummmph' said Nadoo haughtily and went straight over with her wares, making sure that they were labelled correctly. 'Hummph' she exclaimed again.

This time, Garrow, who had joined Nadoo in her drop off task, said, 'Don't worry my precious, those cakes are the best I have ever tasted, you will win for sure. Let's go outside to enjoy the merriment.' Nadoo who had forgot for a moment that Garrow was even with her looked and saw his jovial dancing eyes and couldn't help but get caught up in his happiness and nodded, barely glancing behind at her prized cakes. Garrow was still camouflaged as a Nipoo and they looked a handsome couple walking hand in hand at the fair. Nadoo had not told anyone about Garrow being a Vindervay and thought those discussions were best after the fair when everyone had more time.

Little did Nadoo and Garrow know that the still rather furious Bulbrook had followed them all the way to the fairground. He sat in a nearby tree with full vantage of the foods within the hall. He had previously watched in horror at Nadoo's home, seeing one by one all of his delicious berries from his tree being placed in a strange bowl of thick liquid then placed in a large box only to emerge now covered with a strange substance. Now they had travelled them to this place!He was both curious and determinedly indignant about all of his berries being harnessed in this way. He was going to retrieve the food that he relied upon to sustain him. He had fought off many other Bulbrooks whom dared come near his tree, he fought those off and he would fight these big pink beings off too. He had followed Nadoo and Garrow all the way to the hall jumping from one canopy of tree to another, hiding behind bushes, stealthily with a quiet determination and now he sat high in the Colo Tree next to the Hall and watched and watched and watched, never taking his eyes off his belongings, his treasures, they would be reclaimed!

He gnashed his teeth and growled low and repeatedly to try to frighten off the residents that were streaming in and out of the hall. With all the merriment below, none of the bakers heard the threatening cries of the Bulbrook above in the boughs and went about their business handing in their baked goods for judging. The Bulbrook seeing that his threatening growls had no measure upon this crowd sulked, placed both his clawed hands over his face rubbing his eyes then settled in to sit and wait, ready to pounce as soon as he had an opportunity. It would be nightfall soon and he knew villagers were nowhere to be seen at night time.

He spent the afternoon unnoticed by the crowds, perched on his branch, becoming more and more agitated at the perceived increased threat on the food that his life depended on.

CHAPTER 8

ASHANTI MEETS PERINA.

If you refuse to accept anything but the best outcome, it will always come to you.

Ashanti and Truscott, although on a very important mission, urged themselves onward in a calm and steadfast manner. They focused on the task ahead but still enjoyed their surroundings on the way and pointed out to each other red climbing flowers on vines and sweet-smelling powder puff like blossoms on the trees. They felt energised and elevated by the greenery and beauty around them.

Ashanti broke the silence by saying to Truscott, 'I have never been to Badon Town before. What is it like?'

Truscott replied, 'It is a town in healing. The townsfolk previously managed the pain in their lives by seeking comfort in substances that made them forget temporarily. It was Perina's, whose life is currently in balance, who was the catalyst for the changes in the townsfolk.' Truscott then divulged the journey that Perina had been on and the effect that the substances had on her. Ashanti looked concerned and hastened her step.

Ashanti stopped Truscott for a minute on the track. 'In her mind she was preparing on how she could attempt to heal Perina. 'You are adept at meditation?' she asked. She hoped that he was as he appeared to move in a meditative way.

Truscott bowed and replied, 'I am a humble fledgling in the matter, though I try my best.'

Ashanti laughed and smiled, 'I am sure your enlightened presence denotes more than a novice in such matters.'

Truscott blushed a little and laughed, 'I will be guided by your healing expertise Ashanti, and do my best to support the process.'

'From what you have told me, we will need the energy of many to regenerate Perina's failing body,' stated Ashanti. 'You will be needed, Truscott', Truscott beamed upon hearing Ashanti saying she needed him.

'I will do my best,' he added with a bow.

'I am sure you will,' responded Ashanti and they again joined hands and walked in a mindful hum of ambient love until they reached the outskirts of Badon.

Jardjon, who paced outside his Tavern, spotted Truscott and an unknown female Fallon walking towards town. He flailed his hands and shouted towards them. Truscott and Ashanti noted the small but frantically waving figure in the distance and sensing the urgency, quickened their step to a jog. They reached the verandah of the Tavern and Jardjon wrung his hands in despair.

'It may be in all too late,' he said, holding back his tears as best he could. 'Hurry please, this way.' Jardjon ushered them into the room where Perina lay. There was no time for cordial introductions. Ashanti cringed when she saw the withered and greying body of a Fallon laying lifelessly on the bed. A weeping Wilmsea was bending over her, stroking her face with a damp cloth. Wilmsea sensed the intrusion into the room and looked up with tear-stained cheeks.

'I am not sure if there is any life in her at all,' she said, though was not able to speak any further for the sobbing that engulfed her. 'It is my fault,' Wilmsea added and cried now uncontrollably. Jardjon reached out for Wilmsea and gathered her in his arms carrying her out of the room.

'I hope it is not too late,' he said to Ashanti and Truscott. 'If there is anything you need, please let us know.' He carried his grieving wife into the kitchen to pour her a cup of tea.

Ashanti felt Perina's body, which was cold to touch, she then quickly placed her hands under Perina's nose and after a few minutes declared that there was a slight breath. There was no time to waste.

'Truscott, place your hands on Perina and I will place my hands on top of yours and let's begin with a meditation,' she said.

Truscott obediently placed his hands on Perina's heart and Ashanti placed hers over his. They both closed their eyes and focused their attention on Perina's body and health. Ashanti and Truscott melted into a harmonious trance.

Ashanti begun, 'Perina, you have the wonderful capacity to heal. You have a miraculous healing energy within you. Be aware that this energy comes from the very centre of yourself. Gather up that energy and direct it to the part of the body where you instinctively know it must be directed. You can trust your intuition. Truscott and I will offer you energy that you need, just draw on it. We have enough. Your body is now being filled with loving, light energy which will help you recover, repair, and energise. Truscott and Perina remained by Perina's side holding their hands gently and tenderly on Perina's heart.

A spark in Perina's knowing awakened, words were being said which allowed the spark to flourish into several, they joined together began moving throughout her body. Truscott and Ashanti noticed movement under Perina's skin, a fluid and gentle movement that moved in a figure-eight pattern up and down her body.

Truscott shot a glance to Ashanti who reassured, 'All is going well. You are doing really well, Perina. Your body is hearing you and healing you. You are glowing with healing. Your skin is becoming pink and your heart is flowing joyous blood throughout your veins. Every tiny cell is restored and your body's functioning is restored. You are masterful at detecting where the healing must occur and you can trust all your decisions in regard to this as you are a perfect healer.' Perina's body began to pinken and her breath was becoming audible.

Perina's essence began a silent discussion within. *Is this Truscott? He is back, but who is the women? Where is Zaphod? And the wedding, oh the wedding!*

Perina was paid attention to the female voice.

'Begin, Perina,' continued Ashanti. 'Begin to recover. Look in your mind's eye at the image of you, your body, your healthy you. You have the power you have what it takes, remember who you are, what you love.'

It was at this that Perina murmured, 'Zaphod…' '

'Yes,' Ashanti affirmed, 'you love Zaphod. You will get better for him, though more importantly, you will get better for yourself. Continue to heal Perina, continue to heal. Truscott and I will prepare some herbs for you to drink, we will return.' Perina was delightedly shocked that they heard her. 'I must be healing' she heartened and continued to focus her mind on health.

With that, she and Truscott left the room to prepare herbs that Ashanti had carried with her. The herbs were detoxifying herbs that were full off phytonutrients which reduces inflammation of the digestive tract, which Ashanti had correctly guessed was the cause of Perina's ill health.

'She is not out of the woods,' declared Ashanti to Truscott as they left the room, 'though she has a fighting chance and her condition has improved slightly.' 'She spoke' said a heartened Truscott, 'This is a great sign.'

You were amazing in there,' Truscott declared, beaming at her. Ashanti blushed this time. 'You must teach me your healing methods,' he added. They locked eyes and both blushed.

'Time for our feelings and teachings later,' Ashanti said with a smile.

In the kitchen, Wilmsea and Jardjon were still huddled together comforting each other's despair.

'She has improved slightly,' declared Truscott as he and Ashanti entered, to which both Wilmsea and Jardjon both shrieked with delight.

'She still has some way to go,' cautioned Ashanti though added, 'I am, however, glad of the progress and feel that Perina is a strong soul who can make it all the way back.' Seeing a handful of herbs in Ashanti's hands. Wilmsea offered her the whole kitchen and any help she could render. 'What are you like at stirring?' Ashanti queried.

'At your disposal' Wilmsea answered, jumping to her feet and bowing before her.

As Ashanti and Wilmsea began cutting, chopping and stirring the tonic Truscott and Jardjon retreated to the verandah of the Tavern. A big sign had been posted: Closed for business today. Many a villager were noted to climb the stairs in the expectation of a great meal from the kitchen, though saddened to see the sign which stated the closure and retreated back to their own lodging's to fashion their own sustenance. It was on the verandah that Truscott saw two figures swiftly moving towards the Tavern. As they drew closer he noted the familiar though expedite walk of his good friend Zaphod with the ever loyal and courageous Danio struggling behind him in an attempt to keep up with his grief-driven pace.

Truscott waved to his friends and Zaphod upon seeing the familiar figure of Truscott increased his pace then gave way to flying to greet his friend on the verandah.

'Where is she? How is she?' spewed the grieving Zaphod, his brow furrowed, sweating with fear and worry, as he spoke.

'Improving', said Truscott in an authoritative tone. Zaphod in a state of exhausted panic pushed him aside and headed for the room where his beloved lay. Hearing the door open and slam a curious Wilmsea poked her head through the door.

Zaphod, upon seeing Wilmsea began a violent tirade, 'You filthy scum! Whore! You are the vilest, vilest being, I have ever encountered!' he began.

Ashanti upon hearing the commotion came out of the kitchen drying her wet hands on her apron. 'Zaphod is it? I am Ashanti,' and she held out her hand. Zaphod however, had found the perfect release for all his pent up fear and anger and looking away from Ashanti continued.

'You old crone, you leave you son, incapacitate the town, imprison my beloved with a chemical cocktail of death—'

Wilmsea who already was blaming herself nodded in agreement. 'I am so sorry, I have changed my ways.' she stammered.

Zaphod gave her a shove that so forceful it knocked her to the ground and without even turning around to see what had happened, he stormed into each room until he found Perina, whom whilst improved from before, was still lifeless with eyes shut though a strange movement of skin rippling throughout her body. Zaphod feared that this was a deathly tremor and the end was near. He tore himself away, as he could not bear to see Perina in that condition and returned to the kitchen with renewed righteous anger. Ashanti was attending to the fallen, though unharmed, Wilmsea, Zaphod was about to deliver heightened words of vicious anger and had both fists high in the air when Truscott, who by now had hastened inside, lunged towards Zaphod and held him tightly around the waist.

He dodged Zaphod's punches repeating over and over. 'It's ok, it's ok Zaphod, it's Ok.' Zaphod who became a little subdued struggled out of Truscott's grip and looked towards Wilmsea who was now protected by her husband Jardjon. Zaphod shot a scornful look towards them and pushed past Truscott and the hapless Danio who had just made it to the verandah and took to the skies again, flying around and around in circles above the tavern creating a casting a fury of wind rather like a tornado in its beginnings.

'I have an idea!' exclaimed Ashanti, seizing the opportunity of energy created. Quick all into Perina's bedroom. They all obeyed. With the tonic in her hand, Ashanti quickly maneouvered teaspoons into Perina's mouth and gently encouraged her to swallow. After several teaspoons Ashanti directed everyone to hold hands around Perina which they obligingly did.

'Perina your friends are all around you, your beloved Zaphod is outside flying, the medicine is creating more healing and you yourself are healing.'

Perina's consciousness sparked, *Zaphod, Zaphod flying.* She remembered, she remembered them laughing and flying one wing each, *how could he fly?* she wanted to move her mouth to ask, but it didn't obey.

'There is extra energy around you Perina you can tap into energy of those who love you look for it.'

Perina retreated into the energy swirling inside her and sought to strengthen it she felt a strong energy nearby a whirlwind that she knew well. Her energy flowed out like clouds in the sky and swirled into the swirling force that Zaphod was unknowingly creating. Perina was able to focus on Zaphod, his higher consciousness and tap into the excess energy he was creating. The energy was collected by her life force which now transformed wafted gently and calmly into Perina's body. Perina's body shook a little as Zaphod's energy settled within her.

Ashanti could sense Perina's awakening and continued to encourage, 'You know exactly where to send your energy to revive pathways so that all your body parts harmonise again. Send energy to these parts.'

Perina wondered who this enchanting voice belonged to and she began to explore her body. She could feel an energy circulating and with her mind's eye she directed it towards her mouth and face, to her eyes, to her nostrils. She willed the energy to move her eyelids and to everyone's amazement her eyelids flickered. They all gasped. As Zaphod's fury was being expelled in clouds of love and energy to his beloved, he met with his higher consciousness and calmed immediately.

His calmness allowed him to hear that gasp and, still stricken with grief, he feared the worst and dropped to the ground, peering through Perina's bedroom window to see Truscott, Danio, Wilmsea and Jardjon surrounding and Ashanti leaning over Perina. He wailed with howl that filled the skies. He dropped to his knees and bowed his head with such sorrow that he never thought he would be able to lift it again.

The silence filled every space until a sound so slight leaked into the void, 'Zaphod,' came the meek voice.

Ashanti wasted no time, 'that is great Perina, Zaphod is outside, my name is Ashanti, you are healing, Zaphod' is outsi—' but before she could finish the sentence, Zaphod had clambered back into the room and rather clumsily pushed through the circle to kneel next to Perina, kiss her face, and hold her hand.

'Perina, I am here!' uttered Zaphod. Perina's eyes fluttered and the corners of her mouth elevated slightly. 'Thank god, Thank god!' repeated Zaphod and held her hand tightly. 'Our house is ready,' he told her, 'I can't wait to show you our new home.' Again a smile was weakly fashioned by the convalescing Perina.

'She will heal,' Ashanti declared. 'If it wasn't for your energy source Zaphod, she may not have made it.'

'Oh yes, s—s—sorry,' stammered Zaphod glancing at Wilmsea.

'No harm done,' said Wilmsea, who was actually slightly bruised.

'I think we need to talk about anger management, Zaphod,' said Truscott.

'I have changed Zaphod! Wilmsea interjected. 'You were right to be angry and blame me. I cannot deny my wrongdoing and I owe my life to Perina because it is from her suffering that changed my life and me. You can count on it Zaphod, I have changed forever and will strive to correct all the wrongdoing I have done in the past.' Jardjon hugged his wife and Danio could not help feel proud of his mother for her forgiveness and change in character. He ran up to them both and the three hugged for a very long time. In the end, it was Wilmsea who retreated from the tangle of love. 'Well,' Wilmsea said, brushing down her apron and rubbing her bruised leg, 'I expect I should go and make some food for all you hearty travellers and some broth for the patient.'

Truscott tenderly held Ashanti's hand and drew her close to him, falling into a loving embrace.

'Let's find a quiet place to talk we have a lot of catching up to do,' said Truscott warmly.

'We sure do', Ashanti replied and they withdrew into the empty tavern to sit in a large comfortable lounge where they could while away the afternoon in delicious discussions.

Zaphod remained by Perina's side and vowed to not leave until she had fully recovered. He settled in next to her and cradled her hand in his.

As Perina settled into a healing sleep the colour purple infiltrated her dreams and her body,golden rays of light immersed her every cell. For the first time in a long time, she felt content and relaxed into a prism of delight.

CHAPTER 9

THE BAKERS IGNITE.

Life keeps us balanced between certainty, uncertainty, order and chaos.

Cashan, the Judge shut the doors of the hall firmly where all the delicious goods were kept. She put a padlock around the link that jutted out of the large wooden frame and locked it, checking that it was in place. Once convinced of this, she took her very weary frame home. She was going to stay in the fair ground, though she had exhausted herself with today's events. She chuckled slightly at some of the entries that came in from Tremlite. She had never seen such intricate icings and decorations in elaborate forms such as towers and ships. Nor had she seen such delicate sweets made into small petalled flowers. She had not as yet met the judge from Tremlite and shuddered at her task in hand. There definitely had to be more categories, such as decoration and taste. She hoped that the judge from Tremlite was an agreeable woman and began her journey home when she met, almost bumped into a very strange looking unwinged Fallon who was wearing a long black coat and a large top hat above his head. He, like her, had bony fingers and a long neck.

'Oh I am sorry,' she said as she ducked on the path to avoid contact.

'Not at all,' came the rather loftly reply. 'I was actually coming to the hall myself.'

'It's all locked up now, tell your wife it is too late for entries,' replied Cashan. 'Entries? My wife?' he said rather indignantly. 'My dear, my name is Trulio and I am the tasting judge from Tremlite.'

'You? The judge?' Cashan replied with bewilderment, 'why of course you are, you are—'

'A male,' came the haughty reply. 'Yes, I am aware of that.'

'Yes, sorry,' now stammered Cashan, 'it's just that we have never had a male judge here before as—'

Before she could finish the sentence, he interrupted, 'We males don't cook? Well, I can tell you dear, that I am a very accomplished cook and have been judging Tremlite shows for years.'

'Oh dear,' replied Cashan, 'We certainly have gotten off on the wrong foot.' She held out her hand to shake his to which he readily received. 'Well then, let's go back to the Hall, shall we? You can help me make the categories for judging.'

'Delighted, I am sure.' The two walked back to discuss all things baking. They quickly noted that they both loved cooking and held great knowledge and between the two had set out categories in no time as they walked through the display of entries in the hall.

'I can't help but notice how plain the baking is in Scaysborough,' Trulio announced somewhat tentatively.

'And I can't help but notice how grandiose the cakes and decorations are in Tremlite,' replied Cashan.

'The truth will be in the tasting, no doubt,' smiled Trulio and he looped his elbow with Cashan's and stated, 'I would love it if you showed me around Town a little.' Cashan suddenly forgot how tired she was and with an unexpected burst of energy she locked the door to the hall a second time and almost skipped down the stairs with her new found friend.

'I would be delighted to,' she replied. The pair set off chatting animatedly. They relished the opportunity to discuss their passions and had a twinkle in their eyes that was new and refreshing.

Finally, finally, a small furred creature was thinking in the tree above, finally, I will get my treasures. I will find a way I will find a way. And for the umpteenth time today he shrieked, unnoticed and jumped with a thud onto the roof of the Hall. Bulbrooks, like a lot of other forest creatures, appeared to be able to fit through spaces much smaller than themselves and he was determined and hungry enough to find a path. He started furiously searching this way and that this way and that!

Nadoo had met a Nipoo from Tremlite on her way back to the fair. Nadoo had hoped to catch the Judge Cashan before she locked up for the night just to check that her cakes were correctly labelled, though was disappointed to see it all shut off. Nadoo scanned the crowd and another Nipoo, of similar age to Nadoo caught her eye. This Nipoo was obviously from Tremlite Nadoo thought, she was wearing a straight dress that was brightly checkered with large squares of yellow and pink. This was unusual enough, thought Nadoo, though this Nipoo was also sporting a pink and yellow striped hat that spiralled above her head like a mountain. The hat was adorned with little colourful spheres that looked like candy. Nadoo was enchanted with the structure and colours of the hat and could not take her eyes off it.

This Nadoo, whose name was Astrid, became aware that she was being stared at and in typical abrupt Nipoo fashion, instantly took offense and barked, 'Do you mind?'

'Well, I never!' replied Nadoo equally as gruff. 'It was your stupid hat I was staring at, not you,' continued Nadoo. Even though Nadoo really admired it, she was too cross at being spoken to like that to reveal her true feelings.

'I expect you don't see any real fashion in this backwater,' countered the Nipoo.

'Backwater?!' It was at this point that Gallon walked past on his post of meeting and greeting townsfolk from Tremlite. As Truscott had raced off to Badon, Gallon had joined the other elders of the town to greet its foreign guests.'Good evening Nadoo, and who may this other Nipoo be' Nadoo was taken aback from Gallon's presence and remembered he was part of the greeters to Scaysborough.

Nadoo blushed a little at her rudeness towards the town's guest and stammered.

'I don't think we have met quite as yet,' then curtsied at the strangely clad Nipoo. 'Nadoo at your service,' Nadoo politely added.

'Hummphh, well my name is Astrid,' replied the newcomer, throwing Nadoo an accusing glance.

'Welcome Astrid to Scaysborough,' replied Gallon. 'I see you have met our finest baker Nadoo.'

'Baker, is it?' replied Astrid. 'That would explain the drab clothes then, did you just come from your kitchen?'

'Drab! well I—' started Nadoo though Gallon quickly interjected.

'Astrid, my dear, we in Scaysborough are simple folks and are astonished at the fine clothes and fares that Tremlite residents are bringing to our town. We have a lot to admire and learn from each other.'

This somewhat softened both the Nipoos, and Astrid replied. 'Yes, there are curious differences. I too am a baker and I have entered the competition to be judged tomorrow.'

'Then I will wish you two ladies all the success for tomorrow and will be on my way.' Gallon bowed and continued his way through the crowd smiling bowing and greeting folks. Astrid and Nadoo just stared at each other though not a word was spoken and they both turned their backs and walked towards their destinations quietly though audibly hurrumphing. Nadoo returned to her home and Astrid to the celebrations in the fair ground. Another curious difference between Tremlite folk and Scaysborough folk is that Tremlite residents love to stay up late and dance in the moonlight, whilst Scaysborough residents enjoy a quiet evening and rise early to tend to the fields and enjoy the day break. There was a lot to learn about each other indeed!

Nadoo reached home and was in quite a sulky mood. Garrow was also at her home and quietly reading a book in a rather comfortable lounge chair.

'Do you think my clothes are drab?' she enquired.

Garrow, who was slightly startled at her entry and question, took his nose from beneath the book. 'Why would I think that? Clothes are clothes.'

'Exactly!' replied Nadoo and seemingly happy with his response began humming and clucking and preparing a hearty meal for them both. Garrow shook his head, quite bewildered, and placed his nose back firmly into his book.

CHAPTER 10

DANIO WANTS TO PLAY.

Let your soul dance and your heart sing.
Joy refreshes our spirit.

Perina continued to make gains. Every day Ashanti and Truscott held morning meditations with Perina at her bedside, encouraging healing and restoration. Perina was fed broth and herbs by Wilmsea under instruction by Ashanti, whilst Zaphod remained at Perina's bedside most of the time holding her hand. Perina sensing the warmth, knew it was Zaphod and her spirit was moving continuously throughout her body, restoring every cell one by one. Jardgon and Danio spent the time ensuring everyone was fed and that clothes were washed and the Tavern was clean. It was in the Tavern where Jardgon noticed a very subdued Danio.

'Danio,' he enquired, 'Is everything OK?'

'Sure,' replied Danio and continued with his task of sweeping though with slumped shoulders and a sullen expression.

'Hmm,' said Jardjon who was not convinced. 'Let's sit a while and take a break.' Danio obediently sat with his father though hung his head low swinging his legs absentmindedly whilst sitting in the chair. 'You can tell me,' said Jardjon with such compassion that Danio began.

'It's just that the fair looked like so much fun, there was rides and candy and…' Danio then felt guilty and pulled himself up, 'though I know my place is here to help Perina… so.' Danio himself was surprised at his desire for fun as he had spent all his tender years helping his carers Jyno and Shona to cook and clean and to find food and berries in the forest. He had never had time to play, there were no children in Badon and when he'd seen other children playing when he was in Scaysborough he had so wanted to join in the merriment.

'I see,' said Jardjon who was infinitely aware of the sufferings of his son who by the grace of good fortune and kind carers had become a beautiful caring Trehwell who was growing stronger and taller by the day. 'Let me discuss this with your mother,' said Jardjon. 'We can see what we can come up with.'

'I have no right to want this,' said Danio with a hung head.

'No,' countered Jardjon, 'You have every right to want to have fun like any child and you had little opportunity until now.'

As he said these words, Wilmsea walked onto the verandah they were cleaning and said, 'Perina is getting stronger every day and Ashanti thinks it won't be long until she can sit up and talk.'

Both Jardjon and Danio called out in happiness, 'Fabulous!'

'Well then, Wilmsea, as things are improving, if it is ok with you, I would like to take our son to the Scaysborough fair. If we hurry now, we can make it by daylight tomorrow.'

Danio's eyes were full of hope. Wilmsea, who like Jardjon, was becoming increasingly aware of the sufferings and neglect Danio had been subjected to was delighted with the idea. 'What a fabulous idea, a father and son trip. Let's get you packed.' Danio shrieked with delight and jumped around and around in circles of happiness.

'I won't be needed then?' Danio questioned now feeling guilty of leaving Perina.

'Noooo, we have plenty enough helpers. It will do you the world of good. Now, like I said, go and get packed.' She gently patted Danio on the back as he raced towards his room to grab belongings for the journey.

'You sure?' questioned Jardjon with a smile.

'Definitely,' answered Wilmsea whilst stringing her hands over his head and drawing him in for a large hug. 'We have got this, so now you, off, off and pack.' Jardjon obediently went to back with a grin from ear to ear. He was astonished at how great his life now felt compared to the unhappiness, pain and anguish of his past. Shuddering at the mere idea of the past made him vow again never to return to that chaos. Peace and happiness now reigned in his world and with joy in his heart he packed his bags adding delicious food that Wilmsea had laid out for them to take and with a kiss to his wife and a wave to the others, Jardjon delightedly set off with his son on his first ever trip to Scaysborough. He too, was excited about the prospect. Jardjon and Danio chatted and walked, walked and chatted hand in hand, arms swinging from side to side in a connected ambience that enriched their very beings. It was like this that walked all the winding way to Scaysborough surprising themselves when they effortlessly arrived in the Town just as the 8 moons rose to the skies.

The fair was in its night-time full swing. There were wandering clowns walking on long sticks giving children balloons, persons selling candy on sticks and merry go rounds that spun round and round. The Scaysborough fair however shut down at 9pm sharp which even though seemingly still early for some was rather quite late for the Scaysborough crowd. They had planned more merriment and dancing for the morning so were keen to get back to their homes to get enough shut eye and rest for the events of the next day.

This was in contrast to the Tremlite folk who were mainly fishermen and fished late in the afternoon and night, sleeping up to noon the next day. The Tremlite folk had mainly all set up their camps at the far side of the fair ground and were sitting in a large circle clapping, singing, dancing and twirling. They had no intention of sleeping as yet and their camp was pulsating with noise, merriment, colour and excitement. The happiness and buoyance however were dotted with some sentiments of disdain.

As the Scaysborough residents made their way home Danio overheard some of their conversations towards the Fair exit, 'Look at those noisy Tremlites at their camp. Don't they ever rest?'

'They are a noisy lot, pompous and noisy.'

'Their noise will keep me up for sure, they have no respect,' and so on.

Danio however was having too much fun with his father to give these conversations any deeper thought. He and his father were there to make the most of this rare occasion and journeyed over to the noisy fun of the Tremlite camp, where they were instantly swept up by the dancers. The dancers who now had joined a circle grabbed their arms and linked them with their own and to their great merriment Danio and Jardjon spent most of the night, singing, dancing and revelling beneath the moonlight in delirious, delicious, luscious joy.

The Tremlite townsfolk continued this way until early hours off the morning by which time Danio and Jardjon had pitched their own Cassocks and set themselves down to rest for the remaining dwindling hours of the night. They slept together and held hands, tired and happy, grinning from ear to ear easily spinning off into wondrous dreams.

They awoke early, startled by the sounds of one of Scaysborough's Townsfolks favourite songs, Country Rock. The song was being played loudly over a loud speaker:

Country rock and it's ok,
Country Rock and it's here to stay.

They peered through their cassocks to see the fairground alive with Scaysborough residents holding hands and kicking up their heels to the infectious tunes of this gay and happy song. Before they could eat breakfast, Danio and Jardjon looked at each other, grinned and ran swiftly over to have more merriment.

Country rock and it's ok,
Country rock and it's here to stay,
so spin your partners, spin your cow,
doeseedoe if you know how.

The music continued and Danio and Jardjon gleefully found themselves kicking their heels, bending their knees, and following the boot scooting steps set by the Scaysborough folk.

The Tremlite camp were indignant at the early morning intrusion and some were heard to say things like, 'What is wrong with them? Why get up so early, can't they see we only just got to bed? How rude'

By midday however, all of the Tremlite residents from their camp had risen, put on their best attire and prepared themselves for the various competitions. There was flying competitions that Fallon's entered, woodchopping that Trehwells enjoyed, running competitions that Garnio's delighted in, debating and chess for the Etruscans and if they knew they had a Vindervay in their midst, they would have had a chameleon contest to see which Vindervay hid the best in their surrounds. But of course, only a few knew of Garrow's true identity as he kept his promise to Nadoo staying in a Nipoo form and a handsome one at that. For all the fun and enjoyment of these challenges, it was perhaps the baking competition that Nipoo's took part in that was the most contested and competitive.

Nipoos loved their food and spent most of their time cooking creating and, of course, eating. The Judging of the cakes was left to last. Some residents left the area as they did not like the quarrelling that would result of the fierce tempers of the Nipoos. Nadoo had won this prize many times and was determined to take out the prize again. She had put all her effort into the JimJam cakes and felt that no one could beat her. Especially given the fruit that Garrow had picked was so vast, plump and delicious. She and Garrow were already at the fair and spotted Danio boot scooting with his father. She hurried over, desirous of news of Perina.

Danio was twirling around with his head high in the air when he was tugged out of line by a firm hand. He turned to find Nadoo smiling. She hugged him so hard he could hardly breathe.

'How is she? How is she?' she asked Danio, though as he tried to speak, he could only manage a gasp.

'Release him Nadoo,' cautioned Garrow, 'The poor lad can hardly breathe.'

'Hi Garrow,' smiled Danio upon release.

'Well?' demanded Nadoo with raised eyebrows.

'Oh, she is doing better. So much better.' And before he could expand his answer, he was pulled back into the line by his father and they joined elbows, kicking their heels up once more.

'My word,' clucked Nadoo. Whilst she was happy that her friend was improving, she wanted much more information. Though upon watching Danio and his father engaged in such joyous commotion she resigned herself to the fact that she will have to wait to hear further. Waiting was not one of Nadoo's strengths and she shook her head with disdain. Garrow grabbed her by the arm and escorted her to watch one event after the other to soothe her gruffness. Nadoo succumbed to Garrow's scheme and before long was thoroughly enjoying the shows of strength and cleverness, clapping her hands in delight.

The tally between the Tremlite wins and Scaysborough wins were neck and neck: 14 wins each. Before too long, the final event of baking judging was ready to proceed. Judges, Cashan and Trulio were hand in hand climbing the steps to the Hall for the Judging. They had spent the evening discussing all things cooking and judging and were in great agreement on most things. They were committed to judging with complete integrity, no bias, no affinity to either town, just simple taste, texture and decorations.

It was a very well attended event as after the tastings and judgements, the cakes were cut up for all present to eat. It was especially busy today as two townships of people hungrily lined up for entry. Cashan extracted the key from her neatly ironed apron pocket and placed it into the lock with her bony hands. She entered the hall with Trulio in tow and they gasped together at the setting before them. There were tables overthrown, food displaced everywhere, and one table in particular devoid of any food at all. Only crumbs of obviously devoured fare were left.

Cashan attempted to close the doors so that she and Trulio could try to ascertain what had occurred, but the throngs of the expectant crowd stumbled in with such large numbers that it would need 200 Cashans to keep them at bay. Nadoo and Astrid were amongst the first to enter, with the intention of ensuring that every move of the judges was followed to ensure no unfair judging took place. They both screamed in horror. 'What the, what!!' A maelstrom of emotions erupted into the hall. Nadoo instantly saw that all of her baked goods were missing the whole table depleted.

She scowled at Astrid and said, 'Why you scheming, toff nosed—'

Before she could finish, Astrid who had seen the fate of her own creations (the table overturned and her decorated cakes strewn all over the floor) shouted in reply, 'You despicable, jealous—'

Trulio was right beside them both and said, 'Ladies, ladies, calm down. We will get to the bottom of this.' Though for all his calming attempts the hall became stormier and stormier.

Crowds of Tremlite and Scaysborough folk poured through the doors and upon seeing the mayhem and hearing the two Nipoos pouring out blame to each other, they themselves took sides.

Scaysborough folk let loose on all their Tremlite guests, criticising their dress, their pompous attitude and accusing them of cheating to win. The Tremlite fold retaliated, returning their taunts and accusations with fresh ones of their own. Accusing Scaysborough folk of being lazy, tiresome and boring. Well, this only poured fuel onto flame and the whole hall erupted in a stormy tirade.

'I am sure that the Lurkin is still alive and that these folk from Tremlite brought it with them.' One Scaysborough elderly resident was heard to say. Tremlite folk also were accusing Scaysborough of themselves hosting the Lurkin. The talk had taken hold and the Lurkin be ripe for satisfaction.

Nomad, the Trehwell King pushed his way through the maddening throng and was dismayed at the hostilities being thrown around. He turned to see Gallon, whom also had also heard the affray from outside and was now alongside him with an open mouth and bulging eyes.

They looked at each other and shook their heads.

'I thought we put the Lurkin to rest,' Gallon said to Nomad.

'Me too.'

'Let's try to stop this,' Nomad replied and in the most regal voice he could muster he called out, 'Stop! I say Stop!'

At this time, Isotar a leader from Tremlite, had also entered the Hall and upon seeing the wretched scene of upturned tables and sizzling emotions he immediately agreed with Nomad.

'Tremlite folk, please move outside. Isotar bellowed above the din.' Myself and others will certainly get to the bottom of this,' he added with certainty. The Tremlite residents recognising their leader's voice subdued somewhat. Seeing this calming effect, Nomad followed this lead.

'Scaysborough folk also need to leave so that Gallon and I can work out what happened,' Nomad's reassuring voice calmed the Scaysborough folk long enough to listen though some took back to their quarrelling as soon as he stopped. 'Now!' he cried loudly with an authorative voice, motioning all bodies outside with his hands.

The crowd reluctantly though obediently left the hall though were still unable to contain their animosity.

'You Scaysborough mob will be found guilty for sure, working with the Lurkin no doubt,' spat some Tremlite Townsfolk.

Similarly, Scaysborough folk were heard uttering statements such as: 'Such horrid people upsetting the tables and ruining the show like this, wish they stayed at their homes, the Lurkin is with them for sure.'

The crowd piled outside the Hall, though the unrest went with them and they milled about outside, barely managing to keep the hostilities at bay. Danio, who had just been given candy floss by his father, looked towards the disarray, perplexed.

'What is happening?' he said.

His father shook his head and said, 'I don't know everyone was happy a minute ago.' Their answer came swift enough as Nadoo stormed past them, so caught up in her fury that she barely noticed the stunned Danio watching her every move. He put out his sticky hand to touch Nadoo on the shoulder.

Upon feeling the intrusion, she turned around and began, 'How dare you touch me don't you know—' Though as she turned to see who it was, she came to her senses. Upon seeing a startled Danio and his father staring at her, she calmed somewhat.

'What is happening?' queried Danio.

'Those malicious and evil Tremlite folk, stole my cakes and ruined the whole fair!' spat Nadoo 'They have the Lurkin with them for sure,' she continued, her face reddening and her fists clenching into a white knuckled grip. 'I am sure Astrid did this. She wanted to win.'

Garrow, who had witnessed the disruption, had finally caught up to Nadoo and began his best effort to subdue her. 'No, Nadoo. Calm my precious.'

She shot Garrow a glance so flaming that he was taken aback.

'Nadoo,' Danio began, 'I will go and find out what happened.' Even though he was only 9 he knew to say nothing more, as any further words would only inflame her. Nadoo looked at Danio, who had such innocent, pleading eyes that she could not do anything else but relax.

'Ok. Thanks,' she said.

'Let's get you a drink,' said Garrow and led the still simmering Nadoo to the Tea stand. He looked over his shoulder towards Danio, who was already running towards the Hall with his father only a few steps behind.

By the time Danio reached the periphery of the Hall, the anger between the two townships milling outside was palpable. It was a writhing mess of accusations and retorts,flaming and lit, ready to explode into physical aggression. Danio shook his head, exasperated at how this wondrous fair had turned so sour.

Danio pushed his way through the tangled crowd and stood before the Hall. He jumped and jumped to see through the window as the doors were locked. He could only see glimpses and was surprised when, on one jump, he felt two strong hands catch him and keep him up high. Danio turned to see his smiling father.

'You may need some help lad,' Jardjon offered and Danio replied with the biggest smile in return. Danio could see the Judges, Gallon, Isotar, and Nomad in animated conversation. He could also see upturned tables and crumbs of cake strewn.

'Something has eaten them,' Danio said. He peered up at the eaves and could see a broken board that offered a small hole.

'Hmm' he said and craned his neck over the terrain above. 'Ah ha' he said. Danio had spent a lot of his 9 years young,in the natural habitats around these areas and saw at once what had occurred. He also spotted the culprit, as fat as a buttery pig, high in the tree sleeping with the crumbs of his spoils dotted around his mouth and his hairy back. A bulbrook! Odd behaviour for a Bulbrook Danio said. 'They usually only eat berries.' His father followed his sons gaze and concurred with his thinking. Danio attempted to call out that he had found the culprit, though the crowd was now dangerously fired up and his voice was not able to be heard. The doors of the Hall opened as those inside could also hear the unrest reaching a crescendo.

Garrow had left a now calmer Nadoo to drink her tea and had journeyed to the Hall to see if he could help somehow. Garrow liked to stay out of trouble,though also would hand to whoever needed it. He managed to squeeze his way through the throng and upon seeing Danion and Jardjon squeezed his way up to them, shaking his head at the scene before him.

Jardjon knew that the crowd needed to be silenced so as to listen to Danio's discovery and when Garrow arrived it sparked an idea. Remembering when Garrow had managed to get past his guards when they had the Tavern by changing his appearance he thought of a way to shock the crowd into silence. Jardjon spied a nearby log left after the wood chopping event and whispered his idea to both Garrow and Danio, who nodded in agreement.

Garrow climbed up onto the log and screamed, in his loudest ever voice: 'Stop!' His voice thundered again, 'Stop!' This time it was so loud that the crowd, curious about the command, turned towards the sound. Garrow then promptly turned into a Vindervay the craggy, rocky creature that was misunderstood and feared by both Townsfolk. The crowd gasped in unison and pointed at him.

'Is that the Lurkin?' called out one small child. The crowd now curious and fearful of the craggy rock creature paused and before anything else could be said.

Danio climbed up next to Garrow and began. 'No, this is not The Lurkin. It is a Vindervay. Vindervay's are wonderful people. They do not harm or molest anyone as you may have been told. May I introduce you to Garrow,' he said. The Vindervay kindly bowed.

Nadoo watched this from afar and shook her head. Oh well, at least they know who he is now, she thought.

Danio continued, 'I can see that a lot of people are upset at the ruination of the cake hall,' he said, and was met with grumbles of agreement from the crowd. 'I can see the culprit before me,' he continued.

The crowd rose to these words, 'Who? Why? I will!' they said.

Danio interjected and pointed to a bulbrook, who unaware of the commotion below, was sleeping soundly with his back resting comfortably on a branch and his large belly facing the sky. The crowd looked upward and they too saw the sleeping assailant.

'It is rare for something like this to occur. Something or someone may have taken all his berries on his tree as this would make him look elsewhere.'

It was Garrow who now was perplexed. 'Why, I recently took all the berries from a tree for Nadoo. I didn't know I was meant to keep some for creatures,' he said and his honesty was a candle of light.

'Ah,' interjected Nadoo who had maneouvered herself through the crowd to stand with Garrow. 'I guess I know why he ate all my cakes then. I forgot to mention to you, Garrow, that you need to leave many on the tree for the Bulbrooks.' Nadoo hung her head, 'I guess that escaped me.'

With all the wisdom he could muster-year-old Danio continued,

'I would like to say that as frail beings on the planet we, at times not having the full knowledge at hand, make assumptions and cast blame. My life living in nature has taught me to be curious and watchful. If we place ourselves in others shoes, we can understand fully who they are and why we act or think a certain way. We all strive for the same goal for peace, happiness and prosperity. My home is in Badon and I have journeyed to Scaysborough and Tremlite and enjoyed the customs and fares from both Towns. I have danced in the moonlight with Tremlite folk and boot scooted in early the early sunshine with Scaysborough residents and I say both times were fun. There are differences for sure, though these are wonderful to behold. As you can see for a second time, there is no blame; only discovery. Look around for answers put yourselves in each other's shoes. Delight in new awareness's, taste new tastes, wear new clothes try new things and enjoy each other's company. Please put the Lurkin to rest as I believe there is no such creature. Suffer the fool who delves into the truth of the whisperer. The tormentor is just ourselves. Look within to find fault there and think with more love and understanding. Let's continue our festivities and enjoy the rest of the time we have together.'

Danio's father was so proud of Danio and he grabbed his son off his makeshift podium and hugged him tightly.

'He is my boy,' he said proudly to the crowd. The crowd again was softened by someone so young and wise and they spontaneously apologised to each other. Handshakes and back pats were heard as well as admiration.

'I love that hat. How do you make such a thing?'

'Your cakes on the stall were delicious, can you tell me the recipe?'

The crowd dispersed throughout the fare and friendships between the townships were being made.

'If only Perina and Zaphod could be here,' said Nadoo to

nobody in particular. Nadoo was now completely calm and sorry for her fury.

'Yes,' said Danio in reply and hung his head slightly hoping that she would be completely well soon.

'Come on lad,' motioned Jardjon, 'there is plenty of fun still to be had.' He grabbed his son's hand and lead him to a table where there was a pyramid of balls on display. 'Try your hand at knocking these over,' he said, as they his ventured to the stall with an excited Danio in tow.

Day turned into night and Nadoo's heart was bursting with love and splendour as she held Garrow's hand. She spontaneously burst into song, singing from her heart, creating words to a tune she already knew:

> *'If we all pull together, you know that we can,*
> *we can meet any problem and make a new plan,*
> *with a host of awareness from all the good souls*
> *the wisdom between us will reach any goal,*
> *there is beauty and passion in all that is here*
> *let's remember this joy and renew it each year*
> *our soul does not flourish in blame, fear or hate*
> *let's rise up above it and open the gate*
> *for peace, understanding, and awe driven love*
> *the kind that is kindred from the love force above*
> *we can dance in the morning, and boot scoot at noon*
> *and come back all together to sing a good tune*
> *It is love that will conquer and make all things right*
> *And with love all around us there is no need to fight*
> *If we all pull together you know that we can...'*

It was at this point that Nadoo had become aware that her voice was the only sound audible. She opened her eyes to find all eyes from the crowd on her.

'Keep singing, that is beautiful' some cried.

'Teach us the words,' others called.

'Let's sing together,' said Nadoo in her loudest voice and before long the whole crowd were singing and dancing, smiling and loving. What a day! The crowd continued until the ebb of the moons calmed and cautioned them into their need for sleep. Even though the spirit shines, the body wearies and needs its rest. One by one the revelers succumbed to tiredness and may their way home. Soon the Scaysborough Fairground was emptied. Scaysborough and Tremlite folk slept peacefully with a new found enlightenment, that difference is just difference. They learnt that it would serve both townships and individuals well to judge less and learn from each other more. Nadoo said a special prayer for Perina just before she closed her eyes and had a dream that Perina was next to her dancing. Nadoo slept peacefully that night. The first peaceful sleep she'd had in a long time.

The bulbrook was content and full. Unaware of all the fuss he had caused, he climbed clumsily down the tree and waddled back to his Jim Jam tree knowing that the blossoms would soon turn into the delicious fruit and his belly would keep him in good condition until that occurred. He shimmied up to his favourite branch and too slept a deep profound sleep, knowing that he would wake to abundance of food.

CHAPTER 11

PERINA AWAKES.

When we are fully awake, our soul sings.

Morning had arrived and Zaphod woke from his rather uncomfortable position. He was still sitting in a chair next to Perina's bed with his body twisted towards her, His hands cupped hers and his head lay next to hers on the pillow. He twisted his spine to straighten up and disentangled his hands from hers. Perina stirred at this interruption and instinctively reached out for Zaphod's hand. 'Zaphod saw this and swiftly grabbed her hand cupping both of his over hers.

'I am here, I am here,' he said.

'I know that,' came a reply somewhat faintly. As Perina gently opened her eyes slowly, taking in her surroundings.

'She's awake! She's awake!' hollered Zaphod. He kissed and hugged Perina, who squirmed a little in his firm embrace.

'Maybe not that tight,' cautioned Ashanti whom upon hearing Zaphod's cries had entered the room.

'Ooh sorry,' said a jubilant Zaphod and he relaxed his grip.

'Hello,' said Perina weakly, 'you must be Ashanti, I heard you in my dreams. Where am I exactly?' Truscott laughed at these words as he too had ventured into Perina's room and right behind him was Wilmsea. 'Oh!' started Perina at the sight of Wilmsea.

'I think an explanation is in order,' said Truscott who promptly discussed all things that had occurred since Perina lost consciousness, including Wilmsea's changed ways. Perina after hearing all this, said, 'Thanks to everyone who has had a part in my recovery. I too have had an epiphany in my dream state. I know that happiness and enjoyment cannot be procured from any brew or berry. I am grateful and a second chance of life and vow to live each day with blissful gratitude.' Perina attempted to pull herself out of the bed to bow before everyone, though her wasted muscles collapsed under her weight and she fell back on the bed with a thud. She forlornly looked out at her friends despairingly, confused at her bodies disobedience. It was then that she noted that it was arms and not wings that she had attempted to pull up her weight with and that Zaphod was bearing two. She managed to rub her eyes in disbelief.

'It is Ok Perina,' Ashanti said, noting her confusion. 'You and Zaphod created change in your last crystallisation. You now have two arms and he has both wings. Your muscles need a few days to get used to carrying you again. This is normal, and we will have you up in no time.

'You could always try to crystalise again for wings,' added Zaphod. Perina firmly shook her head.

'You can be the flyer Zaphod. Between us we will find the lows and the highs together.'

'Well, I better fix us all something to eat,' said Wilmsea and exited swiftly to busy herself in the kitchen.

Ashanti and Truscott developed a convalescing plan for Perina and Zaphod took the lion's share of the tasks. He helped her sit, stand and finally take small steps. He bathed her dressed her and fed her tiny portions of food until she could eat more and more. He refused most help, though on occasion when he was visibly exhausted, he nodded to Ashanti and Truscott who happily attended to the task at hand. Wilmsea was always on hand to provide the freshest and healthiest food. It was not long before Perina could walk unaided and her body plumped ironing out the withered affect of her sagging skin.

Perina began to look like her old self and was heard joking around with Zaphod, 'I know! You could carry me in the skies, drop me and catch me. That would be sure to win the flying contest at the fair.'

'You, my dearest, have slept through the fair. We will have to fly at next year's contest,' replied Zaphod.

'Slept through?

'Yes I am afraid s—s—so' stammered Zaphod now aware of the effect.

'So the wedding?' she enquired forlornely

'Should take place right away,' smiled Zaphod as he scooped her up in his arms.

Perina was caught up with his flamboyance and giggled, 'I can wait. Let's start preparing for home!' she added. 'It may be more than one wedding,' Perina knowingly murmured to herself whilst packing. The silhouette on the verandah sported the unencumbered embrace of Truscott and Ashanti delighting in the rising of the seven moons.

As it always appeared to do the party were packed and ready in unison the very next morning. The healing healed, the regrets realigned, hunger fed, learning learnt and the souls satisfied and stronger. Truscott, Ashanti, Zaphod and Perina stood on the veranda of the Tavern reformed to say their goodbyes and gratitude to their wisened host Wilmsea. Wilmsea hugged each and every one of them ardently with the strength and meekness of a soul reformed. 'Be sure to send Jardjon and Danio back when you find them,' said a quavering Wilmsea as she hugged them soundly and surely good bye.

And so they went, all with new vigour, new knowledge, new courage, back to the lands once divided now knitted together with hope and wonder. A new beginning, a new journey, to a changing landscape with their constantly changing selves.

And of course a wedding to prepare for, or maybe two? Three even? It may surprise you who, but that my friends is, of course another story.

CHAPTER 12

THE WEDDING

Let the treasures of beauty and the magic of love
dance in your heart eternal.

They did arrive back in Scaysborough. There was much rejoicing at their return, frantic hugs by Barnio, solid square ones from Nadoo and jolly greetings from Gallon and the others in town.

Somehow, Nadoo had managed to subdue the impulsive Perina not to wed straight away to plan and prepare to ensure their wedding was as magical as their love for each other.

Perina of course protested saying, 'Oh Nadoo, don't be such a fuddy duddy. We can just make sandwiches and have the wedding on the lawn at our house. Why we could plan it for tomorrow!' Nadoo gave her such a stare of horror that it sent shivers down Perina's spine.

'Harumph,' she said still glaring at Perina, 'The whole town coming down for such a thing. Over my dead body! Just once Perina, curb your impulsive nature and plan properly!' It came out rather harshly and Nadoo flinched with regret about serving Perina some home truths in that manner.

Perina however took it on the chin and replied, 'Nadoo, you are right, I certainly have messed up by not being prepared so I will take your advice. You are now my Wedding planner,' she said firmly pointing towards her.

Nadoo was chuffed and chortled a little, 'Well, I'll be. I better hop to it then.'

With Nadoo in charge of all things Weddings things got done! Orders were barked out, food and cakes made and the dress, of course the dress was sewn and stitched by the towns best seamstress who also happened to be Nadoo's good friend Gida.

The Wedding date had been set for a few weeks time and all those involved in its creating were bustling about with their tasks. Weddings in Scaysborough and Tremlite were very much like ours except that the whole town were invited. A Wedding in Scaysborough was a huge event and sent the Town into a flap. The showground was being prepared and fetes and stalls erected. It was a Wedding though it was also a gigantic fair as well. The Villagers enjoyed Weddings very much equally for the celebrations as well as the opportunity to catch up with others in the community unburdened by their usual work routines.

Barnio had also been given a task. He was to be the ring bearer. Barnio was delighted when Zaphod had asked him to stand by his side and hand him the ring at the right moment. When offered by Zaphod, Barnio snatched the shiny piece of gold fashioned into a small band to fit Perina's finger, spinning it around and around. 'Pretty, pretty,' he commented.

'Hold onto it tight, keep it safe!' ordered Zaphod rather sternly as he was concerned about Barnio's tossing of the ring around.

'You can count on me, count on me,' replied a transfixed Barnio. And with that he took off like the wind with the ring in tow. He couldn't help but marvel at the way it shone and flipped it this way and that in the sun to see its golden hues glisten. This is the way he continued until it happened, it happened.

The ring was suddenly plucked from his hand without any warning. 'What the what? He gasped, looking up just in time to see a large Truon flying to its nest in a nearby tree with its golden prize neatly tucked under one of its feet. It was swawking with delight at its treasure and was seen to place it gently in his newly constructed nest. The Truon proudly poked and prodded the ring with its beak until he seemed satisfied it was in the right place and settled down on top of it. Barnio went white with fear, his heart sank and sickness rolled around in his belly.

'Oh, dear oh dear,' he stammered and walked up and down in front of the tree with his hand on his head. 'I will have to climb, have to climb' he stated as he came fully to this realisation that this was his only hope to retrieve the ring, he didn't even want to think about telling Zaphod he lost it as he knew how hard gold was to come by.

Barnio was actually afraid on heights, he clutched his stomach and wiped his brow from sweat and slowly began the climb. He dared not look down and inched himself higher and higher using branches as footing. Higher and higher he climbed, feeling more nauseous with each inch gained. He craned his head upwards and saw that the nest was nearly in reach he swung one arm up to catch the branch where it was nestled and attempted to pull the rest of his body after it. His second arm however missed its target and his body swung from side to side.

Whist swaying, he inadvertently caught sight of the ground which appeared to him a tremendously long way down. Panic fluttered in his heart creating sweat, sweat was making his grip looser when all of a sudden, he felt a hand on his shoulder. Looking up he saw another Garnio resting on her haunches on the branch. Barnio seizing the opportunity before him grabbed her hand and with her assistance was able to clamber up to crouch alongside her.

Astonished, he stared and stared.

She broke the silence, 'That was lucky, lucky I was on the other side, other side, are you watching the nest too? There is two eggs there, two eggs.'

Bewildered, he answered, 'No, no, what?

'Hi I am Berelda, Garnio from Tremlite, Tremlite,' she repeated as Garnios often do.

'Berelda,' he repeated, scratching his head. 'I am B—B—' he stammered as he took in her beauty and looked into her emerald eyes. 'B—B.'

'B. B is it?' enquired Berelda,

'No,' said Barnio, this time holding his nerve, 'Barnio, at your service.' Amazingly Barnio forgot about his fear of heights and was captured by Berlada's beauty She had long dark hair from which her two pointy green ears poked out, she was also sporting the biggest and greenest saucer eyes he had ever seen. The proportions of her long dangly arms and legs seemed perfect. He stared again transfixed.

'Barnio, Barnio,' she repeated, reddening at his stare. 'I love watching the birds, they are nesting, nesting. I was hoping they would have hatched by now, by now.'

'They have my ring, my ring,' Barnio lamented and pointed to the nest. 'That Truon is sitting on it, on it.'

'Your ring, your ring? Oh they do like shiny things, shiny things,' Berelda replied. As it was she that was the closest to the nest she promptly placed her hand under the Truon's belly who protested with a squawk. She gently felt around his feathers until her hand touched a hard round object which she pulled from under him. The Truon responded with a peck to her tiny hand. 'Ouch, ouch, ouch' she bemoaned. 'We'd best be off, off, he looks angry now, angry now 'she added. And they shimmied and scrambled their way down the tree with the Truon glaring daggers at them.

Now both on the ground, they brushed themselves off. 'Want a race, a race?' suggested Berleda who loved fun and action.

'Yes, Yes,' replied an equally eager Barnio, 'though ring first please, ring please,' he commanded with an outstretched hand. Berelda, laughed at her forgetfulness and gave Barnio the ring which he promptly tied into his jacket's button hole with a hanky. 'It's for my friend's wedding he explained as he double knotted it to be sure and then without warning ran straight up the hill towards Town. 'Catch me if you can, you cannnnnn,' he called, though his words trailed behind him. Berelda caught unaware by his cheeky head start zoomed off after him and they zig zagged this way and that laughing all the while at the game.

Scaysborough had changed somewhat since the Fair. A slow and gradual change for the better. Some of the Tremlite folk had loved the quiet nature and country side of Scaysborough Town and decided to move in. They brought with them new clothes, new food and new ideas. Some Scaysborough folk were very curious about Tremlite and wanted to see for themselves the tower houses which lined the cliff streets as well as experience their different lifestyle and taste their unique food stuffs.

Some Scaysborough peoples even relocated there loving the ocean and the sea breeze along the cliffs. So things were changing. Why some even wanted to visit Badon to see the kid who spoke so elegantly, taste the fare from his parents Tavern and hear stories of its darker days.

Some wanted to visit the Vindervay's though they being quite shy camouflaged themselves so well that no one ever was able to discover their abodes. Garrow and Nadoo knew, of course, though they would never reveal.

Both towns had lost their fear of The Lurkin and were realising that people in the two towns were just different. There was a blending of ideas, a teaching of ways and for the most part harmonious relations.

Barnio was delighted in his new found friend Berelda, they were often seen in animated conversations together, flitting this way and that, sharing giggles and laughs.

The wedding loomed. The townsfolk worked together like

clockwork. Chores were distributed, food was collected and cooked and all the while Nadoo was at the forefront barking orders and being the quality controller. 'Nope, not good enough,' she would growl. Only when she was pleased would she give them the thumbs up. It went like this until the day finally arrived.

It was a magical day, the skies were sunny the fields were green and lush. 'Humph, perfect,' said Nadoo to no one with her hands on her hips smelling the air which was pleasant and sweet. Decorated stalls dotted the perimeter of the fields with specially baked ordained by Nadoo fare. A large structure, containing a wedding stage was erected in the middle of the field with drapes of gold material weaved around the posts and bunches of wild flowers neatly tied around the sides.

It was a sight to behold, all the villagers wore their best clothes and the Tremlite folk who were in town paraded around in their fancy hats and tailored suits. Some of the Scaysborough residents, influenced by Tremlite attire, also wore hats and even brightly coloured clothes. One by one they settled into their seats and began waiting expectantly. It was a day Wedding and Perina was due to arrive at around 11am. 'Wonder what she will be wearing,' some pondered, other comments were, 'It's about time. Weren't they going to marry earlier?' Some commented about the clothes of others, 'Oh I like that hat' or 'Can you believe she is wearing that?' Others sat patiently, just in awe of the what was turning out to be a magical day.

Perina was at home climbing into her long elegant dress. It was made from pink silk with flowers stitched on every part. It was a kaleidoscope of colours with the pink underneath matched her cheeks perfectly. She was indeed the blooming bride. Her hair was pulled back and a long flowing scarf of pink silk trailed behind it. She had a bunch of the most beautiful forest flowers in her hands. Reds, and yellows, pinks and blues. Nadoo was fussing around her making sure everything hung where it should. Perina was too joyous to let her friends prodding and poking annoy her. She just beamed with happiness that finally everything turned out all right.

'Ok, let's go,' signalled Nadoo rather abruptly when she was satisfied all was well.

Perina, still nonplussed, made her way to an ornate cart with four carefully preened horses awaiting. The cart was white and decorated in flowers with painted jewels dotting the top, the horses manes were platted with long flowing ribbons creating the most ornate effect. Perina and Nadoo settled into the padded seat in the back of the cart and when completely settled Garrow pulled gently on the reigns sigalling the horses to move forward. The horses obeyed and trotted rhythmically into town with their long yellow ribbons attached to their manes flowing steadily behind them. The whole Town lined up on each sides of the road to see the bride arrive whilst Zaphod paced up and down in the golden draped stage nervously waiting.

'Nothing will go wrong. Nothing will go wrong,' he said over and over in his mind. Barnio picking up on Zaphod's nervous tension darted this way and that, this way and that to calm his own nerves.

Red jacketed Trumpeters stood at the fairground's perimeters and sounding at the sight of the horses arriving. The audience gasped and preened their heads to get the first glimpses of the bride. The cart finally arrived and came to a halt. Perina, disembarked as elegantly as she could with Nadoo behind her clucking this way and that ensuring the folds in her dress fell in the correct way whilst she walked. Nadoo finally gave her the thumbs up, Perina smiled and nodded knowingly and walked stoically through the crowd, smiling and acknowledging all whom her eyes met. The whole town attended as well as the specials guests from Badon Danio, Jardjon and Wilmsea, even Hely and Trival had made their way to Scaysborough for this dazzling event. Shona and Jyno who yearned to be at the festivities decided the trip would be too much for them. They gave Danio a specially wrapped gift to give to the pair. It was a special rainbow rock that they had found alongside the river near their home exactly like the one that Nadoo had found. They hoped it would bring smiles to their faces and add a tiny dash of colour to their home. Danio who had just turned 10 and had a party for same for the very first time, guarded the unique gift on his lap. He held his mother's hand whilst his father had his hand around his shoulder. He was getting used to loving touch and liked it.

Nomad was sitting nearby with the other Trehwell's previously known as Vingoos though now were well accepted citizens of Scaysborough, Gonza, Jansto, Pento and Chinto. They had set up a Cafe in Town and sold their delicious fare from Nadoo's teachings. Nadoo and Garrow were regular patrons at their Café. Nadoo marvelled delicious their food was and how they had improved on her recipes. I am in for some competition at the next baking contest, she mused when she ate at their premises. Naturally, she took all the credit when she ever heard anyone comment on the great food there. 'It was me that taught them,' she was heard to say.

The Badon crew were at the very front of the crowd and the first to gasp at Perina's beauty. Danio's jaw dropped, 'She sure is pretty.' Both Jardjon and Wilmsea nodded in response. Trival and Hely nodded.

'She is alright,' came Trival's reply. He was not one to make a fuss.

Zaphod relaxed upon seeing Perina and was in awe of her elegance and grace as she moved towards them. She was radiant and shone like he had never seen her shine. Gallon, who was conducting the ceremony stood on stage at the front of the wedding party. He greeted Perina motioning her to stand on the right hand side next to Zaphod, Truscott and Ashanti were situated on the left side readying to deliver a wedding speech. Perina now by Zaphod's side turned her head towards his grinning from ear to ear 'We made it,' he said to her quietly winking at the same time with twinkling eyes. They poised for a few minutes whilst the crowd stealthfully found and settled into their seats.

The ceremony began.

'Let us begin,' boomed Gallon in his most official voice.

'Today we are witnessing Zaphod and Perina giving their vows of marriage. They are committing themselves to continue the journey of life together and give all around them their pledges as proof. I will hand you over to Truscott and Ashanti who have been asked to say a few words about marriage.'

Truscott began. 'Marriage is an oath that people will continue the journey of life in each other's company to learn and grow from each other and the world around them.'

Ashanti was next. 'They entrust each other with the sacred aim of evolving to the best being they can be. Kindness, wisdom, love and peace is their primary goals, not only for each other but to radiate in the world around them'

Truscott continued, 'Marriage is a union of souls. Souls who can look into each others' eyes and see a perfected mirror of themselves in return.'

At this point, Truscott looked into Ashanti's eyes next to him who responded by looking into his. The very words Truscott described was happening to them, they saw themselves in each others' eyes and momentarily they felt their souls were dancing together. The sensation was so exquisite that they could not drag their eyes from each other. Nadoo who was in the front row saw this protraction. It was sweet she thought, though it was halting the progress of the next task. She was close enough to prod Truscott on the leg which she did with a small 'Harumph'

Truscott came to his senses, shook his head a little and stammered, 'Oh, oh, I will now hand you over to Zaphod and Perina.'

Zaphod smirked in regards to Truscott and Ashanti's obvious love for each other.

'You're next,' he whispered in Truscott's ear as he brushed by him on the way to the front of the stage.

Zaphod commenced his vows, the delight in his voice shining through.

'I honour Perina. To honour is to love,

I give my thanks to the 7 moons above,

to be in this moment of love satisfied

is a treasure of heart that I will for ever abide.

Adventures and journeys are sure to abound,

though we will have each other and our life will be sound.'

Zaphod surprised everyone with his rhyming vows. Especially Perina whom knowing it was now her turn to speak nodded towards Zaphod with a look of awe and admiration. It was not all Zaphod's work if truth be known Barnio did assist him though this did not deter Zaphod from feeling proud in the moment.

Perina started. She was a little nervous as she had not spoken in front of such a large audience and stammered a little in the beginning.

'Za—Za—Zaphod,' she started, turning her head away from the crowd. She happened to see Zaphod staring back at her radiating earnest love and compassion, This melted her, calming her body, she collected herself and continued, braver and with more confidence. 'Zaphod. Your strength has carried me through the toughest of days. It was your energy that saved me. I am indebted to you. I am in love with you. I vow to stay by your side come what may. I vow in front of all the Town to become the wisest woman I can become to honour you so that you can walk proudly by my side.' Perina had a tear forming in her eye as she spoke as she was truly sorry for all the trials that he as well as others had to endure due to her poor self control and unpreparedness.

They held hands and stared lovingly at each other. Nadoo pressed Garrow's hands wiping a tear from her own eye.

Garrow responded with a firm hug. 'We should be next,' he whispered, making Nadoo cock her head towards him in a moment of ecstasy.

'Yes,' she whispered back. They were not the only one's moved Barnio who standing on stage waiting his turn to hand over the ring, craned his head this way and that to search for Berelda in the crowd, finally finding her, he met her eye and shot her a glance that contained so much love she blushed and giggled knowingly, on her seat.

Gallon took the lead again. 'Then, Zaphod, will you place the ring on Perina's hand.'

Barnio knowing his cue, handed the ring to Zaphod, who promptly placed the ring on his beloved's hand. Perina beamed. Gallon continued. 'Zaphod will you take Perina to be your wife from now until the end of your days under the seven moons of Scaysborough with all its residents your witness?'

Zaphod replied with a clear and resounding, 'Yes.'

'Perina,' Gallon questioned, 'Will you take Zaphod to be your husband from now until the end of your days under the seven moons of Scaysborough with all its residents your witness?'

'Yes!' replied Perina, profoundly matching Zaphod's enthusiasm.

'Then I declare in front of Scaysborough and all that dwell in it, Zaphod and Perina are now man and wife,' concluded Gallon. 'You may now kiss the bride.'

And kiss they did, a delighted kiss, a fervent kiss, a kiss that carried all their previous troubles dissolving them into happiness. The audience rose to a cheer, laughing and clapping.

Nadoo took her cue, walked to the front of the stage and began singing. It was a song that she had written especially for Perina and Zaphod and it went like this.

Love is the beauty that we all can behold
With love you are cosy away from the cold
Companions forever through the journey of life
Defeating together any trouble or strife
Love one another through the trek to the end
Loyal and trustworthy bestest of friends
Love conquers now, love conquers all
Axes and swords never again fall
Follow these lovebirds and follow their ways
Love will grow with them til the end of their days

It was a beautiful song, sang sweetly, the audience was moved an applauded profusely. Perina stood next to Nadoo, bending down to kiss her gently on the cheek. 'Thanks, Nadoo, thanks for everything,' she said, Nadoo nodded towards her and their eyes said everything. A journey of friends the highs, the lows and the knowledge that they have both been better for the input from each other.

Perina gathered Zaphod's hand tightly and threw it in the air with hers, shouting out. 'Lets party!' and with that, the crowd dispersed and music began. Some would say it was the happiest wedding they have been to.

It was certainly a changed Township. The seven travellers who embarked on a journey, learnt together, grew together. They discovered truths and unravelled mis-truths. A new knowledge was developing in both Townships and The Lurkin was hardly mentioned except to discuss its myth. Life was becoming more logical, more balanced,thought was placed before judgement. You could say Tremlite and Scaysborough and all those living in it were now living together more perfectly imperfect than before. Of course, grumbles happened, tiffs and misgivings occurred though wars and weapons were buried deep never to be unearthed. And yes, Garrow and Nadoo were married as were Barnio and Berelda. Truscott and Ashanti however could not see the point, they knew their love for each other and had no use for such ceremonies.

The world turned, the moons rose and life continued, more soundly, more peacefully a kinder hum ensued. And this, my friends, is the very end of the story.

THE END

Shawline Publishing Group Pty Ltd
www.shawlinepublishing.com.au